Re-discove
kind of

Praise for the early works of Victor Canning:

'Quite delightful … with an atmosphere of quiet
contentment and humour that **cannot fail to charm**.'
Daily Telegraph

'There is **such a gentle humour** in the book.'
Daily Sketch

'What counts for most in the story …
is his **mounting pleasure in vagabondage
and the English scene**.'
The Times

'A paean to the beauties of the English countryside
and **the lovable oddities of the English character**.'
New York Times

'His delight at the beauties of the countryside
and **his mild astonishment at the strange
ways of men are infectious**.'
Daily Telegraph

'A swift-moving novel, **joyous, happy
and incurably optimistic**.'
Evening Standard

'His gift of story-telling is obviously innate. **Rarely
does one come on so satisfying** an amalgam of
plot, characterisation and good writing.'
Punch

POLYCARP'S PROGRESS

Victor Canning

This edition published in 2019 by Farrago,
an imprint of Prelude Books Ltd
13 Carrington Road, Richmond, TW10 5AA, United Kingdom

www.farragobooks.com

By arrangement with the Beneficiaries of the
Literary Estate of Victor Canning

First published by Hodder and Stoughton in 1935

Ebook ISBN: 978-1-78842-172-0
Print ISBN: 978-1-78842-176-8

With grateful acknowledgment to John Higgins

Have you read them all?

Treat yourself again to the first Victor Canning novels –

Mr Finchley Discovers His England
A middle-aged solicitor's clerk takes a holiday for the first time and meets unexpected adventure.

Polycarp's Progress
Just turned 21, an office worker spreads his wings – an exuberant, life-affirming novel of taking your chances.

Fly Away Paul
How far could you go living in another's shoes? – an action-packed comic caper and love story.

Turn to the end of this book for a full list of Victor Canning's humorous works, plus – on the last page – the chance to receive **further background material**.

To my mother and father

Contents

1

The attainment of a majority becomes an excuse for truancy

The road came sharply up the steep curve of the hills, pushing its way through the thinning larch and spruce woods as though in a hurry to leave behind it the shadows and dust of the valley, and swerving aside only for the great spurs of rock shoulder that sprawled across its path and frowned at its impulsive eagerness. When the road reached the crest of the long, rolling ridge of hills it moved for a while, contented with its victory, across the wind-ruled plateau, and then tiring of the heights dipped to the farther valleys to seek the cool water splashes, the wide beech-tree shadows, and the noise of bees and hens about the cottage gardens which a few miles back it had pretended to despise.

It was no Roman road moving resolutely along the ridge of the hills, and joying in the intoxication of heights and the splendour of long vistas; it was a creation born of the cities that had lost itself in the country and passed with careless cruelty across field and wood, scarring the side of grass slopes and disfiguring the bold beauty of the hilltops with its stiffly bending lines. It was an ugly road, its white length laid like stamp edging across a quiet-toned stained-glass window. No sooner did it find one joy than it tossed it aside in its eagerness for another. It willingly deserted valley for hill and hill for plain and plain for city ... always pressing eagerly forward.

But not everything shared the white road's desire to leave the wide hilltop. The wind-blown hawthorns remained to live their deformed lives, crouching in the meagre shelter of the low stone walls. The rabbits that honeycombed the long tumuli, and in their delvings unearthed shaped flints and broken pottery, had never known any life but the life of the hilltop. The green plovers manoeuvring in the breeze about the cropping sheep; the whistling curlews that passed in dark flight against the fragile sky, and the golden stonecrop which clung to the grey walls in thick bosses of rich velvet—all these were part of the true life of the uplands, the life which the white road no more than hastily touched. Not everything hurried away from the wide hills so quickly as the road.

A young man had been sitting for half an hour on the low wall which bordered the road. Behind him was a clump of Scotch firs that held their crimson trunks to the westering sun. The careless splotches of sunlight slipped through the barricade of trunks and fell upon the young man, bringing a transient brightness to his fair hair, and striking little spurts of light from the growth on his upper lip, which at times he fingered gently as though to reassure himself that it still existed. He was a slender, wiry young man, and as he sat on the wall he swung one foot to and fro, kicking at the uncurling bracken fronds and whistling softly through his teeth. One hand was in the pocket of his sports jacket, and the other was engaged in tossing little pieces of stone into the upturned crown of a shabby, comfortable-looking trilby hat which lay on the wall by his side.

One out of every four stones went into the hat, for he was not looking where he threw them, but gazing out across the distant sweep of hills. Before him the road dipped slowly in a long descent to a low valley where a trout stream twisted between outcrops of limestone. Sitting where he was, he had a view of ten miles of country which had once played a part in the development of Britain's commerce as valuable as any Welsh mine or Black Country pottery. At one time these hills had been rich with long-fleeced sheep, whose wool had made the fortunes of hundreds of mercers and formed the principal industry of Britain up to the time of the Industrial Revolution.

But the Cotswold woollen trade has long been dead. Fortune travelled north to blacken the clouds with her smuts and paint the night sky with searing flames, and now the mercers lie beneath their long tombs in the valley churches, content to let the verdigrised brasses that hang in the shadow of the church naves tell, in archaic lettering, the story of their past. The hills have gone back to wasteful nature. The forgotten pack-roads that once sounded to the tramp of horses burdened with double panniers of staple now make runways for the rabbits and hunting weasels. The valley streams, once dirty with woollen washings, now flash and murmur over little lashers, and are bright with the quick turn of trout. Over the whole countryside has settled a quiet peace and charm.

It lay breathing slowly under the summer sky; its fields fashioned to mad geometric patterns by stone walls, long reaches of hillside blazing with tansies and silverweed, and, where the valleys grew towards the waterheads, harbouring little patches of buckthorn and alders. Lower down the valleys came the burgeoning woods of fir and spruce—astir with rabbits and jays, and, lower still, the dignified silences of the beech, the elm, and the waving ash prevailed. Between the trees was an occasional grey glimpse of quiet mansion house, chimney-stacks smoking slowly, and the twists of the valleys sheltered clusters of cottages and almost concealed the sober towers of churches. Everywhere was a living quietness and a harmony of pleasant, subdued tones that seemed to have taken their dominant colour from the pale sky above and wrapped it about field and village, draped it over hill and valley, until the whole land lived and glowed with a vigorous, controlled beauty.

The young man who was sitting on the wall let his eyes travel along the miles, from nibbling sheep to hovering hawk, from sheltered valley to brackened slope, and as he looked he shook his head slowly and stopped whistling. He was not thinking of the beauty which spilled itself before his eyes; he was not thinking of the departed glory of Cotswold mercers; he was thinking hungrily of sausages, and wondering how long it would be before the blister on his right heel burst. Perhaps his indifference to the beauty before him may be forgiven.

It is impossible for a hungry man to appreciate beauty, though it may be possible for such a man to be aware of beauty; but it is utterly impossible for a hungry man who has a painful blister on his heel even to be aware of beauty. Blisters and hunger are the handmaids of vandalism.

At that particular moment John Polycarp Jarvis would cheerfully have sacrificed the whole content of the National Gallery, every one of the six thousand acres of beauty before him, and each of the Miss Europes for the last five years to gain a large plate of sausages and mash. After satiating his hunger he would not have deplored his act, for Polycarp never regretted what could not be remedied; he would have made a resolution not to allow himself to become so devastatingly hungry again. It was perhaps the mental counterpart of Polycarp's present physical mood which set Cromwell's men whitewashing mural paintings and docking church spires, started Henry the Eighth upon a career of decapitation, and prompted Potiphar's wife to have Joseph thrown into prison.

At that moment Polycarp's one desire was symbolised by the word sausages. He sat on the wall, and thought of the ways sausages had been served to him in the past. The dishes passed slowly before him, bringing a saliva to his empty mouth. Sausages in rich brown gravy and surrounded by flocculent clouds of creamy mashed potatoes; sausages neatly encased in tender layers of flaky pastry; sausages mired in pleasant depths of batter; sausages whose skins were golden brown from trial by fire; cold sausages with the white fat gleaming icily on their rounded flanks and sentinelled by pickled onions and gherkins; sausages ensconced in the ripped carcasses of long rolls, and eaten inch by inch, anointed at each inch by liberal libations of French mustard; sausages in the friendly aromatic company of liver, kidneys, and onions; sausages spiced with tomatoes and sage—the ghosts of the sausages he had eaten rose tantalisingly before him and passed in fleshly review. Polycarp lit a cigarette, and groaned as he thought that the nearest sausage was a good five miles away. He had to choose between breaking his blister or breaking his fast, to choose either the pangs of hunger or the pains of a broken blister; it was a situation that Polycarp resented.

If Bacon had written an essay entitled "On reaching Manhood," it is possible that his didactic phrases and Latin quotations might have offered Polycarp some guide as to the right conduct of a young man on attaining his twenty-first birthday.

Polycarp reached his majority on the twenty-third day of June, nineteen hundred and twenty-three, and—had he wished to seek advice—the only person to whom he could turn for counsel on the perils, joys, and responsibilities consequent upon this minor climacteric was his middle-aged Aunt Felicia, with whom, after the tragic death of his father and mother at sea, he had lived since the age of six.

His parents had been returning to Africa, where his father held a minor post in an obscure mining company, when their ship had piled itself up on the rocks close to Start Point on the Devon coast. The only survivors were the captain and two of the crew, from whom it transpired at the enquiry that the captain had been drunk since the ship had left Gravesend. The captain pleaded that his intoxication had been necessary to deaden the thought of his wife's infidelity, she having run away with a former first mate of his three days before he sailed. The befuddled state which had made the captain confuse the Start and the Ushant lights had also made Polycarp an orphan. All that Polycarp's father left was a small sum to be handed to him when he became twenty-one, and a Christian name which he had unsuccessfully attempted to hide from his schoolmates.

Polycarp's father had been a man of sudden enthusiasms. A week before Polycarp was born it became apparent to his father that very few Christian names were really Christian names, but survivals from the pre-Christian era. No one bothered to confute his argument; so his son was christened with the names of John, of whose Christianity there could be no doubt, and Polycarp, first Bishop of Smyrna, who had imbibed his Christian principles direct from the great John. Polycarp's companions at the Bristol Grammar School had not allowed him to conceal his strange second name, and for ten years he had borne it like a cross, and then from resentment he had passed slowly to a state of mind which found a queer pride in the name until the day came when he could write boldly across the top of examination papers and on free library membership forms—*John Polycarp Jarvis*.

Advice is something which twenty-one years considers unnecessary in a life which is absurdly simple. At eighteen, when he had left school; Polycarp had been excited by the possibilities which work and the possession of pocket-money offered to him. There was so much to do, and so little time to do it in. At twenty-one life held no further mysteries; he had exhausted all its possibilities, and was waiting for an opportunity to remodel and scrap the old, cumbersome institutions and dogmas which surrounded him. He had passed from the adventurously poetic to the contentedly pessimistic.

He sat at breakfast on his birthday morning, and pretended to be reading the serial story in the *Daily Mail* while he spread butter and marmalade thickly on his toast. He was watching his Aunt Felicia over the top of the paper, and wondering whether she had heard him come in the previous night, when he had been late from a dance. She was a thin, bloodless-complexioned woman who always wore high-necked black silk dresses, set off by a long gold chain with a watch hanging like a dull sun at the end, and she had a mole on the left-hand side of her upper lip which advanced three stout hairy feelers in the fashion of a lobster's antennae. She and Polycarp had lived in the little bay-windowed house by the Downs—so close that at night Polycarp could hear the cargo boats come hooting up the Avon Gorge—for seventeen years, and in all those years Polycarp had been amazed by the miracle of those hairs which never varied in length. He wondered if, as they grew, she kept them carefully trimmed.

She looked up from her plate, and said to him

"Well, boy"—she always called him "boy," a practice which irritated him—"how does it feel to be a man?"

"No worse than I expected. It's pleasant to have a cheque for eighty pounds in one's pocket. I wonder what I shall do with it?"

"If you are wise, boy, you'll put it in the bank and save it for a rainy day."

"Bank, aunt? But it's been lying in the bank for donkey's years. It's time it saw daylight for awhile. Don't you know, aunt, that it's the duty of every citizen to put money into circulation? Creates prosperity for a country that way."

"And creates spendthrifts, too," she said, with a prim wisdom which was always at hand to damp Polycarp's flights of specious logic. "Some day, perhaps, you'll need that money badly. When you come to think about marrying, for instance."

Polycarp stood up, folding the paper under his arm. "Me—marry!" he said humorously. "I'd sooner jump off the Suspension Bridge with

14

a paper-bag for a parachute. Marriage is an antiquated social custom which has survived from the days of nomadic life and—"

"What book have you got out from the free library now, boy?" She looked at him with a little smile about her lips. She knew her Polycarp better than he knew himself. Now that he was away most of the day, at work, their contacts were less frequent, and she could only guess at the influences which played around him; but she was a good guesser, and to help her she had the knowledge of his father's character. Polycarp was very like his father in many ways. He had the same wild enthusiasms, the same quick stubbornness, and the same ready allegiance to any new idea which came to him through books or conversation. He was as selfish and self-centred as most young men of his age; but with his extravagant self-sufficiency he combined a quick generosity which, although he was at times ashamed of it, by its awkward manifestations and sudden strength showed that it would be part of him long after he had ceased to regard the world as his own particular plaything. Because of his youth he endeavoured, with never more than partial success, to repress his generosity and sympathies, regarding them as weaknesses in his character.

"It's no good trying to alter your views, is it?" said Polycarp. He took his hat from the sofa, and, smiling at her, left the room with the feeling that he was leaving behind him the nineteenth and stepping out into the twentieth century.

Not a bad old girl, his aunt, but hopelessly behindhand in her views. She would not join the municipal library because it was free, but preferred to pay a large subscription to a London library for books which Polycarp classed as narcotics. "You might just as well chew tobacco as read those things," he had told her more than once, and had been slightly annoyed when she just smiled and shook her head at him.

He had half an hour to spare before going into the office, and he decided to walk into the town by way of the Downs.

It was a lovely morning. There had been an early shower of rain, which had washed the dust from the streets and gardens so that they stood up proudly under the bright morning sunshine. The modest villas held the light to their stucco and grey stone façades, and the garden plants splashed the sunshine in little shards of silver reflections over their green leaves and flowers. Half-way up the street a great bush of white roses sagged over a garden paling, flecking the slate pavement with white scollop-shells and softening the air with heavy perfume. Polycarp drew a great breath as he came level with the roses, and then, with a quick movement, nipped off a bud and concealed it in the cup of his hand for a few yards before pinning it into the lapel of his coat. Flowers, he argued to himself in defence of this act, were the gifts of a benevolent nature to mankind, and men had no right to withhold them from one another. He screwed the *Daily Mail* into a baton, and as he marched he smacked one thigh with it in tune to his whistling.

A tram clanged down the hill with a noisy, merry dipping and bowing. A dustcart climbed slowly beside him for a while, the driver eating his breakfast from a paper bag, and higher up the hill a milk-float was drawn into the curb, and the milkman stood, with his hand on the horse's mane, talking to a grocer who was changing the price labels on the boxes outside his shop.

The summer sunshine cast a warm spell over everything. Dogs slept on the top of cool, recently swilled steps; cats stretched themselves on back-garden walls, and snapped at the flies which buzzed round the ivy and the yellow-tongued bunches of purple toad-flax; the milkman laughed at a joke from the grocer; the dustman winked at Polycarp, and then shut his eyes as his great mouth opened to receive o piece of cheese almost as big as a church foundation-stone, and Polycarp whistled with greater zest at the beauty of the morning. It was a fitting day to mark his entry to manhood. He breasted the hill and faced the open Downs.

A fresh breeze blowing up the Avon Gorge came tumbling towards the city, shaking the may-blossoms down from the hawthorns, and ruffling the leaves of the elms and chestnuts. Polycarp took off his hat to allow the wind to move about his hair, and then, as the intoxication of the morning worked into his body, he started away in a steady trot—which he designated as training, and which he performed every morning when he had time to spare for the Downs. He stumbled and lolloped over the uneven ground, kicking at the plantain tufts, and performing imaginary rugby passes to the shrubs and trees. To an onlooker, watching him dart and swerve and flourish his arms, he must have given the impression of harmless insanity, but to rugby enthusiasts it was obvious that he was keeping in training. Perhaps the enthusiasts would have been disappointed had they known that Polycarp never played rugby. Still, Polycarp argued, there was no need to play rugby in order to appreciate the sanity of keeping the body fit and strong.

He reached the extremity of the Downs, where they dropped in a tangle of trees and bushes through sheer cliff-face to the gorge. Here he found a seat and flung himself upon it. For a few moments he sat panting and fanning his face with the newspaper. His yellowy hair was awry with his exertions, and his face was flushed with quick circulation. His tongue hung out, pink and trembling like a puppy's, and in some unfathomable way his tie had slipped thirty degrees round his neck and his stud had broken loose so that his collar and shirt flapped in the wind like a loosely furled sail.

When he had regained his breath, he adjusted his shirt and tie, and then stood up. Below him the river flowed quietly between its rocky gorge. The tide was just on the ebb; and the brown mud-banks were hidden. From the cliff top the river seemed to pour sluggishly from the direction of the black and grey huddle of buildings, smoke coils, and church spires which were Bristol, like a turbid vein carrying away all the filth and detritus of the city. Only where the slant of the sun struck it did the dark tide quicken into mercury; but mostly it was brown and viscid, the surface scarred with floating refuse, broken pieces of wood, limp paper, and water-logged straw-cases from bottles. Polycarp turned away from the city, and let his eye rove down the twisting gorge where it worked its way towards the Bristol Channel. Thick glaciers of wood moved down the gorge-side to the river in green patches of flaming beech and dark firs. From somewhere in the blackthorn tangles below him a blackbird volleyed away and left a linnet to sing alone to the sun. Looking seawards the distance took the murkiness from the water, and aided by the sun slowly transformed the river into a thing of light and brilliance. As Polycarp looked a handful of gulls came drifting up the gorge on idle, erratic wings; falling and cavorting in the air like pieces of torn white paper. They reminded Polycarp of the sea, and then he became conscious of himself and remembered for the first time since he had started running that he was twenty-one.

Twenty-one and he felt happy and care-free ... The very thought robbed him of the glory of his state. Carefree—yes, for about another fifteen minutes. Then he would be at his desk. The thought that on this day, when symbolically he became a man, he should have to turn automatically towards the office and incarcerate himself for long hours at a desk, filled him with resentment. He did not mind office work. An office where everyone was divorced from the urgent necessity of making a profit for something or somebody suited his compromising, easy-natured ways. He found it a very pleasant sanctuary; but today things were somehow different. After all, he argued to himself, a fellow could only be twenty-one once, and on that day he was entitled to some special consideration. Obviously—he developed the argument as he stood gazing down the gorge—a fellow who was twenty-one, and had in his pocket his own good pounds to do as he willed with, was not subject to the same rules and conventions as any ordinary mortal. The argument seemed flawless, and, with a logical promptness which characterised all Polycarp's actions, he decided that he would not go into the office that day, but would spend it in his own fashion. Tomorrow he would return, and say, unblushing, that he had been ill. Not an untruth, he argued to himself, for was he not suffering from a mental illness which would be further aggravated by attendance at the office? Indeed, he was. Having made his decision, he sat down upon the seat and began to plan what he should do with his day, to celebrate his new-come manhood.

II
Polycarp leaves the present for the future

The clocks were striking ten in the city behind him when Polycarp left the seat where he had remained, pondering and frowning in thought, since his great resolution to forgo the office for that day.

He would have moved away before, but until the banks were open and he could cash his cheque all his schemes for employing the day in some fitting manner to mark his new maturity were crippled. He took his bundle of crisp notes from the clerk behind the grille, winked at the man, who wondered what he had done to deserve such a salute, and then, whistling a shrill tune which he stoutly imagined to be Schubert's *Marche Militaire*, Polycarp walked down the colonnaded, brass-plate-flanked steps of the bank into the sunshine and petrol-fumes of the city.

He knew exactly what he was going to do. He walked slowly down Wine Street, feeling his young moustache, and stopped at a tobacconist's shop. The window was resplendent with huge polished bowls heaped high with various mixtures of tobacco, and beyond these regular molehills of cut shag, curly cut, and best Virginia rose a precipice of gay-coloured cigarette cartons. Polycarp did not waste any time looking at the window. He knew exactly what he wanted. He bought two ounces of the most expensive tobacco in the shop, a tobacco which Polycarp only smoked when he was left alone in his chief's room at the office long enough to fill and conceal a big cherrywood. He stood chatting for a while to the shop assistant as he filled his pipe; then with clouds of smoke shredding themselves in the breeze behind him as he walked, he made for the Tramway Centre. He skipped across the traffic-lines and came to his objective : a large garage, half faced with a showroom. On the showroom window was a large card:

THE CALL OF THE ROAD
WHY WAIT UNTIL YOU OWN A CAR
DRIVE NOW!
HIRE A CAR—FULLY INSURED
FROM 3Os. PER DAY

Polycarp did not look long at the card. It had appeared in the window for the last two summers, and since that day when a distant cousin had spent a month's holiday with Aunt Felicia, and had taught the schoolboy Polycarp to drive his car, the card in the window had irked Polycarp. He did not earn a high wage, and it was as difficult for him to save thirty shillings as thirty pounds. They could be saved if he rigorously denied himself his weekly shilling seat at the pictures, or if he gave up smoking for a few months; but the subordination of these lesser delights would militate against the pleasure ultimately derived from the joy of a day in the country with a car. Polycarp was not the sort of young man to sacrifice the known joys of cinema and cigarette for the transient joy of a day's outing. In his cosmic scheme—at least, in the cosmic scheme which he favoured at this phase of his life— there should be no necessity for life's minor pleasures to be sacrificed on the altar of its more profound joys. Man, the thinking logical beast, should be able to manipulate the economic system so that he obtained both the minor pleasures and the major delights that life offered.

As it was, man, in the shape of a drunken ship's captain, had manipulated, not the economic system, but a ship's steering system to such effect that Polycarp was enabled to walk boldly into the garage and say to a brown-overalled mechanic:

"I want to hire a care for the day—and I don't want any old crock. It's got to be a car capable of—"

The mechanic interrupted Polycarp's burgeoning specification with a thick and oily thumb. The thumb, travelling in a plane parallel to the cracked concrete floor of the garage, pointed backwards over the man's shoulder as he said tersely:

"Hire cars over there."

"Over there" was a small glass and wood cubicle. Inside the cubicle sat a plump-faced man with pale, bulging blue eyes and a flabby, unshaven chin whose bristles had torn at the knot of his tie until the material was frayed into greasy ravels.

Polycarp repeated his request, and the man sucked at a stump of pencil for a moment before beginning to write on a form. He asked Polycarp several questions, filling up the form as Polycarp replied, and then he said:

"Got a driving licence?"

Polycarp nodded and pulled out the little red book. After his cousin had left them, Polycarp had scrimped and dodged bus conductors in order to save enough money to obtain a licence, and each year he managed to obtain the money for his subscription. The driving licence was a matter of pride with him, and also of wonder; wonder that the State should be so willing to give him official sanction, without so much as taking a look at him, to drive a motor vehicle of any class or description. It is a satisfying feeling for a car-less mortal to know that by paying five shillings he acquires full authority to drive any motor-propelled vehicle, from a three-wheeled invalid chair to a six-wheeled milk-lorry. The easy facilities granted by the State to lethal-minded head-hunters to harry the roads in any class or description of motor vehicle must be taken as in accord with the truest concept of democracy and as one of the hall-marks of a free country. Polycarp was a true democrat and lover of freedom, if not lethal-minded, and had paid his five shillings gladly.

Half an hour later Polycarp was seated at the wheel of a smart two-seater Morris Cowley, sweeping steadily along the wide road to Weston-super-Mare, and by his side was a girl. At a first glance one might have said that she was just an ordinary girl: a cheerful, attractive girl, a girl who looked as though she combined a pleasant face with a fair amount of intelligence, so that neither suffered. But it was not her beauty or her good sense which alone had attracted Polycarp.

He had met her, almost run into her, as he had turned away from the garage after filling up with petrol and oil. She had been about to cross the road as he started. When he blew his horn warningly, she had halted, with perfect pedestrian obstinacy, dead in front of his radiator.

She was a girl of moderate height, dressed in a short skirt of some red material, a blouse of white silk divided down its front with a tie of the same colour as her skirt, and on her head was perched a little black felt hat with a tiny touch of red feather at the side.

She looked round at the sound of his horn, and Polycarp seeing her face for the first time, exclaimed:

Why! Fancy meeting you! This is a pleasure. And to think that I nearly had the honour of knocking down my respected chief's daughter!" He laughed and honked the horn out of high spirits.

The girl, Gracie Hayward, came round to the door of the car.

"Polycarp Jarvis! How you surprised me! I didn't expect to find you in a car. Whose is it? And"—she stared at him oddly—"why aren't you at the office?"

"Ah!" Polycarp shook a finger mysteriously. "Ah! Wouldn't you like to know a lot? Come on, get in beside me and I'll tell you about it. Can I take you anywhere?"

She climbed into the seat beside him, and Polycarp drove off towards the Downs, on whose open roads he could spend half an hour getting used to the feel of the car before he ventured far away from the town with it.

"You see," said Polycarp, "this is a special day. Do you know what day it is?"

"Special day?" She repeated his words curiously and her brown eyes were mildly enquiring.

"Yes! Today I am a man. A grand thought. Today I am a man; yesterday I was a child. In one night the scales have been weighted down and life has become a grave responsibility. And do you know what all that means?"

Gracie shook her head. The only special days which she could think of were flag-days.

"It means that as from today I am legally responsible for all my debts! I'm twenty-one today ..." He finished by breaking into song.

Gracie laughed at his fun. "Congratulations, my little man! Polycarp, you're quite mad. You had to be, of course, with a name like Polycarp; but I like you to be mad. It makes you interesting, you know. I get so tired of boys who are prim and proper. Half of them are afraid to say boo to a goose—"

"The only goose I know lays golden eggs. I had some for breakfast this morning."

"I don't know what you mean, and, anyway, you haven't explained about the car or why you aren't at the office."

"Because of the special day. Surely, Gracie, you couldn't expect me to go into the office on a day like this!" He flourished one arm, and the car sidled immediately towards the opposite gutter, frightening a large Airedale which was sitting in the roadway reflectively scratching itself.

Polycarp explained to her what he was going to do, and finished more seriously:

"You'll be a sport, Gracie, won't you, and not say anything to your father about having met me—"

"Don't worry! I never mention you since he told me that as the daughter of a higher municipal official it was not fitting that I should associate with the two-a-penny clerks in his office. You, my dear Polycarp, are obviously not one of his favourites—though I like you." She said this with an ingenuousness which captured Polycarp's admiration. "I won't say anything. If he knew that you'd taken me to a dance last night—" She threw her hands in the air expressively.

While she was talking, Polycarp did some rapid thinking. Birthdays, it seemed, and especially twenty-first birthdays, were much the same as peppermints, impossible to be enjoyed secretly. The only thing necessary to complete his day of liberty and celebration was a companion, and what better companion could he have than this nineteen-year-old goddess who confessed that his madness amused her? If only his Aunt Felicia were as appreciative ...

The idea was scarcely fully materialised in his mind before Polycarp had asked her to go with him and had overcome her objections with ruthless logic. Before his shower of words Gracie became helpless and a little hysterical. Finally she acquiesced.

"You must stop and let me 'phone mother that I'm going out to lunch with a friend and may not be home to tea," she insisted.

Polycarp nodded indulgently, with an air which seemed to imply that mothers were biologically necessary nuisances, and, as Gracie came out of the telephone-box, he bowed low and handed her with mock courtesy the rose which he had pilfered early that morning.

"Oh, thank you, sir."

"Not at all. Dans la rue de ma tante il y a beaucoup de rose-bushes. Tomorrow I will pick a red one for you. Red for Lancaster, eh? And now speed for Weston!"

They had their lunch at a cafe overlooking the marine lake. They did not waste long over the meal, for both of them were anxious to sample the pleasures of the resort. Polycarp took his bill to the cashier and handed her two half-crowns. The woman was about to slip them into her fill and count his change when she paused and glanced at Polycarp questioningly.

Polycarp raised one eyebrow and stroked his moustache, wondering why she was hesitating to take the money. Seeing his uncomprehending look, the cashier picked up one of the half-crowns and said laconically:

"Dud coin!"

She let the coin slip on to the hard counter of the desk, and it thudded without the least suspicion of a ring.

"A dud?"

"Yes. About as much silver in it as there is in a tuppenny bangle. Someone must have given it to you with your change somewhere. There's a lot of these coins going around just lately. 'Fraid I must ask you for another one, sir."

"Well, I'll be—" Polycarp picked up the coin and handed her another. "You understand I didn't know—"

"Of course."

"Bother it!" He was slightly annoyed. "What a despicable thing to do! Debasing the currency—my currency! Anti-social morons! I don't know—"

He picked up his change and joined Gracie, who was waiting outside for him. He told her about the dud half-crown, and all the sympathy he received was a light laugh.

"The trouble with women," he said bitterly, "is that they look upon money as something which comes, like dew, without effort out of nowhere. But that dud half-crown which has taken the place of a real one represents so much wasted energy, so much fruitlessly expended time and thought, so much—"

"Rubbish!" she finished for him. "Now come and enjoy yourself. Remember, this is your birthday party."

Polycarp shook his head sadly and then completely forgot the coin as he lit a pipe of his expensive tobacco and sent fragrant clouds of smoke curling into the sea air that came sweeping across the wide bay.

Within the next three hours they made a noble, but unsuccessful, effort to exhaust the entertainments which the town offered.

"To derive the utmost satisfaction from pleasure or business it is essential that both should be approached methodically and without prejudice. Therefore, Gracie, we will begin at the far end of the town with the old pier and work our way backwards, attempting everything and scorning only that which is obviously not worthy of our exalted attention. Come on!"

"Oh, Polycarp, you are the limit!" For the daughter of a high municipal official Gracie at times displayed a sad propensity for the mannerisms and vulgarities which are supposedly the prerogative of the misunderstood class from which are drawn thirty-shillings-a-week clerks, honest artisans, dishonest rent collectors, overworked prolific mothers, and unemployed factory hands. Sometimes she even giggled, as though she were a plebeian and not the daughter of a high municipal official; and if Polycarp had not been blinded by his own excess of spirits he might have wondered why she screwed her body in imitation of a carved chair leg every time she laughed at his jokes. Her laughter came from her like paint popping from a tube, only instead of pressing the bottom of the tube, with Gracie the extrusion of mirth was achieved by a quick spiral twist from hips to shoulders.

This depravity for the pleasures of the *hoi polloi* she now indulged to the full, with Polycarp for company.

They went on to the old pier, a gaunt construction of rusty iron piers and long planks that shot vicious little wood splinters into the soles of people's feet as they passed along the causeway. The pier lay out in the muddy sea like an enormous black frying-pan raised on numerous stilts and anchored by its handle to the rocky foreshore. In the centre of the frying-pan simmered and spluttered a batter of astonishing ingredients, and into this churning mass went Gracie and Polycarp.

They passed the next hour like a pair of wasps in a well-stocked confectioner's shop. They threw narrow little wooden rings in an attempt to encircle sparkling brooches of diamanti and cuff-links worked in Birmingham mosaics, while a dark-haired woman with long blue stones dangling from her ears flourished a cane at them, a cane ribbed with half a hundred other rings waiting to be thrown by them.

"Here y'are, sir! Four for tuppence. Win yer lidy a lovely ring and marry her tomorrow. Wot, yer married already? Well—I wouldn't have berlieved it, yer looks so happy! Come on! Life's a gamble, as the man said when the bus went over his wife!"

They threw pennies over a black-and-white checkered cloth studded with metal discs so that each time a penny fell upon a disc a bell rang, and you won sometimes fourpence, sometimes sixpence, but most often tuppence. Polycarp, after a succession of throws, won sixpence, and went on to the next stall uncaring that his sixpenny gain had been at the cost of one-and-sixpence output.

They rode in the gondolas and a saccharine organ poured a thick molasses of amorous dance-music and jazz over them, so that Polycarp had to put his arm around Gracie to guard her from the very remote danger of falling out.

In the centre of the pier was a tall pole, round which they danced together, bumped and pushed by other couples intent upon enjoying themselves. There was a big excursion crowd from Birmingham and London, and two or three paddle-steamers had disembogued hordes of hatless youths and short-skirted girls from the Welsh side of the Bristol Channel. Paper hats made a brave but fluttering show in the wind, and the thin pipe of penny horns and the fluting whine of squeaker balloons voiced an ineffectual protest against the noisy competition of the gondolas' organ.

Polycarp spent money like water. It flowed from his pocket as freely as the brown tide swirled under the pillars of the pier causeway, and with less effect. Gracie threw darts at cards pinned on a board and giggled when an errant dart nearly pierced the right eyeball of a mordant individual who had informed them, "S'easy! S'money for nothing! A child can win a prize! H'yar, sir! 'Ave a go!" This man seemed scared of Gracie's tortile giggling humour, and shook his head as he picked the dart from the matchboarding behind his head.

"Y'better go and have a glass of lemonade," he said. "That'll steady yer hand!"

But they did not want lemonade. They invaded the water-ride and sat hunched up in a little barrel while it bumped and floated its way through dark caverns where skeletons stretched out phosphorous arms at them and skulls grimaced with red and yellow eyeballs from the top of sea-weedy rocks, and past well-lit patches of desert where drooping palm-trees displayed witty mottoes and interrogative questions.

WHY HAVEN'T YOU KISSED HER YET?
FORGET YOU ARE A GENTLEMAN AND BE A MAN.
WHAT HAVE YOU GOT TWO ARMS FOR?

If the barrel-loads of pulchritude and manly restraint which passed along the amorous water-lanes had taken full advantage of the advice of the mottoes the hire-purchase furniture firms would have been working overtime and the marriage-bells would have filled the land with their monotonous clangour. Polycarp proved manfully capable of controlling his emotions. He was no misogynist, though he affirmed at times that he would rather have a pint of old dark beer any day than kiss a girl. As there was no beer in the caverns, he kissed Gracie, and the resulting spiral movement nearly capsized the boat.

"Oh, Polycarp, you've made my hair awfully untidy! What would father say if he could see us?"

Polycarp resented this intrusion of office into his pleasure.

"Keep that man out of this day, will you? I want to enjoy myself. The trouble with England today is that it is governed by men of your father's type. Men of little minds and big—begging your pardon— bellies."

"Oh, Polycarp! What things you say at times! If I told father that, you'd get the sack. But I won't, of course, old thing—" She hastened to assure him of her fidelity.

"Don't," said Polycarp, "call me 'old thing.' It's a term of affection I loathe. And of course you won't tell your father. I know that. Do you think that I'd have brought you with me and let you into my secret if I'd not known that you were the kind of girl I could trust? Let me tell you, Gracie, I may look like a ginger-headed nitwit, but if only some people had my brains there'd be less tragedy and poverty in this world. And when I see a girl of integrity and splendid fidelity, I grab her and say 'Come on, we'll celebrate our mutual intellectual isolation from the masses'."

"And is that what you said when you saw me this morning, old thing?"

"Of course, not! I said, 'Damn, here's old Warhorse Hayward's daughter. If I don't do something quickly, the game's up.' So I had to bring you—you lovely lump of nonsense." He kissed her again quickly to stifle her laughter.

They left the water-caverns for the shooting-gallery, and Gracie watched Polycarp break bottles. They had their weight told. Then they saw the performing fleas, and Gracie wondered for a second or two whether the man was telling the truth when he said that some of the fleas were real Chinese—"You can tell by their slant eyes!" They watched fleas fight a duel, ride bicycles, play hop-scotch, and drive a little coach over a field of green cloth. From fleas they went to skittles, from skittles they wandered to the boating-lake, from boating they hastened, demolishing ice-cream as they went, to donkey-rides, and from donkey-rides they hobbled to the putting-green, and on the putting-green Gracie's twisted humour as she putted landed her ball into every bunker, and once clean out of the putting-ground, so that Polycarp had to climb, clutching for support at a statue of a maiden gleaning corn, over the heavily balustraded wall and rescue it from a terrier dog on the lawns.

"Your putting, mademoiselle," he said as he restored her ball, "is as erratic as the aim of Cupid and about as dangerous."

"But, Polycarp, I do try, old thing. Only it's so difficult to waggle this thing properly, and the holes are so small. I think there ought to be a separate hole for women, and a bigger one at that!"

Her efforts to waggle the putter properly despoiled a lovely hydrangea bloom, razed several glorious spikes of lupins to the turf, and cut the smooth sward into jags, so that her progress round the green was marked by a succession of mangled turfs and decapitated plants.

The putting was definitely not a success, so Polycarp led her away, refusing to listen to her plaints.

They had their tea in a High Street café, and, as they were hurrying along the front to sample the pleasure of the further end of the town, Gracie caught at Polycarp's arm and said:

"Polycarp, look! Do go in and have your fortune told."

She had halted him before a tall boarding-house. In the front garden was a red-and-white striped square tent. From the top of the tent a little pennon of blue cloth flapped in the breeze and displayed the name—Madame Zenovia—to the passing crowd. Madame Zenovia announced, through the medium of various notices on the tent and wall of the garden, that she was at home to reveal the possibilities of the future, between the hours of 10 a.m. and 7 p.m. Outside of those hours the future would remain a closed book, so that if a man were seized by a sudden desire at breakfast-time to know whether he was to travel a long journey by sea, or have an accident involving three distinct modes of conveyance, then he had to possess himself in patience for an hour until Madame Zenovia had thoroughly digested her own breakfast and could apply her mind to auguration instead of mastication; for gastronomy has little in common with crystallomancy. And if a travelling salesman found the mystery of his sales for the coming year too much to bear as he tossed upon his hotel bed, he could expect no help from Madame Zenovia. He would have to lie, hour after hour restless and worried, fretting over the number of calico lengths or sparking-plugs or leather gardening gloves which a fickle public might demand in the year ahead. Only after ten would Madame Zenovia, for the modest sum of half a crown, tell him whether the year was to be a good or bad one for him. For that modest half a crown, Madame Zenovia was prepared to rip back the whole dark curtain which covered the future; the power was hers to give or to withhold, and, like a philanthropic goddess, she offered the fruits of her gift to mankind for the insignificant sum of two shillings and sixpence.

"Go on, Polycarp! Just for fun. See what she says. Go on, old bean. Sometimes they tell you the most amusing things. They never come true, of course, but it's interesting."

"But I have no desire to be informed of my future. It doesn't interest me. And, anyway, I don't believe in fatalism."

"In what?"

"Never mind. I don't want to have my future told. If you are so keen, why don't you have yours done?"

If Gracie had been endowed with acute introspective powers, she would have replied at once that hers was a case for geloscopy, not crystallomancy. She flirted her red skirt as she twisted, and said:

"I don't want to … They make me feel such an ass … Go on, you go. You can tell me what she says and we'll have a good laugh."

Polycarp rubbed his moustache meditatively. "So you'll sacrifice me for a good laugh? Ah, woman, woman … Still, seeing it is my twenty-first birthday, I suppose it wouldn't be amiss to know what lies ahead of me in the gallery of years. Let's hear what Zenovia has to say …"

III
Of doubtful divination, spiritual intoxication, and bad driving

It is not unnatural that, in a world which accepts with ignorant acquiescence the mystery and miracle of wireless, the lesser bruited miracle of accurate prophecy passes without comment. And in the same way as the quacks and charlatans who take shelter under the robe of spiritualism tend to obscure the essential truth which underlies spiritualism, so is it with divination. The foretelling of the future has been the fair game of scores of plausible exploiters of man's ineffable credulities ever since man began to find enough leisure in the present to allow him to meditate upon the future. All classes and times are involved: the Greeks had their Delphian oracles, the Caesars their hieromancy; the men of the Renaissance had their blazing comets, and the city dweller today often consults his dream-book.

That man's future should lie hidden in the entrails of animals, or flash amongst the reflections made by the sun upon nails, or be revealed by dots made at random on paper, by passages in books, by walking in a circle, by pebbles drawn from a heap, or by the position of stars at birth, is an indignity which rarely troubles the minds of honest men, who are content to fill up their football coupons each week, to drink their nightly beer, and who find their present life so full that they have little time to worry about the future. Into this class of indifferent materialists came Polycarp.

When he envisaged the future it was as the future of the race, not the individual. To him the future of the individual was embodied in, and revealed by, the future of the community; but for all his altruistic ideas upon evolutionary Socialism or benevolent dictatorships he could still appreciate the pleasures of a few minutes' dalliance with his own individual future.

There was a little card on the flap of the tent. The side facing him read "Not Engaged." He turned it over so that it read "Engaged" and entered the tent. Gracie watched him go, and then sat down on a seat to wait for him.

Polycarp found himself confronting a dark-green curtain decorated with a rich spangling of white and yellow silk stars. As he stood hesitantly in front of this curtain a voice said in low, clear tones, like the vibrations of a deep gong

"Will you please enter and be seated"; and at the same time a hand slipped round the edge of the curtain, drawing it aside to allow Polycarp to see the figure of a woman seated at a table. Opposite her, on the far side of the table, was an empty chair. Polycarp sat down in the chair and the curtain fell back into position.

"You wish to consult me?"

"That's right ... I want my fortune told ... you know, my future."

"Ah, my good sir ... if I could tell you your whole future I should indeed be a clever and gifted woman. I can only tell you what the crystal reveals to me, and sometimes it remains clouded, wrapped in a fog that lifts but for a second to show some small incident and then is murky again. Do you wish to have a half-crown or a five-shilling consultation?"

"No ... no ... just a half a dollar's worth, please," Polycarp hastened to assure her. No man's future, he thought, could possibly be worth as much as five shillings, and, anyway, he didn't want a five-shilling future. A half-a-crown one was good enough for him.

"Very well."

For the first time Polycarp had a good look at the woman. Her whole body was draped in a black silk gown that gave her a vague, formless appearance. Her head was covered by a cowl of the same material as her gown, and from the black depths of this a thin white face regarded him; a face which, accompanied by normal clothes, might have been commonplace, but now in its macabre setting seemed somehow to be pregnant with prescience. There was a deep cleft between her eyebrows that followed a natural line into the sweep of a long hooked nose, on each side of which, like a warning beacon, blazed a dark, lustreful eye. Below the nose a thin faded red line of mouth emphasised the severity of her narrow wedge-shaped chin. Madame Zenovia had the appearance of a cruel hawk, ready to sweep scornfully on any trembling mortal who had the temerity to ask for a half-crown instead of a five-shilling future.

Polycarp fronted her glare without alarm. He could always appreciate the beauty of a tasteful theatrical note introduced into business. If he had known the woman he would have suggested that a large silver triangle across the front of her gown might be even more impressive than the austerity of its present sombre folds; as it was, he sat with his hands on his knees and watched her as she rolled a green baize cloth from an object on the table and revealed her crystal.

"Look into the crystal as I do," she uttered in solemn tones.

Obediently Polycarp looked at the crystal. They both concentrated their gaze upon it for a few seconds and then the dull sphere suddenly brightened with light, and the reflected gleam danced in Madame Zenovia's eyes like splinters of ice. Idly Polycarp wondered where she concealed the battery and switch which brought the ball to life. Outside he could hear the whirr of motors passing along the front, and catch the low murmur of the returning tide and the screams of children playing on the sands. His attention was drawn from these exterior interests by the sound of Madame Zenovia's voice. She spoke like the grumble of a steady avalanche rumbling down some interminable mountain-side.

"The crystal clears and I see many faces ... There is confusion and strife. I see a change for you, a change of position ... Now the crystal dims ... Ah, there lie before you many journeys, long journeys through blackness. I cannot tell what the blackness means; but at last I see the blackness fades and the sun shines with brightness upon you and you are happy ... The crystal is troubled. ... Yours is a curious future ... The crystal tells me that you will rise to a great height only to fall back, but after your fall you will find something to make you forget your reverses … You will make long journeys in search of happiness … but in the end you will find it. There will be many men pass through your life but few women, though in the end you will meet a woman whom you cannot escape, a dark-haired woman … The crystal changes and I see great crowds waving their hands, and there is a black shining machine that beats up and down and is surrounded by men. I see men running about … The crystal tells me that, although you are honest by nature, you will not always find it wise to be too honest, though you will never take advantage of those unable to look after themselves … Ah …" She clutched at the edges of the table, with a fine histrionic effect, as though the efforts of her divinations were too much for her. "Ah … the crystal dims again and all is black—"

All was black because just then she switched off the light and with a deft movement swung the cloth back over the ball.

"Is that all?" enquired Polycarp.

"That's all. The crystal divulged much to you. Usually it reveals little that is definite. Thank you." She held out her hand and took Polycarp's money.

When Gracie saw him come out she hurried to him.

"Well, Polycarp? What did she say to you? Are you going to marry a fair woman or go for a long journey?"

"Yes, it's all coming to me," answered Polycarp as they made their way up the road. "Only the woman's going to be dark-haired—that puts you out of the running, I'm afraid, Gracie, unless you dye it! All the usual junk; long journeys, ups and downs, men running about. And then she insulted me by saying that the crystal said I was an honest bloke. What's my morals to do with a crystal that was born in the Midlands and will finish life as a garden decoration?"

"But it may all come true, Polycarp, old boy. And what's there to be annoyed about in finding out that you're honest? You knew that, didn't you?"

"Of course, I did," said Polycarp. "But why pay half a crown to be told something one already knows? Telling me I was honest! Anyway, I got my own back. I passed her that dud half a crown!"

"Polycarp! You didn't?" Gracie was shocked.

34

"You bet I did! Someone passed it to me. The rule in any bimetallic country is an eye for an eye … and so on. Come on and I'll treat you to a glass of sherry. With a future like mine I can afford it."

"Oh, Polycarp! I don't know how you can have the cheek to do and say such things. You are interesting. I wish father didn't disapprove of you." Gracie laughed, and condoned his moral lapse as she clung to his arm.

"You forget," said Polycarp severely, as he stood with his hand on the door of the Hotel Metropole, "Zenovia said a dark-haired woman."

They entered the Hotel Metropole at a few minutes after half past six. Drinking, far from being one of their vices, was not even entitled to call itself a habit with them.

There were only a few times in the year when Gracie indulged in intoxicants; Christmas-time, when there was liquor in the house—for her father was one of those fortunate men who always seem to win prizes in draws; on the twenty-ninth of April, which was her birthday and always honoured by the ceremonial drinking of grocer's port while her family and friends wished her luck and all the things which go with birthdays; and on the rare occasions when she was permitted to attend a dance which was enlivened by the presence of a bar, and then she guardedly fortified herself with not more than two cocktails in order that she might not be execrated as a wet blanket by her more vinous friends.

Polycarp drank beer on the isolated occasions when he found himself in the company of men who treated beer as though it were as innocuous as weak tea, and he did so then merely to prevent himself from being regarded as a raw youngster. The only time he enjoyed a glass of beer was after a long walk, when he sat down before a plate of bread and cheese. At other times his drinking was a pose, and a dangerous pose, for Polycarp had early found that he was one of those unfortunate (or fortunate—it, depends entirely upon your outlook) individuals who can become happily oblivious of decorum and pleasantly regardless of propriety on three half-pints of mild ale. Later in his life he was to find that his defect presented an economic asset and a social drawback.

But today was a special occasion. A human being reaches—though he may regret it many times—manhood only once in his life. And

Gracie and Polycarp drank without any feeling of hesitancy. It is true that they only had two drinks each, but the warmth and pleasantness of the room, the long, deep lounges, the palms in their neat brass-bound tubs, the obsequious waiters, the thick carpets and quick gushing sound as beer-handles were drawn; the gay appeal of coloured advertisements by which five different whiskeys, four kinds of beer, and numerous liquors announced, through the medium of horses, dogs, Highland chiefs, pretty girls balanced on apples, bearded octogenarians, and a blindfolded man in evening dress, that each was the only drink worth taking; the soft chatter of other people about them; and the casualness of other glasses being filled and drained quickly—all combined to induce in them that pleasurable, daring feeling which assails those whose mental state is not far removed from that which apprehends that to taste a glass of beer is to be immediately seized with the craving to go on drinking and drinking until life leads to the drunkard's grave. Gracie had two glasses of sherry and imagined that she was slightly intoxicated; her face grew a little flushed and she a little excited by the thought of her utter demoralisation and intrepidity. She knew that sherry made one merry, and she was determined to be merry merely because she knew that it was against all her principles to be in such a state. Merriness belongs to the drinker; teetotal folk must be content with solid mundane happiness. Polycarp drank two glasses of beer and his reaction was much the same as Gracie's, for his social ethics, when stripped of their extravagant trimmings, were almost identical with hers; but his assumed gaiety was heightened and enriched by a moiety of abandon which was directly due to his peculiar inability.

Between them they had not drunk enough to make a stork uneasy on its legs. They left the Hotel Metropole with all their faculties quickened, and possessed of a sense of their own depravity and daring in having publicly taken beer and sherry in a hotel when one should have been at home sewing and the other recuperating from a strenuous day at the office.

As they stood outside the hotel, Gracie said solemnly:

"Polycarp, we must go home. It's getting late and my people will wonder where I am."

Having delivered herself of this remark, she hitched herself sideways and laughed as though each one of her words was the quintessence of humour.

"Home!" Polycarp mouthed the word sadly. "Just think, Gracie, there are thousands of people without homes. There's something wrong somewhere—"

"Of course, Polycarp. But we haven't got time to bother about them at the moment. Things always work out, don't you think so?"

"No, I don't, Gracie. Come on, let's go home!" He caught her arm and started away towards the sea front. If she had not restrained him he would have been involved in a steeplechase over the geraniums and tulips of the ornamental gardens.

"That's not the way to the garage," she giggled.

"I know that!" said Polycarp sternly. "But there's a very fine specimen of a *macracarpus cascarasagrada* in the rockery over here which I wanted you to see ..."

The keen air of the returning tide and the erratic swirl of lights and moving people about him all tended to enhance Polycarp's delight in his ethereal feeling. The beer played little arpeggios of exaltation in his mind, so that his brain functioned with cinematographic quickness and brilliance. Gracie watched and listened, and the disarming spectacle of Polycarp's apparent tipsiness made her forget her own slight exhilaration. Gracie discovered for herself the old truth which is sometimes unpleasant—that drink can so change men within half an hour that the influence of a thousand years of traditional restraints and prides and the effect of twelve years of the most expensive and cultured life in school and university may be nullified and reveal man as a pitiable or humorous cipher whose cerebellum has for a while lost control of his cerebrum. Gracie rapidly reverted to normal in the fresh air, and was a little frightened by Polycarp. She need not have been, for Polycarp, although a little more extravagant in his utterances when in a state bordering upon ebriety, was always the soul of propriety.

They reached the garage where the car was parked without any misadventure, though Gracie had an anxious, giggling moment in front of a greengrocer's shop when Polycarp almost decided to go in and ask the shopman if he might show him how the various colours of the different fruits might be utilised by way of contrasts and harmonies to form a perfect aesthetic unity. For one moment his mind had dwelt lovingly on long rows of bright oranges, pyramids of pomegranates, and bold Byzantine columns built of pineapple.

"I will fashion for Mother Ceres a temple such as no Greek ever conceived …"

Gracie tactfully got him away before he could lay a hand to a banana.

Gracie was distinctly feminine in outlook; when confronted by the possibility of danger her reaction was more inclined to panic than philosophy. She sat now at Polycarp's side and wondered fearfully while he played about with gear-handle and brakes as though his profession were that of a motor-racer. He had decided—and would not listen to her contrary arguments—that they should return to Bristol by way of Cheddar Gorge. And by Cheddar Gorge they went.

The twin beams of the headlights bored into the night so that the blackness leaped to life in a succession of hasty film scenes. Trees, powdered with light, bowed before them like lofty-coiffured ladies and waved their wide skirts over the edge of the road as they passed. Stiff white gate-posts, like the spindle legs of gallants who held their bodies high in the hidden sky, stood in steady pose, and occasionally one of the legs would reveal the flash of jewelled garter where a prowling cat crouched on top of a post waiting for the voles that whispered in the dried grasses of the ditch. Sometimes the side of a cottage would start across the screen in whitewashed wonder, with dark black window-eyes staring at them as they roared by. On and on like a buzzing, disturbing insect the little two-seater hurried through the country roads, and Polycarp gripped the wheel as though he were at the helm of a tea-clipper tossing in the Indies. The balmy June air filled his lungs with a wine compressed of all the sweetness of the land about him; there were in it the scents of the thyme on the hillside, the beauty of the evening flush on a lark's wing, the richness of the purple knapweeds that stained the hayfields, and the sparkle of the starshine that wavered in the dark pools which were guarded so closely by hanging larch and trailing alders. The air filled him with a stronger, more riotous intoxication than any alcoholic spirit could give. He sang aloud for joy that he was alive and healthy and twenty-one.

The curlews roosting by the grass tufts on the upper slopes of the hills lifted their arched bills in the air and stood ready to rise into the slight breeze as the sound of *Down Rio* came trolling across the night.

Just before they reached Cheddar a hare started from the road ahead of them, and, dazed by the headlights, leaped away deer-fashion along the road. The animal seemed unable to break away from the fascination of the lights, so Polycarp stopped the car and switched off the lamps to allow it to escape.

When the hare was gone, he started the car, and in two minutes had forgotten the animal.

"Oh, Polycarp, darling, do be careful!"

Another car suddenly leaped from the night ahead of them. Polycarp swung the wheel with a magnificent sweep of his arm, and Gracie was thrown against the side of the seat as they swerved. Dusty briar-stalks scratched at the canvas hood and then they were back on an even course.

"S'nothing!" said Polycarp calmly. "You should have seen me bring her through an equinoctial monsoon in ninety-eight, when the whole of England was waiting for the tea I had on board; Noah wasn't in anything like as bad a fix. It takes a lot to get Polycarp down. Driving's like swimming. If you've got the confidence you can do it. Without the confidence—" He flourished his hand expressively, and Gracie was impressed by the scorn on his young face. His eyes were wild, and in the blackness of the car she could sense that his hair was blown awry. So completely out of himself was he that she had not observed him to stroke his moustache since leaving the Hotel Metropole.

Polycarp's dictum that confidence was the chief part of driving may or may not be correct; though it seems very obvious that a man who drives without confidence is in the same position as a doctor who is seriously ill and has to prescribe his own medicine—he may survive. Anyway, from the moment that they turned off the main roadway and began to mount through Cheddar Gorge, Polycarp gave Gracie as superb an exhibition of confidence as ever Blondin presented on a tight-rope. He passed what few cars there were with a daring assurance that looked like safety; he changed up and down through his gears with crisp crescendos and diminuendos that reverberated up the grey cliff side and started little stones into avalanches; he swung round hairpin bends so that the crushed road-grit spun away from his wheels in a fan, to fall amongst the paper-bags and cigarette-cartons that littered the lower part of the gorge, adding a defiantly domestic touch amidst such soaring grandeur, and at intervals he honked his horn to clear the way before him. Gracie had never had such a wild ride.

She sat shivering and frightened in the car, waiting for death. For her there was no sky, no gorge, no road, no sanity; only was there a mad vortex of twisting macadam that danced and writhed under the lights, great vicious patches of grey rock-face, deformed blackthorn-bushes sprouting from the cliffs like shaggy eyebrows; and rushing black gulfs of star-lit nothingness that was the sky; and all the time Polycarp's exultant voice and horn shredding the night to screaming echoes and turning peace to pandemonium. The small soul of Gracie could not rise to the flighting heights where Polycarp's roamed. The effects of his beer had long worn off; he was filled now with the intoxication of the ride, of the fresh air, of the dark, star-stippled night, of his grand disregard for conventions and of his daring at taking a day off. She had tried to accommodate him at first, but when they had stepped out of the Hotel Metropole she had been left behind, and the person who now sat by his side was no longer Gracie, but a slim bundle of frets and worries. Polycarp, however, did not think so. She still looked like Gracie to him, and when they were at the top of the Gorge he stopped the car with a vicious jerk to receive her congratulations on his driving. At least, so he expected. Gracie's first words were far from admiring.

"Oh, Polycarp, why are you stopping? Please hurry home! And try and drive more carefully. It's so late, and father will be angry."

"Who cares about him?"

"Stop it, Polycarp. You mustn't talk about my father like that! If you don't take me home immediately I shall tell father ..."

Polycarp laughed—hollowly, as he thought, though the sound was no more than a discordant jangle of coughs.

"Who cares? Not I ... me ... not I. Gracie, you are lovely. Here on this wind-swept hill you blossom in the dark corner of the car like a tiger-lily, like a Woolworth's tulip, like a ... By George ... I never knew till now how much I loved you." He leaned forward quickly and kissed her. She pushed him away and wailed, "I'll tell father, if you don't go at once!"

"You're divine. The colour rushes to your face, though I can't see it in the dark, like the sun warming the clouds to send them out for the day. Stay there. I feel the stirring afflatus of poetry. You are so beautiful. The organ-grinder—crystal-gazer was wrong, with her dark hair ..."

Polycarp descended from the seat, and to a chorus of Gracie's "I want to go home. I'll tell father!" he walked over the road and sat himself on the low stone wall. For ten minutes he completely ignored Gracie, resting his chin on his hand, muttering to himself and beating one hand in the air.

"Polycarp, you are mean! I want to go home. Oh, why did I come?"

"Gracie, Gracie, how can you want to leave me now? You belong to me for ever. Listen to me, listen to my song! For you I declare my love." He came back from the wall, and there was a happy look on his face. He felt like Milton, though his actions gave Gracie every excuse for regarding him as a madman. He began to declaim:

> *"Still is the air*
> *As still as the sea,*
> *And heavy my heart*
> *That yearns for thee.*
>
> *White is the thorn*
> *That stands by the wall,*
> *And whitest thy face—*
> *And fairest of all.*
>
> *Bright is the sun*
> *That springs from the hill,*
> *And strong is my love*
> *That—"*

"Polycarp! Take me home! You must! You're crazy! And I hate you! And I wish I hadn't come!"

Polycarp stopped, and for a brief moment he was sane, as sane as he had been at breakfast that morning. He saw for the first time that he really was frightening Gracie. He climbed into the car, a little chastened at the vision of his own uncouthness, then the warm comfort of his exultation came back to him, and he smiled.

"I'm sorry, Gracie. Didn't mean to scare you. I thought you were enjoying it as much as I was."

The car started, and they now drove silently through the night.

41

IV
Polycarp loses his temper, his job, and his suitcase

Polycarp awoke the next morning possessed of an ill-defined feeling of apprehension and seventy-five of his eighty pounds.

His Aunt Felicia gave him a curious look at breakfast, and said:

"What ever happened to you yesterday, boy? You didn't come into lunch or tea. If I did not know you were capable of looking after yourself, I should have been worried."

"I know, aunt ..." Polycarp had no desire to go into ong explanations. "You see ... we were rather busy at the office. A big committee in the morning and there wasn't time to come home for lunch, and I didn't bother about tea because I worked late."

"What a busy day! You'll have to hurry this morning; you must be tired ..." Something in the timbre of her words suggested to Polycarp that his aunt did not believe his explanation. He looked across the table at her, but her fine, perfectly composed face gave no hint. She sat there, as she had been doing for as long as he could remember, one hand warming itself under the tea-cosy, and the other fiddling about with the brittle piece of toast which she called her breakfast. He had never seen her excited or moved to emotion; life seemed to pour over her as though she were a smooth, well-polished boulder standing splendidly in the centre of a swift stream. He believed that if he said to her, "Aunt, yesterday I killed a man," she would reply calmly, "Yes, boy, and why did you do that?"

He rose from his breakfast, and this morning an impulse prompted him to move over to her and kiss her lightly on the forehead. As he bent to her, his hair fell in sunlight across hers, which for years had been a dull pepper-and-salt colour.

She smiled at him as he left the room, and thought to herself, "That young rogue has something on his conscience." And she was correct in her assumption, for Polycarp knew quite well that he was going into battle, and like a wise general he wanted to make sure that his reserve line was secure from disaffection.

As he walked to the office his sense of guilt grew steadily within him. Now that he could view the whole of the proceedings of the past twenty-four hours divorced from the excitement and exhilaration of the previous day, he saw that he had behaved rather badly and he was sorry, though he would not have admitted his sorrow to anyone. He thought of Gracie and her quaking, almost tearful state when he had restored her to her home, and he wondered whether she had kept the secret of his truancy or whether she had blurted everything to her father. He hoped she would prove staunch and keep her faith with him; but the more he considered the matter the clearer he saw that she would have every justification for ignoring the promise which she had made to him before they had started for Weston-super-Mare. His feelings as he walked up the slope to the Guildhall were tending to be misogynistic. Why, he asked himself, had he clouded the joy of his day off by taking a girl with him? It had complicated the pleasure of his day, and finally left him stranded with this horrible feeling in his stomach as though it were a ship's hold which a couple of million rats were vacating at short notice. He remembered the last time he had had a quivering sensation vibrating about his large intestine; that had been before he took the Senior School Certificate examination. He bit the nail of his right forefinger reflectively, and the passers-by, observing this pensive, keen-faced young man, might have been forgiven for thinking that the problem which exercised his mind was more weighty and serious than it really was. His problem was—Had Gracie told her father? Mr. Hayward, he knew, would not hesitate to bully the truth from her if he guessed she was trying to lie to him.

At the entrance to the office he made an effort and threw off his gloom. He entered the building, whistling and fingering his moustache.

The other clerks in the room nodded good morning, and in reply to their enquiries he said : "Yes, I felt a bit off the mark yesterday. Been overworking myself lately ..." This effort at a joke produced a roar of contemptuous laughter and rude replies, under the cover of which Polycarp entrenched himself at his table and began to frown at his papers.

At ten o'clock a clerk came out of Mr. Hayward's room and called across to Polycarp.

"Polycarp, Hayward wants you—and the old boy's wearing his war medals this morning. As lovely a temper as ever came out of Hell!"

Polycarp went like a lamb to the slaughter.

Mr. Henry Isaac Hayward was a tall, middle-aged man who never liked to be reminded of the Isaac and could never forget that he had been a captain in the Great War. He suffered from a permanent superiority complex, occasional gout, and a temper as raw and more frequent than cold November mornings. He was in a permanent state of bad temper towards his clerks, who disliked him with a consistency as unchanging as his own spleen, and they had long ago abandoned any hope of ever doing anything right for him or gaining any praise for their work. He wore his hair in a convict's crop, so that his white scalp showed through his scrubby gorse-like growth as though it were a chalky downland; and he believed in running his office staff as if they were army orderlies, and very bad orderlies at that.

"Ah, Jarvis!" he barked, as Polycarp came in and shut the door. "Why didn't you report for duty yesterday?"

And that, thought Polycarp, who was facing what he liked to think was his destiny, was just the sort of awkward question the man would ask. Polycarp hesitated to tell the lie. If he told the truth, there was sure to be a row. If he told the lie, he might be caught out ... Morality, mused Polycarp at that moment, was entirely an affair of compromises.

"Haven't you got a tongue, man? You let us down badly. What happened?" Mr. Hayward's steel-grey eyes caught Polycarp in their gaze and forced a reply from him.

"I'm sorry if I caused any inconvenience, sir. I was quite unable to come ... er ... er ... I was indisposed."

"You mean you went sick?"

"Yes, sir."

"Then why can't you say what you mean? Indisposition is a woman's complaint!"

"Yes, sir." Polycarp breathed a little sigh of relief. If the old fool was picking him up on small points, then it was pretty certain he knew nothing about his truancy. Gracie had been faithful to him. He would see Gracie and repay her somehow.

"So you went sick, eh? Well, Jarvis, we all have our infirmities, I suppose. You your indisposition and I my gout, curse it! But"—and as he mouthed the word Mr. Hayward seemed to swell up like a balloon until he filled the room, and the veins on his forehead were like main roads on a white map—"when I have gout, I stop at home and keep warm. But not Jarvis, eh? Not Jarvis! What kind of malady was yours, sir, that you had to go to Weston-super-Mare in a hired car? Did it need ozone treatment? Did it? Did it mean that you had to take a nurse with you? Did it? And did you persuade my daughter to be a nurse for you? Did you? And did you have to drown your pain in swilling beer? Did you? And did you have to scare my daughter out of her wits almost by furious, mad driving? Did you? Aaaaaah!" He drew breath for a fresh discharge. "A curious, convenient malady, Jarvis; very curious, but not very convenient for the office—"

"My illness, sir," Polycarp broke in boldly, "was more mental than physical. I wasn't suffering from such bodily infirmity as gout or headache. I was ..." Now that the hostilities had begun in earnest Polycarp strangely found himself able to stand up to the battery of his chief. No man should browbeat him while he called himself John Polycarp Jarvis. "You may be unaware, sir, but yesterday I was twenty-one, and the entry to manhood—"

"Manhood! Why some of the lice in our army blankets were better men than you'll ever be! And if becoming a man entitles you to drive irresponsibly, become intoxicated, and frighten innocent girls out of their wits—"

"I am sorry to have frightened Gracie, sir. I apologise for that. But I was not intoxicated, and I would remind you that Gracie came with me of her own free will, and, what is more, gave me her word that she would say nothing to you. It seems strange"—Polycarp, realising that his boats were blazing merrily, could not resist the dig at the pompous old war-horse—"that the daughter of an officer and a gentleman should find it so easy to break her word—"

"Jarvis!" Hayward exploded like Vesuvius. "This is impertinence! I won't stand it! You deliberately play truant from the office at our busy period, and then you come back and insult your chief. Have you lost your senses? You seem to treat this affair and the whole of your work as a comedy! I'll report you to the committee!"

While the chief was speaking, Polycarp was doing some quick thinking. He had said enough to get him the sack from any ordinary commercial office, though perhaps not enough to merit the committee to whom Hayward was responsible being justified in dismissing him. Local government committees are more tolerant than company directors. But Polycarp knew that even if he didn't get dismissed for his impertinence the rest of his time at the office would be a hell, for Hayward would always remember the insult and would do his utmost to humiliate and pester him. The thought of a few more years at the office with Hayward to harry him did not appeal to Polycarp. He had made up his mind long ago that he would forsake the service as soon as possible for something which would offer him more scope for his ambitions, and now, it seemed, the gods were engineering a way for him. He had enough money to keep him for a while, and the thought of this gave him a comfortable feeling of assurance. He would not let Hayward have a chance to threaten him with dismissal, or humiliate him with badgering forgiveness.

Polycarp smiled for the first time that day.

"I should hardly say that I treat it as a comedy, sir," he said politely. "Let us rather call it a comedy of errors. After all, what is local government but an epitome of democracy, and what is democracy but a fundamental error which has possessed the minds of men—"

"Jarvis! Are you utterly mad? You've said enough to get you dismissed from the service."

Polycarp waved a conciliatory hand towards his chief. "Not mad, sir. Not mad; but gifted at this moment with a divine acuteness of perception. I've stayed so long in this place that I've almost become blinded. Now I see again. Office work was never intended for men of ambition and courage. It saps those qualities. I know"—Polycarp flourished his hand as the man started forward, and there was an imperial quality about him which kept Mr. Hayward dumbstruck in his chair—"I know exactly what you're going to say. I'll help you out. You can't get me sacked, because I'm giving in my notice—now. Yes, I'm leaving, and before I go I'll say something which every one of those clerks out there and a few million in other offices in the world would like to say to you and your kind. You think, because you get a few hundreds a year more than they ever will, that you own 'em. Remember, won't you, that they're human; that they appreciate politeness, and that they do their best when you acknowledge it. You curse their occasional mistakes, but you forget the hundreds you make. Don't expect infallibility in others if you can't achieve it yourself."

"Jarvis!" Mr. Hayward waved a ruler. "Stop, I tell you. You're insane. You don't know Someone take this fool away—"

"Don't bother, I'm going by myself. And the next time you are in a furious temper because you've got gout and your wife.served you with fat bacon instead of lean, come into the office and work yourself up into a real paroxysm and then go out and jump off the Suspension Bridge. I can promise you that the whole office will give you the biggest cheer of your life. By that one act you'll endear yourself to them for ever. Good morning, Mr. Isaac Hayward, and convey my respects to the committee for the many pleasant hours I've spent in their offices."

And, without giving the astonished man a chance to speak or act, Polycarp scuttled from the room, walked quickly through the clerks' room, and, snatching his hat from its peg, went out into the street. It was not until the noise of the traffic came flooding round his ears and the sight of people hurrying about their business cleared his head of its rampaging emotions that he realised acutely what he had done. And, when he did realise, he refused to regret it. He stared reflectively into the gutter.

"What's the matter, mate? You look as though yer'd lorst summat!" A G.W.R. motor-man stooped to crank his engine. Polycarp shook his head and grinned. The world didn't stop going round just because he had given up his job.

"I'm all right," he said. He turned and made his way over the road, and so, stroking his moustache, he found himself at last sitting on an iron bollard by the dockside, watching a Swedish timber boat being warped into her berth.

"One crowded hour of glorious life is worth an age without a name," he murmured slowly to himself. "And I wonder what Aunt Felicia will say. This looks like the end of Bristol for me. What a damned fool I am at times ..."

It was four o'clock when Polycarp reached home, and by that time he had walked and thought himself back to his normal state. He had spent the latter part of the morning and the early afternoon lying on his back underneath a tree on the Downs, eating ices from paper cartons, and making plans. The ices had been runny with the heat, and the plans sketchy from the confusion of so many potentialities. Only one thing emerged from his welter of ideas and plans; that he would leave Bristol and make a name for himself so that no one should ever be able to reproach him for what, he now saw, was no more than a deplorable, but exciting, lack of self-control. At twenty-one the human mind is as adaptable to fresh material as a puppy's stomach, and Polycarp entered the house with only the slightest qualm of apprehension at what his aunt would say. He guessed that she would be sensible about everything.

His aunt was sitting by the open window, sewing, when he walked into the room. She looked up in surprise as he shut the door, and cast a swift glance at the marble clock on the mantelshelf to see whether she had mistaken the time.

"Why, boy, you are home early. I thought you were very busy at the office?"

Polycarp came over to her, and, sitting on the window-sill, put his hands into his pockets. For the first time in his life he began to appreciate fully the quiet wisdom and unexcitable good sense with which his aunt was endowed.

"I hope you won't be upset, aunt, at what I'm going to tell you; but you see, the truth is that I've given up my job at the office. I resigned today, and walked out ..." He waited for her.

Slowly she put down her sewing and looked up at him. "You've resigned your position?"

He nodded. Then she added, with a half-smile playing around the corners of her mouth. "You're sure you resigned, and not ..."

"Yes. I beat them by a short head that way, otherwise it was bound to be ... I don't know, I suppose I've been a silly fool, but I simply could not help myself. You see, aunt, yesterday I didn't go into the office."

"I guessed that much," she put in quietly. "Go on. ..."

Polycarp went on. He recounted the whole story to her, censoring and abridging only those portions which it seemed to him were entirely irrelevant. He finished talking, and waited for her to say something.

"When you do a thing, you do it in style, don't you, boy? If you wanted to resign, why didn't you do it less flamboyantly?"

"I ... well, I didn't know I did loathe the place so much until it came to me today ... and then it was too late to think of the proper procedure. Besides," he added more cheerfully, "if I'd done it in the proper way, I couldn't have told old Warhorse Hayward just what I thought of him and his kind ..."

"You haven't told me about that."

"Oh, that was just by the way. The point is now ... is ..."

"Is what are you going to do with yourself. Have you got any plans about another job?"

Polycarp got down from the window-sill and stood in front of her.

"Yes, I have, aunt; but I'm afraid that you may not like them. You see, I want to leave you and Bristol."

"Yes, boy."

"Oh, I know you'll have a lonely life when I'm gone, but honestly, aunt, I'm a man now, and I've got to make my way in the world. I've got a little money, and with that I shall be able to live until I find something which I like doing. I won't, at least, impose upon you in that way. Oh, aunt, don't you see"—Polycarp's visions which he had enjoyed on the Downs came back to him—"don't you see what an opportunity this is for me to find my right place in life? There are too many round pegs in square holes. I was one, but now my chance has come to discover the life I want to live, not what someone else wants me to live. And I'm going to do it. I'm going to leave Bristol, and I'll make a fortune, and then one day I'll come back for you ..."

"It sounds like Dick Whittington, boy. Do you think it's wise to go out into the world with so little money?"

"No, it's not wise. That's the beauty of it! Don't you realise, aunt, all great men have had to take that chance, to gamble as it were on their luck, and look how they came through."

"I know, boy, but the world never hears of the million sad failures who also started out with the few fortunate ones, and on whom luck never shone. Still, I don't want to discourage you. You're your own master. I shall be lonely, but I'd rather be lonely than be selfish and keep you. And you know that at any time there's always a place for you here …"

He put his arm around her, and held her comfortingly. "I know, aunt, and I'm sorry to have to go."

She smiled and patted his hand.

"And when are you going, and where?"

"The day after tomorrow. I haven't many arrangements to make or business to clear up. I thought about going to Oxford first of all. I've always sort of wanted to see the place."

Whether his Aunt Felicia understood Polycarp's desire to go to Oxford is a mystery which may safely be left with her. She was a wise woman, and, what is more rare, a wise woman who was unconscious of her wisdom. She just accepted his statement without question. When a young man starts out into the world to seek his fortune, he might profitably begin either at Golder's Green or Christianshaab, for Fortune left the City of London a long time ago. But Polycarp's choice of Oxford had a very definite genesis. Although his aunt was comfortably situated with a small private income, she was by no means wealthy, and the most which she had been able to afford for Polycarp was a grammar-school education. Polycarp's dream had been a course at Oxford University. Unfortunately for him he was far too unstable and sciolistic to win a scholarship, but all his life he had dreamed his own private dream of Oxford, and, now that he was free to do as he liked, he had decided to go to Oxford and live for a while in the atmosphere of the unattainable. Browning once said that a man's reach should exceed his grasp, which probably accounts for the fact that the Wessex labourer on an excursion to London spends his time gaping in Park Avenue, and forgets his wife as he looks at the bare beauties displayed on bills outside the West End theatres. A man can only live his own life, and often how very narrow and irksome it is; but there is nothing to stop a man from dreaming—nothing to stop a cow-hand from dreaming of cocktails instead of milk, of clipping Venus in his arms as he lies by the side of his hard-breathing wife, and thus it was with Polycarp. Only now, he was determined to live for a moment on the edge of a dream. So he decided to go to Oxford to begin his search after fortune.

At nine-thirty two days later he was standing outside the coaching office on the Tramway Centre, waiting. Aunt Felicia was not with him. They had said their farewells in the house, and she had cried a little as she watched him, from behind the pink curtains of her bedroom, walking away down the street with his suitcase in hand. She watched him go, and the picture remained with her for the rest of her life as the true Polycarp, the Polycarp she knew and loved. She never lost her love for him, but somehow he was never the same person after that morning. He walked quickly, for he was anxious not to remain under the barrage of inquisitive eyes which he knew must be concentrated upon him from the houses in the street. His trilby hung on the back of his head, his brown sports jacket swung open, and his grey flannel trousers were marked about the turn-ups with grease which he had encountered during his drive to Weston-super-Mare. After he had turned the corner and gone out of her sight, his aunt went, sniffing, to make her beds and resume the routine of her quiet life.

Polycarp was no young man of good family and fortune who decides to abandon wealth and walk round the world, and, coming back after four years, writes a book entitled *World Trek* or *Round the Globe on Five Pounds*, and tactfully forgets to record the wired remittances which reached him at New York, Buenos Ayres, San Diego, Melbourne, Parang, Calcutta, Suez, Cannes (slightly larger remittance than usual), and Rome, or to mention that he was well known to the officials of half the world's consulates, and consequently traded his acquaintance for food and shelter. No one objects to such books, but it is regrettable that truth is as great a stranger to such young men as a good hard kick in the pants. Polycarp had no real friend but his aunt; he had no money beyond the seventy-two pounds seven and eightpence which now remained from his eighty, and his only possessions were the clothes in which he was dressed and the contents of his suitcase, namely: two extra shirts, one blue striped, the other plain white, with a darn close to the neckband, which was hidden by his collar; four collars to match shirts; an extra vest and pair of pants; six pairs of socks, five of them plain, and the sixth, his pride and delight, a work of art in circles of colours drawn straight and indiscriminately from the spectrum; a school tie, slightly stained with perspiration where the knot came under his chin; a navy-blue serge suit, with a camphor ball in in each pocket; a pair of black shoes; and wedged into the sides of the case, next to the Woolworth's washing-bag which contained his toilet articles, his books. Three books Polycarp considered necessary to his comfort, for the rest his literature could be supplied by the free libraries; one was *Chambers's Etymological Dictionary*, which he had pilfered from school, and whose fly-leaves were adorned with slightly bawdy verses, another a small octavo leather-bound volume entitled *Disraeli's Curiosities of Literature* which had enlightened Polycarp on subjects as varied as old English drinking customs and the origin of Dante's *Inferno*, and the last, a Bible, which was a purely artistic and orthodox concession to the generally accepted, but less generally appreciated, dictum that it contained the best and all that man could want of literature.

And there Polycarp stands, waiting for the coach. What little other odd and ends he owned had been left behind at his aunt's. That was at nine-thirty. At twelve-thirty he possessed even less, for he was without his suitcase.

The coach came in, and Polycarp, after handing his case up to the driver, who was stowing the passengers' luggage on top of the roof, found himself a seat at the back of the coach. There were a lot of people travelling, and the coach was uncomfortably full. Before starting Polycarp bought a weekly, but after a half-hour's determined effort to read he put the paper aside and contented himself with watching the flying scenery. The coach went north from Bristol to Cheltenham, and then from Cheltenham struck due eastwards towards Oxford.

Some time after the coach had left Cheltenham it drew up at a neat little wayside hotel to give the passengers an opportunity of obtaining refreshments and exercising their legs after sitting in a cramped position for several hours. Polycarp was not interested in the other travellers, and in his present mood he was not interested in refreshments. He stood for a few moments outside the hotel, and then walked round to the yard at the back of the building.

In the yard was a small smithy, and through the open doorway he could see the forge fire glowing like an enflamed eye. The merry bastinado of hammer on steel attracted him, and he walked over to the door and, leaning against the upright, watched the smith. The man was bending over the socket of a scythe and hammering it into shape while his assistant worked at the bellows. As Polycarp's shadow fell across the doorway the smith looked up and winked. Polycarp returned the greeting, and for five minutes he witnessed a display of hammering and fireworks. The smithy was like a pleasant, echoing Hell. Everywhere was dust and soot from the fire, and the walls and floor were littered with lengths of iron rods, rusty agricultural implements, broken ploughshares, cracked horseshoes, pieces of iron railing, and large steel plates. Each time the smith struck at his red-hot iron a cascade of bright sparks splashed away from the head of the hammer in dwindling meteors, and the draught soughing at the forge fire made it blossom into a small patch of strange, twisting, exotic flame-flowers—flowers of purple sheathed in long green leaves, red spreading poppies, and tall blue irises of flame; all springing from a mass of deep yellow moss and black soil. Polycarp looked on, entranced by the beauty of the scene.

"How'd you like to have to work for a living?" said the smith suddenly, in a pause between hammering, and he nodded affably to a seat inside the door. Polycarp sat down, without replying, as the smith went on with his hammering, occasionally heating the socket to white-hot pitch and hammering again, and sometimes plunging the hot metal into a trough of inky-black water. The water writhed and hissed at the heat, and sent up spurts of steam. Polycarp let himself be carried away by the noise and colour and warmth about him. At that moment he felt, though he would not have said so, a little lonely and dispirited, and the friendly presence of the smith soothed him. The smithy was so pleasant that he was quite unaware of the swift passage of time and, after twenty minutes that seemed to him like ten, he stirred himself and, nodding goodbye to the smith, he went back to the front of the hotel and was surprised to find that the coach had proceeded without him. There was no doubt about it. He had been left behind. He asked a small, thin-faced man, in tight trousers and a Norfolk jacket, who was standing in the hotel porch, how long the coach had been gone.

"Went about two minutes ago. Pretty full up, too. Did you want to catch it?"

"No, I just wanted to know," lied Polycarp proudly, and he started along the road in the direction which the coach had taken. He was not going to let the hotel people think he had been such a fool as to miss the coach. And, he argued, possibly the driver would find out that one of his passengers was missing and turn back, so that the farther he walked along the road the shorter would be the distance the coach would have to retravel.

Polycarp walked for an hour, buoyed up by the hope that the coach would return, and at the end of that period he had given up hope. He was feeling hungry, and the back of his shoe was chafing his heel in preparation for a blister. He swore once, to give himself encouragement, and lit a cigarette. For the next hour the road went up and down gently, but always rising. Then, as though tiring of the subterfuge of rising and falling, the road began to climb steadily until Polycarp found himself walking along the top of an undulating plateau. He was tired and hungry, and the promised blister had arrived. He looked at his watch. It was three o'clock. He swore again, cursed his luck, and wondered why no one in a car had overtaken him from whom he might beg a lift. He came to a clump of Scotch firs and, feeling the need for some rest after his long walk, he sat himself down moodily on the stone wall where we first made his acquaintance.

V
The Red Dragon

It would be interesting, but perhaps idle—for many things which interest one are a subtle waste of time—to speculate upon the parallelism between the state of mind of Dick Whittington and that of Polycarp during the first brief days when they found themselves faced abruptly with the disconcerting fact that life went on just the same whether they were working or sleeping, whether they were about to make a fortune or a bloomer. It is one of the most disheartening discoveries in the world that mankind generally is more interested in men than man; the dyspeptic householder in Peckham can sense with proper sorrow the tragedy of a mass pit disaster—the enormity of a hundred lost lives stirs his turbid imagination to pity or anger—but the tragedy of one lost life, though it belong to the publican of the Blue Pig at the end of the street, generally leaves him untouched.

When a man has been part of the clumsy machine of existence for years, when he has risen regularly at eight to reach his work at nine and shouldered his way through seven, eight, nine, ten hours a day, contributing his quota to commerce and industry, he begins to arrogate to himself an undue pride. He tells himself that he is an indispensable unit in the great intricate machinery. If he fails, the whole machine fails. And then one day he does stop, or is stopped. He stands back with a smile on his face and waits for the inevitable chaos in the office or factory, and the smile changes to chagrin as he sees the work of the world go on as though he had never been part of it, as though he had never influenced it in one minutest particular. Then is the tragedy: the discovery of man that other men can do without him; that there is no such thing as indispensability; that one man is as good as another and that men are easily replaced when one falls out. Man is akin to the leaves which draw the precious sun-energy into the tree through the medium of their chlorophyll. Without the chlorophyll of the leaves the tree must die, but when one leaf falls the tree lives on as strong as ever. And when one man withdraws his precious contribution to the mechanics of life, life goes on and leaves the poor man feeling bitter and depressed. If a consensus of the motives which lead to suicide could be taken, the realisation of the dispensableness of the individual would probably rank highest.

And, on the morning after his arrival in Oxford, Polycarp was almost depressingly aware of this grand all-embracing indifference of his fellows. He stood on the pavement of the Cornmarket at ten o'clock and waited for the world to acknowledge in some way the fact that he had nothing to do. The world just roared rudely in his ears and continued with its business of making money, and all the incidental manufactures such as food, cars, clothes, poverty, tobacco, dishonesty, lechery, furniture, and war which cluster round the main industry of money-making. Tradesmen's vans rushed up and down the road; buses nosed their way through battalions of bicycles and cars; clerks on errands crowded one another off the pavement; girls in shops cleaned glass shelves in readiness for cakes and displays of shoes; porters yawned behind their calloused hands; solicitors read their letters and rang bells for their clerks; newsboys shouted morning editions; dogs sniffed around the garbage-tins in the gutters and, high above all the turmoil of the city, an aeroplane wrote laboriously across the sky *Jixo, the Summer Drink*, though no one in the roaring canyon of the city seemed to take any notice except Polycarp, who alone had time to crane his neck backwards to watch. This was not true, of course, for there were plenty of other people who stared at the smoke-writing, but to Polycarp it seemed that he was the only one with leisure. At first he was a little hurt by this apparent unconcern of the city with his presence. Then, when the first bitter moment had gone, he laughed to himself and started off to explore the town—the town which had occupied so large a place in his pubescent dreams.

He had arrived in Oxford at six o'clock the previous afternoon, having begged a lift from a passing petrol-wagon. All the way the driver had forced him to talk of football, and the respective merits of Chelsea and the Arsenal. For an hour the driver had compared players, matches, and performances, and Polycarp, who from boredom had developed a mild speculation as to which team the driver favoured, was unsettled when that worthy remarked:

"But for real football there's no team to beat Manchester United. They've got everything the others are trying to get. I'm a Manchester man."

"Is that so?"

"Yes. No place like Manchester, lad."

At Oxford he had gone straight to the coaching office and, although no one offered any apologies for something which they clearly considered to be his own fault, his suitcase was restored to him and he set out to find a lodging. Like a sensible British citizen Polycarp asked the first policeman he saw if he knew of any lodgings suitable for him and, like a solid, resourceful policeman, he did know of a lodging.

Policemen are wonderful people. They may not be at home in the higher realms of philosophy or art, may not care tuppence whether Kant or Schopenhauer ever lived or that there were such persons as Gauguin or Picasso—and, after all, life may be lived very comfortably and happily without one's ever having seen Holbein's *The Ambassadors* or read Goethe's *Wilhelm Meisters Lehrjahre*—but ask them the quickest way to the station, for the best barber's shop, what hotels to avoid, the time of the next train to London, the names of the shows at picture-house or theatre, and it is seldom that they disappoint one in these human essentials. Some day the policeman will have his superb qualities suitably recognised in literature, and the book will be a best-seller.

"Mrs. Anstruthers of Kingston Road's the place for you," said the policeman, and he gave Polycarp the number of the house. "Tell her I sent you—P.C. Wimple. That's all right. Glad to help you." He smiled, and Polycarp started off for Kingston Road, trying to remember the man's instructions.

The house, when he found it, was a tall, three-storied building, standing a few doors away from a confectioner's shop and overlooking a garage and an ironmonger's yard on the opposite side of the road. At the back of the house was a cramped rectangle of garden where grass and a few forget-me-nots and wallflowers battled desperately with cats, which took refuge from Mrs. Anstruthers in an apple-tree that might have been transplanted straight from the backcloth of a Russian ballet. When Mrs. Anstruthers opened the door after Polycarp had rung the bell, he decided that he was not going to like her. She was one of those women whom nature has unkindly fashioned from remnants. Her hair was brown and glossy, but there was not enough of it, so that its short ends stuck out from her head like a rotating mop-end. Her features would have been comely if her skin had not been stretched economically over her chin and cheek-bones, giving her face a drawn look, as though she were continually sucking in her cheeks; her hands were knuckly, her body straight and stately but skinny, and she crossed her arms inside the front of a rubber apron, pressing them outwards as if she were trying to disguise the fact that she had flat breasts. From her head to her knees nature had been relentless, and then, where niggardliness was a virtue, in a Puckish mood had endowed her with the biggest pair of feet which Polycarp had ever seen on any woman. She stood on the doorstep confronting him, and he said to himself decisively, "I am not going to like this woman."

"My name is Polycarp Jarvis," he said. "P.C. Wimple recommended me to come to you. I want lodgings ..."

But when Mrs. Anstruthers opened her mouth Polycarp was not so sure that he disliked her.

"My!" she said, and her face wrinkled with a smile. "I thought you were going to try and sell me brushes. They carry big suitcases like that, you know. Come inside. P.C. Wimple, did you say?"

Polycarp nodded.

"Ah, he's a good boy. I used to look after him when he was a youngster, while his mother went out charing. Many's the time I've had to smack his behind for him, his poor ma being that tired she couldn't manage it. But he's a good lad. Poly—what did you say?"

"Polycarp Jarvis ..."

"My, with a name like that you should be staying at the Mitre; but never mind, this isn't the Mitre. I'll show you the room, and you can have it if you like it ..."

She led him up a flight of narrow stairs, that twisted at each floor, until they reached the top floor, which contained two rooms. She showed him into the front room, which overlooked the road.

"Here you are. Comfortable bed, a gas fire when you feel cold—though it's an electric fan we want just now—and a view of the elms on the Woodstock Road and the use of the bathroom on the floor below. Twenty-five shillings a week if you have your meals, and seventeen-and-six if you don't, and you can come in as late as you like as long as you don't wake me up."

"I'll take the full course—meals, elms, and bathroom," said Polycarp. "Do you want me to pay in advance?"

"No; pay at the end of the week. You've got an honest face even if you have a heathen name."

"My name," said Polycarp, who was regretting his first opinion of the woman, "is as Christian as anybody's. It belonged to one of the first bishops."

"Is that so? My! Well, you can never tell, can you?"

She gave him a few more instructions about meal-times and then clumped out of the room, leaving him to unpack his few belongings.

He spent the rest of the week looking about the town and university, and it was not until he lay in bed on Sunday morning that he faced the fact that so far he had done nothing towards achieving the object which had sent him away from Bristol.

There are rules for doing most things, but there are no definite rules about the game of fortune. If Polycarp had wanted to learn to play the ukulele he could have bought a shilling primer; the presses of the world offered advice at a price on almost every subject except that of fortune. There was nothing to tell Polycarp how to come to grips with fortune. He lay in bed with his hair awry over the pillow and stroked his moustache and wondered what he should do. He had to begin soon or his money would be gone. Success, it has been said, is ninety-nine per cent perspiration and one per cent inspiration: Polycarp scoffed at this idea. Success came from wisdom, and wisdom had nothing in common with perspiration. Who had ever heard of a sweating Sappho or a panting, perspiring Plato? Polycarp lay back in bed and tried to be wise. He was still trying to be wise on Monday morning as he left the house. As yet he had no plan as to how fortune was to become his.

But fortune does not work to any schedule or routine. Polycarp might have spent the whole of his life wondering what to do had he not stopped in a doorway of an office building in a street leading off the Cornmarket. He stepped aside into the doorway to light his pipe, and as he bent his head to the bowl his eye caught a paper pinned against a notice-board on the wall. The notice was brief.

THE RED DRAGON MOTOR COMPANY
Drivers wanted at once—must be keen, sober,
and experienced. Apply inside. Good wages.

That was all. And it was enough for Polycarp. He had no particular desire to be a motor-driver, but there was something about the name of the firm which appealed to him. The Red Dragon. The orientalism in the name caught at his love of colour and pomp and held him. He knew a little of the company—it owned a big service of motor-coaches and was offering a formidable opposition to the railway companies—and there was the lure of good wages. His money was dwindling, and it was hopeless to think of starting any of his dream-schemes or any business until he could augment it. Good wages; that sounded hopeful He put out his pipe and applied inside.

Inside was a small office, containing a table at which sat a girl typing. Along one side of the room ran a low seat occupied by five men of varying ages.

As Polycarp entered, the girl looked up sharply.

"Well?"

"I've come about the notice outside."

"Fill this up, please." She produced a form from somewhere behind her and handed it to Polycarp, with a pen. Using the corner of her table, Polycarp filled up the form It was not a long or a difficult form to complete, but it asked one or two questions which Polycarp found were awkward to answer with veracity. His age he put as twenty-three, and his driving experience he euphemised as "mainly with private cars for the past five years," which was not altogether incorrect, since it was on a private car he had learned to drive five years ago. When he had completed the form he handed it to the girl, who disappeared through a door behind her which led into another room. She came out almost immediately.

"Wait here, will you?" she said, and then went back to her typing. Occasionally a little bell would ring on her desk, and she would nod to one of the waiting men and usher him into the room behind her. Polycarp watched the men come and go. They were not a very prepossessing lot, and he thought to himself that he would have very little confidence in reaching his destination safely if any of them was driving the coach. His turn came, and the girl conducted him into the next office.

In the middle of the room, which was lined with green cabinet-files, stood a huge desk, behind which sat a fat, bald-headed man in a morning coat and pin-striped trousers. He indicated a chair, and went on tapping the butt of his fountain-pen against his teeth. In front of him lay the form which Polycarp had completed.

"So you want to be a driver, eh?"

"Yes."

"Good—or may be bad. Let's have a look at you. Stand up."

Polycarp stood up while the man ran his eye over him. He felt like a horse in a market-place.

"Good," said the man, and he tapped his teeth quickly. "Do you know anything about the Red Dragon Company?"

"I know that it—"

"It's the finest company in England!" The man was evidently not interested in how much Polycarp might know. He told him all about it. He had the aims and specifications of the company worked out to a fine formula, and Polycarp, as he listened, guessed that each of the other applicants had been subjected to the same disquisition. The Red Dragon Company was a high-idealed, almost philanthropic institution for the transport of anyone anywhere in England. It was starting slowly, yet surely it was going to throw a network of routes over the whole of the country. From Edinburgh to Penzance, from Rhyl to Hunstanton, the symbol of the Red Dragon would soon be flaring along the high-roads. Already it covered a considerable portion of the home counties and Midlands. Did Polycarp realise how much safer, more comfortable, and pleasanter was a coach trip compared with a train journey? Never mind; even

61

if he did, he should be told again. And the man told him, tapping his teeth at intervals.

"And the Red Dragon Company looks after its passengers' comforts like a mother over children. It pays its employees good wages in return for good service. It has no place for slackers." In three years' time there would be no other company on the road. Its motto was, "Red Dragon first, Red Dragon second, and Red Dragon for Safety and Speed."

"It sounds," said Polycarp, as the man stopped to tap his teeth, "almost like a secret organisation. The Red Dragon."

The man ignored him and took up his form.

"John Polycarp Jarvis, age twenty-three, five years' driving experience; last job, clerking. Why did you leave that?"

"I found I wasn't suited for indoor work—not enough exercise—so I gave it up."

"Ah!" Which might have meant many things. "And so you want to take up driving? Well, you'll get plenty of exercise at that."

During the next ten minutes the man asked Polycarp questions and answered most of them himself. Then he terminated the interview with a curt:

"You seem all right. We'll write to you shortly and let you know further."

And Polycarp departed, followed by the faint sound of teeth being tapped by a fountain-pen.

Apparently at the next meeting of the sacred Red Dragon circle it was decided that Polycarp was "all right." Two days after his interview he received a letter requesting him to report at the company's garage on the Botley Road. The headquarters of the company was at Birmingham, but the Oxford branch was almost as big and important, so Polycarp discovered ten minutes after he arrived at the garage. His informant was an instructor who had fastened on to him when he had reported at the office. He was a big, double-chinned man with fair hair, blue eyes, and a sandy-coloured stubble, and he wore a long white driving-coat emblazoned on the breast pocket with a red dragon rampant.

"Your name Jarvis?"

"That's it. John Polycarp Jarvis."

"You can forget the trimmings. Jarvis is good enough. So you want to be a driver, eh? What of—a fairy cycle?"

His tone was far from affable—due to the fact, though Polycarp was unaware of it, that he had spent several weeks trying to make a succession of muddle-headed men, who thought they could drive, distinguish between a hand-brake and a gear-change lever.

"I understood," said Polycarp airily, "that I was to have the privilege of driving a Red Dragon. But if you've got a magic carpet or a witch's broom I'll have a shot at that."

The instructor ignored Polycarp's remark.

"Red ruin, that's where I'm driving. Red ruddy ruin—just because a lot of fatheads who know nothing about it at Birmingham imagine that it's possible to make good drivers out of nit-wits in a week. Here, put this on and we'll soon see."

He threw Polycarp a coat similar to his own and led the way to the end of the garage.

They stood in front of an enormous motor-coach. It rose above them like a liner, a long, squat-faced thing of red and white paint with bulbous tyres that reminded Polycarp of the curving legs of a fat woman. On the flaps of the windows were gold-leafed names of towns, and on each side and across the front of the coach were painted three red dragons.

"This," grunted the instructor, whose name was Webb, "is a Red Dragon, but don't let that frighten you. When you can take it across three hundred miles of country at an average of forty miles an hour, scrape through six-feet openings in traffic while you keep your eyes on traffic signals, change gear on hairpin bends of one in four without attracting attention, and decarbonise it and put in a spare piston while your passengers sit in the hedge without making 'em wait too long—then you'll be a damned good driver, and, such is Willy Webb's luck, you'll probably smash the ruddy contraption to pieces by trying to light a fag coming down Whitchurch Hill. Well, come on, let's see what you know."

Now, Polycarp was not entirely ignorant of the internal combustion engine and his driving skill was moderate. Within the next hour, however, he realised, without making it apparent to Webb, just how much he did not know about driving and engines. The instructor talked glibly of camshafts, valve guides, big ends, crankshafts, clutch plates, differentials, magneto brushes, plugs, tappets, oil gauges,

petrol consumption, batteries, needle-bearings, bowden controls …
and every now and again he would dart under the bonnet of the Red
Dragon and illustrate his remarks by pointing into the dim interior
and saying over his shoulder: "See what I mean?"

Polycarp decided that it was wisest to admit that he did, and nodded
an affirmative. In order to implement his supposed knowledge he
even asked one or two questions, and Webb gave him a grateful look,
but Polycarp was heartily glad when the instructor closed down the
bonnet and said:

"Now then, I'll take her out and you can show me what you can
do."

He did take her out. He took her out five miles from Oxford to a
comparatively quiet roadway, and there, on an open stretch of a mile,
Polycarp showed him what he could do. He climbed into the driving-
seat and Webb crouched beside him, ready to correct any mistake.
Polycarp felt much the same as a small boy who has been riding a
Shetland pony for years and then one day finds himself squatted on
top of the head of an elephant—his perspectives were all upset and
altered.

"Remember—if you want to stop suddenly, step hard on the
clutch and brake, and don't be nervous … See what I mean?"

Polycarp nodded and grasped the driving-wheel. Driving, he
told himself, was like any other thing: if you said to yourself firmly
you could do it, then you could do it. Everything depended upon
being able to impress yourself with a sense of your own competence.
Polycarp smiled at Webb, and then said to himself firmly: "I can drive
this Red Dragon easily. I could drive anything!"

And he threw the gears into place and moved the clutch. He
absolutely refused to acknowledge that it was difficult to manage
a Red Dragon, and to his surprise he found that it was far easier
than even his superb optimism would ever have deceived him into
thinking. He drove steadily at thirty miles an hour along the road,
and the great machine answered to the wheel as sweetly as a private
car. Webb watched him as he sat perched up on the seat and breathed
a little sigh of relief as he saw that he had got someone who, if he
obviously knew nothing about the innards of a car, could at least
handle it with some assurance. As time went on Polycarp grew more

and more confident. He began to get the feel of the wheel and to know just how much turn to give at corners. It was so easy that he could have sung aloud.

When they were back at the garage Webb said to him:

"Young fellow, you did very well. You've got the knack of it. These Red Dragons are beauties to drive. I'd rather drive one than any small car. In a week you'll be able to do anything with one."

Polycarp nodded. He was pleased with himself.

"I reckon you can do anything if you only make up your mind to do it. It's like the Yogi philosophy of life—if you have the faith you can move mountains or drive Red Dragons. It's all a question of faith …"

For the next week Polycarp came daily to the garage and underwent instruction, and he proved himself an apt pupil. Webb was so proud of him that on the last day of training he took him up the road and bought him a drink.

"And that's something I don't do for more than one out of every twenty drivers that pass through my hands," he explained as they drank their beer. Then he went off into a monologue on drivers and driving, and allowed Polycarp to buy him three beers without protest. The beers tended to make him morose, so that when they parted he said sadly:

"I'll keep my eye open for your name amongst the accidents. All the good drivers get busted up sooner or later. They get too confident. Choose a thick hedge. Goodbye."

So Polycarp became a motor-coach driver at a salary of three pounds ten shillings a week, plus uniform and an allowance for the nights when he had to sleep away from Oxford. He had been chosen to operate on the Oxford to Brighton route. He was to start from Oxford on a Monday at a late hour of the afternoon and drive through the night, rest during Tuesday, and return, driving through the day, on Wednesday, to start for Brighton the next day, and so his duties alternated from night-driving to day-driving, allowing him one free day on Sundays in Oxford.

It was nearly the end of July before Polycarp began his duties and by that time he had come to know Oxford very well He loved the cool charm of the city, which combined without discord the slow beauty of mediaevalism with the hard glitter of modernity. He hardly ever bothered to enquire the names of colleges. He was content to walk through the quiet quadrangles and the sharp shadowed cloisters and immerse himself in the serenity of the peace which seemed to dwell eternally with them. Sometimes he lay by the river in the Parks and watched the long punts, full of laughing, gaily dressed women and students, go drifting by and the riot of colourful blazers and blowing dresses filled him with satisfaction. He loved bright colours and full laughter and the lifting sound of music; and Oxford gave him all these. There was colour everywhere, splashed in great white daubs of paint where the college barges lay anchored below Folly Bridge, in the sudden curve of the river, in the quick flirt of a dabchick's rudder as it crossed the stream, in the soaring heights of the elms and the dropping wonder of tall willows and birch-trees. In the evening the colleges were grey and gold against the sun, and the towers and pinnacles stood enfolded in a glory of purpling sky. Everywhere was colour, rich and satisfying, and with the colour went laughter and music: laughter that came from the throats of a thousand young men, all facing life eagerly and with the spirit of youth warm in their veins. They laughed as they played, laughing as cricket-bats vibrated beneath their fingers, as long oars bent pliantly to their shoulders, shouting as they dived from tree-stumps into the cool, jewelled waters of the Thames and Cher. When they were sober they laughed and when they were drunk they laughed, and their laughter built for them a freemasonry which swept aside all the barriers of life here were congregated duke's son and doctor's ward, the miner's son and the brown-skinned heir to an Indian throne. Every class of society made its contribution to the life that swirled between the narrow streets. They laughed in the tones of Northumberland and Wales, they spoke with the soft speech of Devon and the uncouth tongue of Yorkshire. Some took into their dark wainscotted rooms the vision of Scottish hills and Hebridean seas; others saw the snows of Helvetia; some the hot steaming dankness of Amazon towns; and a few saw the drab misery of empty factories and idle shipyards, of wet streets evil with flickering gas-light and nauseous with smells of garbage and humanity ... but no matter what their vision they laughed here, where all men sought one thing, and nothing could rob them yet of their exuberant enthusiasm and optimism. Even their morbidness was an unconscious pose, only the shadow of a real thing. The city held them in its shining hollow and glowed like an old woman's cheeks when her singing grandchildren crowd about her. And from the colour and laughter was worked the music of all being the music of joy, of endeavour, of despair, and of triumph. It was all here, a grand orchestration of emotion that filled the mind of the onlooker with an immutable sense of the majesty which dwelt in the heart of humanity; a work not of one composer but of a million composers, and a work which was interpreted by each listener differently ... And Polycarp walked through the spectacle, glorying in it so much that he forgot to regret that he had no real part in it.

VI
A butterfly and a miracle

In May, nineteen hundred and twenty-four, Polycarp ceased to be the driver of a Red Dragon. Whether the company regretted losing him is a secret which will remain locked for ever in the heart of the little teeth-tapping man who was in charge of the routes covering the south of England. Regret or pleasure—public companies seldom betray themselves by such emotions—one thing is certain, that the manner of Polycarp's going did occasion a definite, though temporary, state of anxiety for the higher officials of the Red Dragon Company.

For nine months Polycarp worked as one of the vast brotherhood of commercial drivers, of men who for small wages accept responsibility for the safe transport of milk, petrol, flowers, meat, groceries, and human beings. It was like entering a new world, a world of greasy-uniformed gods and be-muffled Mercuries. As Polycarp swept over the same route day and night, he came slowly to know and recognise them one by one, and in the rapid lift of their raised hands there was greeting and fraternity; that quick movement symbolised their common purpose and readiness to help one another. As he sat cooped up in his little driving seat, with the big engine drumming smoothly beneath his feet, he watched them start into the halo of his lights and drop into the darkness behind him. Lumbering fat-bellied milk-wagons that came tearing through the long night from Wiltshire to London, their white-painted tanks shining through winter squalls and summer moonlight and their heavy wheels growling over the road with murmurous impatience, as though the lorry were alive and fretting to get its precious fluid quickly to the thirsting metropolis, where milk had no connection with cows that moved hock-deep through farmyard muck, but was something found on doorsteps; gaudy, swaying petrol-tankers, with fat arteries indecently exposed along their sides, arteries through which would be disembogued petrol that had begun life three thousand feet down in the Mexican oil sands, to end as choking carbon fumes spouting from the exhaust of the labourer's motor-cycle as he hurried to work through the frosty November mornings; tall, high-vanned provision-lorries that sprang from the twilight like moving houses, well stocked with gay packets of tea, sugar, and groceries that, before the sun was well up, would be resting coldly upon the marble slabs of the multiple stores that stretched over England in a network of public pantries ... Polycarp came to know them all and watched with delight the passing pageantry of food, fuels, and folly—for often roaring, drunken charabanc parties would swing into life round corners, coaches packed with tipsy skittle-teams and driven by well-treated drivers. The whole brotherhood formed an army of jolly, swearing, joke-telling servants who moved across the fair face of the country while people in towns and villages slept. They brought at night fresh supplies which the daylight would soon diminish. So it went on night after right, never ceasing; lorry after lorry leaving London crammed with carcasses of meat and boxes of fruit from the Dominions and the United States, and as they rumbled eastwards, westwards, north, and south, they passed other lorries speeding towards the great city, heavy with their vegetables and milk or swaying lightly with a fragile load of Scilly Island flowers—narcissi, daffodils, and jonquils that let their rich perfume escape into the crisp spring air, so that the scent, catching at Polycarp's nostrils, woke him to the memory of pleasant days on the Bristol Downs and long walks through Somerset valleys and across the Mendip Hills. He revelled in the life and was glad that he was part of it. So entranced was he with the magic of the road that he forgot about his quest after fortune and let himself be immersed in the clangour and splendour of the changing scene.

For those nine months he drove across his sector of the country until he came to know its every turn and twist as if it were the wrinkled face of an old, beloved man: from Oxford to Reading, slipping through the tram-lined streets, from Reading to Guildford, and from Guildford to Horsham across the burgeoning North Downs and through oak-covered slopes and hillocks to the sharp scarp of the Sussex South Downs and the long run into Brighton.

He saw the seasons slip across the country, passing from the colourful glory of summer, when the flags waved yellow blossoms by the streams and pale scabious flowers shone from the meadows, to the pregnant sorrow of autumn, that littered the roads with sharp chestnut husks and studded the hangers of the downs with amber beechmast. And then followed the wet, drizzly days when the roads were treacherous with a damp coating of beech-leaves like enormous copper coins, and leafy spearheads where, as winter overcame them, the chestnuts threw down their weapons. Within a month, winter was all about him and the trees were frost-rimed in the glow of his headlights, the eyes of hunting fox and rat moved swiftly across the roadway, and cold winds came cutting into his driving-box with all the sting and bite of their icy journey over the sea and barren fields. And in a while winter changed almost imperceptibly to days of brief summer sunshine and cold squalls, until that time when Polycarp saw the first primrose pads signal to him from the mossy woodsides, and pale spikes of snowdrop rose timidly from the leaf-mould around the base of the shining limbs of the beeches. Spring came, and the buds made a green mist of loveliness to cover the carpet of anemones and daffodils and the wheatears returned to the bare rolling crests of the Downs; and with the coming of spring there came a restlessness into Polycarp's blood which made him resent his enforced captivity in the driving-box. He was no longer content to ride in Roman state through his domain; he wanted to escape and to linger in the woods and fields.

At first he had not been interested in his passengers; they were his merchandise, and his job was to get them to Reading, Guildford, and the towns along his route. The coach was generally fairly full, and he had no time to speculate about passengers, for there were too many for any particular one to occupy his attention. When they stopped at the resting-points for food and refreshments, he ate by himself or sat reading in his box, waiting for the time to move on. During the summer the passengers were mostly holiday people going to Brighton, going with high expectations and laughing and talking, their bags bursting with summer clothes and tennis-rackets, and when he brought them back, their faces were sad because the holiday was done, but their bags were still bursting and now adorned with knobbly excrescences that were presents for friends. But as summer waned and winter stepped softly about the land, the passengers diminished in number until there were times when he went from point to point with only a single fare behind him, and sometimes ate with them.

There was a man who took food with him at a roadside café some miles from Horsham one day. He was a tall, dark-haired, dark-skinned, middle-aged man who spoke with a foreign accent. It was late at night, and they both sat close against the fire at the end of the room, waiting for the proprietor to bring them the soup which they had ordered. The soup came, and after the first mouthful the man put down his spoon and wrinkled his face.

"Anything the matter?" enquired Polycarp, who was enjoying the steaming hot broth.

"This," said the man; "it is terrible. This is not soup; it is dishwater!"

"Tastes all right to me. Why don't you put some salt and pepper in it?"

"Ah, you English! You would eat anything so long as it is hot enough to burn the skin from your mouth. Food, my dear sir, is as important as clothes; a good suit makes a man feel like Napoleon, and a good meal—ah, it makes a coward feel brave enough to twist the nose of a policeman. I have been in England too many years now and never have I tasted a *minestrone* as an ordinary Italian peasant will make for you. No, not even in the best hotels, and I have stayed in most ..."

"Perhaps the Englishman's disregard of food accounts for the position which he holds in the world. Why waste time on food when you can spend it making money? The commercial prosperity of England is probably responsible for the indigestion which afflicts most of its people."

"That is so; they eat quickly, like the animals. Eating should be slow, and should be seasoned with talk and laughter. This stuff"—he prodded the plate with his spoon—"is like, what do you say? hogs' water."

"Hogwash?"

"Yes, hogs' wash. Food is a science. In England the only place where you can sometimes get good food is in London—that is because there are so many Frenchmen and Italians there. In your country places they have minds which do not rise above potatoes boiled and a plate of ham. Yes, in London I have eaten well."

He began to tell Polycarp where, in London, to obtain good food. His dark face flushed with enthusiasm as he spoke slowly and reverently of *hors d'oeuvre, purée, bouillabaisse, salim, croquette,* and *borsch*. He grew more enthusiastic, and told Polycarp where he had obtained *beignets* that filled the soul with immutable glory, of *bouchées* that made the weakest men strong and the strongest men gentle, of *kromeskies* that could win a woman's heart for a man, and of *soufflés* which had influenced the political opinions of statesmen.

"And to think," he wailed as he grew more excited, "that you have the places where they make a meal of hors d'oeuvre!"

"Ah, give me a plate of fish and chips," said Polycarp iconoclastically, "and a pint of bitter!"

"Bitter beer! Ah!" He went off again, and his talk flew from beer to wines, and, when he had finished, Polycarp's head was a whirl of hocks, moselles, brandy, red wines, white wines, Sauternes, Italian, Greek, and other wines. He flung about Chianti and champagne, and denounced all cocktails and beer as concoctions of the Devil and fit only for the northern and American people. Polycarp, having finished his soup, sat and listened with delight. He was a willing listener, for in that way he came by most of his knowledge. He stored up the Italian's—for so he judged the man to be—dissertation on food and wine, and reproduced it a few days afterwards as his own for Mrs. Anstruthers's benefit when she insulted him, so he said, with an omelette.

A week later he was disappointed to discover that the distinguished passenger, whom he had taken to be a real gourmet and a man of wealth, was a waiter at a large Brighton hotel.

Once he ate with a tall, gawky young man who seemed far more misanthropic than any man-eating lion. He was, so Polycarp discovered as they ate, an assistant in a big multiple shop and was travelling from Brighton to Oxford to take up duties in one of his company's shops in that town. Polycarp felt sorry for the man as he sat opposite him and recounted his woes. He complained of the very long hours of work, of the coldness behind marble-topped counters in the winter-time, of the surliness of customers and the savagery of over-managers, and his raw, red face as he spoke was as chilly and uninviting as the last slice of pressed beef upon one of the counters which he hated so much.

"You certainly don't seem very pleased with life, do you?" Polycarp said.

"No, I don't. I never do when they transfer me to Oxford. Why they have to do it I don't know. They treat us like slaves—sending us all over the country—but I wish they wouldn't send me to Oxford! Any other place would be better than that—"

"You don't like Oxford?"

"I like it. It's a fine city; but it isn't that. You see—" The man's watery blue eyes threatened to dissolve and streak his red face. "You see, when I travel from Brighton to Oxford on the coach it means I pass within three miles of the village where I was born and where my mother keeps the post office. If you saw your people only twice a year for very short spells, wouldn't it make you sad to think that you passed within a few miles of your village about ten times in the year and yet couldn't step off to see them?"

"Oh, I understand why you feel a bit blue. Bad luck, old chap, bad luck; but a train wouldn't stop to let you pay a visit en route—why should a coach? Must stick to regulations."

I know all that, but it's sad all the same. Specially when your mother's getting up along and any time you see her may be ... you know ... folks don't last for ever, do they?"

"No, that's true. What was the name of the village?"

The shop-assistant mentioned the name of a small village near the Berkshires on the other side of Reading.

When the coach started, Polycarp sat in his driving-seat thinking of a white-haired, wrinkle-cheeked, blue-eyed postmistress who was probably the chief exchange for village gossip and the mother of the unlovely face behind him. Life was very hard on some people, he thought. It served people right for indulging in sentiment. Any man who was worth his salt could get along without sentiment and all this mother business ... He could not remember his own mother.

Two hours later the coach came slowly to a halt in the darkness.

Polycarp got out and went into the coach. The assistant was his only passenger.

"Something's gone wrong with the engine. Sounds like magneto trouble. It'll take me about an hour to fix, and in addition to that I seem to have strayed off my path a bit. Funny, but there's a signpost on the corner there pointing to your mother's village half a mile away. You'll have time to walk there and see her while I'm fixing the engine, if you care to."

"I say, you know, this is most awfully good of you. You know——" The man shot forward and attempted to take Polycarp's hand.

"Don't get sentimental, please. It's just a coincidence. I lost my way and now the engine's failed. You mustn't think I've done this deliberately. I've got my job to think of and can't afford to break rules. About an hour I shall be." Polycarp went round to the front of the coach and watched the man dwindle in the beam of the headlights and then turn the corner towards the village.

"People always jump to wrong conclusions," he muttered to himself, and then climbed back into his driver's seat and took out a copy of *John o' London's Weekly*. When the assistant returned, Polycarp had read right through the weekly from the front page article to "Questions and Answers."

"Have you fixed the engine all right?" asked the man.

Polycarp nodded. "Yes, took me some time, but it's all right now."

"Good. Mother was glad to see me. She sent you this." He held out a small paper-bag hesitantly.

"Uh, cake I Looks good!"

"It is—the best in Berkshire!"

"We'll see," said Polycarp, and for the next half-mile he imperilled their two lives by driving a Red Dragon with one hand, while he used the other to feed his mouth with cake which was far better than anything he had ever tasted before.

It was not often that Polycarp broke the company's rules, but when he did they were broken before he had time to stop and think about them. There was a rigid rule about giving people lifts which Polycarp obliterated from his memory. When he was driving along the road with an empty coach in a heavy rainfall, it seemed sheer inhumanity to pass a tramp or labourer without offering him a lift, and many a tramp in the southern counties slept comfortably along the back seat of the coach while Polycarp tried to dry his coat by the engine in his driving-box before setting him down on the outskirts of Brighton or Guildford.

Of his women passengers, when they attempted to make friends with him, Polycarp was definitely wary. Since Gracie—as he imagined—had betrayed him to her father he had developed a determinedly misogynistic attitude. Women were a snare and an empty delusion, and he wanted nothing to do with them. He never ate with them, not even when a good-looking girl was his only passenger, and if they sometimes tried to induce him to be friendly—for in his white driving-coat with its flaring red dragon and his smart peaked cap, worn a little to one side, Polycarp was an attractive figure—he quickly showed that he wanted to have no nonsense. He could not understand the mentality of some girls who would go so far as to ask him for a kiss. It was an Eleusinian mystery which even Mrs. Anstruthers could not solve for him when he talked about it in her kitchen one day.

"It's just life, Mr. Jarvis. That's how I explain it—just life. I wish someone would ask me to kiss 'em. I ain't been kissed by a man since poor Bill died, the year before the war, and he never kissed me with anything like the interest he showed for his pigeons. But he was a good one, was Bill, though I don't believe he would ever have married me if my dad hadn't asked him how much longer he thought he was going to get free suppers at our place. Ah, well, some gets all the luck—that's life. Eleven years without a kiss, I've been—almost as monotonous as these 'ere new by-pass roads they're making, ain't it?"

Polycarp agreed, and then made an excuse to leave the kitchen before his chivalrous emotions got the better of his good taste.

All these little incidents of the road served to cheer Polycarp when he first became aware of his growing dissatisfaction with the dull routine of driving and to help him forget the wearisome repetition. But after a while he found himself performing his duties in a monotonous, mechanical fashion, without deriving any pleasure from his job. When he reached this state, he decided that the constant travelling across the southern part of England could not content him much longer and he began to think of other things. There was still that fortune waiting for him somewhere, and now he began to dream of it more and more.

He reached the point eventually when he loathed going into the garage at Botley Road and donning his uniform for the long night run. He did not know what to do. He felt that he had to have some excuse for leaving the company, and, still more important, something to do when he left them.

From his wages he had saved a fair amount of money, and he went through, in his mind, the ventures into which he might put his capital, but none of them seemed attractive. He might have gone on for a long time in this unsettled state had not something happened which forced him to a decisive act.

How often have very small incidents—the fall of an apple, the boiling of a kettle, the song of a lark, a chance word, a look between passers-by—altered the whole of a man's career and sent him flighting towards genius and fame, or plunging into poverty and pessimism; and it was a very small thing which altered the whole course of Polycarp's life; a member of the lycaenidae family—a Chalk Hill Blue butterfly.

It was early on a May morning. The coach had been travelling through the night and Polycarp had not long switched off his headlamps. They were travelling through the grey light which precedes the dawn and were about eleven miles from Brighton.

Away before Polycarp the long Downs were strung in a series of black heaps against the dirty sky. He was holding the wheel gently and humming *I'm for ever blowing Bubbles* to himself when the blue butterfly appeared. It landed in some miraculous way on his windscreen without smashing itself to pieces.

"Hallo, old feller." In his driving-box, Polycarp could speak aloud without fear of being heard by his passengers. "Where did you come from? You're up early. The sun won't be with us for another twenty minutes." The butterfly took no interest in these remarks, and, as the wind pressure prevented it from taking off again from the glass, it began to move across the windscreen. Polycarp watched the slender black legs tensed against the glass and the antenna waving as the wind fretted at the pale-blue creature. The butterfly slowly traversed the expanse of glass until it reached the edge and the wind caught at it, sending it whirling safely into space. Polycarp followed it with his eyes as it went flighting over the top of a blossoming may-bush. When he brought his attention back to the road, he had a shock. Directly in front of him the road forked, and he had to take the left-hand prong, but coming from a gateway just ahead was a horse and cart. The horse was a quarter of the way across the road when Polycarp saw it. There was no time to draw up, so he swung the wheel over and the red-and-white coach slewed across the tarmac, whizzed by the horse's head, and, unable to get safely back on to his correct route, Polycarp steered the Red Dragon up the right-hand fork. The whole incident occurred so quickly that the passengers were unaware that anything unusual had happened. They were not familiar with the road, and if Polycarp took the right- or the left-hand bend it was a matter of indifference to them, provided that they arrived in Brighton on schedule.

To be on time—that was the chief concern of the passengers. There was a fat-fowled, unpleasantly bald-headed man wearing a black coat and pin-striped trousers—a traveller for a Manchester firm of leather merchants—who talked patronisingly to a thin-faced chemist's assistant sitting by him, who was going to take up a new appointment at a Brighton shop, and at the back of the coach sat a roughly dressed, broad-faced labourer from Newbury, who had joined the coach at Reading, going to see his married daughter who kept a boarding-house at Hove. He held a withering bunch of early roses and tall tulips in his hand throughout the whole journey, as though the flowers were a talisman to guard him against the rigours of the road. The rest of the passengers were women; a big, buxom, overflowing countrywoman taking a whole seat to herself, and then overlapping into the gangway, and a young girl from a Reading factory who was going to Brighton to recuperate after having her arm mangled in the machinery at her works. And not one of the passengers noticed how narrowly an accident had been averted.

Polycarp had driven the coach a hundred yards up the strange road before he had time to think. His heart was still fluttering from the proximity of the disaster. When he composed himself, it was clear to him that as a matter of pride he could not stop the coach and retrace his route to the correct road and thus make his incompetence plain to the passengers. He might have done wrong, but Polycarp certainly had no intention of advertising the fact. If he did so—he remembered incidents earlier in his career as a coach-driver—the passengers might doubt his ability and make complaints; although, he admitted to himself, he didn't care much now whether they complained or not. He decided to drive on and later to swing off to the left and so come back on to his original route.

The road went straight across the plain towards the rising Downs, but nowhere did Polycarp get an opportunity to work around to his original route. They passed through a village where a square-towered church showed above a barrage of dark yew-trees and an inn-sign flashed a scarlet and gold Rose and Crown before him, and then the road began to climb through the mists towards the heights of the Downs. The coach sped through deep little combes where the mists and vapours of the passing night still lingered, and then began to mount into the hills. To Polycarp, who was so bored with his familiar route, this fresh ground was exhilarating. No longer did he know exactly what lay beyond each curve and turn, or the name of the public-house whose sign swung towards him in the fast growing light; no longer did he know each detail of the view that would break upon him as the coach swung round the side of copse and hill, or that the shadowed form under the laburnum was the village constable standing as he had stood every morning throughout the year. This was virgin ground to him, and he took in every detail. Before him, the slopes of the Downs lay interlocked like the fingers of two hands. In the twilight they slept grey and sombre, as though the sunlight were all that was needed to wake their dormant beauty. On their slopes the gorse-bushes smouldered with latent fire and the dew pricked out the silver webs from spike to spike and strung the gossamers in globules of light. About the valley-bottoms, sheep moved restlessly in their pastures and thought perhaps of their freer brethren loose on the open Downs. The coach climbed through a combe overhung with tall beeches and green with fresh-leaved oaks. A handful of wood-pigeons flapped into the wind as it passed, and a kestrel, sitting on the topmost branch of a fir, lifted into the wind and went drifting like a plume of dark smoke across the fields to hunt for the hedge-sparrows and finches, which were filling lie morning with the noise of their chittering and song. Higher and higher the road wound, as though it had forsaken the plains for ever, and meant to reach heaven.

The character of the country changed. They left behind the dark pools and ditches, red with campions and meadow crane's-bills, and came into open rolling Downs, where the road stretched ahead of them, unshadowed and unobscured by trees, like a great tape drawn tight across the smooth folds by a hidden hand. Rabbits flirted on the slopes; from the tips of the furze, yellow-hammers sang in rivalry to the swelling chorus that poured in a refreshing summer shower over the earth from the larks hidden in the lightening sky. And the higher the road climbed, the narrower and rougher it became, until, in one last wild swoop, it rushed up the steep scarp-side and, flinging the coach to the top of the hills, left it there. Polycarp pulled up. There was nothing else to do. The road had disappeared into smooth green turf and hummocks of grass flowered with yellow trefoils. For the first time the passengers realised that all was not well. As the coach halted, they stopped talking or listening and stared at the back of Polycarp's neck, which was the only portion of his anatomy granted to them from his driving-seat.

Polycarp frankly did not know what to do or say. Whereas he had been unable through pride to admit his mistake a quarter of an hour ago, he was now reluctant to indulge in a long explanation. The pleasure of the ride up the new valley had filled him with a wild, impatient intoxication. He was tired of the perpetual fret of the long journeys, and the whole of his spirit rebelled at the feeling that, on a morning when all nature quivered expectantly, he should be bound to a hideous, gaudily painted motor-vehicle and have to serve imperious men and chattering women as though he were a slave. The independent spirit which had sent him to Weston-super-Mare to celebrate his birthday was now fermenting within him, and at that moment the only master he acknowledged in the whole world was John Polycarp Jarvis—and he was ready even to disobey that erratic personage.

He got down from his seat and walked round to the door of the coach. He did not know what he was going to say to the passengers; he only knew that he was sick of being a coach-driver and that today he wanted to have his freedom.

He opened the door and looked inside without saying anything. The passengers waited for him to speak, but he said nothing. He left the door open and then rested against the warm side of the Red Dragon's radiator. As if by some instinctive impulse common to them all, the passengers, headed by the commercial traveller, rose from their seats and tumbled stiffly from the coach.

"What," said the commercial traveller, whose name was Percy Smithers, "what have you brought us up here for?" He asked the question in the guarded tone of a man who knows that he may receive a perfectly reasonable reply. He did receive a reply, and Polycarp contended that it was perfectly reasonable.

As Polycarp opened his mouth to speak, a miracle happened: a miracle which is the most frequent in the world and perhaps the most disregarded, a miracle which occurs every morning and brings to the world fresh beauty.

"I brought you," said Polycarp, and as he spoke he felt like a character from a Russian novel, "to see that!" He pointed to where the sun was rising over the long stretch of the Downs. At the very moment when he had wanted an excuse for his waywardness, the sun had not failed him. "I brought you to see what some people never see in the whole of their lives—the sun rising over the Downs."

He spoke so calmly that it might have been his single intention to bring them to view the sunrise. The passengers did not fully understand. They followed the line of his arm turning towards the rising sun, and then so compelling was the scene that they stared in silence for some moments while the beauty caught at their hearts and awakened in each some long overlaid desire. They gazed without speaking.

VII
Polycarp loses another job

At one moment the long stretch of the Downs was lying grey and quiescent under the darkling morning sky, with only the song of birds, the swaying of flowers before the wind, and the crisp sound of the sheep as they cropped the grass, to give life to its greyness; the land was a sombre oil-painting, wrapped in the dust of the departed night. But now the sun tipped the eastern ridge of the Downs and a great shaft of light played like a searchlight over sky and hills, and the great oil-painting was immediately cleansed of its dust and sprang to a vivid colourful life. The dull huddles of sheep were bathed in yellow light until their fleeces shone against the fresh green, and they moved, etched in silver outlines, against the sun. The growing light caught at the flowers and painted them with rich colour, so that the trefoils made a royal gold to frame the stately purple of the knapweeds. The long slopes and curves brightened with the charm of the new day. Around the edges of the deep copses the trees flung the colour about until the landscape blazed with changing greens. The beeches extended their new leaves towards the dark moss-banks. The birches filtered the light lingeringly through their fluttering fingers so that splashes of it clung and glittered amidst the foliage in bold yellow streaks, and the firs and spruces tossed it in a thousand silver sparks from their needles' points; and far below, in a valley dip, the weathervane of a church stood up to the advancing light and gilded itself in the sun's glory. Far away, on a spur of the Downs, a windmill which had been a dark plug against the sky now revealed itself, white and impressive as a lighthouse, and below it a chalk quarry reflected the light as though it were a whirling bowl of mercury; and across the crests of the hills came a warmer, softer, fragrant wind, a wind that rioted through the gorse blooms, pilfering the scents of cowslip and may-blossoms and bearing them on and on as if it were charged to carry the precious balm across the whole of England. Bees stirred and straddled their black-banded bodies across the slender thyme flowers, butterflies chased one another over the thistle heads in zigzagging flight, and a stallion, with dew wet on his flanks, kicked up his legs and thundered across the springy turf, prancing and curvetting as though he carried upon his back the joyous, invisible spirit of the Downs.

The people by the coach were stilled by the majesty of the moment, and all their little hates and concerns dropped from them before the splendour of the new morning. They saw the country with different eyes. It was no longer merely hedges and fields and cows and flowers, but a living, breathing, splendidly arrayed body upon whose firm breast they were cradled; a fine-limbed Titan who sprawled across a hundred miles of land, thrusting his feet down into the depths of cool forests, and bathing his shoulders and arms in the sunshine.

"Look! The sea!" It was the factory girl who spoke, and her eyes were wide with wonder, and her thin lips trembled with excitement. She had forgotten the long workrooms noisy with the incessant din of wheels and swiftly moving conveyors; forgotten the shoddy contacts of the streets and the cinemas; forgotten the cramped houses with garbage-littered gardens and dark passages; forgotten the clanging trams and the scabby plane-trees ... She was transported into a new world where everything was clean, alive with health and afire with beauty.

They all turned at the words, and followed her gaze. Away in the distance a trembling blade of light flickered and danced, more dazzling than the sun, between a dip of the Downs. And then a messenger from the tall white cliffs and the tidal pools, a black-headed gull, came rising and falling on white wings across the hills towards them, and they heard in memory the pliant cry of gulls and the wash of waves over rocks. They looked in silence. Then from behind them rose the sharp echo of a dog's bark and, carried by the wind, came the raucous beat of a car's engines and the dying whistle of a train as it plunged into a tunnel. The noises brought them all back to their normal selves. They were civilised again, and immediately repented that they should have been lifted out of themselves even for so short a period.

"I should like to know the meaning of all this?" said Mr. Smithers sharply. "This is not part of the company's regulations, is it? Sunrise—what do you mean, young man?"

"The company's regulations are fashioned for men," said Polycarp gravely. "The company is only concerned with getting you to Brighton, but surely you have no objection to sharing godlike emotions for a few moments. Is it so important for you to reach Brighton that you would forgo all this?"

"Brighton is where I paid to be taken, and Brighton is where I want to go!" put in the countrywoman. "The country is nothing new to me. When you've been up at five nearly every morning of your life to milk cows, young man, you don't think so much of a sunrise!"

"That's right," agreed Mr. Smithers. "I shall report you to the company for a breach of rules and for annoying passengers!" Mr. Smithers's correct body contained the genesis of a fine anger. "Brighton is where! want to go, and that's where I'm going! I'm a business man, and time is money to me. Sunrises!"

"Ah! you business people—always talking about time and money. It would do some of you good to watch a few sunrises!"

"That's your opinion, young man, but it isn't mine! I'm a plain leather salesman, and I haven't time for fripperies. Please get back into that coach and take us to Brighton. You'll hear more of this. Sunrise, indeed!"

The rest of the passengers, except the factory girl, who was still clinging to the beauty around her and hardly heard what was being said, nodded agreement.

The ungrateful intolerance of the passengers annoyed Polycarp. They had no souls, he told himself; they were clods.

"So you're not interested in sunrises, eh? You'd rather spend your lives thinking about attaché-cases and dog leads, and buying morning papers and eating, drinking, and sleeping in unhygienic houses. Well, if the sunrise is too much for your febrile little brains, consider the clouds. Perhaps they will appeal to you!" Polycarp waved a hand towards the sky, which was decorated with lofty banks of cloud. He was feeling as reckless as he had been in Bristol before Mr. Hayward. Now he didn't care what happened. He only knew that he had driven a Red Dragon too long. It had seemed as if he would never be able to escape from the harsh influence of petrol engines and the deadening mechanisation of his life. He was ready now to welcome the slightest excuse for effecting a break from the company, ready to seize any opportunity no matter how fantastic.

"Clouds?" They repeated the word slowly, as though it were a shibboleth, and looked at him.

"Yes, clouds." Polycarp began to quote slowly, "*Clouds, fogs, or mists formed at some distance from the ground, and composed of tiny water particles floating in the air.* You wonder what it means? It comes from an encyclopaedia, but don't let that frighten you—"

"You're mad!" burst out Mr. Smithers, who really was growing alarmed at the unusual excitement which was shining in Polycarp's eyes. Mr. Smithers could understand an enthusiasm for superior grades of cowhide, a transferred player to Manchester United football team, a laughing gramophone record, or a new joke ... but an enthusiasm for clouds and sunrises—it was indecent and unmanly.

"It's not me but you who are mad! What do you know about Cirrus, who tells us of coming storms? Nothing! What do you know about his brother Cirro-cumulus, who brings the fine weather and delights the fisherman's heart?

Still nothing! And of pleasant Strato-cumulus; and of jolly Cumulus, who floats above you now, telling of the fine day ahead? Nothing, still nothing! You're ignorant, and so would I be if I hadn't read the encyclopaedia yesterday. Here we are, sitting on top of the world, looking at the sun and the clouds. What more could a man want?"

Polycarp was so excited that he could not keep still. The dullness of the passengers was beginning to egg him on to an extravagant excess of feeling. He did not care a straw for anyone.

Mr. Smithers's paunchy face whitened with apprehension, and he whispered into the chemist's assistant's ear : "He's quite mad. Quite mad! No other explanation. We shall have to humour him."

"He isn't safe! I'll have something to say to the company about this! Sending us out with a madman for a driver!" The countrywoman shook her head angrily.

"Maybe the laddie is touched with sunstroke," suggested the labourer, who still held his flowers in moist hands. "He seems harmless enough." He offered no explanation for his theory, though the sun was hardly yet powerful enough to evaporate the dew.

" 'Tis often the harmless-looking ones that turn out to be the most vicious," snapped the countrywoman.

Polycarp broke in upon their discussion.

"I'm mad, am I? Mad …" The fact that they thought him mad only made him more anxious to fulfil their opinion of him. He would be mad. "Come on, get into the coach and I'll take you to Brighton, and you can report me—that'll prove my madness! I'll drive like a demon downhill, round corners as though the Red Dragon were a chariot of fire, under the viaduct and into Brighton. Come on!"

But none of them was at all anxious to come on. They stood in a ring together, like wild cattle, for mutual protection from his animus, and eyed him as though he were some wild-eyed woaded savage who had sprung mysteriously from the turf before them.

"In you get! I'll take you to Brighton!" Then, seeing their hesitation, he laughed. "Why, I really do believe that you think I'm crazy. I'm as sane as you are, but a man must have his enthusiasms. Come on, get in please, it's all been a mistake, and I promise not to do it again. I always seem to be putting my foot into things …"

Mr. Smithers rubbed his chin. "I'm not trusting myself any further with him. I'd rather stop here."

They all seemed to be of the same mind.

"Are you coming?" Polycarp faced them. "I assure you I'm quite sane." The passengers took this profession of sanity as a sure indication of his inherent madness.

"No … and you'd better keep your distance."

The sight of the fearful group filled Polycarp with mirth. He put his hands on his hips and roared with laughter. His action only served to convince them more than ever of his insanity.

"So you won't come? You're afraid of me! Well, if I've been adjudged *non compos mentis*, I'll be *non compos mentis*!" He danced round the coach, and, throwing off his uniform and peaked cap, he took his own clothes from under the driving-seat. He came back again, and, still grinning at their consternation, said : "One more chance. Are you coming?" There was no answer.

"Very well, goodbye, ladies and gentlemen, and if I come across a telephone I'll let the company know where you are." He turned to the factory girl, who was watching him with bewildered eyes, "Don't be frightened, miss.

You'll be all right. And if you feel cold there's a thick rug under my driving-seat and some sandwiches. Don't let hog-face there pinch them from you!" And with this Polycarp was away, running from sheer light-headedness.

"We're lucky to get out of that so easily," said the labourer as he watched Polycarp disappear over the brow of the Downs. "Madmen take queer ideas into their heads ..." And he, who had been so silent all the journey, began to regale the party with stories of lunatics.

For the rest of the morning Polycarp wandered about the Sussex Downs enjoying himself. He came down off the hills to the little village of Poynings, and telephoned to the company's garage at Brighton, telling them that the coach was stranded, and giving such details as he could of its position. The garage overseer wanted to know who was speaking. Polycarp chuckled and said:

"The coach is already overdue, so you know this message isn't a fake. It comes from a madman. Yes, that's what I said, a madman. The passengers will tell you all about it."

At nine o'clock he was back in Oxford, having reached that town by way of bus and train. As he walked up Kingston Road none of his recklessness had departed from him. He knew that, so far as he was concerned, the Red Dragon Company had seen the last of him, though it was far from likely that the company would, if they could help it, let him go without some explanation. Probably by this time, he mused, they had telephoned through to Oxford, and if they caught him he would find himself in a bother. And bother at that moment was the last thing which Polycarp wanted. He had severed his connection with the company cleanly, and he did not propose to suffer any enquiries or recriminations.

He went round to the back of the house and tapped on Mrs. Anstruthers's kitchen window. After a few raps she came to the back door.

"Has anyone been enquiring for me?" were his first words, as he slipped into her kitchen.

"Now then, Mr. Jarvis, what have you been up to?" she asked severely.

Polycarp waved a hand dismissing her question.

"Has anyone been after me?" he enquired again.

Mrs. Anstruthers eyed him suspiciously and nodded her head. "Yes, someone came down from your company late this afternoon, asking for you. They want me to let 'em know when you come in. What have you done?"

"Never mind about that; I must get out of here without them knowing. Look here, Mrs. Anstruthers, you'll be a brick and not let on that you've seen me until, say, tomorrow morning, won't you?"

"That depends, Mr. Jarvis. Is it anything criminal? I don't mind helping anyone, but if it's criminal that's another thing. I won't stand for any dirty business."

"Oh, it's nothing like that," he assured her. "I just got fed up with being a driver and I left the company in my own way. Honestly, I just played 'em a harmless little joke, but they won't see it like that. Do I look like a criminal? It was just fun."

"Fun, eh? Well I suppose you're like the rest of men, you have your bit of fun and then you come to a woman to help you out. If you won't tell me, you won't, and I ain't going to lower my pride by trying to wring it from you."

"You're an angel. Lord, you know I don't want to be rude Mrs. Anstruthers, but all this history talk about Cleopàtra, Lady Hamilton, Beatrice, Helen of Troy, and the rest of the good-looking bunch—they may be good-looking, but after that there's nothing in them. If you want a woman who'll stick by you and help you and be faithful, choose one that isn't quite so good-looking. That's what I say."

"That may be so, Mr. Jarvis. Though only, I reckon, because the plainer ones don't get a chance to be unfaithful. Now, what are you going to do?"

"Well, it's like this. I've got to leave Oxford right away. I'll slip upstairs and pack my things, and—I'm sorry to leave you, of course—I'll pay you a week's board in lieu of notice, and tomorrow you can tell the Red Dragon people that I came in without your knowing and slipped off with my things. That's easy enough!"

"Ay, it sounds easy. Where are you going?"

Polycarp shook his head and pulled at his moustache. "I don't know until I get to the station."

"Ah, well it's nice to be a bird of passage, stopping where you will. Some folks get all the luck. Go on and pack, and I'll make you some supper before you go."

Half an hour later Polycarp had finished his packing, eaten his supper, and was ready to leave the house. He stood with his case at his feet and his hand on the kitchen door preparatory to slipping out into the darkness.

"Goodbye, Mrs. Anstruthers. Some day I'll remember your kindness to me and repay you."

"Easy said, easy forgotten, Mr. Jarvis: though you're welcome. And, if you ever feel like it, you might write and tell me what happened."

"Perhaps I will. Well, goodbye."

He picked up his case and held out his hand to her. Slowly she took and shook it. She stood, a grim, thin figure, her face lined with a passing sorrow, for they had been good friends, and Polycarp had come to appreciate her mordant humour and pessimism. As he held her hand a thought flashed across his mind. His face wrinkled into a grin, and he dropped his case.

The next few seconds were the most astonishing which the good lady had experienced for the last eleven years. One lean arm went round her waist, another held her behind the shoulders, and, without giving her a decent opportunity to pretend to protest, Polycarp's moustache was tickling her face as he smacked three loud kisses on her lips.

"Don't say that I never give you anything, or that you're unlucky!" he called, as he ran, laughing, out of the kitchen with his case. "You're the first woman I've kissed for almost a year. Goodbye!" And he was gone, leaving her supporting herself against the kitchen table and listening to the mingling sound of his footsteps and the ticking of the clock on the mantelshelf.

"My!" she murmured to herself, feeling her lips gingerly. "My! When things happen, they do happen."

VIII
An architect with plans

It will always perhaps be a matter of dispute whether the real tragedy of the Great War lay, not in the thousands of young lives lost in battle, but in the thousands of disappointments which faced the survivors of the great upheaval when they returned to England. Men came back from Flanders and Mesopotamia somehow expecting to find their England unchanged and still the country of four years before; but the times had changed while they fought. And the men who came back, as well as the times, had altered. Many of them had gone to the front carrying with them the idealisms and enthusiasms of youth; they went from school, from university, from factory, field, and mine, from the cities and the villages of England to answer the call, and behind them they left the dream of their peace-time ambitions. The schoolboy forgot his vision of scholarship and shouldered a rifle; the factory youth stifled his longing for a home and children and went away to slay and be slain; the labourer ceased to dream of seven milking cows instead of his one, and learned to finger the trigger of a Lewis gun instead of the teat of his mild-eyed Jersey—everywhere men interrupted their labouring after their ideals and ambitions to forget everything in the debacle of war. And when the warring and horror was done they came back to their fields where the golden-faced dandelions still starred the grass, to their cities where the same church bells marked the hours, to their delayed visions and waiting ambitions, and tried to recapture the impetuousness which they had been forced for years to curb.

Some of them found that it was impossible to regain their youthful fire and ambition. The times had changed, and they had changed, so that against the bulking background of the carnage in which they had lived for so long all ambition appeared trite and transient. When such men thought of fame and distinction their thoughts were clogged with the cries of the dead, and their minds retained indelibly the memory of companions who fell on the Marne and at Passchendaele. A restlessness was upon them which neither scholarship, nor home and children, nor beasts standing in the morning mist could allay. The memory of the war years lay across their minds, staying them from the execution of their young ideals. If the memory could have been blotted out, they could have taken up the strings of their interrupted lives, but the memory remained and, for some, civilian life offered no balm. They found themselves to be people apart from the generations who had not known the immediate contact of war. They did not fit, there was no place for them, so they drifted into lives whose one objective was to achieve a forgetfulness of the past years. In blood and horror they had baptised their youth and manhood, and for these unfortunates the peace of a natural life was withheld ...

Such a man as this was Frank Burns. At the age of nineteen he was a student in the Liverpool School of Architecture and convinced that the world only waited his coming to acknowledge the renaissance of architecture. He was the son of a Keighley engineer and a Yorkshire farmer's daughter, and had spent his boyhood roaming the fells and moors above the Aire valley and bathing in its limestone pools and becks. And while he was still nineteen he had, through audacious lying, changed from a student of architecture to be a pilot of a Bristol Fighter. He went through Arras and Messines unscathed, and at the end of the war found himself practically alone in the world, his father having been killed at Ypres while serving in the Army Service Corps, and his heart-broken mother having returned to her parents. He borrowed two hundred pounds from his farmer grandfather to continue his course at Liverpool, and within three weeks found that when a man has seen heavy shells destroy in an hour the slender beauty of a Gothic cathedral representing the life-labour of skilled craftsmen over hundreds of years, he can entertain little faith in the aesthetic permanence of architecture. Where once architecture had posed itself as his gateway to the world, now it reminded him only of tumbled ruins of once lovely buildings. If a long-range gun could knock a Gothic cathedral to hell in an hour, what, he wondered, was the use of his spending four years training himself to design beautiful houses and public buildings if the same thing were to happen to them? Architecture saw him no more.

At the age of twenty-six he was sitting by himself in the far corner of a public-house in Corporation Street, Birmingham, still wondering. Wondering whether he should spend the whole of his remaining twenty-five pounds in one last fling, or whether he should try again somewhere to make a success of a life which since the war had graduated from architecture through clerkship, farming, and adventure to a general despondency lit at times with wild, uncontrollable bouts of gaiety and inebriety.

He sat at his table, tapping one finger on the glass top, and playing at times with his half-empty glass of beer. In his pocket he had twopence-halfpenny, not the price of another glass, and he did not want to go back to his room behind Snow Hill Station. It was just past one o'clock, and the day stretched ahead of him interminably. He was not a remarkable young man to look at; a thick-set, dark-haired fellow, wearing a dirty grey polo jumper and grey flannel trousers and a checked sports jacket. His face was broad, and his deep-set eyes were overhung by thick eyebrows. He was short and broad in the chest, and his whole being gave one a general impression of hairiness. He was one of those males who, one instinctively knows, possesses a thick mat of hirsute growth over arms, legs, and chest, so that when they go bathing small boys shout "Yah, monkey-man!" and then run. There was nothing animal about his face, it was pleasant and honest. And Frank Burns was, for the most part, pleasant, becoming bad-tempered when he thought too much, and his honesty, though never prominent, was strong enough to keep him from deliberate crime.

He was still playing with his now empty glass when Polycarp walked into the public-house, carrying his suitcase. If you want to know how Polycarp had arrived in Birmingham, you must consult a Bradshaw for the times of trains between Oxford and Birmingham and into this weave some of Polycarp's erratic nature to account for his missing connections. When he had approached the ticket-office at Oxford the word Birmingham had come from him without any definite volition. It had surged up from his unconscious mind—and here he was at Birmingham, still a little dazed with the roar and clangour of New Street Station.

The public-house was crowded with lunch-time business men assaulting Basses and Worthingtons, and when Polycarp was served with his beer he carried it away from the bar and looked for a place to sit down. The only vacant seat was at Frank Burns's table.

"Mind if I sit here?"

"Not at all." And then, as Polycarp's suitcase hit him in the shin, Frank added, "Stranger to the town?"

Polycarp nodded as he drank, and, putting his glass down, said:

"Yes. Haven't been here long. I've been wandering around a bit trying to get my bearings. You know—General Post Office, public lavatories, free library, Woolworth's, and the pub where they dish out free olives and gherkins."

Frank nodded. "All towns are constructed round those essentials—those and a cast-iron fountain commemorating the jubilee of Queen Victoria. Some of the finest pieces of Chinese Chippendale in the world came into being just after Queen Victoria's jubilee—you can see 'em in every market square."

"Chinese Chippendale?"

"Never mind. Let it go—it's a joke, but in better taste than the façades of most Methodist chapels. I was nearly an architect once, but don't hold that against me. Where are you from, and what do you do—if you do anything? Don't answer if the questions offend you."

Polycarp smiled. "They don't offend me. Politeness has been supported by ignorance for too many years, questions that should have been asked and weren't. You know—Daddy, where did I come from? Still, I can't tell you for private reasons." Polycarp did not know whether the Red Dragon Company would make police enquiries after him, and he did not wish to take any unnecessary risks.

"In trouble, eh?"

"Something like that—nothing criminal though, as my late landlady would say."

"Uh, people in trouble are generally more interesting than the ones that ain't. What are you going to do in Birmingham?"

92

"I don't quite know. I'm a sort of rolling stone, seeking the goddess Fortune as it were."

"One of those? That's even more interesting. I'm in something the same boat myself. Let's have a drink together to mark the occasion. I'll toss you who pays."

"I don't mind. Got a coin?"

"Here you are." Frank Burns handed him a penny, and, as Polycarp tossed it, he cried "Heads!" and so it was. Over the drinks he gave Polycarp an abridged version of his life story. By the time he had finished the glasses were empty.

"Have another?" he asked affably.

"I don't mind if I do."

"Tell you what, we'll toss for it again and see if your luck changes. I'm a great believer in luck. Heads you pay; tails I pay."

He tossed and won. The drinks came, and they sat talking. The beer warmed Polycarp, and he contemplated confiding to Frank the reason for his leaving Oxford. He told him something of the events which had brought him to Birmingham, and the talk drifted to various topics. The glasses were emptied, and before they were filled they tossed to see if Polycarp's luck would change, but it did not. He bought beer, and, when they discovered that neither of them had cigarettes, they tossed, and Polycarp bought a packet of Players. When the glasses were empty again, and Frank suggested that they should toss for a last drink before going, Polycarp agreed, but, as the coin fell to the ground, he picked it up and examined it. He looked at Frank.

That worthy nodded sadly: "You've guessed my secret. I get quite a lot of free drinks from that two-faced friend. It's one way of getting my revenge on life. Silly and mean perhaps, like some of these council houses, but, there you are, I am silly and mean at times."

Polycarp was more amused than annoyed. There was something about the fellow which attracted him, an air of careless disregard for everything.

"I don't blame you, though I can't say that I agree with such forms of economic sadism. Still, that's your problem, and, if people are fools enough to be taken in, why shouldn't you rob 'em this way just as they are robbed by pseudo-legitimate business men?"

"I agree. I dunno quite what it all means, but as long as you're not annoyed I can still like you for it. In fact I'll give the coin to you to show my generosity. Here, take it."

He pressed it on Polycarp, who was unable to refuse.

"What are you going to do now?" said Frank.

"Look for a lodging, I suppose, and then try and find some way of making a fortune." He smiled.

"Fortune! Some people only think of money. The truest saying in the world is that money breeds money. If you've got plenty, you can make more. I've got a little, but it isn't enough. If I had, say, another hundred pounds, I know where there's a small fortune waiting to be picked up—"

"To be picked up?"

"Yes, just swiped from the ground."

Polycarp did not know whether the man was a grand liar or in earnest. From his demeanour he might quite easily have been either.

"How?" he asked.

Frank shook a finger at him. "Ah, you can't expect me to give my ideas away, can you? If I had someone who would invest a hundred pounds in my scheme, I could treble it within four months. Absolute certainty—but who will?" He looked at Polycarp suddenly, as though an idea had occurred to him.

"Say—you haven't got a hundred pounds, have you?"

There was a pause, punctuated by the sighing of drawn beer handles and the clink of glasses.

"As a matter of fact, I have." Which was perfectly true, for with his initial capital and his savings he had a little over that amount.

Frank whistled slowly. "You have?" He was serious. "Listen, I don't know anything about you, and you know very little about me, but I'm in earnest now. You come back with me to my room. You can dump there as long as you like. And we'll put all our cards on the table. I think we could get along fine. I was acting mean just now. I apologise. That's how I am until I know a feller. You play straight with me, and I'll stand by you. If you give me your word, I won't let you down—not even if you are a criminal."

"It sounds as though it may be worth looking into," said Polycarp cautiously, stroking his moustache.

"It's worth more than that—it's worth hundreds to the right people."

"A fortune, eh? All right, let's go and talk about it." Frank grabbed Polycarp's suitcase, and they went out into the street. As they went the barmaid watched them, and then turned to her assistant, saying: "There goes a couple of good-for-nothing nobodies!" Which, had she but known it, was very untrue, and proves how singularly inapt barmaids are at assessing human character. Perhaps it is that they see men only as so many pale ales, double Scotches, or tonic waters, and imagine them all to be as volatile as the spirits they drink, or as dark-souled as the ale they quaff. Anyway, she was quite wrong about the two, for both of them were good for a great many things, and both of them were one day to be well known.

Frank occupied a front room on the third floor of a large apartment house. The only time he saw the landlady was when she emerged from her basement retreat to take the rent. The room was fifteen feet long and twelve feet broad, but by reason of the furniture, which was packed into it without regard for convenience or design, it looked like a more than usually untidy rabbit's hutch. In one corner was an iron bedstead, which had once been white but was now suffering from scurf, so that large black patches stared about the room from its curves and creaking legs. During the daytime the bed served as a general depository for papers, clothes, and food parcels, which were all swept on to the floor at night. Under the window a rickety table complained of weak legs, and enlisted the aid of several old copies of *The Motor Cycle* to wedge its quavering flap into alignment. This table was covered with a red cloth that shook dusty tassels towards the worn oilcloth, and the cloth in turn was covered with an unlovely detritus of crockery, books, pipes, saucepans, and food stains, above which, like the grey columns of lighthouses at sea, showed the necks of milk bottles. When Frank wanted a meal he cleared a space in the morass with his arm, and hoped that nothing would fall from the table; if anything did fall, it depended upon his mood whether it was picked up. Against the wall was a tilting set of bookshelves, furnished mostly with old library copies and pilfered volumes which he had acquired in his peregrinations. An armchair, excreting black filling over the room, and whose springs voiced a hymn of hate on three notes when sat on; a kitchen chair; a presentation picture of a small boy in velveteens blowing soap bubbles; and an heterogeneous litter on the mantelshelf, crowned in macabre glory by a sheep's skull which Frank had picked up in the Doone Valley and for years had cherished as that of a deer, completed the furnishing of the room. It was into this bachelor slum that Polycarp was conducted.

"This," said Frank proudly, "is where I live. Difficult to believe, isn't it? But man is a tough creature—he gets used to anything. Here is perfect peace except for the other roomers. Above me is an Egyptian university student, who is under the impression that he can play the guitar—some day I mean to disillusion him. Below lives a small-part man from the repertory theatre, who seems to have great difficulty in learning his parts. He bawls them out loud most of the day, and shouts them out in his sleep at night. To the left and right we have respectively a welfare worker, who is prepared to talk about lost souls and fallen-women-I-have-met by the hour, and a gas-fitter, who is studying languages on the gramophone. Together we make a harmonic quintet of the arts and humanities, but don't let that worry you. Take the seat ..." He pointed to the armchair.

Polycarp dropped his suitcase on the bed and sat down, while Frank lit the gas-fire and, placing a kettle on an ingenious trivet, began to prepare a cup of tea.

Polycarp never got that cup of tea. They began to talk, and what remained of a shilling's worth of gas in the meter expired quietly without their noticing it. They talked on and on, and Frank outlined his scheme. He went into details and costs, and Polycarp examined the idea from every possible angle until it seemed to him that it was as perfect as Frank had originally stated. At half past six they stopped talking for a moment, and then they were conscious of their hunger and thirst.

"You stay here and I'll get some food. Lend me half a crown, will you? The rest of my money's in the bank."

Frank disappeared, soon to return with a jar of pickles and a loaf of bread and a long red Bologna sausage.

At half past eight the food was gone, and they were still talking. Frank was lying on the bed, while Polycarp was seated on the kitchen chair at the table. The table had, after Herculean efforts, been entirely cleared, and the contents now reposed on the floor beneath the bookshelves. Spread over the tablecloth were large sheets of white foolscap paper, borrowed, at risk of a long eugenic conversation, from the welfare worker, and upon these sheets of paper Polycarp was busily writing.

Occasionally he would stop writing and read aloud. "How does that sound, eh? Pretty good?"

"Like poetry. Like poetry, Polycarp. You're a genius, and so am I. The world is waiting for us."

"It won't be long now."

Polycarp went on with his writing. There was an interval while his pencil made a soft noise over the paper, and Frank lay on his back, looking at the cracked ceiling, and humming gently a refrain from the *Gondoliers*.

"Polycarp!" He shot upright on the bed. "We've forgotten the most important thing of all!"

"What do you mean?—everything's been thought of." Polycarp stopped writing.

"No!—what chumps! We haven't decided where we're going to start!"

"But here in Birmingham, of course. I thought that was obvious?"

"We can't start here. Must start somewhere where we are complete strangers. You know, a prophet without honour, and the rest."

"How are we to decide? One place seems as good as another."

"It shouldn't be difficult, then." Frank lay back on the bed, and considered the question to the tune of *Take a Pair of Sparkling Eyes*.

"I know what we'll do!" Polycarp sat back.

"What?" Frank rolled over on the bed and looked at Polycarp. "Is the seed of a great thought germinating under that ginger thatch of yours?"

"Wait for me." Polycarp goo up and left the room. In the hall of the house, by the telephone, he had noticed a Bradshaw. He brought it up with him and waved it over his head.

"Here," he said, spreading out the map of England which was folded into the book, "we have a map. With the aid of a pin and a circling hand, we should be able to decide. Got a pin?"

"The only piercing things I have are my intellect and a dart which I purloined once from a pub in Chester." Frank was standing at his side. "We'll do this in style, my lad. No half measures about this firm. We do things properly."

Frank took charge of the proceedings, which, being construed into action, means that he ripped the map from the Bradshaw, smeared small portions of butter on its four corners, and then fastened it to the wall of his room, under the picture of the bubble-blowing infant. From the mantelshelf he unearthed the dart, and handed it to Polycarp.

"As titular head of the firm, you shall have the honour. Throw it good and hard, Polycarp! And if your aim is going to be so bad that you miss the map altogether, I hope the dart sticks that velvet-trousered infant in the gizzard and destroys for ever his bubbly propensities. The thought of children like that turns marriage into a lottery."

Polycarp bowed ceremoniously, spat on the point of the dart for luck, and threw it at the map. The point pierced the paper and a half-inch of plaster and lath.

They moved to the map and examined it. The dart was firmly embedded in East Anglia, and the point had entered the paper at a spot about an inch below the Wash.

"What's the name of the nearest town?" asked Frank.

"March," read Polycarp, as he extracted the dart and tore the map. "March? Have you heard of it before?"

Frank shook his head. "I've heard of Nineveh and the buried city of Ur, but March! I'm only familiar with the unpleasant month of that name."

"Well, there must be a town of that name, otherwise it wouldn't be on the map, would it?"

"True, true. There must be a town of that name if Bradshaw and the railway companies say so. And that is where we commence operations. Little do the inhabitants of March know of the good fortune which is to be theirs."

"Let's hope that's how they look at it," said Polycarp, pulling at his moustache.

"Don't worry. You and I were fated to meet and go into this venture. I have a great belief in Fate. We instinctively recognised in one another the favoured of the gods. Come on, put away that writing, and, if you'll lend me ten bob until tomorrow, I'll take you out and treat you to the pictures or the theatre to cement our already lusty friendship."

He caught Polycarp's arm and pulled him from the table. As they passed along the corridor a voice suddenly demanded, through a half-open doorway:

"Est-ce que les abeilles sont méchantes?" and then, in different accents, came the reply:

"Elles ne sont pas méchantes, mais si nous les derangeons elles nous piqueront …"

While from above came the jangling twang of a guitar and a discordant voice rising and falling.

"We were just in time!" Frank made a grimace, and Polycarp laughed as behind them a voice began in petulant tones:

"Ceci est un éléphant. L'éléphant est un quadrupède. C'est le plus gros des quadrupèdes …"

"Ceci est un éléphant! As though one could mistake an elephant in any language " exclaimed Frank.

IX
A demonstration of crowd psychology

The chief characteristic of March is a quiet, leisurely uneventfulness. It is a town in which, although there is a great deal of movement, nothing ever happens. It lies in the heart of the fertile fen country on the bank of the old River Nene, a slow-moving, sluggish stream as earthy and ill-favoured as the fat tench and coarse roach which swim through its waters. At one time its geographical position in the fens isolated it from the successive civilising influences which moved across the country, but since the fens have been drained the town has become an important railway junction, and the influences which formerly it resisted have now invaded the town. Yet their victory is far from complete. There is a cinema and a library, inns and concerts, clubs and churches, a market-day, and a drinking-fountain which never functions. It has most of the adjuncts of a small country town, but, despite an importance slowly being forced upon it by its position in the fens, it refuses to relinquish the atmosphere of isolated intimacy which characterised it as a village long before steam became of industrial significance. It is as though some of the sturdy spirit which fired Hereward the Wake to resist the Normans at Ely, twenty miles away, has been captured by the townsfolk and transmuted into a naive denial that existence anywhere but in March must necessarily be a sorry affair. The fundamental truth of this denial will probably always be a matter for contention between the true-born natives and those migrants from other towns and districts who, for business reasons, come to live in the town.

And it was in this town that Polycarp and Frank had decided to begin their business enterprise. And it was here, by the side of the river on the outskirts of the town, in one of the few pasture fields which star the countryside like green jewels dropped amongst the leagues of sugar-beet and potatoes, that Polycarp sat and waited for Frank. Behind him lay the town, the red tiles of its houses showing through gaps in the elms and poplars, and, topping the tall willows where the stream curved, there rose the square tower of the Town Hall crowned with a verdigrised figure of Britannia, who averted her eyes from the town and, as it seemed, stared rather wistfully across the flat country towards the distant North Sea, and thought, if her copper head were capable of thought, of its grey rollers and battleships, of the cargo-boats, tramp steamers, and Yarmouth smacks that exemplified the glory which she symbolised. From her exalted position she commanded the whole town the river, with its twisting row of cottages on one bank and its market square on the other, the occasional mansard roofs, the flash of green ivy on walls and yellow hotel signs, the scuffle of loungers on the river bridge and the row of parked cars in the High Street.

Normally the whole town breathed quietly, pursuing the steady trend of its daily functions, but today there was a quicker tempo in its breathing, though not so quick that it might be termed excitement— excitement had been unknown since Hereward defeated the Normans at near-by Witchford—yet there was a definitely briefer, livelier cadence. The loungers on the bridge were fewer, for some of them had shifted to the front of the Golden Barbel Hotel and were looking at a large red and white notice posted on a board. About the town there were similar notices: clinging to the sides of shops, hanging from hoardings, blazoned on boards, enlivening the exit of the public lavatory—Polycarp had audaciously fastened that one himself under cover of darkness—and flaring in cautionary colour from the rough barks of the elms along the main roadway. Polycarp had done his work well. He had been in the town two days and by this time there was not a man, woman, or child who was unaware of his presence. It was impossible for any inhabitant of March to move three yards from his doorway without encountering one of the advertisements. He was referred to when he appeared as "That's him." He frankly enjoyed the publicity and made the most of it, and now he sat on a hummock of grass in the field which he had hired for a week and waited for Frank. In his hand he held, and contemplated with the tender eyes of a creator, one of the red and white notices. He read it through slowly to himself for what was easily the hundredth time:

FLY!! FLY!!! FLY!!!!
THE ATTRACTION OF THE NEW AGE!!!
THE GREATEST THRILL SINCE STEPHENSON'S "ROCKET"
MAKE THE AIR YOURS

Enjoy a thrill a hundred times greater than travelling by train, motor or liner—Fly with the
NEW AGE FLYING COMPANY
which is visiting this town for one week from Monday, May 19th.

Trip round the Town.........................5s.
Tour round the surrounding countryside 10s.
Loop-the-loop.............................. 20s.

FLY!! FLY!!! FLY!!!!

Experience this New Thrill with a Famous War Ace—Frank Burns, the British Immelmann!!!!
FLYING IS THE THING OF THE FUTURE!!
BRING YOURSELF UP TO DATE

Proprietor—Polycarp Jarvis.
Pilot—Frank Burns, late R.A.F.

Certainly not a work of genius or even a work of great merit, for any statement which relies upon a plethora of exclamation marks tends to create an impression of falseness and unforgivable ostentation, but it was Polycarp's own creation and he could see nothing wrong with it. He smoothed it, and his eye strayed to the corner of the sheet where the red letters cried out "Proprietor—Polycarp Jarvis." He was a proprietor, and the feeling was good. Proprietor of the New Age Flying Company, capital originally one hundred and twenty-five pounds cash, now reduced to twenty-five pounds cash and the valuable asset of one aeroplane which Frank Burns had purchased for the company from a London acquaintance for one hundred pounds.

Polycarp had never seen the aeroplane which Frank had gone to London to fetch. It was, so he understood, an old army machine, and he sat now in the flying-field waiting for the arrival of his partner so that they might begin business. The town of March waited to be tempted to the new experience of flying and Polycarp waited for Frank. This was to be, he mused, one of the great moments in his life, this venture into aviation and big business. He sat and dreamed with the poster on his knees.

Flying had increased in popularity during the six years since the war, and there was, so Frank had declared, pots of money waiting to be made from people who were anxious to sample the pleasure of the new thrill, and Frank was surprisingly correct in his estimation of the public's desire. A new generation was ripening of men and women eager for fresh thrills, for new sensations; already they had tired of the old, well-tried joys, and now they were seeking new fields in which to sport their vicarious enthusiasms. The world seemed to have forsaken all its old channels of conduct. People were overwhelmingly anxious to submerge their individuality in any meretricious, flashy amusement, and a new conception of entertainment began to develop in their minds, a conception based, it appeared, on noise. Everything had to be raucous and noisy: they left Strauss for jazz; research workers were struggling to perfect the new technique of sound so that talking pictures might become commercially possible; the pleasures of the countryside were exploited and spoiled by cars and charabancs : this was the day of speedways and huge crowds yelling under arc lights, and even the starry depths of the ether were riven by the electric discharges of broadcasting stations. No one ever dared to think for very long, because sustained reflection induced a state of melancholy, and rather than find the sanity beyond melancholy, people bathed themselves in the oblivion of new experiences, welcoming any fresh device to charm their fretting souls from the contemplation of the purpose of life. Everywhere—in the theatre, in politics, in sport, and even in religion—there was a growing tendency to forget and forgo honest cogitation for gaudy spectacle.

And Polycarp was part of the great turmoil. He sat now on his hummock of grass in the flying-field, with a wind-cone bellying like a fat white maggot above him, and dreamed great dreams of sensational success. Twenty-two years of age, with his mental eyes really not fully open, he dreamed of great conquests and fame, dreamed of Polycarp the Great and Polycarp the Splendid, and as basis for his dreams he had no more than a ready, flashy wit, an errant impetuousness and generosity, a ginger moustache, a body subject at times to twinges of indigestion, twenty-five pounds in the Post Office Savings Bank, and, somewhere in the cerulean blue above him, an old army aeroplane which was probably unsafe; and—so superb is the optimism of youth and youth's visions—he saw nothing paradoxical or ridiculous in his dreams. To him dreams and hopes were solid stuff from which he had but to shape the future and from which he could hew himself a fortune as easily as a white-coated grocer's assistant carves cheese; and perhaps it was from the very fervency of his dreams that he did later in life manage to achieve so much of his desire; for fervency, like flatulence, marks a man from his fellows.

Polycarp sat in his flying-field, rented at one pound for the week from a local horse-dealer, and dreamed his private dreams of great publicity and fame, and waited for Frank. He had not long to wait.

Through the stillness of the early summer morning a low note burgeoned, swelling and deepening into a steady drone, and growing from a drone into a pulsing roar.

Polycarp stood upon his hummock and gazed into the almost blinding brilliance of the sky. Away in the south he could make out a bright red shape, that swelled quickly and took the form of an aeroplane flying fairly low. Polycarp's face broadened into a grin; he had never for a moment doubted Frank's integrity, but he was glad to find that the aviator had kept his word.

The aeroplane roared above the town, making a wild din, and Polycarp ran into the middle of the field, waving his arms violently when it passed overhead. As Polycarp ran into the middle of the field, so did every inhabitant of March, beyond the sick, the paralysed, the unconscious, and the sleeping, run into the street or throw up windows and crane their necks to observe the gorgeous sight. The potman at the Golden Barbel threw down his napkin and tankards and came out on to the river-bank; the shop-assistants sidled towards the windows in an attempt to view the aeroplane, and cursed beneath their breath the pernicious economic system which forced them to remain at their counters while the masters of the shops calmly walked out on to the pavement and stretched their skinny, fat, or wrinkled necks to the sky; the policeman on point duty left the traffic to control itself, and, forgetting to lower his signalling arms, stared aloft in a crucified attitude; the loungers on the bridge pressed their elbows against the parapet and looking up said, "There 'tis!"; the boys in the Grammar School yard dropped their tennis-balls and *Nelson Lees* and wondered how they could find five shillings for a flight; the girls in the confectionery and hairdressing shops patted the sides of their heads and thought of Polycarp's dinky moustache and pictured what the famous aviator would look like; the clerks in solicitors' and the local government offices made for the windows or dashed with spurious excuse to the outside privies and then stopped to stare and dream wild dreams of the joys of flying; the operator at the cinema interrupted the cleaning of his projection machine and, leaning against the placards, speculated as to how much the attendance at the cinema might suffer by this new attraction; and, as the pigeons who whitened the robe of the copper Britannia rose up in alarm at the noise of the engines, the statue seemed to sigh contentedly and her face brighten with interest. Things were looking up in March at last. In fact, everything and almost everybody looked upwards at the aeroplane and, as if in recognition of this general adulation, Frank decided to give March something to look at. He gave a ten-minutes' exhibition of flying which absolutely disproved the growing theory that man was fast becoming the slave of his own machines. Frank forced the aeroplane to do nearly everything but land on the cobblestones of the market and peck at crumbs like a hen. He banked the machine round and dipped down over the town, the engines screaming and shrilling as though the aeroplane were a vicious red bee. He shot up into the air at terrific angles, climbed in long spirals until the red machine was lost in the blue, dived straight towards the earth until the spectators winced and stepped for shelter into their doorways and breathed with relief when the aeroplane flattened out to safety, and he looped the loop so that his last downward swoop brought him almost to the tips of the elms, and, while he pirouetted in the air, Polycarp shivered alternately in fear and wonder as he watched the machine swerve and glide, curve and fall like a leaf, twist and revolve, stand on its head, balance on its tail, fly upside down, fly in zigzags, and behave in a dozen other impossible ways. It was the worst and yet the best ten minutes of Polycarp's life. To the hundreds of inhabitants of the town it was only an aeroplane demonstrating in the sky, but every time Polycarp saw it dip towards the Britannia or fall towards the river or miss the elms, he saw a string of one hundred pound notes fluttering in the air, and the mental vision was almost distracting enough to destroy his pleasure at Frank's obvious skill.

Polycarp's first words when Frank landed were:

"Why on earth did you do that, man? You had my heart in my mouth!"

Frank stepped out, smiling and ruffled by the wind; he was wearing an old stormgard motor-cycling coat, a leather helmet, thick gloves, and grey trousers that were well protected by grease stains.

"Best advertisement in the world. If I hadn't been afraid of annoying the town council, I'd have flown under the river bridge, circled round the War Memorial, and parted the hair of the policeman on point duty, but I didn't want to put us in the wrong from the start."

"You might have smashed the thing up!"

"Not me! I never take those kind of risks. What I can do, I can do. That was nothing; some day I'll take you up and we'll have an afternoon's fun. And, besides, think of the advertisement! Everyone in the town saw that, and they'll tell one another what a skilful chap I am; that'll increase their confidence in us, and in another two hours we'll have taken ten pounds."

"I hope so, anyway. Did you have any trouble with the plane?"

"No. She's a little beauty. Dirt cheap at the price. Come and have a look."

He began to show Polycarp round the machine, explaining the technicalities so that Polycarp was reminded of the day when Webb had led him round a Red Dragon for the first time. In the end he knew little more about the aeroplane than that it looked neat and trim, had room for two passengers behind the pilot, and was painted red. When they had finished the examination Polycarp said:

"I've been thinking. What about the Air Ministry's regulations? Do we have to register it or notify them about this? You know there must be certain formalities."

Frank looked at him and laughed.

"Sure there are formalities. Where would the Air Ministry be if there weren't a few formalities and regulations to occupy their minds? But don't you worry about that, Socrates—I've fixed all that up. All you have to do is to take the money at the gate while I give the passengers what they want. Let's eat, and then we'll begin business."

"I've taken rooms at the Castle of Comfort Inn."

"What sort of joint is it? And are the maids dark-haired or blondes?"

"Quite a respectable place. The food's substantial and sometimes good, but it's never both. You know, good and not much or a lot and not good! The barmaids are blonde and plumpish. Why?"

Frank wagged his head. "Always as well to know these things."

At the hotel Frank soon showed that his principal concern with food was that it should be substantial. He engulfed a huge plate of soup, made eyes at the waitress and got another plateful, and then on this brothy basis he built up a store of reserve energy from a plate of chipped potatoes and a steak which looked as though it had been carved from a brontosaurus. The whole of which repast was firmly cemented by bread and frequent half-cans of ale, and embellished with several sticks of celery, which he ate travelling between the sideboard and the window as he talked about his trip from London and their plans for the future.

"As soon as we've made a little working capital from this town we'll move to a seaside resort, and then we'll rake the dough in. We shall catch them at the right time—the beginning of the holiday season. By the end of September we should be quids in pocket and have enough to keep us until next summer, when we can start again."

"And in time we can have two or three planes and hire more pilots—perhaps I can learn to fly—and become fat and wealthy. Gosh! Just think of the possibilities!"

"I have, I have. Boy, I believe I'm going to like this job. You know, I've started several stunts full of enthusiasm, but it goes. Today, though, when I got up aloft it seemed different. Sort of gave me a new confidence. Polycarp, I'm damned glad I met you. I think you've saved my life! Anyway, let's drink a brandy to the New Age Flying Company."

They called for brandies and drank a solemn toast. Then they went back to the flying-field to begin the great work. When Frank said that his stunting exhibition would prove an advertisement for them, he was quite correct. The general topic in the town that day was of the flyers. But when he said that within two hours of his arrival they would have taken ten pounds, he was a long way out.

They arrived at the flying-field at two o'clock and stood expectantly at the door of the bell-tent which had been erected by the gateway as a pay-box and petrol-store.

"This is the great moment!" Polycarp was enthusiastic.

"Great moments always give me a headache," said Frank cynically. "I'll go and look over the plane while you wait for 'em to roll up in their thousands. Most of 'em are still digesting dinner, I expect, and don't forget that it is Monday—never a good day in any trade. But they'll come in time."

It was, however, a long time before they did come, despite the endemic of red and white notices, despite the flying exhibition of the morning, and despite the signboards which pointed from every available corner: "This way to the Flying-Field."

Polycarp could not sit down. He flipped the bunch of tickets in his hand—red for a town flight, blue for round the country, and green for a loop. He walked restlessly to the gateway and, leaning across the top bar, stared down the short lane towards the town and waited. Nothing happened. No dark crowds churned the dried furrows of the lane to powdery dust, no pressing crowds brushed down the hawthorn hedges and trampled the long quitch grasses underfoot. The world went on just as though Polycarp and Frank and the New Age Flying Company did not exist. It was a typical Monday world. The sun shone; the birds sang when they could spare a moment from their momentous tasks of building nests, laying eggs, and feeding their broods; the flowers were busy spreading their pollen by bee, fly, and wind; the trees sucked in the sunlight with their leaves and drew sustenance from the earth through their roots and only incidentally gave Polycarp shade beneath their outflung branches; the cows munched and chewed to fill their smooth udders; worms and moles worked through the ground bringing the precious oxygen to the pale mould; hens pecked at shell-forming grit; and fat shopmen, replete from their dinners, picked at the crannies of their teeth—everyone and everything seemed to have something to do far more important than sampling the thrill of the new age, and the greatest thing since Stephenson's "Rocket."

But was Polycarp downcast? Not at all. His knowledge of human nature told him that with this business it would be the same as every other. People were timid about flying. They would all be waiting for someone else to try it first. There would be a general hanging back, although all of them wanted to fly, until some Columbus or Cortez arose from their homely ranks and led the way to a new experience. Patiently, then, Polycarp waited for the new Columbus and Cortez to appear in the lane. He waited for half an hour and nothing happened. Frank did not appear to worry. He was lost in the internals of the machine, happy with a spanner and memories of the war flying days. And then, when it seemed that no one was ever going to come, Polycarp's patience was rewarded. A small figure appeared at the top of the lane and came towards him. It was a woman; a middle-aged woman, respectably dressed in a blue coat and skirt, with a small grey hat on her head which was of the same colour as the wisps of hair that strayed from under its brim. Her face, though naturally timid, was now stiffened into fines of forced determination, making it obvious that she was conquering a desire to hold back from something she wanted yet did not like to demand.

Polycarp was overjoyed. As she came up to the gate he could not restrain himself. He burst out:

"Madam! I congratulate you! You are a credit to a sex which has too long held an unjust, inferior position, but now you are about to take your place alongside the dominant male. It is fitting that a woman should be the first to patronise the New Age Flying Company. What do you want, a five-bob, ten-bob, or a pound flight?" He held up the coloured clutch of tickets hopefully, tantalisingly, temptingly.

The woman drew back from this flood of words and gestures and shook her head wanly as she produced a bottle from behind her back.

"Do you mind," she said, half apologetically, "filling this bottle with petrol? I ... you see ... I don't want a flight. I want to get some stains off Johnnie's best suit. Do you mind? ... I live in the cottage at the end of the lane ..." She added this in a hopeful tone of voice, as though it gave her some esoteric claim upon the New Age Flying Company's stock of petrol.

Polycarp repressed a frantic desire to laugh aloud at the disappointment and ridicule which struggled within him, and then he said, controlling himself

"Certainly, madam, the New Age Flying Company is always willing to oblige." He took her bottle and, going within the tent, filled it from a container.

As he handed it back to her, he felt half sorry for the woman, she seemed so apologetic and depressed about Johnnie's suit.

"And don't forget," he reminded her, "if you do want to fly, there's the New Age Company at the bottom of your lane waiting for you." He was not going to let her go without a struggle.

She shook her head again and this time managed to smile. "No, I don't want a trip. If the good Lord had intended us to fly, he would have given us wings. Thank you for the petrol, sir." She went, leaving Polycarp grumbling quietly to himself.

A few moments after she had gone, Frank came back from the aeroplane and Polycarp told him the story.

"We shall have to watch 'em," he said; "otherwise they'll be asking us to start up the engine so that they can dry their clothes in the draught from the propeller."

He went into the bell-tent and left Polycarp at the gate. After the woman had gone the lane remained empty for a long time. Polycarp began to lose some of his first enthusiasm, but he was still far from downhearted. Then, when he was beginning to think that perhaps they might have to take some decisive action to rouse the town, a man came slouching down the lane towards them. From the slovenly state of his clothes Polycarp was assured that he was not the type to want petrol to clean the stains from his trousers.

The man came up to him. He was a typical corner-house propper and upholder of bridge parapets. Before Polycarp could say anything or flourish his tickets the man nodded to him curtly and, pushing his cap back from his eyes, said

"You the flying chaps, ain't you?" As he was speaking, Frank came out of the tent and stood beside Polycarp.

"Right first time," said Polycarp. "Do you—"

"Have you a cigarette to spare?" The man shot out the request with an air of perfect command, and so unexpected and almost authoritative was his manner that, before Polycarp could really appreciate what he was doing, he found himself holding out his case towards the man. The fellow took a cigarette and stuck it into his mouth.

"Nice machine you've got over there. I used to drive a motor-plough myself once." He patted his pockets for a match and then, looking at the two, said: "Got a match on yer?"

Still in a humorous daze at his audacity and presumption, Polycarp took out his matches, and, when the man made no move to take them, he struck one. As the flame flared up, the man jerked his head forward and lit his cigarette. His whole attitude was lazy and indolent, so much so that Frank could not control himself any longer.

"Is the cigarette drawing all right?" he asked. The fellow nodded an affirmative.

"That's good," replied Frank. "We like to satisfy people. How are you fixed for blowing your nose?"

Even this sarcasm went unheeded. A man who has propped up the side of a town hall for years becomes almost insensible to the human emotion of resentment. His is a philosophy of. stone, susceptible only to slow attrition.

"S'all right, thank you," he replied, making himself comfortable against the gateway.

He stayed with them awhile. When he had gone Polycarp turned to Frank.

"It wouldn't be a bad idea if you went up and did a trip round the town as though you had passengers. Give people the impression that we are doing some business."

Frank took the aeroplane up, and when he came down they waited a while to see what would happen. Nothing did happen. He took the aeroplane up again, and still nothing happened.

"Seems as though they're boycotting us," he said as he threw his tenth cigarette stub into the ditch.

"They're not boycotting us, don't you worry," snorted Polycarp, pulling at his moustache. "They're afraid. That's what it is—fear! Waiting for someone to take the first step! Well, I'll soon settle that for them. Polycarp Jarvis isn't the sort of fellow to let fear interfere with his business schemes. You wait here and I'll show you something about crowd psychology."

He left Frank at the gate and darted away towards the town.

It was just after four o'clock, and the town was emerging from the deep afternoon somnolence. He went into the town, past the market square and bank, to the bridge over the river. There were three men keeping the stone warm which commemorated the building of the bridge. With an unusual fierceness in his grey-blue eyes, Polycarp walked straight up to the first lounger and blurted in a rapid voice:

"Pardon me, sir, but have you ever heard of Wilbur Wright and Blériot? Did you ever hear of Captain Sir John Alcock—"

"T'aint no good asking him that, sir," interrupted the middle one of the three men; "he's as deaf as a post and couldn't tell if you was swearin' at him or offering him five pounds to get drunk with. Could 'e, Bill?" He turned, laughing so that his cracked, nicotine-streaked teeth showed like misshapen iron-stained stalactites in a cave. "And I can tell 'e, mister, there ain't no gentleman of that name in this town. I've lived here forty years and I know."

"Oh!" Polycarp threw his hands into the air in a gesture of despair. "Listen," he almost shouted. "I'm Polycarp Jarvis, manager of the New Age Flying Company—"

"Ay, us 'ave heard about 'e."

"That's gratifying! Now look here. None of you men are employed, I suppose, and you've very little money to spend on entertainment? Right. Then, in the spirit of true philanthropy, I'm going to lighten your dull lives a bit. If you'll come with me, I'll see that you get a free trip in the aeroplane. What do you say?"

They said nothing for a moment. The major portion of Polycarp's mouthings was unintelligible to them. Only the words "free trip" had any significance.

"A free trip, eh? Is there a catch in it?"

"None at all. Just sheer generosity. Come on!"

Polycarp took one of them by the arm and led him away. Their curiosity was stirred, and the others followed him; the deaf man talking volubly and wanting to know what was going to happen. On the way back to the field they were almost knocked over by a sudden spate of knicker-bockered, tousle-headed humanity that burst from a school. Boys of all ages and conditions of cleanliness swarmed around them. Polycarp caught one lad by the shoulder.

"Ever been up in an aeroplane, my lad?"

The boy shook his head and, like his elders, wondered at first whether there was a catch in the question.

"No, sir. Only the chair-o-plane at the Status."

"Status?"

"He means the Statute Fair what comes in September," explained one of the men.

"Oh. Well, son, come along with me and you shall have a free trip in my aeroplane. Come along, and bring a couple of pals to keep you company."

The boy was much quicker in appreciating his good fortune than the men had been. After a scuffle and babble of high voices his two pals were chosen, and then, escorted by a bellowing mob of other boys, indignantly, piteously, truculently, outrageously, and loudly demanding why they should be left out of the chosen ones, Polycarp headed the band back to the flying-field and on his face was a smile of triumph. At last he had aroused real interest and was going to break the barrier of fear which prevented the townsfolk from taking trips.

The crowd stood outside while he swiftly explained to Frank inside the tent what he was to do. The aviator soon grasped the idea and, very shortly, an aeroplane load was circling the town with a lounger and a schoolboy seeing their home-town from an entirely new angle and their first rapid fear being smothered by the strength of their interest and wonder.

Three trips the aeroplane made, and then Polycarp announced that the free trips were over. The loungers and lucky schoolboys departed after a while; only the other schoolboys, full of noisy hope, remained, waiting for the miracle to happen again.

Polycarp had done his work well. The loungers and three schoolboys spread the tale of their experiences round the town within an hour. Mothers and fathers were regaled with vivid accounts of just how the back garden and fowl-houses looked from the air, and how funny the old church and various citizens seemed from the top, and the loungers stopped every acquaintance and imparted the news of their infinite superiority to mortals who were unfortunate enough to have passed the whole of their life upon mother earth.

Flying was the thing of the future. Did anyone ever hear of fellows called Wright and Blearyo? Or Oldcock? Ah, they were men.

Such a state of affairs could not last long. It could not be said that a few loungers and schoolboys were the only persons in the town who had sampled the joys of the air. The interplay of envy and class-consciousness worked to a ferment, and fear vanished, and as soon as the shops began to clear of assistants and the offices of clerks, Polycarp saw how successful his scheme had been.

The whole effect was very much the same as the scene at any bathing-place on a cold morning. All the swimmers stand grouped round the diving-board waiting for someone to give them a lead, and not until some heroic individual breaks the steel mirror of the waters will the others dive in. Someone had flown, and immediately all those who could afford it were determined to fly as well.

The first two fares came half an hour after the schoolboys and loungers had left—they were the fathers of the two boys, who wisely saw that unless they, too, had shared the experience of flight, life at home would be a merry, puerile torture. Polycarp handed them their five-shilling tickets and rubbed the coins lovingly as Frank taxi'd away down the field.

The New Age Company had started to function and, as the red machine circled above him, Polycarp shook his head in approval and smacked his hands together. Life was grand. Life was good and the best thing in it was Polycarp, who could charm fear from these morose, hidebound fenmen. Oh, he was a great fellow, was Polycarp.

The rush to the field was not enormous. When they had to break off because of fading light, they had taken fifty shillings in five-shilling flights, but success was a matter of time, and convenience. The others would come before the week was out.

114

The two pulled the tarpaulin cover over the aeroplane, roped up the front of the tent, and went, laden with their wealth, back to the Castle of Comfort Inn to eat a well-earned meal.

"Polycarp," said Frank as he leaned back, refreshed and contented, "you'd probably make a lousy pilot, but I must say that you've got a way of getting what you want. Tomorrow we'll make the bell ring!"

"Tomorrow and for always—we'll keep the bell ringing! The New Age Company. Aaaah! A smart pilot and a clever proprietor. Let's drink to them." And they did.

X

A launching ceremony at the Golden Barbel

Once the element of awe behind their reluctance to taste the new experience was banished, the people of March soon showed that they were no cravens. For a week the New Age Company, to borrow a theatrical term, flew to a full house. In the morning there was little doing, but in the afternoon the tradesmen slipped away from their shops for a flight over the town, and some, as the result of bets in the Castle of Comfort and other inns, even defied gravity and their stomachs by looping the loop. The evening was devoted to satiating the desires of shop assistants, clerks, and the daring girls who believed themselves to be ultra-modern, although as Frank said to Polycarp, they probably all of them wore combinations.

Polycarp had never handled so many half-crowns in his life, and long before the week was over the green flying-field had blossomed into exotic patches of discarded red and blue tickets. The company achieved what is so essential for the success of any company—popularity. This popularity came in devious ways. The woman who had borrowed petrol fostered it in her small circle; the smoke-cadging lounger extolled the praises of the two in every public-house where there was a possibility of a free drink; the bridge loungers were as near ecstasy as they could ever come over the pleasures of aviation, and shifted their pitch from the bridge to the flying-field for the week, and consequently picked up a lot of erroneous aeronautical details from the ignorant Polycarp; and at evening the girls and young fellows of the town came and sat round the field, watching and talking to Polycarp, who soon installed himself in their affections by his good humour and jokes. His sturdy disregard of the girls' attempts at flirtation not only made them more determined than ever to conquer him, but also served to endear him to the pomaded and flannelled swains, who saw in him a person of stout integrity and one unwilling to take advantage of his exalted position to transgress their amatory rights. Polycarp was popular, and so was Frank, though his popularity was not of the same order.

To Frank the girls were fair game, and twice he had disappeared in the evenings, leaving Polycarp alone in their room making up the company's accounts. Frank, from the very volatileness of his character, achieved more popularity than Polycarp. Whenever he went up in the aeroplane it was impossible to tell what would happen. You bought a five-shilling ticket, and when you came down you had possibly flown round the town, over the countryside, and looped the loop—all for five bob. Polycarp tried to correct Frank's extravagant tendency by pointing out that it did not pay. People were beginning to buy only five-bob tickets and speculate as to what would happen, whereas they might otherwise have purchased a blue or green ticket. But all Polycarp's entreaties did not affect Frank's waywardness.

"We mustn't be niggardly, Polycarp. Bad for business. Keep 'em guessing. And, anyway, I don't feel like just buzzing round the town sometimes. The air's free and petrol's cheap, why should we be mean about things?"

"Preserve a balance in all things, Frank. Balance, the great thing in life. You're too irrational and unbalanced. Some day you'll be looping the loop with a nervy dame on board, and she'll jump overboard in fright, and then where should we be?"

"Rats! I tell you that half the people don't know they've looped the loop even when it's over. They all expect so much from a loop that when it comes they don't recognise it. Leave it to Franky—the British Immelmann—you awful liar!"

By the Friday of the week they had collected the magnificent sum of sixty pounds. Both of them were jubilant. The fame of the company was spreading, and although the labourers were busy in the fields many of them were finding time to cycle in from outlying villages and have a five-shilling flight. Those flights produced dissension, discord, and diversion in a hundred villages long after the company had passed on.

Polycarp was interested to observe the attitude of the people who took flights. Most of them came up timid and apprehensive, not quite knowing what to expect, but half hoping and half fearing that it was to be something unique and sensational. They climbed into the aeroplane, and were scared a little by the flimsiness of the fuselage. Polycarp watched them come, and saw them when they came down; saw with amusement the quick metamorphosis of mind. They came swaggering back from the centre of the field, treading like lords, and ready to laugh to scorn all the unfortunate mortals who had never been up in an aeroplane. A new aristocracy arose in a week, dividing the town into two classes: those who had and those who had not been up in an aeroplane.

All sorts of people flew. Clerks from the local government offices in the town came dressed in navy blue suits and black ties, and because he had once been one of them, Polycarp sometimes handed them a ten-shilling ticket in return for five shillings, and stilled their enquiries with a look—he liked to fancy them up aloft, forgetful for once of filing cabinets, clacking typewriters, dictating voices, and shiny office-tables littered with the miscarriage of files and crumpled papers; young railwaymen and their girls, with shingled hair and rouged lips, and dresses that revealed their knees as they stepped into the aeroplane under Frank's anxious, watchful guidance—it was extraordinary how complacently and naturally most of the girls accepted the little squeeze which he gave to their hands as he helped them in; farmers with heavy, black-muddied boots and high-collared jackets; sporting lads in checked coats and yellow polo jumpers, or flaunting ties with a design of horseshoes and hunting-crops; cowmen and beet-pullers, who cycled ten miles across the straight fen country on creaking bicycles and missed the monthly instalment on the perambulator or gramophone to have a flight—all sorts, all conditions, all kinds came, and almost invariably there was the same timid, half-wondering approach, and then the godlike swagger away from the field to celebrate their mastery of the air in a beer, the films, or the family circle. And all as they passed Polycarp abated their swagger a little for fear that he might smile in a superior, ridiculing way—he to whom an aeroplane was as commonplace as a bus, and none of them realised that he had a far greater experience than Polycarp of flying, for the company had been so busy since Monday that his only flight was a very short trip round the town as an advertisement on their second morning.

On Friday morning Polycarp decided that the time had come for him to alter this sad state of affairs. The first enthusiasm of the town had passed and business was steadying, so that the company could afford to indulge in a little relaxation.

"Say, mister"—he went up to Frank, who was tinkering about with the engine—"what about giving the proprietor of this company a really good flight. So far I've not been further than the end of the Town Hall. We can spare an hour off duty today."

Frank's dark head came out of the internals of the engine, and his grimy hands clutched the lower wing. "Getting ambitious, eh? Hop in, sonny, and poppa will show you the countryside."

He waited for Frank to climb in the pilot's seat and then swung the propeller. The engine fired, and Polycarp dodged round the wing and took his place behind Frank. The machine bumped and jolted across the field, and then lifted into the air and was away over the town, rocking in a slight easterly wind as they headed almost due south. For a time Polycarp was conscious only of the vicious snarling of the engine and the bite of the wind, which beat back into his eyes and sent long streamers of tears rolling over his cheek to his neck. Then slowly the sound of the engine was assimilated by his senses and became an unheeded background. He leaned over the side of the aeroplane, and let the wind take his hair as though it were water swirling about a knot of seaweed. Before him the propeller screamed and cut the bright sky into white flittering shards of light, and the fuselage and his own body trembled with the rhythmical shock of the pumping pistons and the lifting valves. Below him there was no noise and little movement, only a vast unbroken plain that stretched away into the blue distance until the eye confused it with the downward sweep of the sky.

All this flat arable land had once been virgin fen, a land of marshes, of wide sedge-lined pools where heavy-headed bulrushes swayed in the wind, of tangled islands formed from decayed vegetation where wild swan and grey-plumed herons nested, a land rich in fish and fowl and impassable to any but the native Saxon. Long ago, through the marsh water had moved fat carp, broad-nozzled tench, and heavy barbel; eels had twined about the mud and under-water flag stems, and across the tops of the wide water-lily leaves dainty dabchicks had walked with red feet and upraised rudders. In springtime the fens had lived with the noise of nesting birds; sheldrake, widgeon, pintail, mallard, and coot had found a home in the spreading maze of yellow irises, and water-oaks had lifted their branches into the bright sunshine and bathed their roots in the dark waters, and over the tops of the reeds had fluttered splendidly coloured butterflies, now extinct, and after the butterflies had dipped the screaming swifts and swallows. From the tips of the flags the reed warbler had made his tender song and the black-capped reed bunting had flirted, watching his reflection in the waters beneath his swaying perch. It had been a land fat in food. The fenmen had netted the wildfowl for the priors of the surrounding monasteries, fat, tonsuded monks fished in their wide pools, and great flat-bottomed fen boats had moved slowly along the waterways laden with ale, butter, cheese, and grain.

It was in this impenetrable tract of still water and sodden land that the last of the English had held out against the Norman invaders, and in those days the marshes had seen bloodshed and sudden death. The sleeping widgeon had been roused by the sharp flight of feathered arrow and the choking, gurgling cry of men as they clutched at the willow shafts that pierced their throats. At times the quaking marsh paths had swayed and sunk beneath the tramp of horses sweating from the weight of armoured knights, and bright green bog had held and sucked down many a valiant chevalier from Normandy.

It was in this land that Lord Hereward of Brun defied the Norman conqueror for years, and showed that to hold London was not to subdue the English. The fens were the true England, not the narrow alleyways of London. The fens were the cradle of the true spirit of the people, as were the Welsh mountains, the sweeping dark-crag Pennines, and the heather-strewn heights of Exmoor and Dartmoor; it was in the wild places of the land that there existed a spirit which no sword could hew down and against which the stoutest chain armour could not prevail. Each of the four conquests in the history of Britain has been more a compromise than conquest, conquered and conqueror both giving and taking until time made it difficult to say where was conqueror or which was subject.

And then what sword and fire could not accomplish, a few drains and dykes had wrought. The fens were drained and became flat, monotonous countryside, rich and dark-soiled. The heron and the geese were gone, the coot confined to long, narrow waterways as straight and grim as a main road and filled with the puny descendants of the fish which had once known the unchannelled freedom of the marshes; the wildfowl nested no longer, for briar-tangled withy island and whispering reed bed disappeared; the fenmen forgot their rod and line and fowling-net, and took up spade and hoe, and of the fens there at last remained no more than a few protected acres as lonely and pathetic as a solitary polar bear in a zoo.

From the aeroplane, Polycarp saw only league after league of flat field, green with ripening corn and squat potato plants, and ruled by thin lines of beans and peas. His eye encountered only monotony of cultivation stretching away and away, broken at intervals by a clump of elms or a row of young poplars, no hedges, no hills, no nestling groups of cottages, no bright glimmer of wayside pool, no dark copses alive with the swearing of jays, no working yeasts of wandering sheep, nothing but field after field, alone with the company of scarecrow and stranded farm machinery. Square, dirty-bricked houses, straight roads, straight drains, straight furrows of plants, straight telegraph wires, straight, straight … this was a man-made countryside, and man's passion for unbroken line and geometrical economy had been granted full play, until from the sheer ugly monotony of line and unbroken distance there grew a queer, thwarted beauty which was further enhanced when the sun went tumbling in bloody humour into the west, and the poplars held some of the gold to their trembling leaves and the elms shone with passing glory against the flanking rows of beet leaves that were etched with silver contours for a few precious seconds before the day died and the night came down, like an avenging Assyrian, upon the fruitful ugliness.

For ten miles southward of March the countryside remained unchanging, and then slowly the drains developed errant loops and twists, the fields gave up their rigour to patches of wood and rising mounds crowned with oak and silver-barked birch. Hawthorns shook white petals over the clover and grass, and by a drain a windmill revolved in dignified movement. Polycarp welcomed the change with gladness. He let his eyes run over the low ridge before him, from tree clump to tree clump. The sun bathed the country in light, picking out the spire of a church and setting the sides of cottages blazing beneath their canopies of hanging laburnum blooms. And then, almost before he was aware of it, they were flying over a town, a little grey huddle of houses perched on the end of a low ridge of hills. About the foot of the hill curved a shining river, hidden in places by crowding, fragile willow forms, and spanned by a white bridge. The streets of the town ran up the hillside in radiant lines, as though they had their being and drew their life spirit from the tall plug of the cathedral building which dominated the hilltop. Polycarp recognised Ely Cathedral, and he tapped Frank on the shoulder to draw his attention.

The wind was too fierce to allow any speech, but his friend nodded, and the aeroplane swept round in a gigantic circle above the town. Twice they circled the town, and the great tower of the cathedral seemed to rise threateningly into the sky before them, daring them to approach too closely. It stood like some grim old Roman father, guarding the town and facing all comers, its weathering lantern tower and tall front almost as high as the plane, and its feet thrust firmly into the smooth sward. For years it had stood, looking out over the countryside, watching the houses below grow and rot, and watching generation after generation pass along the pavements and linger in the market square. From its commanding position it had seen the slow conquest of the fens, the coming of the railway, and the erection of cinema and schools. Along its aisles had passed dean and chorister, in its transept had prayed farmer, labourer, clerk, spinster, sinner, soldier, lover, teacher … age after age, and their passage was marked by no more than slight depressions on the wide stone slabs. It was a work of man outlasting man, and its erection had taken shape through the centuries until it stood, not the concretion of one man's ideal, but a beautiful hybrid evoked by the dreams of many men. Each stone, each pinnacle and carved gargoyle had levied the toll of all great work; the building was bought at the price of blood and death. About its thick columns and tiny clerestories walked the spirit of the dead, of men who had fallen, twisting from lofty perches where they carved, of masons blinded by flying stone-chips, of labourers crushed by sliding quarry blocks, and peasantry starved to pay the price of fine stone and expensive craftsmen. And now it stood a monument to man's conquest of his own physical infirmities and an architectural poem to the glory of God.

Polycarp leaned over and watched the grey pile revolving as they circled, and something of the tragedy of life, and the triumph of human spirit which had wrought the miracle of stone, entered into him and he was shrived for a moment of his fleeting, youthful ambitions. But not for long. He was suddenly cold, and, tapping Frank on the back, pointed northwards. Frank nodded agreement, and the aeroplane was soon speeding back to March.

"By Jingo! It gets cold after a bit, doesn't it?"

"That's because you're not used to it," said Frank, as they walked towards the tent. "After a while you don't notice these things. When I get up aloft I'm a different man. I feel as though I meant something. Once I'm on the ground I sink back into a kind of slothfulness which, though I hate it, I can't resist."

"You should have been an angel or a pterodactyl—then you could have flown all day long."

Although he made a joke of Frank's mood, Polycarp was actually far from understanding his friend's feelings. In fact he was still puzzled at the other's attitude to life. Frank possessed all the qualities which made Polycarp pleasant to other people. He had the same engaging carelessness, and the same easy manner. They both liked food and laughter and pretty girls, they were both honest enough to pass in a crowd, and they were both capable of affection and sincerity, but always with Frank there was a grim feeling and spirit behind his carelessness and mannerisms which made them appear false or far-fetched. His love of food and drink at times approached greediness; his friendly attitude was sometimes a cloak for an acquired hatred of everyone and everything; his glance at a girl in the street held a covert lewdness, and his friendship for Polycarp was, Polycarp thought occasionally, perhaps not so sincere as it seemed. Polycarp did not know these things definitely, he could only feel them, and for the most part he loyally stifled them. The trouble with Frank was, he said excusingly, that he had gone through the war, and the war had changed men until they were somehow different from ordinary people.

The rest of that day they did good business, and when it was too late to continue flying they returned to the Castle of Comfort Inn. Over supper Frank suggested that, as they had been hard-working all the week, they might allow themselves a little relaxation that evening.

"We shall have to clear off tomorrow," said Frank. "I don't know where to—we'll have to decide that. It's easy enough to hire a field and get some bills printed, though in future we shall have to get that sort of thing done in advance. Tonight, I think, entertainment is indicated. We haven't celebrated our success yet. Besides, I'm getting tired of seeing this town from the top; I've got a desire to see it from the bottom."

"Very good, my dear aeronaut. I think, as you say, we have earned some little pleasure."

So a-pleasuring they went, and, as is so in most small towns, they found that entertainment was not to be bought but had to be made by themselves.

First they inspected the cinema. The placards outside decided for them immediately that there was no entertainment of the type they desired : Pearl White in a thrilling serial, *The Wheel of Chance*—a vivid chromatic poster showed poor Pearl struggling in a pool to escape an advancing octopus, while a fat, long-whiskered mandarin sat on a high throne and watched through half-shut eyes and rubbed his hands together like a pawnbroker.

"I'll bet she had to choose between her honour and the octopus," grinned Frank.

"Very likely, and woman-like she tries to persuade herself that her virginity is more precious than her life. If she'd half the intuition women are supposed to be endowed with, she'd have known Wun Lung didn't want her virginity, he wanted to see the octopus doing its stuff. The right way to have disappointed him would have been to offer her virginity with a song and dance, as though it were something given away with a pound of tea. That would have revolted his oriental fastidiousness and secured her immediate release."

124

"You do talk beautifully, Professor Polycarp. And what about Fatty Arbuckle—do you want to see him?"

"Custard-pies, Frank, are like double-sixes—unless you do the throwing yourself there's no pleasure in it. Let's see if we can find something else."

The only other thing was a concert in aid of a local Methodist chapel, at which, it was announced, a collection would be taken in silver. There were to be songs by a local baritone, choruses given by members of the choir, and a sketch entitled, *Fanny's Dilemma*.

"Phew! Fanny's Dilemma! That puts me off right away!" said Frank. "Come on, let's have a drink."

So they went and had a drink, and then, because there was nothing else to do, they had another drink. They went, drinking ale and playing darts, table skittles, and dominoes, from the aristocratic patronage of the King Alfred to the democratic atmosphere of the Spade and Shovel. Then, to pay their respects to the large number of railwaymen in the town, they visited The Rocket, but the beer was so bad that they soon left for the Cock, and from the Cock they wandered to the George, where they started an interminable argument as to whether the George was the Dragon George or the infant-minded George the Third. Then, tiring of so much royalty, they embraced heraldry at the Griffin.

By this time Polycarp was beginning to feel heady and unsteady on his feet. He could not take much drink, but, rather than confess his unmanly weakness to Frank, he drank his beer and tried to keep his foot firm on the rail beneath the bar, and, when he stretched out his hand for his glass, he hoped that he would grasp it without knocking it over.

"Say, Frankie, don't ... don't you think we'd better go home?" he enquired, as they came out of the hot bar into the night.

"Home!" exclaimed Frank, in horror. "We're homeless! We're outcasts. Don't weaken, brother, don't weaken!"

"I'm not weakening, Frankie, not weakening ... just vacillating. Beer always makes me vacillate. I shouldn't wonder if I don't start writing poetry soon."

"Good Lord! Here, come and have a brandy. That's the stuff to cure you of poetry." He took Polycarp by the arm and dragged him along the road. The town was crowded with men and women doing their Friday-night's shopping, and the lighted fronts of the stores cast square panels of yellow light across the streets.

They turned aside from the main thoroughfare and walked along the river bank. From the purple dusk of hanging willows and dormer-windowed houses ahead of them came bursts of laughter and the sound of singing, and then, above them, in the reflected light which poured from between the slits of the curtains of the tap-room, they saw the swinging sign of the Golden Barbel : a huge fat, lumpish, cigar-shaped object whose only resemblance to a fish lay in the fins which projected from its body like the atrophied wings of a deceased bluebottle.

"The Golden Barbel!" exclaimed Frank, with a dramatic gesture towards the hanging sign.

"Sounds like a Ruddy Babel," said Polycarp, but he allowed himself to be drawn into the tap-room.

Immediately they opened the door of the room the noise and mirth swept out about them and drew them into the warmth and comfort. The tap-room was a long, low room, furnished with straight high-backed settles that ran around the walls from one end of the bar to the other. The dark roof overhead was traversed by five warped oak beams, carved with a Jacobean egg-and-dart pattern, and hung with branches of sage, ropes of onions, and, in a position not far from the log fire which burned in an open grate, a side of bacon. The Golden Barbel was among the oldest inns in Cambridgeshire, and the oak beams and thatched roof, that now echoed with the tinkling of an old piano and the voices of singing men and women, had once echoed with the voices of the ancestors of these same men and women, and some of the faces they looked down upon now perpetuated the memory of other faces that had shone with drink and good humour two hundred years before.

The people in the room were mostly rough labourers and a few workmen with their wives. Everyone except Polycarp and Frank had the stamp of those who work with their hands under an open sky. Their faces were reddened and browned with cold and wind, while their hands were knuckly and calloused from spade and trowel.

Their lives held little beyond work, early rising when the mists lay heavily along the dykes and drains, and lonely evenings in cottages filled with the smeech of oil-lamps and the damp of drying clothes, but on Friday night they forgot their hardships and privations, if they ever looked upon them as such, and came to the Golden Barbel to drink and be happy. Happiness is a blessing which not even poverty can rape from a man, and a glass of beer and a song meant as much to these ploughmen and labourers as a fine dinner and a stall at the theatre to a city magnate—more, in fact, because these men were, at least, conscious that they had more than earned their pleasure.

When Polycarp and Frank entered, they were recognised at once, and the landlord beamed at them over the bar.

"Two brandies, please."

They took a seat by the fire, and a tipsy old man rose from the other end of the room, and, waving a stumpy clay-pipe in the air for emphasis, began

> *Me and Jane in a plane!*
> *Soaring up to the clooouds!*
> *What could be sweeter—*
> *In our two-seateeeeeer …*

Here the piano caught him up and the whole room was singing the song, and, conscious that it was a loud but genuine compliment, the two joined in with gusto. Polycarp was touched by the demonstration. When the song had finished, he rose to his feet and held up a hand for silence.

"Ladies and gentlemen. My friend and I thank you for your welcome. As proprietor of the New Age Flying Company, I ask you to drink with us. Landlord, drinks all round!"

The applause was terrific, and, as the drinks were served, the piano started *Annie Laurie*. They drank to Annie Laurie, and then listened in respectful silence while a wizened little man sang a song about his dear mother who was watching his every action from heaven and was waiting for him there. He sang in a dirgeful tone, and punctuated the end of each phrase with a sniff and a quick wipe of the back of his hand across his nose. Then three youths with large caps and voices like the jangling of cracked bells got up and persisted in singing *Way Down Upon the Swanee River*, and the whole company had to restrain its resentment until the chorus, when it thundered and roared in an attempt to intimidate the three, but nothing could stop them. The youths floated the whole way down the Swanee River, and would have gone marching through Georgia, if the pianist had not confuted them by playing a medley of war songs.

For a while they contented themselves with a succession of old favourites. They "daisy-daisied" and did the daring young man on the flying trapeze, and then a tipsy old lady with a black crest of feathers upon her bonnet got up and bewailed the fact that her daddy wouldn't buy her a bow-wow.

Polycarp listened to this solo with sadness. He tried to picture her daddy, but the sight of her standing by the piano, her big body bursting at her shabby coat and skirt, and her bosom rising and falling like a lake of lava, held his attention.

He leaned across the little table, and, taking a carnation from its vase, pinned it in Frank's buttonhole.

"A flower to encourage you, *mon brave*," he said. "Why don't you give us a song?"

Apparently this thought had not occurred to Frank. He immediately got up and approached the pianist. And then, as the piano started, he broke into song and, to Polycarp's surprise, revealed that he had a fine baritone voice, but the virtuosity of his voice was forgotten in the roars of laughter which punctuated his verses. Long afterwards, when Polycarp tried to recall the incidents of that night, the most salient thing he could remember was Frank standing before the room, swaying a little, his forehead beaded with perspiration, and his red carnation flaring against the loud checks of his coat as he sang the bawdy and interminable saga of the disillusionment of a country maid in the metropolis.

The song was a success, and earned for the two free Worthingtons from the landlord.

As the evening wore on, the table-top became ringed with glass-marks and the company lost a little of its cohesion. In various parts of the rooms different songs had their genesis and persisted against the piano. A little group of men and women nourished *It Aint Gonna*

Rain No More in their midsts, while from the opposite side of the room another group bewailed the fate of Clementine. Men kissed their wives with healthy, smacking sounds, and later indulged in an indiscriminate freemasonry of kissing around the bar.

Polycarp and Frank let themselves go. Polycarp had been struggling to preserve his decorum all the evening, but the power of drink overcame him, and he laughed with the best of them and sang until his throat was dry with a dryness that no amount of liquor could assuage. He and Frank gave a demonstration of an apache dance, in the middle of the bar, and all the flowers in the table-vases gave up their sweet odours as they lay, crushed and mangled, on the floor. The air was tenebrous with smoke, and from the background of bottles and tankards behind the bar the fat face of the landlord beamed and blossomed in exotic growth. He was a great fellow, the landlord, great in girth and soul. He thrived on noise and laughter, and the noisier the room became, the bigger he seemed to grow, until his presence filled the place with a jolly, roguish, Falstaffian atmosphere, as he superintended the drawing of beer and the handing down of bottles without ceasing his joking and laughing, and always keeping a watchful eye on his two assistants.

The room was a cheerful universe filled by a shouting drinking nebula which, as it whirled, flung off little planets and young worlds into the different corners; two men argued endlessly about the prowess of Carpentier and Joe Beckett; a man offered to race his greyhound bitch Nell against any other dog in March, over five hundred yards for a pound, and forgot that the day before he had sold the dog to make up the arrears on his bicycle payments; two women loudly discussed the bed-time habits of their husbands, and their husbands gravely sat over a game of dominoes though their eyes were bemused with the dancing white spots before them. Polycarp borrowed a cap from a man and, using it as a tray, went round the room, making a collection for the pianist. He got fivepence in coppers, two half-crowns, four mangled carnations, number twenty-six of the *Do You Know* series of picture cigarette cards, and an old regimental button—all of which he presented gravely to the pianist, who was drooping over the keyboard, playing with one hand the harmony to "God, Save the King," and, with the other, what he proclaimed to be the first movement of a Chopin waltz.

As closing time drew near, the babble increased, arguments grew louder, songs more erratic, and Polycarp's head began to spin round and expand. He looked at Frank, and saw that even that stalwart was not in a fit state to pilot an aeroplane.

"You're a melanic individual," he confided to Frank.

"That I'm not. Drink never makes me sick. I'm the reincarnation of Nero. Good old Nero!"

"Good of Nero," echoed Polycarp, and wondered whether the landlord would object if he went to sleep on the floor. He was about to lie down beside the fireplace and test the landlord's opinion, when one of the two men who were arguing about Carpentier and Beckett jumped to his feet and threw sixpence upon the floor.

"Who'll pick that up?" he cried, his eyes flashing with pugilistic valour.

"Certainly, of feller. Anything to oblige a gentleman …"

The unsuspecting Polycarp swayed across the room and bent down to the coin. He rose, and with a silly smile presented it to the man. But the man was not at all grateful. As Polycarp held out the coin, he shot out his fist and struck him on the nose with such force that Polycarp toppled backwards to the floor and lay there with a surprised expression upon his features.

"Say, you shouldn't do that to my pal …" Frank came across to the man. "That's wrong of you. He didn't … didn't understand that it was a challenge to fight. He's a good pal to me … ain't you Polycarp?" He looked down for confirmation, but Polycarp had decided that sleep was better than valour, and was lying happily on the floor while a thin line of bright blood trickled from his nose, rivalling the crushed carnation petals beside him.

"He shouldn't have picked it up, should he then?" snapped the man drunkenly. "He shouldn't have …"

"That was wrong," persisted Frank. Then he turned to the people in the room. "He's my pal, and I'll take his challenge. I'll take it …"

"You will, eh?" The fighter raised his fist. "Well, here's for you!" He aimed a blow, but his fist shot over Frank's shoulder as he swayed to one side. As the man lurched, Frank, with a neatness that came from partial inebriety and experience in Flanders messes, hit him behind the left ear and regretfully watched him fall to the floor.

"Consider yourself launched, lad. Consider yourself launched," he murmured, and, to complete the ceremony, he poured the contents of a beer bottle over the man's upturned face.

The rest of the people in the room looked from Frank to the man on the floor, and there might have ensued an awkward moment for the New Age Flying Company if the fat landlord had not come from behind his bar, and, pointing to the man, said to his assistant:

"Take him into the yard and put him under the pump. He won't hurt. He's got a head like a cannon-ball. Always gets to want a fight when he's had a drop too much. And, mister, you'd better take your friend home and put him to bed. He can't sleep on my floor."

"Right y'are; right y'are ... No offence ... No offence ..."

"That's all right. These things will happen. Now then, now then. Time, ladies and gentlemen! Time, please!"

When Polycarp awoke, it was in the stillness of his room at the hotel, with a sore nose, a thick tongue, a swelling head, and a sturdy determination to eschew all drink in the future.

XI
Mostly flour

The New Age Flying Company was a success. Their total takings at March amounted to eighty pounds two shillings and sixpence and a foreign coin which Polycarp had mistaken for a half-crown. From March they went to Scarborough and did even better business, and the months of June, July and August saw them going week by week from one seaside resort to another.

Polycarp discovered that he had a real flair for publicity. He could wake the most somnolent of seaside towns into an awareness of the presence of the New Age Flying Company. His posters grew bigger, bolder, and better, and no place was immune from them. They obscured the faces of public clocks, they were pasted tenderly across the fundaments of public statues, and in one town, where a nude Hercules flaunted at the top of the main street, the more prudish townsfolk woke one morning to discover with approbation that a large New Age notice had been draped round the figure like a short skirt, thereby satisfying their public demands for decency and Polycarp's desire for publicity. No place was safe from the posters, and when there were any indignant protests—and there were many, both from lovers of art and public officials—Polycarp always had the excuse that he was not concerned with the affixation of the particular notices, but that some irresponsible vandal had done it. He himself, he would say passionately, loved the arts and proprieties as much as any man; he himself, he would say, growing indignant, could not understand why the officials and dilettantes thought he was responsible—it was outrageous; and he sometimes departed from the town hall with a profuse apology, though more often under suspicion, for town clerks are not fools.

Publicity, publicity, and more publicity—that was the company's motto, for publicity meant money. And their publicity brought them patronage. It was an honour to fly behind a man who was suspected of having plastered the backside of a royal statue with a notice declaring:

THIS IS THE WONDER OF THE AGE!!!!
Take your mind off Mundane Things
and Fly with the New Age Flying Company

Polycarp discovered that if he invited the Press, the young reporters, to have a free trip, they gave him good news stories.

At Whitby the company announced that they would hand one quarter of their weekly takings to the town officials for use in connection with any charity, and their receipts that week were among the highest of the whole tour. At Blackpool, Polycarp had the flying-field floodlit and ran lovers' trips by moonlight. If the company had owned five planes they could have kept them going all night. At Aberystwyth, Frank nearly wrecked the machine trying his skill at smoke-writing and after much effort managed to scrawl across the sky the name of the company. At Weston-super-Mare, Polycarp obtained two blue sweaters with the name of the company forming a circle on the front and in the centre of his circle the word *Proprietor*, and in Frank's, *Pilot*. They never appeared in public without them.

Frank discovered that the walking advertisement was good for free drinks, and Polycarp just gloried in the fact that people turned and looked at him. They mapped out no definite route, but went where they willed, without regard for distance or time. They flew from Yarmouth to Hastings, from Hastings to Weston-super-Mare, and then across the whole width of England to Felixstowe. When their funds increased they bought a car and hired a man to help them. With the car Polycarp obtained more publicity. He draped the sides with cotton banners advertising the company, and toured about the town offering free rides to the flying-field to prospective patrons. His one regret after buying the car was that when the day's flying was over

Frank often used to disappear in it with, so Polycarp suspected, one of the local girls, and did not return until the early hours, and when he did return he was not always in a fit condition to start flying the next day. There were anxious moments when Polycarp would watch the red aeroplane circling over the town and wonder why it did not crash, for Frank was often half asleep. But luck was with them and they were involved in no mishaps.

The summer passed away pleasantly and the bank-balance of the New Age Company grew satisfyingly, and then, when September was opening the chrysanthemum buds and touching the countryside with the sobering tints of approaching autumn, the company came again to Brinton-on-Sea.

Brinton—none of the inhabitants or visitors bothered about the "on-Sea" part, for, when the waves at high tide have a habit of splashing into your front garden and the gulls use your roofs as privies and sanctuaries, such a phrase is sheer supererogation—is a modest town on the eastern coast of England whose principal industry is taking in summer visitors. Frank had said on their first visit to the town earlier in the year that, if all the people who were not in some way making money out of summer visitors were placed end to end along the sea front, the barracks would be emptied of its soldiers, for they were the only persons monetarily independent of the visitors, though a few had a pretty large amatory interest in some of them.

The country about the town was low-lying and orderly, with golf-courses and large estates, and the coast presented a range of small sand-dunes, bristling with marram grasses, to the North Sea. The town had a long promenade, a wide bathing-pool, a beach upon which it was sacrilege to undress without the shelter of a bathing-hut, and a pier over-weighted by penny-in-the-slot machines where, by the turning of a handle, clerks and artisans were excited by the tantalising vision of some belle of the nineties nearly undressing herself.

Frank was bitter about these machines. "They're a fraud!" he complained. "They label themselves. 'What the Doctor Saw', 'A Night in Paris', 'Betty's Bath' and so on. And all a fellow gets for his hard-earned copper is a flipping dog-eared series of photographs showing voluminous dames who died years ago."

"I should complain to the mayor," suggested Polycarp.

But it would have been little use protesting to the mayor, for he was married to a woman who might have been the subject of one of the peep-shows, and he would suffer no criticism of Brinton. Briny, beautiful Brinton. Bracing Brinton with its healthy air and, so many people thought, over-lighted shelters. Polycarp liked the little town, so he made no protest when Frank suggested that they should revisit it. He liked the people, he enjoyed the theatre and the comfortable cinemas, and he had made friends with the librarian and was accorded the facilities of the public library, a privilege which he appreciated and exercised, for during their erratic life wandering round the coast he had been sorely starved of literature. The town was split into two sections by a deep-cut estuary, the main part of the town, the promenade and amusements and public buildings, lying on the south side and on the north was the substantial residential quarter. Polycarp and Frank stopped at a small hotel on the north side, ferrying across each day to the main town, where was the flying-field.

And it was here in this town that the luck which had accompanied the company for so long gave out and occasioned the abrupt termination of the New Age Flying Company, proprietor, Polycarp Jarvis; pilot, Frank Burns, late R.A.F.

When luck comes it may be for a day, for a week, or for years. One day a man serves nothing but aces at tennis and the next he smashes every window in the clubhouse, while luck goes flighting across the greens to help your rabbit to hole long putts. It puts a fortune into the pocket of a wheelwright in Hackney by way of a spinning lottery drum and it makes a pauper of a Lancashire mill-owner by a vicious interplay of loin-cloths and stock markets. Most great works and fortunes owe more to luck than their creators will ever acknowledge, though nearly all failures readily ascribe their downfall to its absence. When you have it you deny its influence and when it goes you bewail its departure. But not everyone. When it went from Polycarp and Frank, neither of them bewailed. They just accepted it as part of the normal routine of life and looked around for some other lure with which to bring it back. Luck left Polycarp and Frank by way of one hundred babies. The one hundred babies were all suffering from varied complaints; some of them were spotty like Dalmatians with measles, and most of them much noisier. Many were unsightly with mumps, and all of them suffered from some disease. In fact, as they lay in their cots, they presented a pathetic but instructive object-lesson in therapeutics. They included every ailment, from diseases of respiration and of digestion to derangements of the nervous and endocrine systems. And for the convenience of the townsfolk, the postal authorities, and the kindly doctors and nurses who tended them, they were collected in one building which declared itself through the medium of a large board bearing yellow letters: *Brinton Children's Hospital. Supported by Voluntary Contributions.*

The "voluntary contributions" was, of course, the cruellest part of the whole affair. That so many children's lives and their welfare should depend upon the vagaries of voluntary contributions, and not upon a wise provision made by the State, was a shameful exposure of the inadequacies of a civilisation which ignorant folk are fond of boasting as being the highest the world has known. No civilisation can be worthy of the name while children's suffering or cure depends upon coppers tossed into collecting-boxes in the street.

And it was the fact that these contributions had lately not been so prolific as they should be that brought about the downfall of the New Age Flying Company. The Mayor and Corporation of Brinton decided that there should be an "End of the Summer Season Carnival" in aid of the Brinton Children's Hospital, and, the word of the Mayor being law, there was a carnival.

The promenade was strung with bright bunting and floodlights illuminated the public buildings and statues and, incidentally, Polycarp's notices. Young girls altered their dance-frocks for the Carnival Ball, while their young men worked feverishly in their garages disguising their Ford vans and two-seater Morris Oxfords and baby Austins into the semblance of dragons, baskets of grapes, scenes from Shakespeare, tableaux of Sir Walter Raleigh's boyhood, the Wreck of the *Hesperus*, and the Dying Child. Some girls bought new bathing-costumes to flash before the eyes of the crowd and judges at the Bathing Belles Competition and young men enlisted the aid of sisters and sweethearts to fashion grotesque costumes to disguise them while they should prance about the streets and promenade of Brinton collecting money for the hospital. The whole town, young and old, was fired with this great philanthropic spirit, and while the

Mayor and his male and female advisers of a more sedate age wielded pen and ink and formed committees, the young folk wielded paint-pot and scissors and formed dresses of silk and strange headgear of cardboard boxes.

All Brinton was *en fête*, and it was to this fête that Polycarp and Frank were invited to contribute. The invitation came by way of the librarian, who was on the Entertainments Committee of the Carnival Association. He interrupted Polycarp as he was glancing through a copy of Wyndham Lewis's *Tarr* at the library.

"Could you spare me a moment in my room?"

"What's the trouble?" asked Polycarp, raising an eyebrow.

"I'm going to get something out of you, young man, something for nothing."

"You know they say that a friend is only a friend until he begins to borrow money …"

"Come inside and be sensible."

The librarian sat him in a chair and, sitting on the corner of his book-littered table, explained what he wanted.

The Mayor was anxious that the carnival should be a success. The hospital was in very low funds and he wanted to attract as much attention as possible in the neighbourhood: Polycarp, no doubt, had seen the various shows and competitions and galas which were advertised?

"I have. Frank and I thought about entering for the beauty competition, but his legs are too hairy and I won't shave off my moustache for anyone. He and I are examples of hirsuteness in its right and wrong place. Hairy legs are an abomination and confusion, but a nice ginger moustache … Still, go on."

"I will. In the bathing-lake there will be a beauty parade in the morning and then a swimming and boating gala in the afternoon, but we want something to round off the whole thing. You know—make it end with a bang!"

"What about blowing up the pier and those rotten peepshows? Frank would be glad."

"Too expensive. I've suggested to the committee that you will probably be only too glad—since you've been fleecing this town for two days—to help, and give your services free."

"What is it?"

"Could you persuade Frank to give a flying display? You know, loops and thrills and then, as *the pièce de résistance*, I thought about an aeroplane versus speedboat battle. We'll have a speedboat dodging about the bay and the aeroplane trying to drop very small bags of flour on it. If the boat eludes the plane for more than twenty minutes it wins, but if the boat does not—then you win and have all the honour and glory and cheers and thanks of the Mayor for entertaining the crowd."

"Sounds quite simple. I wish I could do more for the hospital."

"It is, and if we can advertise that, it'll draw more people here for the great day, and that means money for us. We need it badly, you know."

"Don't worry. That speedboat is as good as sunk. I'll talk to Frank. But I know he'll be keen."

"That's good of you. You know, in spite of your ostentatiousness and horrible sweater I believe you're quite human."

"Oh, I am. You'd be surprised. Do you know, I've begun to eat with a knife and fork, and when the man at the hotel says *consommé* or *hors d'oeuvre* I not only catch what he says but I know what he means!"

"Brinton is doing you good."

Frank, as Polycarp expected, was enthusiastic.

"Good," he said. "This has come just in time. You know, I'm getting a little tired of this continual flight-round-the-town business. When we started at March I was keen about flying, but now I'm wearying. It's getting monotonous. I daresay it's all right for you down below, but think of me always in this rattling hencoop. By the way, if she doesn't fall to pieces very soon my name is not Burns. We'll have to buy another if we go on next year. An exhibition and a little bombing, eh? Even though it is with penny bags of flour, it'll pep me up. Boy, I'll give the girls a thrill!"

"You will," said Polycarp sharply. "I reckon that's your trouble in life, Frank, if you'll allow me to say so. You're too keen about giving the girls a thrill. Haven't you any ambition? Don't you want to get anywhere?"

"No. I just want to be where I am at the moment. That's good enough for me."

"I wish I could understand why—"

"So do I sometimes ... Still, don't let's be serious. Come and have a drink."

Polycarp shook his head. "No, thanks. I'm reading." And when Frank was gone he took up his book, but he did not read.

He was thinking of that day—so long ago it seemed, yet not so long—when he had left Bristol determined to seek Fortune. He was doing well, but he hadn't found her. By that rash, impulsive act when he had insulted Mr. Hayward and thrown in his job he had made a compact with himself to achieve something and, he mused somewhat sadly, he was a long way from attaining his ambition. He sat in his chair in the hotel lounge, a long, sprawling figure, and one hand stroked his thin face and smoothed at his fair hair as he stared with the solemnity of youth at the meaningless page before him. The world would have to hear a lot more of Polycarp before he could feel free from his self-imposed vow to find fame and fortune.

On the day of the carnival the New Age Flying Company took a holiday. It was not a brilliantly fine day—carnival days seldom are—but it was not a beastly wet day. The sky was heavy with tall cloud masses and the sun now and then managed to send his warmth earthwards through the blue cracks which sometimes split the white mountains of cloud. A light breeze blew in from the sea and made idling uncomfortable for all those people who were not wearing more than a bathing-costume. But the unkindness of the weather could not thwart the carnival spirit which besieged the town.

The bunting in the streets was grateful for the breeze, which helped to display the fullness of its beauty and colour, and the hordes of people who had come to the town from the surrounding districts to swell the crowd of residents and holidaymakers, filled the streets to overflowing, so that the aggregate warmth from their bodies more than compensated for the niggardliness of the sun.

The eating-houses did a fine trade; piles of food and gallons of drink disappeared into the hungry, thirsty maw of the crowd, and the collecting-boxes of the prancing clowns, whooping Indians, grimacing gargoyles and simpering male ballerinas grew heavier and heavier until it was a difficulty to shake them with a happy flourish before the faces of the milchable onlookers. The pier was crowded and the tin bellies of the automatic machines were gorged with coppers. The pierrot show cracked its faded jokes and got a big hand from the crowd. The tram- and bus-conductors wore gay rosettes. Balloons floated about the street, detached from their owners and meeting death and deflation beneath wheel and before pin and cigarette-end. Confetti littered the pavements, spouting in whirlpools from the promenade gratings as the draught caught at it, and worked with growing eagerness and irritation between vest and skin. Dogs lost their masters and ran bewildered in a forest of legs each emanating a different smell. At the bathing-lake girls walked along a thin planking before the critical eyes of the judges (a local justice of the Peace, the Vicar, the town's wealthiest baker, and the Mayor—closely watched by his Victorian-minded, Edwardian-curved spouse) and tried to forget the remarks which occasionally floated towards them from the tall bank of spectators.

Audacity, decided Polycarp as he watched, was the keynote of beauty competitions, for, although there were some very good-looking girls in the line, it might easily have been a line-up of applicants for the position of a good plain cook for the town's wealthiest baker or a sober maid for the Mayor's parlour. The beauty queen was chosen amongst partisan cheers and scattered boos from dissenting what-is-beauty theorists.

In the afternoon there were the swimming gala and diving exhibitions, which Polycarp did not watch, as he was at the flying-field with Frank waiting for a message to tell them when to start for their demonstration of flying and bombing.

"You're sure you won't hold me liable if anything happens to you?" said Frank.

"Absolutely. I mean to be sitting behind you all the time you're stunting. Do you think I would miss such an opportunity? And, anyway, you'll want someone to help you throw those bombs. That's going to be fun. By jingo!"

"Pity they aren't real bombs. That would wake this joint up." Frank handled one of the tiny flour-bags scornfully and thought of bombs.

"Break it up, you mean!" Polycarp said as he helped Frank to lift in the box of flour-bags.

Ten minutes later the aeroplane bumped off the flying-field and started towards the town. As they came low over the promenade a cheer echoed up from the crowd and they both waved over the side. From his seat Polycarp could see the great curve of the promenade and the black mass of heads where the main crowd was congregated around the swimming-lake. On a high dais overlooking the lake and bay sat the judging committee, with the beauty queen securely tucked between the Vicar and the Mayor. Around the edge of the pool, which was crescent-shaped, sat the higher officials and councillors of the town, and behind them, in inferior positions, the rag-tag and bob-tail disposed themselves as best they could. They swarmed over ornamental gardens, squeezed a dozen on a seat, clung to flagpoles and electric light standards, and sprawled across the roofs of saloon cars. The sun in a generous moment decided to shine and the whole scene was flooded with warmth and light.

Frank lifted a hand to warn Polycarp, and then, with the box of bombs wedged tightly into the bottom of the cockpit, the stunting began.

Polycarp had become inured to flying behind Frank, but he had never done more than loop the loop with him. Looping was child's play compared with the aerial acrobatics which Frank indulged in that afternoon … He did so many things that before he was finished Polycarp was half silly with vertigo. He sat in his seat like a drunken man and just let things happen. He had a sensation of the plane corkscrewing, of houses wheeling round and round, of faces first small and staring and then large and waving. He saw heads, legs, roads, and water dip earthwards and then fade like a film shot to the blue of sky and the dirty piles of clouds. One moment he was staring at the back of Frank's head and the next his stomach had severed all connection with him and he was looking into the face of eternity while his ears were fogged with the roar of the engine and the scream of the agonised wind as the propeller bit into it like whirling knives. One moment they were sailing high above the earth and the next they were under the earth and looking up at it; sometimes the ground retained its usual horizontal sanity and the next instant they were flying up a narrow defile, the wall on one side being white-topped waves and the other wall the solid mass of green, grey, and black from lawns, houses, and crowd. Polycarp felt as though he were riding on an eccentric swing and in the region of his navel was a singing, perpetual exhilaration which gradually spread about his body until he found himself laughing and shouting with the mad joy of uncontrolled space and motion.

After a time the aeroplane righted itself and he found Frank looking back at him. He said something. Polycarp could not catch the words.

"Man beats the birds at their own game!" Polycarp shouted exultantly and then held up a bag of flour and pointed down below. Frank's hairy brows contracted and his dark face moved to a grin. He nodded and, as the aeroplane dipped over the lake in salute, Polycarp tossed a bag of flour overboard to give the signal that they were ready to start. He watched the bag fall and hit the water, raising a tiny spout of white foam. From the seaward side of the wall, which separated the lake from the bay, a long speed-boat slipped across the water, making a shrill crepitation.

"After him!" cried Polycarp, grabbing another bag. "Slip the dogs of war! Hurrah!" He stood up in the cockpit in his excitement and sat down quickly as the force of the wind struck at him like an irresistible hand.

Frank sent the aeroplane after the speedboat and, flying low, quickly overhauled it. Polycarp saw the man at the wheel glance backwards. When the aeroplane was over him he moved the helm and the speedboat shot away almost at right-angles to its course. At the same time Frank banked, and to Polycarp it seemed as if the aeroplane were skidding in the air over the top of the boat. So sudden was the manoeuvre that Polycarp was flung against the side of the cockpit and the bag of flour in his hand fell overboard. And luck decided as part of its preliminary campaign against the two that it should fall fair and square upon the bows of the speedboat. Polycarp could scarcely believe it. Frank turned round and raised his hand in sign of victory.

Below them the speedboat slowed up and then stopped in recognition of its defeat.

"We've won!" shouted Polycarp into Frank's ear. "What a sell! All my belligerent passions are roused! I thought it was going to be exciting!"

Frank did not attempt to answer. He turned round and pointed to the box of flour-bags. As Polycarp handed him one he could see that he was laughing.

The aeroplane banked about and headed back towards the lake. Every face was upturned to watch the machine. Frank brought the machine as low as he dared and then, as he passed over the crowd, he dropped a bag of flour. Polycarp saw the movement and looked back. The bag fell like a plummet towards the diving-platform anchored in the centre of the pool. It struck the platform, and a few seconds before it burst into white powder the board, which had been crowded with bathers, blossomed suddenly into twenty outflung petals radiating away from the bomb into the lake and presenting an astonishing and decorative effect from the air.

Frank twisted round and shouted loudly:

"Let's bomb the town! We've got to get rid of the bags somehow."

The idea, had Polycarp considered for a moment, was obviously a silly one, but at that instant his mind and stomach were in a whirl from stunting and he was a little delirious with speed and the rough caress of the air. The suggestion caused him no concern at all. He did not even stop to think about it, but caught up a dozen bags and handed them to Frank.

Around the lake the townsfolk and visitors had not appreciated that the falling of the first bomb had not been accidental. It had fallen well away from the Mayor and he had chuckled as the bathers deserted their diving-platform. His laughter ceased abruptly as the scarlet machine wheeled into sight again and, swooping over the crowd, rained a succession of bombs over them. From the heavens in substantial manna descended a string of flour bombs and, although they were no bigger than penny packets of sweets, where they burst they caused confusion. The first hit the promenade in front of a bus and sent a white flurry across the road to smother a policeman's boots and trousers, so that he changed—one moment a sober upholder of the law, the next a hybrid baker's assistant. Another finished its journey in an iced sundae which a man was eating in the lake cafe. The sundae exploded violently and, with a vehemence worthy of a Catherine-wheel, flung ice, fruit, and flour in a circle that embraced everyone, without regard for class distinctions. The mayor, who had been wondering whether the beauty queen would object to his pressing her hand, had his thoughts abruptly switched to the contemplation of his wife's face staring through a powdery death-mask, as she vainly tried to rid herself of the flour which had settled like strange leprosy upon her. The Mayor's first inclination was to laugh, and his second to shout for action, but he was prevented from the fulfilment of either by a bag bursting at his feet and toppling him backwards into the arms of his mace-bearer. His gold chain slipped round his neck like a dog's lead and the crowd yelled with delight. The floured unfortunates received no sympathy. The aeroplane swooped again, flinging bombs everywhere, and the crowd spent their time laughing and ducking. If you were hit it was unlucky; if you weren't it was good fun.

Polycarp and Frank were panting with laughter. From the air the scene was ludicrous; men dodging and knocking one another over, women stiff with indignation and women laughing, bathers falling into the water, unlucky civilians crawling out of the water and a malicious mildew of flour creeping over the ground where bag after bag burst with a loud whop!

The noise was too great for Polycarp and Frank to talk to one another. They contented themselves with indicating targets and hurling bombs. Polycarp had never enjoyed himself so much in all his life. The flour was no respecter of persons. It besmirched its donor, the wealthiest baker; whitened that saintly man the Vicar and streaked the justice of Peace with lines of trickling purity.

There were a large number of bags left in the box as they swooped for the last time. Polycarp tipped the bags loose on to the floor of the cockpit and then ripped them open one by one and shook the free flour back into the box. Then as they dipped to the promenade, he raised the box aloft and inverted it over the side so that the flour escaped in a long trailing plume. For a time it eddied and whirled in the wind from the aeroplane's passage, then it settled down towards the ground, drifting with the breeze. Polycarp and Frank watched the menacing white cloud draw closer to the people below and they laughed until the tears came to their eyes. The instinct of self-preservation was strong in the crowd. Everyone tried to avoid the drifting plume of flour that threatened to envelop the bathing-lake. There was a general exodus towards the promenade and side-streets, a wild scramble that embraced all without regard for status or wealth. Respectable citizens, fathers of children, owners of business, churchwardens, prison wardens, Labour men and Conservatives, flappers and high-school mistresses, bank clerks and mechanics, all pushed and ran to get away from the flour which settled upon them like fine snow, and in the hurry and turmoil one or two unfortunate persons slipped into the lake and wetted their trouser-legs and skirts, which formed a tenacious surface for the falling flour. The flour cloud thinned and died on the shoulders of statues and stampeders, drifted leisurely into the crannies of rock gardens and between clothes and skin, dusted the broad leaves of palms and softened the hard lines of monkey-trees and coagulated in the lake and glasses of lemonade on the cafe tables. And as it died the crowd brushed their clothes and some laughed and some swore, and Frank, guessing that the revellers would cherish no feelings of undue gratitude towards the New Age Flying Company, turned the nose of the aeroplane away from the town. It was time they disappeared until the anger and turmoil died down. And it was at this point that fate finally intervened. Their luck deserted them and as it went it stopped the motor of the aeroplane.

The sound of the motor ceased, and in a silence which was oppressive and somehow unreal after so much noise and motion Polycarp heard Frank say: "Now what's the matter with the blasted thing?"

"What is the matter?" enquired Polycarp a little anxiously.

"Dunno. I can't get out and see, can I?"

"But ... but you must do something. We shall crash otherwise."

"Don't be silly, Polycarp. We are crashing."

"Crashing!"

"Yes, that's exactly what's happening. Only we aren't coming down in flames as they do on the films. We're coming down gently and slowly and, although the aeroplane won't be much good, we shall have to swim ashore, I'm afraid. I've often crashed, but this is the first time I've had to swim after it. Life is always preparing new experiences just for me."

Seeing Frank so calm, Polycarp tried to stifle his fear, and he watched the water glide closer as they settled downwards. They were coming down well to the north side of the bay and would not have long to swim before a boat picked them up. He looked back, but the crowd at the lake did not seem to be taking much notice of what was happening to the aeroplane.

It is surprising the influence which the parade of one man's bravery will have upon another. Frank was not afraid of the crash for several reasons : the chief was that he knew he could probably effect the descent in such a way that they would come to no harm, and another that he did not care much what happened to himself. If he were killed he was killed and what happened would happen. Such a philosophy made panic impossible. And seeing Frank's calm, Polycarp, who was human enough to have fears as cogent and spontaneous as any other person, kept his head and waited for the aeroplane to hit the water. He quickly took off his jacket and shoes. The water came up and up and then, as Frank flattened out, glided underneath them for what seemed an age until the undercarriage touched the waves. Polycarp heard the sear of broken water, and as the nose of the machine dipped he was catapulted from his seat and struck the sea in a dive not more than usually ragged.

XII
Polycarp writes his own obituary notice and starts a new life

Polycarp came to the surface and looked back at the aeroplane. It was floating with its nose deep in the water, one wing buckled and ripped, and its rudder stuck into the air like the tail of a diving porpoise. Straddled across the fuselage sat Frank.

"Come on—hurry!" shouted Polycarp, as he trod water. "She's sinking fast!" He could see the aeroplane settling lower into the water as he spoke.

"Don't worry," answered Frank. "Think of Sir Francis Drake."

Very calmly Frank sat on the fuselage and took off all his clothes except his singlet and trousers. Around his neck he hung his shoes and, expressing less concern than a boy wading into the sea-brink to paddle, he slipped quietly into the water and swam with steady breast strokes to Polycarp.

"We came out of that without much personal damage," said Polycarp, as they headed towards the beach on the north side of the estuary.

"You don't seem very worried about things," puffed Frank. "What about that bomb-throwing stunt? We'll get it in the neck for that."

"Oh, nonsense! Just a joke. I'll apologise—you know, high spirits. They'll understand."

"It'll be difficult to make 'em see it your way. I think we must have both been a little drunk with too much air."

"Leave that to me," said Polycarp. "We can afford a new machine, and when we get it the New Age Company will start again; bigger and better!"

They swam on in silence for a time. Before them the line of beach and houses widened, and away by the bathing; lake they could see the crowd dispersing along the promenade towards the ferry. Two motor-boats were hurrying out towards them.

In a way, mused Polycarp to himself, the crash was fortunate, for it would deflect some of the ire of the worthy town officials. He was congratulating himself on their good fortune when Frank spoke again.

"I'm afraid, Polycarp, that you don't understand everything."

"Don't understand what?"

"That the New Age Flying Company is now as derelict as that machine over there."

"Don't be foolish, man. We can buy another."

"No, we can't. Listen, Polycarp. I feel a bit of a worm now I have to tell you, but I never dreamt that anything like this would happen."

"What are you driving at? And, whatever it is, do we have to discuss it in the middle of the bay?"

"This is the best place." Frank stopped swimming; treading water, he faced Polycarp, and spoke with some difficulty because of the lapping waves. "This crash is going to put us in the dirt with everybody. The flour business might be explained away and we could begin again; but the crash—no! You see, in March when you asked me about Air Ministry licences and regulations, I lied to you. Just sheer laziness, I admit, and it's no good your being annoyed, because what's done is done. Still, I know you won't be annoyed, and that's what's making me feel such a rotter. I never bothered about licensing or complying with any regulations, and as soon as the Air Ministry officials come nosing about this crash, or the police—and we can't expect them to overlook it, can we?—they'll discover everything, and we shall probably get a couple of years in clink for not observing the formalities."

"I understand. We've been carrying passengers and endangering human life for months. Does look bad, doesn't it? What a damned fool you were, Frank!" Polycarp found it impossible to be annoyed while swimming.

"I know. I always have been a damned fool. The point is, however, not what I am, but what we're going to do when we land. The best thing is to liquidate the company, share out, and then part, to make the trail harder for the authorities. After all, we've had a good run and done well. We can't grumble. Are you angry?"

"No, not angry—just wondering why people bother to have children like you. Anyway, why talk about that? It seems certain that the company will have to evaporate quickly before the police and other folk become unpleasant."

"I'm glad you aren't livid; though I must say I shouldn't have cared much if you were. Even if this hadn't happened, I couldn't have stopped with you much longer. There's something else—"

"I can guess the answer to that one. Damn the waves! A careless combination of drink, darkness, and passion. Poor Frank, I can't imagine you as a father. My congratulations or commiserations, whichever you like. I hope you do the right thing by her—I feel sorry for the poor girl."

"Oh, I shall do something, but I'm not stopping in this town. Now do you understand how impossible things are?"

Polycarp nodded, and started to swim on. He was not disappointed. He had always expected some catastrophe to result from his association with Frank, and now that the catastrophe had come he found that it did not alter his liking for the aviator. Despite the man's selfishness and irresponsible hedonism, there was an attractive quality about him which aroused Polycarp's admiration. He felt sorry for the girl. She would probably suffer, if he knew Frank, and he made a resolution to get her address and send her something. He felt that he was in a way responsible for her misfortune, because he had brought the company to the town.

And so, all that remained of the New Age Flying Company swam on towards the shore until the motor-boats came up to them and landed them on the quay. They were given a lift to their hotel, and for the rest of the day they were busy making preparations to quit the town. They stalled the police, when they came to make enquiries, with the excuse that they were suffering from the shock and could not go into long details until the next day. Meanwhile, several things happened: the crippled machine sank to the bottom of the bay, to provide a new anchorage for molluscs; Polycarp sold the car and withdrew their capital from the bank, and they shared out the money in proportion to their original investments. Polycarp found himself with approximately three hundred pounds, while Frank was jubilant over his seventy-five pounds.

The next day they disappeared, each in his own way, and the authorities of Brinton knew neither Polycarp Jarvis, proprietor, nor Frank Burns, pilot, any more, and the only trace that remained of the New Age Flying Company's activities in the town were the flour stains that littered the lakeside and the promenade, and the red buoy marking the place where the aeroplane had sunk.

After the disappearance of the two, there was some confusion in the police station, and enquiries were made, but as no trace of them could be found the enquiries gradually lapsed and the whole affair was officially forgotten, though the incident remained an indelible memory for most of the people who had attended the carnival, and the Children's Hospital benefited from the good humour induced by the sight of other folk's misfortune to the extent of a collection half as large again as was anticipated. When a man has just seen someone's best suit ruined by an unexpected immersion in a bathing-pool, he puts sixpence instead of a penny in a collection box, just to mark his own singularity and immunity from such misfortunes.

Polycarp became a hunted man. He was watched from behind every corner: when he looked around, there was a dark shadow following him through street after street; when he stopped, his shadower stopped, and when he turned quickly, the shadower slipped into a doorway from his sight. He passed every policeman furtively, with a sideways glance, and his hand instinctively went up to his bare lip to cover a moustache which had fallen beneath his razor the day he left Brinton. He dyed his hair brown, but as it grew he developed into a half-albino, so that he had to wear his hat everywhere, except in bed and at the cinema. If a man asked him the time in the street, he knew him at once for a police spy trying to detect whether he had a mole under his chin—so he affected high collars that cut his neck and changed the mole into a sore. He enjoyed being hunted. Every town held danger for him. Innocent citizens were in the pay of the police, and even the toddling child who asked him for fag-cards was a decoy. Sometimes he walked alone in the country, swinging a stout stick and starting at every movement.

"I'll die, rather than be taken alive," was his favourite remark, and he composed newspaper headings for himself, and long obituary notices. He could see the notice in the *Bristol Times and Mirror*, under a very bad photograph supplied by his weeping aunt, and announced by thick headlines: "The death by suicide of a once well-known Bristolian … found dead in the gas-filled room of a Worthing boarding-house when the police, who had been searching for him for months in connection with a long series of frauds and misrepresentations, battered down the door. The body was surrounded by rows of champagne bottles and the stumps of burnt cigars … A man, who, had his abilities been directed into legitimate channels, would indubitably have made a name for himself … genius, warped by contact with bad associates … Miss Gracie Hayward, who knew the deceased well … A note by his side …" The note worried Polycarp. Sometimes it was defiantly flippant, that of a man who met death rather than dishonour with a jest on his lips and the spirit of wine seething in his head. Sometimes it was a heavy sociological treatise ascribing his downfall to the immalleable conditions of the present social order, showing him to be yet another victim of civilisation; and sometimes it was an epitaph in rhyme:

> *Here's an end to the tragedy, Stranger,*
> *The days of my terror are done.*
> *Gladly I leave this privation and want—*
> *A roll and a butter for one.*

The last line was always difficult because some ridiculous mundane anticlimax would obtrude, and, when he got the last line to his liking, he found that the first three were inclined to be bawdy. He gave up epitaphs, and decided to stick to cutting sarcasm wrapped up in heavy phrases.

He wrote now to his aunt, with whom he had always corresponded regularly, without affixing any address, and she wondered from the various postmarks just what he was doing. She did not worry unduly even when a short note arrived, enclosing a good photograph of himself, saying: "You may need this some time."

To live in the shadow of an imaginary fear of apprehension opens a man's eyes to things which otherwise he would pass without seeing. The hunted man, so Polycarp discovered anyway, lives in a different world from the rest of humanity. He eats in low cafés; he sinks his identity in crowds and cinemas; he seeks the peace of country solitudes, and suspects even the lonely shepherd and the labourer of espionage. For three months, since he had no imperative need to work, Polycarp played the game of the hunted man about England. A time-table was his chief literature, and he became a connoisseur of cheap lodgings and popular amusements. He knew the best place to get a cheap meal and a bed in Leeds. He knew how to work across the country in a day, from Stafford to Lincoln, by bus routes. He knew the times of the expresses going north, and he slept in rocking sleepers as he fled from the phantom of a Peterborough policeman to the security of Edinburgh. He visited Scotland, and drank, slept, and ate cheaply at little inns along the Kirkcudbrightshire coast. He fled from Blackpool to the Lakes, and spent a few days losing himself on the pikes. He hid himself in Barmouth after a fictitious scare at Liverpool, and, after that, arrived in Bristol late one night and woke his aunt by climbing through the drawing-room window, which he opened with his pocket-knife. He did not stay long, and to all her enquiries remained enigmatic.

"Well, boy, I suppose you know what you're doing. It can't be serious, I suppose, otherwise you wouldn't look so happy about it. What have you been reading lately, the memoirs of a spy?"

"Of course, not! I'm not really happy, that's just a deceptive front. I'm weighted with care."

He told her some of his adventures, and, a few days later, left suddenly because a policeman, so he imagined, had followed him half-way across the Downs.

The whole of Polycarp's erratic movements during that three months would take too long to detail. At the end of three months, when even he had to admit that the police were no longer looking for him, if they ever had been, he discovered that he had got so used to dodging about, and seeing fresh country and new towns, that he had no desire to give up the life. He was faced with a problem. His money would not allow him to roam about from hotel to hotel for any great time, and there was always his vow to make good. He could not forget that.

He wanted to combine the two desires and, as luck would have it, he was enabled to do so. Polycarp became the sole manufacturer, distributor, and retailer of Solomon's Glory. He forgot that he was a wanted man, and immersed himself in his new venture.

It all started with Harry and a black Wyandotte rooster which had strayed into the roadway outside a Hertfordshire egg farm. The fowl should not have been in the roadway, it should have been in its run keeping an eye on the mixed bunch of Buff Orpington and Hamburgh hens, and Harry, too, should not, at half past one in the afternoon, have been morose and saddened so that the future seemed as sombre as his past. He had been travelling across country, in his little motor-van, from Aylesbury to Watford, and had stopped at the Two Brewers Inn at Chipperfield; a village that spread-eagled itself about one corner of a large common that was littered at this time of the year with brown oak and beech leaves, and smouldering with the down-crushed fronds of dried bracken. Harry looked across the common at the tall, scarlet-trunked firs and shook his head sadly. Beauty was nothing to him at that moment. Life was nothing. Breathing was a pain. The only things which still came naturally and easily to him were sadness and drinking.

He went inside and called for a drink. He was tired, he told himself, of the continual hurly-burly of life, he was tired of the continual travelling and shouting, and the continual selling and wheedling, which seemed to be his lot. And, most of all, he was tired of his perpetual bad luck at horse-racing. He had lost money steadily for two years, lost so consistently that he no longer regarded it as bad luck but as a direct equine conspiracy directed against him from every stable between Newmarket and Newbury. If he could obtain enough money he would leave England and try his luck abroad. He had never heard of any horse-racing in Canada or South Africa, so he would be fairly safe from temptation in either of those places, and he could start a new life. That was Harry's forte—starting a new life. Ever since he had been dismissed from his first job as errand-boy for incompetence, Harry had been making new starts.

There are scores of people like Harry. They have ambitious ideas; they start little arty cafés to confound people who suffer with hunger and thirst, and when they find that a café is only a success if it meets the demands of healthy appetites, they start again with a poultry farm and imagine that all they have to do is pick up eggs. They even have the ingenuity and perseverance to invent nests which obviate the painful procedure of bending to pick up the eggs, but when they discover that the processes involved in the production of an egg are as intricate and insistent as the processes governing the production of milk, that fowls have to be fed, pens cleaned, rats killed, hawks watched, and temperatures controlled, they decide that no egg can possibly be worthy of the labour involved. So they go through life starting fresh ventures in the hope that one day they will come across something which will be entirely independent of their labour and yet make a fortune for them. They hate hard work, they hate work of any kind, and Harry was a noble member of the great community of starters. And now as he sat drinking, a red-faced man with George Robey eyebrows and a body as plump as, but less agile than, a sea-lion's, he was wishing that he could make another start.

If only he had enough money. Starting cost money, and starting abroad would mean at least twenty-five pounds. He had thought of selling his stock and car, but even a person of wealthy abandon would only have offered him ten pounds and then considered it a generous gesture, and Harry knew this. He was still thinking of this when he left the inn and switched on the engine, and he was still wrapped in the sad solemnity of his thoughts and the contemplation of the harshness of his particular existence when the cock Wyandotte crossed the road three feet in front of him. The black apparition of flapping wings and cackling calls frightened Harry, and, as the car was travelling downhill towards the dip of a valley, he could not stop. He did not try to stop—he just swerved away from the fowl and then forgot for a moment to swerve back. When he started to swerve back it was far too late, for the front of the car had gone deeply into a thick bank of holly-bush and a shower of ripe berries pattered down into his lap in festive welcome.

"And there's a horse in the three-thirty called Hollybush." The omen seemed so forcible that he spoke the words aloud.

"And is this the way you usually get tips for your bets?" said a voice close beside him.

Harry looked round, and saw that almost at his elbow was a wooden fence, which he had missed knocking down by no more than a foot, and sitting on top of the fence was Polycarp. Of course, Harry did not know Polycarp or he might have answered at once, telling him not to be a damned fool. As it was, he said:

"No; but judging by the bad results of most of my other methods, there may be something in this. What's the good, anyway? I haven't any money to put on it, and I haven't any money to get this crate out of this hedge."

"I'm sorry for you. You seem to be in a very bad way."

"I am—in a very bad way. People ought to control their fowls. I never get a square deal, always something happens to upset me ..."

"You very nearly upset me as well," Polycarp reminded him.

"I apologise, but it was the fowl's fault, not mine. And anyway, we've all got to die some day, and the sooner the better for some people. Sometimes I wish I was dead. There ain't no chance for the underdog in England. You ever thought of that? No chance in England for them that's down. I wish I could get away and start again. New Zealand, now—there's a country. Absolutely virgin. Absolutely virgin ..." He repeated the phrase lovingly, as though the contemplation of absolute virginity was a joy granted to man once in every thousand years. "Or Canada now, I could do things over there—"

"You seem to have a grievance—can I help you at all?"

"I've got a grievance all right. All pedlars have, but no one can help them."

"Don't let it get you down—there's always a bright side to everything. Why, if you hadn't run into this hedge, you wouldn't now be consoling yourself by explaining your woes to me."

"That's humour for a man in my present position, that is! But I don't mind. I get so used to funny remarks being made at me in the market-places that I don't think a person's human unless he tries to score off me with poor jokes. People think that because you're selling them something they've got a right to insult you. The nit-wits! Why, some of 'em, if their brains were gunpowder, wouldn't have enough to blow their silly hats off their silly heads."

"You sell things, do you?"

"Sell things! I sell anything! I sell a cure for every ailment heir to man."

The look on Polycarp's face, though it was not definitely of disbelief, stung Harry's professional pride; and he decided to give a demonstration of his powers. He stood up on his seat, and, waving his fist aloft, addressed an imaginary crowd collected behind Polycarp. "Ladies and gentlemen, and others present! I don't want to insult you. I couldn't if I tried. You can't insult a blockhead, because he doesn't understand. I don't come here today to insult you or to deceive you. I don't have to do that. In fact, I don't have to come here and bother myself with you at all. You may not believe it, but I could, if I liked, open up a practice in Harley Street and make a fortune out of curing the wealthy people in London. In fact, I have made a fortune—and given most of it away again—to the bookies! I don't bother with the rich. 'Let the rich look after the rich,' as a famous man once said to me. I won't mention his name, because you wouldn't believe me, and it might cause questions to be asked in Parliament. Let sleeping dogs scratch themselves and beggars get what they can. And that's why I've come to you. I was the son of a poor man, and my job is to help the poor, to cure their ills. See that card there—" Harry swung round and pointed to a card which hung, invisible, between two hawthorn-bushes on the other side of the road. "See what it says? Frederick William Manning. Do you know what those letters after the name mean? No? Well, I'll enlighten you. I'll let you into the mysteries of the medical profession. They mean doctor of dental surgery—yes, sir— you over there—I can take that rotten tooth of yours out in a second, without you knowing it's gone. They mean doctor of science—there's nothing about the universe and electrons that I don't know. Doctor of medicine—medicine! Why, half the medicine they give you is sugar and water with a little colouring. I know, I was one of them for years. Until my honesty made me give it up—and the bookies, did I hear someone say? No, sir—honesty—the thing that makes the world go round! Yes, ladies and gentlemen, you're listening to a man who's been amongst the highest circles in surgery and medicine. I know what's what, and I'll let you into a secret." Here Harry leaned forward confidentially towards Polycarp. "Don't ever go to a doctor again.

They're a lot of quacks and butchers. Do you know what they were called in Queen Elizabeth's time? Sawbones—sawbones and leeches! That's all they knew when good Queen Bess singed the beard of the King of Morocco. They drained your blood and they cut your body about—and that's all they know today. Believe me, I know. They tell you this and they tell you that—but they don't know any more now than then. No, not a thing; but they never let on. And that's what I'm here for today. Not to rob you—I don't want to make a fortune from you. If I wanted only money, I could get it somewhere else much quicker. I'm here with a purpose. Harry Manning, the Healer with a Mind above Money. That's me, and known in every town in England, and proud of it. Yesterday I was in Swansea, today in Cardiff, tomorrow—who knows? Sufficient unto the day is the good thereof, to alter a famous Spanish proverb which, in the original, if there's any Spaniards amongst the crowd, is *omnia vincit labor*. Listen, Nature is the only healer! Nature, the great healer! You've got a toothache, you're constipated, you've headaches, you've got rheumatism, boils, earache, debility, anaemia, heartburn, high blood pressure, dandruff, impetigo—anything you damned well like to have—and Nature's got a cure for it! No matter what it is, you'll find a cure somewhere in the flowers and herbs of the countryside—" He broke off suddenly and looked at Polycarp.

"Very good," said Polycarp. "Ever thought of going on the stage?"

"Humour again. But I can stand it. That's my job. See the idea? Jolly 'em with talk, make 'em laugh, insult 'em a little, and then sell 'em pills and ointment. Nature, the one healer. It's funny how much people will believe in Nature."

"And are you really a doctor and all that? Your fervour is worthy of a more demonstrative profession."

"Doctor, no! Never was and never will be. And I wouldn't be jockeying around in this crate with my load of cures, from one town to another, if I had enough money to go abroad. Just think—a few flimsy things like pound notes stand between me and starting afresh in Canada! It's sad. It is. It's as depressing as Oxford Cattle Market on a wet Wednesday. But why should you care about it? What does anyone care?" Harry leaned over the driving-wheel and plucked a berry from the hedge.

"As a matter of fact," said Polycarp suddenly, "it happens that I do care."

And he spoke the truth. How he came to be in that particular spot is not a long story. He had spent a week in London, looking round for something to do. During that time he had almost been persuaded to invest some of his money in a little tobacconist's and hairdresser's shop in return for a position as manager; the Jewish proprietor's business methods, as revealed to Polycarp on the first day, had so revolted him that he had walked out in disgust, having taken the precaution of punching the man on the nose to correct his impression of Polycarp's character. He had answered several advertisements with a view to investing some money in businesses, but the only business that seemed genuine and decent wanted more money than he had. The City had depressed him. He could not understand the attitude of people who were either going somewhere as if they would die unless they got there quickly, or coming away from places in a hurry as though they would die if they remained. He left and came by bus to Hemel Hempstead, and if was from his hotel there that he had walked until he had met Harry in the valley bottom.

"What do you mean?" asked Harry.

"Just that I'm looking for something to do, and the idea of selling cures in a market square attracts me. It sounds like a good exercise for one's histrionic powers and also provides a course in crowd psychology. Psychology is the new thing, these days, you know."

"And so were railway engines in my mother's days, but why should we worry about either? You get used to everything. Do you mean you'd like to be a pill-pedlar?"

"The idea attracts me. How does one go about it? Do you have to have a licence?"

"Yes, you get a licence and pay the market square charges, and there you are. But, what a life! Here today and gone tomorrow—never knowing the same town two nights running. You know, like a flea in a warm bed, always moving from one place to another. Oh, it's a great life if you like movement, but give me Canada. Why—" Harry looked at Polycarp sharply, and he saw a fair-haired youth, a dreamer, he thought, filled with the vision of pleasant country towns and open

158

roads and the joys of itinerancy, and he also saw someone who might be instrumental in giving him a fresh start.

"It's a great life, is it?"

"Sure—if you're young and full of beans. And, what's more, there's plenty of money to be made if you can keep away from the booze and betting."

"That won't trouble me."

"I wish I could say the same." Harry paused as Polycarp stroked his new growing moustache. "Listen, Mr. ... what's the name?"

"Polycarp Jarvis." It was the first time Polycarp had uttered his real name aloud for months, and the gesture seemed to indicate a break with the past. He was a free man again.

"Listen, Mr. Jarvis. All right, Polycarp, if you wish. I'll tell you what I'll do. I'll give you an hour's tuition in the tricks of the trade. You know—gags and what to watch for, because the majority of the people on the road are out for number one most of the time, and ready to do you dirty. I'll tell you all I know, and then throw in this car and the whole of my stock, and the goodwill in over a hundred towns of Harry Manning, the Healer with a Mind above Money, for a paltry thirty pounds. And that's cheap at the price!"

Polycarp was impressed and attracted, but his enthusiasm did not decommercialise his instincts. He shook his head. "Make it twenty-five and I'll consider it."

"All right—though it's throwing things away. Twenty-five and the whole lot's yours, plus the tuition."

Polycarp walked around the car as far as he could, and Harry opened the doors of the little van and displayed the stock.

"Well, what do you say?"

"Done, but I think I'm being swindled. I don't mind, I'll pay the price of enthusiasm as a gift to the gods, so that this venture may prosper."

"More humour, but for twenty-five pounds I'd stand anything." Harry rubbed his hands together; a new start.

For the next hour they sat on the running-board of the car, and Harry explained the mysteries of selling quack medicines in market squares. To some of it, Polycarp listened, but after a time he accepted the conversation of the man as inevitable and concerned his mind with ideas for the future. He would burst upon the markets of England like a bomb, a modern Sequah to charm money from the crowd and to relieve their pains. After the lecture they parted; Harry, with twenty-five pounds, in the direction of the main road to catch a bus for Watford and so to Canada for a new start, and Polycarp to get assistance from a Chipperfield garage to haul the car from the hedge and make the necessary repairs.

That night a plebeian tradesman's van rested amongst the autocratic private cars in the garage of a Hemel Hempstead hotel, and Polycarp lay on his bed making plans. For the first time since the abrupt termination of the New Age Flying Company he felt that he was again in the path of fortune.

XIII
Sheba was not the only person to acknowledge Solomon's Glory

Polycarp remained a pill-pedlar for a year, and at the end of that time he was heartily weary of all pills and salves. Even the knowledge that he was making a moderate profit did not compensate for the discomforts and inconveniences of his life.

At first he had wandered about the country, prompted by the fantastic fear of capture by the police. He knew, however, in his heart that he was in no real danger, but the make-believe added a piquancy to his peregrinations and coloured each new scene with alluring tones. He loved the continual movement. When the possibility of police pursuit became too remote even for him to persuade himself that it was real, he looked around for some other excuse for continuing his peripatetic life. Pill-peddling gave it to him, and then, like a young man who would secure the pleasures of courtship by marriage ties and is disappointed because a wife is a different creature from a sweetheart, Polycarp discovered that pill-peddling ceased to be an excuse and became a compulsion. No longer did he wander because he loved wandering. Now he was under the compulsion of making a living and somehow, some day, a fortune. Vagabondage is somewhat similar to good music; most people welcome it when they discover it for themselves, but tell them that they must like good music, that it is a woeful betrayal of their cultural pretensions not to like it, and they immediately hate it. Polycarp, of course, did not immediately hate his new profession. That came later. At first he was wildly enthusiastic.

He bought his licence and started at Watford Market, and from Watford he plotted out a circular tour that took him east as far as Ipswich, south to Portsmouth, west to Gloucester, and north to Leicester. Within that circle of country Polycarp moved and had his being for a year, until he knew every twist of its roads, every commercial hotel and market square; knew just how mean the people were in each town, just what jokes they liked, and just how much he could insult them without annoying them, and he did a small amount of business, though his profits were scarcely more than enough to cover his outlay and expenses—until he concocted his famous Solomon's Glory. The birthplace of this elixir of life was Northampton, and the time a day in December.

Polycarp had not been in a pleasant mood. It was Saturday and had rained all day. He had motored for hours through the driving showers. Everywhere lay mud and slush and wet rotting leaves. The trees were black and bare, their green trunks streaked with runnels of steady rain which, falling upon the windscreen, gave Polycarp a distorted view of the road and country. Cottage gardens were miserable graveyards with the brown, withered stumps of chrysanthemum and Michaelmas daisy leaning like tipsy headstones over the unkempt earth. The fields were untidy expanses of stubble or wide stretches of black ploughed land, and a stiff north-easter was driving the rain into long sheaves that soaked through everything. Great gusts of wind and rain battered the small van as Polycarp drove it along the roadways. He tried to sing to cheer himself up, but the sound of *There's a Blue Ridge Round my Heart, Virginia* only emphasised the gloom of the day.

Wind and rain ravaged the land so that the tall, leafless elms gripped with their roots into the loosening earth and bore their rugged branches aloft defiantly. The cattle gathered in the lee of the hedges and stood stoically as the rain ran off their hides and the wind tossed their ears and manes; the gulls, which had come inland to follow the plough along the tilth, gathered in a wedge-shaped phalanx pointing into the wind, and the water-fowl clung close to the shelter

162

of reed and alder. The wind and rain were cold, cruel pagans, leaping from the distant north and bringing with them the bite and hate of the slate-coloured seas and ice plateaux to scourge the earth. The storm swept from the sea across a hundred miles of land in a rude torrent; past tall church towers, fraying at the brown ivy-leaves and whistling through the rusty and beetle-eaten frames of belfries, past council houses and manor hall, shaking dormer windows and French casements, rattling at crazy shed doors and wide wrought-iron drive-gates. The wind and rain raced by dark fir copses, swaying the thin trunks until the dead needles at their bases quivered in sympathy with the earth's battle. Over field and fen, over quarry and quagmire, making sport with buckets and scarecrows, buffeting tram-cars and electric light standards, tipping up dustbins and scattering the garbage along the streets, rocking shop-signs and filling the gutters with a dark, muddy spate, went the storm.

Nothing was immune. Water soaked through the hood on to Polycarp. The wind choked roof-gutters with dead leaves and forced the accumulating waters to run down roof and walls, percolating through to painted ceilings and plastered kitchens; it overturned the trolleys at the side of sugar-beet fields; it knocked down allotment sheds and tobacconists' kiosks; howled through railway tunnels and snapped telegraph wires; and set dogs barking with fear as it played a vicious bastinado of rain upon tin roofs. It was a royal winter storm, a magnificent wrath of rain and wind that drove all before it, sending men scurrying to the shelter of their roof-trees and their ale-houses, and it put Polycarp into a gloomy mood as he sucked his empty pipe and thought of standing in a damp market square trying to sell ointment for ingrowing toe-nails and salves for boils. He stopped for lunch at a wayside hotel where the beer was so bad that it would have been unworthy even of a railway buffet, and the usual plate of rouged ham and weary potatoes made Polycarp think sympathetically of suicide. The only things that did not seem to mind the wind and rain were ducks and the proprietors of theatres and cinemas. The ducks quacked and revelled in their muddy pools, flinging weed and water over their backs in ecstasy, and the. cinema proprietors stood in their foyers and, restraining a desire to quack, glanced out gratefully at the grey sky and then at the terrific posters advertising *The Lost World*;

there would, they thought, be a damp, close, human fuddle in the ninepennies that night and the glow of many cigarette-ends in the one-and-sixpennies.

But storms have no concern for ducks or cinema proprietors, and by the time Polycarp had reached Northampton and taken his stand in the market-place the wind had gone and the rain was fining to a drizzle which would presently stop.

He glanced round and nodded to the holders of various stalls. He had soon come to know them and all their peculiar histories. They were as constant in their movements as the stars in the night sky: a little floating nebulx of hucksters, tricksters, pedlars, hawkers, rogues, and a few honest men who kept their secret so well that they went unrecognised. There was Bill Brailey, the You-want-it-I-got-it man, who sold anything from alarm clocks, cheap saws, fretwork outfits, nail-scissors, bicycle lamps, to indecent postcards, and had a mistress in every market town to save the cost of lodgings. Not far away from him stood the peppermint maker, who demonstrated his confectionery art in the open and was a great favourite with the schoolboys because of his indiscriminate habit of flinging free samples into the crowd. Next to him a tall, bearded Afghan who was born in Pimlico and dreamed, not of a hill village near Kabul and a long rifle, but of a bungalow at Southend and a fat wife who could cook, as he pared at the nodose feet of country yokels and loudly staked his reputation against any corn in the United Kingdom. There were dark-skinned, hooked-nosed gentlemen who sold rolls of linoleum and caught at your arm as you passed; men who flourished silk stockings and leered; men who proved by experiments performed on a rickety table that it was ridiculous to pay a shilling for a proprietary brand of floor-polish when they could give you the same thing for tuppence. "You pay for the name," was their refrain. There was a stall where a thin, bespectacled individual hid behind his piles of tracts, calendars, religious books, and flowered texts and, scorning to commercialise his wares by crying them aloud, never appeared to sell anything. Polycarp knew them all and he liked them. He liked the glitter and the noise, their quips and weaknesses. Sometimes he drank with them and laughed at their tales, but today the total effect of the market-place was to give him a mental stomach-ache. He had no luck at all. No one wanted to buy his goods. He went right through his stock and sold about three-shillings' worth of goods. The crowd watched and listened to him : a smattering of late-shopping women, unemployed men who found his patter a cheap form of amusement, youths and girls, workmen, clerks, a few labourers, soldiers, bus-conductors coming off their shifts ... a typical market crowd, some come to watch, some to listen, some to forget themselves, some to heckle, and a few to buy.

Polycarp was nettled by their apathy. It seemed impossible to rouse their interest to the point where they would buy from him. He grew angry with them and decided that if he could not stir them from their stupor by flattering them, he would stimulate them with insults.

"You don't want to buy, do you? You think I'm out to catch you? Ah, my friends, what a mistake you make! See that board—" He swung round and pointed to the board above his van.

NATURE THE GREAT HEALER
Let Nature Do the Work—not the Doctor
Rely on Herbs—not Operations
Rely on John Polycarp Jarvis,
the Man with a Mind above Money
JOHN POLYCARP JARVIS, D.Sc., M.D., D.S.

"Yes, that's me. John Polycarp Jarvis. Once I was a doctor, but I left my practice—gave it all up to come to you here in this market-place and to thousands of others like you all over England to tell you the truth, the greatest truth of the age: that you needn't waste your money paying doctors' fees for exactly the same thing as I can sell you here today for a tenth the price. But you don't believe me? If I stepped down among you and started to sell pound notes for a shilling you'd still think I was deceiving you. You're all too smart. You're all expecting to be caught and you won't recognise the truth when you see it. Did you ever hear of Diogenes?"

"Whose colours does he carry, guv'nor?" someone shouted from the crowd.

"There you are. Humour. I can stand it, though. Diogenes, my good sir, was not a horse but a philosopher. And he went through the market-places and streets of Athens carrying a lantern looking for an honest man—"

"Shame! What was wrong with 'is eyesight?"

"Humour again!" Polycarp dismissed the laughing crowd with a contemptuous gesture. "All right, I made a mistake. You aren't interested in the classics. What are you interested in? You stand there with your hands in one another's pockets and silly grins on your faces as though nothing mattered in the whole world. You don't know what's happening to yourself. You're the great working class and you don't know when you're being done down—"

"Oh, yes, we do. When you try to sell us your quack cures!"

"Ah, you're waking up at last! My cures aren't quacks! They're based on the fundamental laws of nature; they don't try to help nature, they only give you in a concentrated form what nature would give you. And if the humorist who made that last remark suffers from bronchitis, cough, chronic catarrh, itches, indigestion, boils, corns, heartburn, sciatica, or any other trouble, and cares to step out here, I'll give him something which will cure him within three weeks or my name isn't John Polycarp Jarvis. Come on, you sceptics!"

The crowd stirred and a big fellow stepped out, a broad-faced garage-hand, his fingers banded with mourning lines of sub-ungual dirt and his dungarees wrinkled with permanent creases, as though he had been born in them.

"Here I am, mister. I'm not afraid!"

"Ah, you're not afraid. Look at the brave fellow. So you're a humorist, eh? Well, if your jokes aren't any better than your repairs to cars I shouldn't like to drive one. And what do you suffer from?"

"It's my left eye. I can't see with it."

"Can't see—do you mean you're blind?"

"Something like that, mister. It hurts around it, too. Been like it for some time now."

The crowd came closer as the conversation became less stentorian, and then retreated as Polycarp jumped on to his box.

"Eye-trouble, optic nerves!" shouted Polycarp loudly. "And what would most of you do? Rush away to an eye hospital and get surgeons cutting you about and charging you fat bills. But not Nature. She has a remedy for every complaint. Never seen a little white flower in the hedges around this town called eyebright, have you? Perhaps you'll recognise it, since you're so clever, as *euphrasia officinalis*. Eyebright—and its name is such because herbalists make an ointment to cure blindness from it. You don't believe me? I don't care. Truth is stronger than disbelief and, as Shakespeare said, truth will out. Here you are, sir. A tin of eye-ointment, price three pence, but free to you. Rub that on every night and within three weeks you'll be able to see even your own stupidity." He handed the tin down to the mechanic, who took it and turned it over. Then he looked up at Polycarp and said slowly:

"This ain't no good to me, mister. No amount of ointment could make me see with me left eye—it's a glass one!"

To prove his statement he slipped the eye out and showed it to Polycarp and the crowd. A howl of laughter went up which attracted attention from all over the market.

"Humour! The humour of the populace! But I can stand it." Polycarp made an effort and controlled his annoyance.

"Here, you!" he called to the mechanic as he stepped back into the crowd. "Take a free packet of poison and kill yourself. Someone'll be glad of your eye then to play marbles with."

And so the evening dragged on to the accompaniment of jibes, laughter, the sound of wavering naphtha flares and shouting men— and Polycarp did very poor business.

No one wanted his famous Etna Ointment for curing all itches, rashes, and eruptions of the skin. No one wanted his Trukure Emulsion for bronchitis, colds, coughs, and catarrh. They made rude remarks about road-sweepings when he tried to sell Hill-Thyme Herbal Cigarettes for nasal troubles, and his Rubbitton for rheumatism, lumbago, and cramp evoked sarcastic guffaws.

He made a last attempt.

"Put 'em all down. You don't want 'em. All right, I won't force them on to you. What is it you want? You're difficult to satisfy. Now I understand why politicians were loath to give you the vote; they knew what you were like. They knew what a shiftless, undecided mob you were and they knew their lives would be hell, one moment giving you free trade and the next protection, one moment shouting for war and the next for peace, one day loving the French and the next hating 'em.

Here, look at this—something you've got to pay half a crown for in any chemist's shop!" He held a small flat tin into the air.

"Half a crown in your shops, but I don't ask you half a crown, I don't ask you two shillings, not even a shilling. And don't think I'm lying when I say that the contents of this tin are exactly the same—in fact a little better, because it contains no colouring material—than the stuff you pay silver for in your town shops. Not half a crown, not a bob—here you are—sixpence, and it's giving it away at the price! The finest skin cream in the world. Removes blackheads, pimples, rashes, blemishes, and all defections of the skin while you sleep. Come on now! Who wants sixpennyworth of beauty? Make your skin smooth as satin, give it that velvet texture which speaks of health. Come on …" Polycarp got down from his little rostrum and walked round the fringe of the crowd brandishing a handful of skin-cream tins. The faces he passed regarded him with amusement, boredom, apathy, and not one of them showed the slightest sign of wanting to buy his wares, though most of them seemed to need skin-cream. Their faces were sallow with life in dark rooms, blotched with indigestion and lack of exercise, or reddened and coarsely pored with exposure to the sun and rain. There were very few brown flushed cheeks and bright eyes. Polycarp noted this lack of blooming youth and health and supposed that all sensible people kept at home on such an evening, and the healthy people were generally the sensible ones.

"You don't want it, eh?" he cried as he went back to his rostrum. "You don't want to have beautiful faces—"

"What do you think we are, mate—a ruddy lot of film stars?" shouted someone from the crowd. "We make a living with our hands, not our faces!"

"You don't have to tell me that. Humorous, ain't you? If you had to make a living with your faces you'd all be starving. With faces like yours it's a wonder you're allowed to live. Here, perhaps this is what you want. Not skin-cream, but sand-paper to smooth out your bumps and pimples. Who wants a penny sheet of sandpaper for his face?"

Polycarp's bitter humour fell flat, and he decided that the Fates were against him. At that moment he regretted his meeting with Harry Manning, and he thought longingly of the long-ago hot days of the summer when he had been proprietor of the New Age Flying Company. He had meant something then, and had been giving the public something which it appreciated. Now he was saddled with a load of quack (he knew they were quacks though he would not admit it to anyone but himself) cures for complaints as varied as mumps and brain-fever. He wondered what Frank was doing and where he was at that moment. He packed up his wares and drove back gloomily to his hotel. He lay on the bed in his room staring at the framed hotel rules hanging under the gas-bracket and allowed himself to sink into a state of delectable misery. At that moment Polycarp was a very sad, neglected person. He was easily discouraged and ready to throw up a venture if he could see that people did not appreciate him. With pill-peddling, however, he could not bring himself to believe that it was his fault that he was not making a success. The fault, if any, lay in the things he was selling, not in himself. If the cures were as genuine as his efforts, then success could not possibly be withheld from him for long.

He began to ruminate upon the fallacies which bolster up the lives of men. Cures, all the things which be tried to foist upon the public, were suspect. People had got into the habit of saying that anything which purported to cure an ill cheaply must, because of its very cheapness, be a sham. It was true that they sometimes did buy his ointments and medicines, but, as they always took them in a spirit of pessimism and doubt, they seldom had any effect. Medicine, Polycarp decided, was merely part of a ritual which inspired fear, doubt, or confidence. If you coloured water and gave it to a man with sufficient impressment to convince him that it would cure his cold within a few days, then the man took the medicine in that spirit and the cold was cured, not by any physical virtue of the medicine but by the power of the man's mind. If a man were ready to believe that coloured water would cure him then it would, but if he was not prepared to believe it then nothing could effect a cure. And Polycarp had to admit that most of his ointments and cures were not of a nature strong enough to take a hold upon a man's mind and work as a hetero-suggestive remedy for his ills. Recovery from disease was like human progress—all cures and progress proceed from the domination and conquest of man's mind over his bodily limitations. Mind over matter. If Polycarp could induce enough will-power in a man then he could cure any ill. He lay for a long time thinking about this and slowly an idea was born. Man, the men and women of the market-places, needed some potent ritual, some pageantry to stimulate their faith. Some people found it easier to believe in divinity and God with the aid of ritual and the ceremony of a church and ecclesiastical pomp, and Polycarp would give them pomp to orient their confidence in medicine.

Within an hour Polycarp had the whole scheme worked out in his mind and was enthusiastically setting to work. He would scrap all his old cures and sell medicine, the universal medicine, along the new lines. And so was Solomon's Glory born, the medicine which would cure anything if man but had faith.

Polycarp's preparations were not involved. He sold his existing stock cheaply to a herbalist, bought five hundred small bottles, and had an equal number of labels printed to his direction. Into the bottles he poured a rosy-coloured liquid, compounded of water from his hotel washing-jug, iodine, a liberal addition of cochineal, and a judicious addition of quinine. This mixture was made in his bedroom hand-bowl in relays, and after the bottles were corked he spent a sticky morning affixing the labels. When the job was completed he got the porter to carry the bottles down to his van and, after making a few more purchases in the town, Polycarp started for Oxford, where he intended to give the world the benefit of his discovery.

Oxford has been called the home of lost causes, and it does seem that revolutionary movements which have their genesis in that city, although they may produce a certain stir for a while, never come to any great moment. But Polycarp was unimpressed by these pessimistic historical associations, and there was never any doubt of the success of Solomon's Glory.

It was a fine, clear, frosty day, with the spirit of Christmas floating in the air, when Polycarp arrived at Oxford. The cattle-pens were noisy with bellowing cows and bleating sheep, and the air was piquant with the smell of exhaust gases and dung. Stalls showed touches of green, and along one side of the market stretched a line of butchers' and poulterers' stalls bright with red and white carcasses and the hanging bodies of plucked birds.

Polycarp was not interested in the rest of the market. He was wrapped up in his own occupation. Over the top of his van he had stretched a long red and white banner which read

NOT THE FABLED ELIXIR OF LIFE
BUT THE ELIXIR OF HEALTH
SOLOMON'S GLORY
Obtainable nowhere else in the World but at this Stall
Sole proprietor—Polycarp Jarvis

Already the banner had attracted attention. A few schoolboys from the school which stood in one corner of the square were grouped about him, watching eagerly, pulling at their yellow and black caps, and hoping that the school-bell would not ring before he commenced selling.

Bill Brailey shouted to him:

"Hey, Polly, how long have you known Solomon?"

Polycarp ignored the remark and began to lay out his bottles along the side of the van. They gleamed and sparkled in the sun like a row of freshly painted toy soldiers, their ruby shoulders reflecting the light and their white label-faces shining in the winter sunshine. By the time he had finished his preparations Polycarp had gathered the nucleus of a respectable crowd around him. Market crowds scent a new stall or new attraction from any distance up to half a mile. Already it was known in St. Aldates that there was a new man in the market.

Polycarp slipped into his little van—the space was restricted, but he did not mind—and the few onlookers lost sight of him. They saw him enter the swinging doors, a tall, awkward young man with auburn hair that struggled against a flattening onslaught of brilliantine, a lean face whose skin was browned with weather and betrayed by freckles around the nose and mouth, and with his body clothed in grey plus-fours splotched in places with grease stains. They were totally unprepared for the figure which emerged. Before them strode a magnificent creature, afire with colour and the barbaric splendour of the East. It was Polycarp—but what a Polycarp! A Polycarp whose head was crowned with a green turban, a Polycarp whose boyish face was stern with the mysticism and inscrutability of a Tibetan philosopher, a Polycarp no longer in plus-fours but graced by a flowing robe of bright scarlet, and caught about the waist with a heavy yellow tasselled cord reminiscent of the bands used to loop up curtains. On his feet he wore long pointed slippers with curved toes, and about his robe and turban glittered the facets of many jewels; a splendid compelling figure who might have stepped straight from the pages of *The Arabian Nights* instead of the interior of a Ford van. The apparition produced a wave of telepathic curiosity which travelled round the market square, so that a slow drift, quickening each moment, began towards the stall.

Polycarp took no notice of the crowd. He had long ago assessed the commercial value of suspense. He walked across to his rostrum and took up a small drum. Mounting the rostrum, he commenced to beat the taut skin, his face remaining perfectly solemn and composed, though in his mind he was saying in time to the rhythm of the drum, "I'll show 'em—show 'em. I'll show 'em—show 'em. Buy, buy, buy— I'll make 'em buy. I'll show 'em—show 'em,

I'll show 'em—show 'em. Buy, buy, buy ..."

He beat at the drum for nearly three minutes, so that its pulsating notes went echoing over the heads of the crowd, over the crowded pens, disturbing the pigeons before the Corn Exchange, rousing the curiosity of the barmaid in the Welsh Pony, and making the schoolboys, who had returned to their classrooms, itch in their seats as they tried to concentrate on French verbs and the shorthand grammalogues for *cannot, gentlemen, gentleman, particular, opportunity*, while their minds were preoccupied with their lost opportunity for seeing the particular gentleman who was going to sell Solomon's Glory and who was making such a glorious row with the drum and obviously fretting the shorthand teacher's nerves.

Polycarp's inscrutability and the insistent drum had their effect and, when he judged that he had a large enough crowd, Polycarp stopped beating. He felt perfectly self-composed. He was one of those fortunate individuals who do not comprehend the meaning of stage-fright.

Polycarp dropped the drum, and as the last note faded he crossed his hands before him and bowed low to the crowd. Now it was so large that the few people who had seen the metamorphosis of a plus-foured man into an Eastern potentate were swallowed up and negated.

"Ladies and gentlemen," he said in a voice which no one but his Aunt Felicia would have connected with his normal tones. "I am happy to be with you this afternoon and I hope you, too, will soon share my happiness, for I come to you with the powers of the East in my hands and the mysteries of the Orient in my heart, for although, as you will see from my notice, I am an Englishman, yet I was born in the East and lived there for many years until I received the great Message from my Master." The crowd shifted a little uneasily, and wondered what was the message and who was the master.

"I stand before you today for the first time, and I stand in the market square because your English market embodies all the traditions and customs of the Eastern bazaar. I could, I suppose, take a shop or consulting-rooms in London, but I come with the message of the East, so I will deliver that message in the manner of the East." The crowd shuffled again and hoped that he would not be long broadcasting it, and Polycarp saw that, although it was still his to play with, he would have to be careful.

"I bring to you the elixir of health, the elixir which gave Solomon his strength and his wisdom, the elixir which made Solomon, the son of David, the most famous king of the Israelites and a man revered and honoured to this day. And now I will tell you my secret."

Polycarp proceeded to give them a fantastic story of the appearance of Solomon to him in a dream. Solomon, he informed his audience solemnly, had claimed him as the son of his loins and had disclosed the whereabouts of the recipe for his elixir of health. He described his successful search for the recipe which contained Solomon's instructions for the compilation of the elixir. The crowd smiled at his story, but Polycarp was undismayed.

"Yes!" he cried. "An elixir such as Solomon himself drank when Sheba lived and Solomon reigned in all his glory. That elixir, my friends and brothers, I bring to you today. The elixir belongs to the past, but its power spreads into the future and lies at hand for you, to help you to gain the strength and the glory of Solomon." Polycarp turned quickly and held aloft a bottle of his Solomon's Glory.

"All disease, all bodily disorders, arise from the disharmony of the brain. All illness comes from the brain; cure the brain and the body regains its strength. A worried man is a sick man. A cheerful man is a healthy man. A contented woman is a healthy woman. A discontented woman is a weak woman. This elixir will cure any ill of the body. I do not say I think it will or that I hope it will; the wisdom of the East which is in my heart tells me that I know it will. I do not care whether you believe me or whether you doubt me. So soon as you take this elixir as directed on the label you are on the way to recovery. It is not a cough cure or an ointment to rub into the tissues—it is an elixir which stimulates the brain and brings the power of the mind to work upon the weaknesses of the body. Skin-diseases, bronchitis, chronic catarrh, coughs, itches, impetigo, indigestion—the Western evil—acidity, wind, nervous disorders, sciatica, rheumatism, cramp, aches, liver trouble, kidney pains, ulcers, eczema ... No matter what you have, my friends and brothers, they come from the brain, and the brain, which is the master of the body, alone can cure them with the aid of Solomon's Glory. And"—this was Polycarp's trump card— "I do not sell to anyone. I sell only to those who, by reason of my Eastern occultism, I know to be worthy of the great Solomon's Glory. Here it is for you, the greatest aphrodisiac of all times, as used by Solomon himself."

He stepped down into the crowd with a handful of bottles. He walked slowly round the fringe of the crowd, scanning their faces, and then stopped in front of a pleasant-faced housewife who had a half-smile on her face.

"You, madam, you are worthy. One shilling is the price." He held out the bottle, and after a momentary hesitation she took it and fumbled in her purse for a shilling. Polycarp could have shouted for joy. His success hinged upon the first offer being accepted. If the woman had turned away, the crowd would have been shy, but she bought without hesitation and he knew that her shilling was worth twenty more to him. He was right. He walked through the crowd, stopping now and then as he picked out the worthy ones. The honour of having one's worth publicly acknowledged by an Eastern mystic was not to be lightly disregarded, and for a shilling, was cheap. Soon Polycarp found men and women trying to catch his eyes, and he passed bottles and gave change, keeping up a running patter of talk to hold the crowd.

Solomon's Glory made a hit. On that day Polycarp sold the best part of his stock. He had gauged the stupidity of the crowd to a nicety. The more fantastic his story the more ready they seemed to believe it. Truth was too soberly clad for them to cherish it. His presence became known, and he had a continual crowd before him. Six times he whanged his drum and brought folks flocking to him, much to the other stall-holders' disgust, and six times he told the story of his vision and discovery, and each time it grew in detail and embellishment, and each time he sold a substantial number of bottles to the worthy people of Oxford, and each time it was remarkable how the proportion of worthy people in his crowd increased.

Solomon's Glory established itself wherever he took it, and so strong was the power of suggestion over the minds of the purchasers that it actually did do them good and effected some remarkable cures. At the end of four months Polycarp had a selection of astounding testimonials to the efficacy of Solomon's Glory. He had put his finger on a great truth—that mind controls the body and can cure it. He had the satisfaction not only of making money but of seeing old men come up and thank him for curing their rheumatism and sciatica, and of patting one-time pimply-faced youths on the shoulder as they presented their rosy cheeks for his inspection. Polycarp Jarvis became in a few weeks a prophet and a curer of a rank far above your ordinary pill-pedlar, and he revelled in the publicity and public approbation. There were even pieces about him and his remarkable cures in the local papers. Polycarp kept these and cherished them, because they consoled him when he thought that if he never did anything else in life he would have the satisfaction of knowing that he had been instrumental in straightening the back of Mr. Herbert Philpot at Gloucester and banishing the nervous fears of Miss Sarah Woolmington of Thame, and when one paper referred to him as the Modern Miracle Worker he bought six copies and sent them to his aunt and Gracie and other acquaintances, and he had one framed to hang upon his van at market squares. He also had photographs taken of himself with a few of his willing patients. Polycarp the healer. He lived in a dream of mental therapeutics for months, and forgot that he had once been tired of the itinerant life, and he never ceased to wonder at the power of a few bright clothes and a simple mixture made in hotel bedrooms.

XIV
Polycarp goes from one thing to another very quickly

A medical student's first glimpse of an appendix lying snugly in a stomach may occasion him the elation of some watcher of the skies when a new planet swims into his ken, or it may provoke a disturbance in the student's own stomach—it depends whether the glory of his discovery affects his head or his appetite. The first time he plies his sharp knife through flesh and tissue to remove an appendix may mean more to him than a century at cricket, perfecting the crawl stroke, or falling in love. But, no matter how ardent his enthusiasm, there must come a time when to doctor or student the appendix ceases to be a thing of beauty and a joy for ever, and assumes its real character of an unnecessary, vestigial organ about as much use to man as a whale's legs or a kiwi's wings, and he finds it as boring to take out an appendix as a girl with protruding teeth. Repetition will take the joy from anything. This is an axiom which children find hard to credit as they dream of unlimited supplies of apples, pastries, toys, and penny-dreadfuls. It is only when the child becomes an adult that he discovers that a joy is only a joy because of its very scarcity and infrequency. That is why the world's greatest love-stories concern those who were forced to live apart or to see one another only at fleeting moments. If Dante had lived with his Beatrice, if Paolo had settled down with his Francesca on a farm, if Sigurd had taken his Brunhilde a-viking with him, and if Romeo had lived to see Juliet grow old and develop a slight moustache upon her upper lip—what then? Would their loves have been any more refulgent and renowned than the courtship ardour and marital monotony of any city clerk and shop-assistant, farm labourer and dairymaid, or duke and duchess? The happy men and women are those who dream dreams and see visions, and wisely never change them for realities.

No matter what man does, be it working wonders, reading the future, creating things of beauty, performing miracles or making pressed-steel panels for motor-cars, there comes a time when he tires of his work, and Polycarp found that he was not different from the rest of his fellows.

At the end of a year he was tired of working cures and entertaining the crowds at market squares with his colourful lies, and he was weary of travelling and looked enviously at the comfortable town homes and citizens. He felt as though he were a piece of paper blown here and there, a thing of no stability. And deep in Polycarp's heart there grew a desire for things substantial and lasting. He came to hate brief contacts and passing charms. He wanted to have his joys and hold them to him, to make friends and keep them, not lose them at the dissolution of each day's market.

Polycarp, the wanderer and healer, found that the itch for movement had left him, and he performed his cures and told his tales in a spirit, though not apparent to the crowd, of resentment and reluctance; and to add to his growing dissatisfaction with his itinerant life, he knew that it was not bringing him much nearer to the fame and prominence which formed the mainspring to his actions and thoughts.

So Polycarp ceased to be a miracle-worker, and the markets lost a little of their colour and fulmination with the departure of his coloured robes and booming drum. His departure, though he had contemplated it for some months, was hastened by the Public Health authorities of Gloucester.

A man came up to his stall at that town and asked for a bottle of his Solomon's Glory, paid his shilling, and went away.

"Know who that is?" Bill Brailey asked Polycarp later. Polycarp shook his head. "Someone with an ache, I suppose."

"That's an official from the Public Health Department. They'll probably analyse your stuff. I hope it's genuine. Those coves make a fuss sometimes."

Polycarp was ignorant of the law pertaining to quack medicines, and the knowledge that his mixture was going to be subjected to a public analysis frightened him a little. Was it possible for them to arrest him for selling a harmless liquid and calling it a medicine? He could think of two or three perfectly sound logical reasons to support the efficacy of Solomon's Glory, but he couldn't get away from the hard fact that its composition was more water than anything else. Ignorance is no excuse before the law; he remembered the old saying, and, partly because he wanted to do so, and partly because he did not know what might happen after they had analysed his mixture, he decided to renounce his filial claim upon Solomon's strength and wisdom. Even if he had known that, although the bottle of mixture had been bought by an official from the Health Department, it was for private use, and not for analysis, it is doubtful whether Polycarp would have remained a pedlar. He had exhausted the possibilities, so he thought, and had made enough money from peddling to justify his looking for something more interesting.

He spent the next four years looking for that elusive something, and during those years he changed a little in build, but not a great deal in character.

He learnt much about men, but very little about himself. He went from one small venture to another, from green-grocery store to travelling library, and, if he had more success selling fruit and vegetables than fiction, he consoled himself with the thought that this was inevitable since man dare not deny his stomach for fear of death, but can happily starve his mind and assure himself an entry into a wide circle of companions. He could not hold himself to any one business or venture for many months. He found nothing that captivated his enthusiasm or prompted his imagination to keenness. For a while he considered going abroad—that was in the winter while he owned a newsagent's shop, and, because of the stringency of the local by-laws against the employment of boys under school age, had to deliver his morning papers himself in a small van—but the summer came before he had made up his mind and early rising became a pleasure, and he decided to stay in England. And so the months went by, and Polycarp grew more tolerant and slowly learned that the greatest factor in any man's commercial success was not so much his own ability but the degree of stupidity and cupidity which marked his customers.

Long afterwards when he looked back on that period the details of his ventures were less cogent than the general impression of the people whom he had met. He came to know and love his fellows, to know their weakness and to love their geniality, and he began to appreciate that if the commonest human trait was optimism then the most universal emotion was disappointment—yet he never considered himself to be compounded of the same fallibilities and emotions which marked his customers. He was Polycarp, alone, different and intended for great things. At twenty-seven he was heavier in body, his hair turning a more subdued shade, his eyes still impudent and searching, and his upper lip loyally bearing its hirsute banner. Of his many weaknesses, none had the dignity of being a vice, and a few were still extravagantly puerile. He loved to see his name, Polycarp, in print and painted in big letters, though this was not an ordinary vanity, for he did not care whether other people saw it as long as he was allowed to stand and expand with esoteric satisfaction. Where at twenty-one he had never bothered to define a man's character until he had known him for some weeks, now he found himself an able judge of types, and could tell at once, with some accuracy, whether a man was trying to swindle or deal fairly with him. He was still single and, since the days of Gracie, had very little to do with women beyond a few innocent, transient flirtations with females as widely distributed along the social scale as chambermaids, cashiers, library attendants, teachers, and the daughters of wealthy councillors, but not one of these affairs was of sufficient importance to take a place in this history; a passing kiss in the dark in the life of a man is seldom of more moment than the pile of used razor-blades on top of his toilet cabinet.

His beliefs were mundane but honest; he liked the smell of fired bracken, the taste of an old pipe, the comfort of well-tried shoes, and the feel of a clean linen handkerchief. He thanked God for well-browned beef, for bridges with wide parapets that cushioned his stomach as he watched his reflection in the water, for public libraries and shouting crowds, and for his health which enabled him to enjoy his life. He wrote regularly to his aunt, visited her occasionally, and steadily increased his bank balance.

For three years he went from one venture to another, emerging from each one with a little extra capital and a great deal of new wisdom, but nowhere did he find that stability and domesticity which had begun to burgeon in his mind as an ideal during his pill-peddling days, and nowhere did he find the entrance to the fabled land of fortune. He was just Polycarp Jarvis, one of the millions of workers that make up the British Empire and the stamping crowds at football grounds. Although he wooed fortune with ambition, he was at first no more fortunate than hundreds of other enterprising young men and women who set out to discover cities whose streets are paved with gold and whose shops hand goods across the counter in exchange for courage instead of silver. His ambition could take him so far, but what ambition failed to achieve it was for luck to complete, and, perhaps because of his singleness of purpose or perhaps because of his ridiculous moustache, Polycarp was picked out from the many contestants for fortune. Luck is something which cannot be explained or elided, it just stands as firmly as Nelson upon his monument, a thing of, and yet not of, this earth, and immune from vulgar analysis.

In his search for domesticity and stability, he was frequently disappointed until he metamorphosed himself into the owner (on a mortgage) of the Polycarp Kennels (formerly the Chessvale Dogs' Home) and five acres of land running down to a river, five acres covered partly by tall dock and thistle growths and mostly by forty apple-trees leaning at various angles to the earth. The fruit-trees were tended with whitewash and spray against the ravages of sawfly and grub by an assistant (John Higgins, one-time barman of the Black Cock near Abingdon), who also looked after the dogs and did most of the work while Polycarp exercised his proprietorial instincts by smoking a large-bowled pipe as he strode around the kennels, inspected the orchard and hens, and talked to worried ladies who wanted their Mamma's-only-ones, Did-ums-thens and Poor-dear-snowballs to recuperate from overdoses of proteins at the Polycarp Kennels. In addition to Pekineses and lap-poodles, Polycarp also had dogs under his care— husky Alsatians, noisy, jolly terriers, gentlemanly Irish setters, morose dachshunds, and sheep-dogs like great bears; and, while Higgins tended to their ills and food with more care than many a child receives from its parents, Polycarp looked after their exercise and education.

Their exercise consisted of accompanying him on walks along the valley of the Chess, and their education in listening to his monologues on subjects as remote from one another as Christianity and modern politics.

He had seen the place advertised in the *Daily Telegraph*, and cycling over from High Wycombe, where he had been trying to find domesticity in a Good-Pull-Up-Here-For-Drivers, had decided that the life of a country gentleman with a piece of land and dogs, even if the land and dogs were not strictly his, was better than trying to impress lorry-drivers with the originality of his meals.

The house to which the kennels and land were attached stood on the side of a hill where a narrow, rough road sloped down to the river Chess. It was isolated deep in Hertfordshire, and Polycarp's nearest neighbours were the inhabitants of the village over the crest of the hill on the other side of the valley. At the dip of the valley the road crossed the river, and then lost itself in a twisting lane as it climbed the opposite slope. The roadway marked one boundary of Polycarp's domain. The river, which spread out into a reed pool and little islands where a pair of herons nested in the spring, marked another, and behind him a cornfield that was dark, ploughed earth when he came, marked the third, and a deep, gloomy fir plantation formed the fourth boundary. Inside this rectangle of river, road, corn, and conifer, Polycarp lived happily with his man Higgins, other people's dogs, and his fruit-trees and hens. He was very poor, for most of his capital had been sunk in the mortgage, but he and Higgins managed to make enough from the dogs for them to waste on the trees and hens and still leave enough over for food and clothes, which, if one is a philosopher, is all that man is justified in asking from life—food, clothes, and a little money to waste upon hens and fruit-trees. And it was here in the valley of the Chess, one July afternoon when the wood-pigeons were sweetening the air with their love-songs and the trout rose lazily to the ebony-topped stream to take the dancing flies, that Polycarp came again under the direct patronage of fortune. He had been happy with his dogs and hens for over a year when life and fortune came to him again—came to turn him out of his peaceful corner to find the turmoil and the glitter of the streets instead of the solitude and peace of the country. And it all began with a naked man.

XV
Polycarp meets a successful man

Tim, Pedro, and Polycarp were walking up the river valley, dividing their thoughts between moorhens, the stupidity of men, and the possible impermanence of the talking film.

Tim, an excitable fox-terrier who had lived most of his life in the West End with no more than brief sights of the moorhens in Kensington Gardens, had forsaken the path alongside the stream and was ploughing his way through the fringe of green flags, routing out the nesting birds and barking at them as they steamed across the river with a piping flotilla of fluffy chicks trailing behind them. Sometimes Tim stopped barking, came on to the bank and standing before Polycarp, waggled his whole body and looked up with his brown eyes to see if his work was being properly appreciated. At such moments Polycarp interrupted his speculations and rewarded Tim with a smack on the rump that sent him flying into the rushes to carry on his noisy work with splashing, muddy energy.

Pedro stalked sedately behind Polycarp as became a Great Dane of royal blood, and brooded upon the infidelity of a master who, because he chose to take an unorthodox holiday on a tramp steamer bound for the West Indies, imagined that he had to leave his dog behind. Pedro was quite capable of looking after himself upon a tramp steamer and keeping out of the way when necessary, but his master had not thought so and Pedro was taking a holiday with Polycarp.

And Polycarp, who had taken a day off and gone into London to see the wonder of the new invention which was to revolutionise the entertainment world, was trying to foresee the effects which the new invention would have upon the existing forms of entertainment.

So the three of them made their way along the river bank, splashing and barking, brooding and stalking, wondering and smoking, and on their left the river sparkled and jumped over its gravelly bed. The air was bright with the sheen of passing wings; from the quick iridescence of the dragon-flies that hovered for a second close to the water and then darted faster than the eye could follow to the dripping shadow of leaning willows to seize the dancing midges, to the sudden curve and flicker where butterflies crossed the river to settle on the meadowsweet that hid the grass on the far side of the valley—blue wings, white wings, red. wings, wings that shivered the sunlight with peacock colours and wings that carried white-rimmed, staring eyes—and dipping after the butterflies came the birds. Swallows skimmed along the stream, tracing their blue-and-white reflections on the water and punctuating their flight with widening full stops where they flicked the water with the tips of their wings; reed-warblers and martins performed little acrobatics and tumbles in the air where they banked and turned to catch at flying insects; a heron, disturbed by the barking of the dog, got up from a patch of flowering reed and went lazily with long, trailing legs away across the tops of the willows and chestnuts to lose himself in the blue distance, where long plantations of fir and spruce stretched down to the river, and from the middle of a green-mossed plank across the stream a robin sang, strutting like a red-robed tenor in opera until the passing shadow of a raven's wing frightened him into the shelter of a clump of white nettles.

Summer had brightened everything to high colour. In the water-meadows the grass was laid with pale, purple cups of marshmallows and decorated with trails of trefoils and convolvulus. Tall magenta spikes of willowherb stood guard beside the frightened blue-eyed speedwells, and purple-decked thistles ringed themselves around the thyme-banked mounds of old molehills, fronting the black-tipped, hardy plantains as though they were defiant savages, spear-brandishing men of Cassivellaunus defending some hill-fortress against the onslaught of Caesar's legions. The meadows were yellow with buttercup, dandelion, and trefoil, blue with speedwell, scabious, and catmint, red with pimpernel and tall sorrel, and white with daisy and bladder campions, and the colours splashed over into the river, invading it with the purple and gold of irises and the soft white of lilies and water bedstraws. The colour bathed itself in the river, changing to leaping browns and quick spurts of silver and the dark wavering green of moss-covered stones. It moved in the wake of wandering trout as they tossed the water from their straining fins. It rippled in dappled reflections up the sides of ash and birch and lost itself in the mystery of summer green, where the leaves talked to one another in the breeze and whispered the secrets of the birds which nested in their arms. It ran up the valley-sides in dark clefts of fir and tall spires of elm and beech, and painted the sides of copse and farm with bold patches of ivy and briar-rose. It stippled the hedges with the faint flowers of nightshade and bryony and livened the dead grey of walls with kidney vetch and toadflax. The country was blazoned with a prodigality of colour that changed as one looked at it, a colour that recognised no proscribed territory but invaded cornfields with its poppy hues and rioted through gardens with the quick fertility of hawkweed and shepherd's purse.

And along the valley went Polycarp with his dogs, following the twisting course of the stream as it widened to gravel shallows, where minnows and gudgeon played and forgot the lurking pike, past dark pools that hid fallen treetrunks which rotted quietly and gave shade to cannibal trout and fat roach, by long, steady reaches where the caddis grub was busy decking himself with the finery of the stream bottom, pausing to watch the water frolic over small lashers as it purified itself by flight through the air from one level to another, and through the dark maws of woods where the water ran black and subdued with the silence of the sentinel trees, a silence that not even the slow call of the wood-doves could lighten. The river looped and turned, first to one side of the valley and then to the other, sometimes running straightly for a while, skirting low willow-beds or circling islands of tangled briars and silver-trunked birch, and occasionally disappearing under the low arches of little stone bridges that showed crescents of bright daylight when Polycarp stooped and looked into their gloom.

And as Polycarp came round the edge of one of the many islands of briar and birch he met the naked man.

Tim was aware of him first. He barked sharply and jumped on to the pathway. Polycarp looked up and was in time to see a white figure jump from the river-bank, where it had been standing by the side of an elderberry-tree, into the river. The figure vanished with a mighty splash and then, as Polycarp, his feelings alternating between alarm, curiosity, and reticence, was about to step back, a head emerged cautiously from the water; a head which, being definitely male, assuaged one of Polycarp's fears. It was bald, with little hairy side-wings that relieved the monotony of the baldness above the ears, and the eyes below the wet whiteness were round and staring. If the head had been adorned with a pair of white whiskers, long and quivering, Polycarp mused, anyone might have been justified in mistaking it for that of an albino seal of prodigious size. Beneath the head a white body, grotesquely distorted by the wavering water, faded into the depths.

Polycarp stood and looked, wondering what he should do or say. His dilemma was solved for him. From beneath the water the man's hand appeared holding a pair of horn-rimmed spectacles, and he adjusted them on his face.

"What a shock you gave me," he said, fiddling with his spectacles. "I thought you were a woman for the moment."

"I thought that about you," said Polycarp as the nude figure stretched up a hand to be helped from the water. He came out, scattering a shower of drops and grunting like a grampus.

"Thank you."

"Come away, Tim!" Polycarp drove off the terrier, which was sniffing round the man's heels. "He won't hurt. He's just curious, like Pedro and I, though we're too well bred to show it. You're shivering; why don't you put your clothes on before you catch a cold?"

"I know that, young man, I know that! You don't have to tell Joseph K. Winterton when he's shivering. But I shall have to go on shivering. I haven't any clothes to put on."

"No clothes!" Polycarp was amazed, and beneath his amazement a little amused and sympathetic. "You're not one of those nudists, are you?"

"Nudist? Nonsense, young man, nonsense! Of course not! I'm Joseph K. Winterton, not a nudist. Young man, you're fortunate; you're probably the only person who's ever seen me completely harmless and helpless, a prey to any wild beast. You don't seem to be very impressed?"

"I am, very. But you can't stand there like Adam, giving me your pedigree while you catch a cold. If you care to try the experiment, you could borrow my trousers and shirt and I could manage with drawers and a jacket until we get to my place—"

"Why, that's very good of you—very good. I can see you're a gentleman. I shouldn't be in this fix, of course, if it were not for—"

"Don't bother about that at the moment. Here, get into these." Polycarp took off his trousers and shirt and handed them to Mr. Winterton. He hesitated for a moment, but, as Polycarp nodded, he began to wipe his body on the shirt and then with masculine wisdom donned the wringing wet shirt over his dry body, satisfied that he had done the right thing.

"I'm surprised at your not knowing my name, young man, very surprised. And glad in a way. It's nice to meet someone who isn't impressed by my good self. Are you sure you can spare these things?"

"Absolutely. You must come back with me and get some warm dry clothes, otherwise you'll be catching some complaint. Come along. We look like something from a comic film—if you'll pardon the liberty."

"Not at all, young man, not at all. 'Always look on the bright side of things' is one of my mottoes. It's very kind of you to do this for me."

Pedro eyed the pair with gentle disapproval. His normal world was not peopled by half-dressed madmen, and he resented having to spend his time in the company of those who imagined that a pair of grey trousers and a wet cricket-shirt, or drawers and a sports jacket, constituted correct sartorial adornment. Tim, however, had no scruples. He danced around Mr. Winterton on his hind legs and shoved his cold, button nose into his face as he bent to turn up the legs of the trousers, which were too long for him.

"Even the animals revel in my misfortune," moaned Mr. Winterton. "If you would be kind enough to lead me to the nearest house, I should be grateful to you."

"The nearest habitation is the Polycarp Kennels, of which I am the proprietor. Polycarp Jarvis is my name. You don't seem to have heard of me? The name is synonymous with dogs, though at one time it was synonymous with aeroplanes, then with the greatest aphrodisiac of the times ... Still, I won't bore you with details. Come along, and look out for the thistles as you walk, otherwise you'll be having sore feet before we get there."

"I'm coming. I'm coming. And now I realise that good Queen Elizabeth wasn't half harsh enough when she started to make laws about vagrants ... "

They started back towards the kennels and Mr. Winterton began to recount to Polycarp the facts which accounted for his present denuded condition.

Joseph K. Winterton was a very rich man, and he had jockeyed his way to wealth upon the backs of men and women of ability and genius. He was not a parasite, nor an idle investor of the armchair type; he was a promoter. He had been promoting all his life from those early days when he had laid the foundations of his rich career by promoting enough bad feeling between schoolmates to make them fight, while he laid penny bets with other boys and then framed the fight by bribing the contestants. His profits on such deals had ranged from as little as threepence to as much as three shillings, and after he had left school his money-making genius had gradually earned him greater profits, though he had never again employed such directly illegal methods as bribery. In fact, as his position became more and more assured, he even stopped employing the sharp business methods which are the legal weapons of all men who have long forgotten that the original function of money was as a means of exchange. In nineteen hundred and twenty-nine Joseph K. Winterton was not only a familiar name to the great British public, but the spirit and controlling motive behind a great deal of their entertainment, and also one of the many well-dressed bulwarks of England's commercial prosperity. He was, as we have seen, a little, bald-headed man with bulgy eyes that hid themselves behind horn-rimmed glasses; also he was a shrewd-headed financier with a gift for divination in the matter of the fluctuations of stocks, and a promoter with a pretty eye for the monetary potentialities of prize-fighters and playwrights. He had an unobtrusive hand in most things which happened in London and drew a crowd of more than a thousand. He was the spirit behind the lean greyhounds which circled under glaring arc-lights, and from him indirectly emanated the noise of motor-cycles as they shovelled their cindery way round dirt-tracks. He inspired the punch that sent heavy-weight champions to dream of Irish homesteads as they lay quietly upon canvas; his spirit danced behind the chorus-girls on more than one theatre stage and was wrapped about the tension of many a second-act climax. He was Joseph K. Winterton, one of those men to whom Fate gives the option of figuring either in the Honours List or the Police Gazette and who surprises Fate, when the time comes, by deciding, quite rightly, that a knighthood is the wrong kind of publicity and prefers to remain a commoner. That was his public figure. Privately he was a generous little man with a weakness for cigars made from leaf grown upon his own plantation in Havana, and with a profound admiration for women, an admiration which he had never endangered by committing the major folly of matrimony. How he came to be naked in the valley of the Chess on this particular July day is not a long or complicated story. He had arisen from his bed in his Kensington house and discovered the whole of London heat-bound by its hot streets, with only chirping sparrows and drooping plane-trees to make summer. He had stood at the window and thought of hot days when, as a boy, he had sun-bathed in Cornish coves reached by cycling from his Truro home. He had decided to sun-bathe, and his chauffeur had, because Mr. Winterton could not afford the time to go to Cornwall and because he shrank from displaying his pandiculated stomach at a public lido, brought him to the quiet valley and left him.

Joseph K. Winterton had decided that he would be independent of a liveried chauffeur and a Daimler for one day, and he had dismissed the car with the intention, when he had finished sun-bathing, of walking to the nearest railway station and finding his own way home. He had picked his bathing-spot with careful regard for the softness of the grass and, after taking off his clothes, stretched himself out in the sun with his middle covered from the sight of bird, man, and wood-sprites by a large silk handkerchief, and, with his horn-rimmed face staring at the clouds, he had slept until the removal of the large handkerchief by a predatory tramp, who saw no reason why he should not steal it as well as the outfit of clothes, had aroused him some few seconds after the tramp had forced his way through a gap in the hedge at the other end of the field. Joseph K. Winterton had not pursued the man—he was always quick to perceive the futile—but had crouched by the side of the elderberry-tree, swinging his glasses in one hand, and wondering what on earth he should do. He had still been wondering and crouching, like a startled obese satyr, when Polycarp had come along and sent him jumping into the river.

"So now you know," he said, finishing his explanation to Polycarp as they neared the kennels, "how I came to be without any clothes."

"Some of my hens disappear like that. Still, we mustn't be too hard on these acquisitive wanderers. One animal preys upon another, and man does the same. The weak go to the wall. Life today, despite all our inventions and laws, is just as primitive in conception and practice as it was when this valley was filled with fighting Romans and hairy Britons."

"Nevertheless, I insist that Queen Elizabeth wasn't hard enough on vagrants."

"Maybe you're right. I haven't studied her much. The nearest I've ever been to royalty is a little King Charles spaniel we've got here—a dissolute dog, unless I'm mistaken."

They approached the kennels and, as Polycarp pushed open the gateway leading into the yard which was lined with the dog cages, Higgins came out of the food-store.

"Higgins, take Pedro and Tim, please. And is there any of that cold ham left? You see"—he turned to Mr. Winterton—"we look after ourselves except on Wednesdays, and then a woman comes in and gets a meal for us. Wednesday is our gala day—for the rest of the week we live on eggs, when the hens feel like it, and ham when there is any. Come inside and dry yourself off by the fire—that's another thing we have to do here. Keep the fire on all the year round for cooking. Never let it out, in fact—saves the trouble of lighting it and the cost of wood to kindle it each morning. Great thing, being domesticated. I've introduced a few new ideas since I've been trying it."

" 'Tis beer and cheese you'll have to have, sir. The 'am went funny this mornin', so I fed it to the dogs. You seem to have got yourself in a tidy mess-up, sir."

"Tidy mess-up is one way of describing it, Higgins. Take the dogs away, will you, and then you know that navy-blue suit you wear when there's a fair at Berkhamsted?"

"Yes, sir? That suit's seen—"

"Never mind what it's seen," Polycarp interrupted the craggy-faced, short-bodied Higgins, "bring it down for my friend, Mr. Winterton.

He wants to borrow it for a day, and you might see if you've got a pair of shoes and the other things that go with a suit. My stuff's too big for him."

"I'll be pleased to do it, sir. You'll look fine in the suit, sir, though 'tis a bit tight in the seat, if I was to speak the truth."

Higgins was, in fact, almost as big a man as Mr. Winterton, but where one's girth came from rich food and little exercise, the other's was the result of plain food and much exercise.

"Good. If I do burst at the seams, I'll see that you don't have to go to the next fair looking shabby," said Mr. Winterton. "And if there are any camphor balls in the pockets, for heaven's sake remove 'em."

"You'll find no camphor balls, sir. Ever since I ate one in mistake for a peppermint, I've used packets of lavender. Here, Pedro, Tim— come up!"

Higgins disappeared into the kennels and the two went into the house. It was not a large house, for most of the ground space was occupied by the outhouses and kennels. There was a large living-room with an open fireplace that took up one wall. The room stretched the whole length of the house and was furnished with a battered refectory table, one large armchair, four Yorkshire ladderback chairs, a sideboard beaconed with bottles, catalogues, fruit-bowls and things which could not find a home on table, mantelshelf, or floor. The top floor consisted of two bedrooms, a bathroom, and a lumber-room. The kitchen and cooking-room were contained in a small outhouse attached to the rear of the house and communicating with the long living-room by hatch. When a meal was prepared, Higgins stood on one side of the hatch and Polycarp on the other, and they used the flat of the hatch as a table, Polycarp making himself responsible for the food and utensils needed from the living-room and Higgins playing a similar part with regard to the articles in the kitchen. If Polycarp wanted to go into the kitchen, he had to go out through the back door and walk around the side of the house, an oddity which soon lost its fascination. Here in this manly home Polycarp and Higgins lived very happily with their dogs and dreams.

In honour of the occasion Polycarp bestirred himself and made an effort at laying a cloth on the end of the table nearer the fire, and here the two sat, eating thick hunks of cheese and new bread, and washing it down with beer. There were only two small bottles in the house, and, as they were very thirsty, Higgins, after being shouted to through the hatch, handed in a brown pitcher full of water.

"This," said Mr. Winterton, stretching his legs cautiously inside Higgins's trousers, "has been a quite exceptional day for me."

"And for me," said Polycarp, who was delighted to have someone to whom he could talk. "I've sunk so deeply into my rustic life that at times I almost forget there's a world outside this. Nothing like domesticity, nothing in the world. A fireplace and a roof over you—that's the secret dream of every wanderer. I ought to know, because I was one for years. Have a cigarette?" He handed Mr. Winterton his case.

"Thank you. Damn that tramp!" Mr. Winterton started up suddenly as a thought entered his mind. "He's gone off with ten of my best cigars—I can spare those less than the clothes!"

"Calm, now, calm—think of the joy he'll get. A good cigar'll compensate perhaps for the hardships of his life. I don't think I should mind being robbed by a tramp—I feel that the fact that I knew he had a greater need than me would soften the pain—but it's when some rich swindler does you in that the rub comes. Ever come across a rich swindler?"

"Plenty. Some people call me one, but that's their mistake. I don't swindle; I earn my money! This is a comfortable place you've got here. Restful—"

"That's it, Mr. Winterton. Restful, peaceful, secluded, and calm. And it's what I dreamt about for years—at least, for some time. You see, I had a drifting life, and it began to get me down, so I decided upon domesticity instead of dreaming wild dreams. Did you ever dream wild dreams of fame and fortune? I suppose it's a weakness peculiar to the young. When you get old you appreciate the material comforts of domesticity."

"How old are you?" Mr. Winterton turned in his seat and looked at Polycarp with a half-smile about his lips.

"Twenty-seven. A responsible age, Mr. Winterton. At my age some men are just beginning to do things, but I've done 'em all and the only thing left for me is a quiet tranquillity. Here, in this valley, I shall finish my days, alone with Higgins, the dogs, and my mortgage. What do you think of that board—nice lettering, eh? Designed it myself." Polycarp pointed through the window to the board which stood at the foot of the garden, facing the roadway. "Polycarp's Kennels—I always like to see words in Roman capitals; gold letters on a green background, nicely proportioned. Proportion and balance are everything in art, you know. I knew an architect once—in partnership with him for a while—and he used to say that no building could be ugly that was correctly proportioned, and the same applies to lettering, I think."

"And is that really your name—Polycarp?"

"It is, and in its way it's been pretty well known at times. If I hadn't seen the folly of ambition and a vulgar seeking after publicity and fame, I might never have known the peace of this valley. I shouldn't have had any private life. You say you're a big man in London—financier, eh? Well, you know what that means, I guess?" Polycarp eyed Mr. Winterton compassionately, as though he were a rat in a trap.

"I do—there was a time when I couldn't go anywhere without a bunch of reporters hanging around me."

"I daresay I should have been like that. But I stopped myself in time. Are you in a hurry? There's a country bus goes by the door every hour—that'll take you into Watford, where you can get the Metropolitan to London."

"No. Today is a holiday for me. Why?"

"Good. I haven't had anyone to talk to, except Higgins and old women with sick dogs, for months. Got so bored I went up to London and saw some of the new talking pictures the other day. Great future for them, I should say. See that bottle on the mantelshelf "—Polycarp reached up and handed down the bottle of Solomon's Glory which held a place of honour on the shelf—"that stuff nearly wrecked the medical profession once."

"Impossible, my boy, impossible!"

"In this world, all things are possible. Here, I'll bring you photographs and cuttings to prove it." Polycarp jumped from his seat and rummaged in the drawer of the sideboard. Presently he returned to the fireplace with a sheaf of Press cuttings and some photographs.

It was two o'clock in the afternoon when he began to talk about himself and Solomon's Glory, and at ten o'clock Mr. Winterton had to dash down the drive to catch the last bus, and by then Polycarp had given the promoter a pretty comprehensive outline of his life history from the cradle to the kennel stage. In the telling they had become good friends and laughed together at the various setbacks and accidents which had marked Polycarp's career. In fact, once Polycarp had set Mr. Winterton laughing, the little man continued to laugh and chuckle for the rest of the story. After a while Higgins finished his work and, with the true democratic disconcern for social differences which Polycarp always induced, came and sat on the floor, smoking a discoloured cob and occasionally interjecting some remark of disbelief or approval, and kept an anxious eye on the rotund body of Mr. Winterton as it quivered and squirmed within the limitations of a high-cut serge suit which had buried three generations of the Higgins clan.

Higgins disappeared for a while, to return with more provisions, and they had laughed, talked, ate, drank, and smoked while Polycarp lived again at Brinton and Oxford; and when Polycarp grew hoarse, Mr. Winterton livened the company with some of his reminiscences; and when he tired, Higgins came into the breach with a few stories of tap-room extraction and Shakespearean antiquity. By evening, they had dispensed with all formalities and were just three happy men rioting in a sentimental wallow of memory and gossip.

Polycarp and Higgins followed Mr. Winterton down the drive.

"Be careful of the seat of them pants when you bend!" shouted Higgins as the stout promoter climbed into the bus.

"Hold your tongue, sir," cried Mr. Winterton over his shoulder. "Polycarp, chain him up in the kennels, will you? Goodbye! I'll see you again soon!"

"Cheerio—and don't forget you've borrowed five bob from me!" sang out Polycarp. As the bus started off into the purple summer night, the two began to sing reverently and incorrectly

My bonnie's gone over the ocean,
My bonnie's gone over the seeeeeeeea!

A frame of yellow window, with a black head silhouetted against it, sprouted an arm which waved until the bus turned a corner and Mr. Winterton was gone.

"A great fellow, eh, Higgins?" said Polycarp.

"He is—and a well-dressed one at this moment. I hope that seat holds ..."

XVI
Domesticity

A couple of days later a parcel arrived, addressed to the Polycarp Kennels in careful Roman capitals, gold against a green ground. Inside the parcel were a case of choice Havana cigars, a five-shilling piece, Higgins's blue suit and another of the same measurements, and a note saying:

"Here's another suit for your Mr. Higgins. I'm afraid I pulled the other out of shape."

Higgins immediately donned the new suit, and he and Polycarp sat in the garden rivalling the scent of the stocks with their cigars and talking about Mr. Winterton.

"He's a fine gentleman, he is. Look at this grand suit! 'Tis neither tight nor loose and, the Lord be thanked, doesn't grip me in the seat. It would be a fine suit to be buried in …" He blew a cloud of smoke contentedly at the roses. "Yes, he's a great chap, and to think that he's probably a millionaire. Him, a little feller like that, a millionaire! It's not proportionate."

A few days later a Daimler drew up outside the kennels, and Polycarp and Higgins wondered what doggy complaint was coming to them as they listened to the insistent horn. They both walked down the short drive and leaned over the gate.

"Open the gateway and let me in, you heathens!" Smiling at them from behind the wheel was Mr. Winterton. But a very different looking Mr. Winterton from the man they had known. He was dressed in comfortable tweeds and cap, and armed against the world with his own cigars and pocket-book. And this time there was no need for Higgins to walk to the village for beer, or for Polycarp to dignify the end of the table with a cloth and a hunk of cheese, for Mr. Winterton had taken the precaution of bringing a hamper with him. Any other person might have regarded the hamper as an infringement of their friendship and as slight upon the culinary and domestic efficacy of the Polycarp Kennels, but not Polycarp or Higgins; food was food whether it came from Winterton or through their own hatch, and they had no compunction about eating more than their fair share.

"You know, Polycarp," said Mr. Winterton, as the two walked alongside the river after their meal, "I've been thinking about you."

"Oh." Polycarp studied the ash on the end of his cigar carefully.

"Yes, I've been thinking seriously. You know, my boy, with all your experience and talent you're wasting your time in this place. How long have you been here?"

"Let me see—about eighteen months. Not very long, but, I daresay I shall say the same at the end of eighteen years. You see, Joseph Kay, this is what I dreamed about all the time I was on the road. This valley is me now. It's part of me. I know each twist and turn; I know the places where the different birds nest; I know where to find fritillaries in spring—I'll send you a bunch next year, you'll like 'em. And most of all it's peaceful. I don't have to be thinking up new dodges to coin money. I've got Higgins to look after the kennels, and we make enough from that to serve us. I used to think that ambition could only be directed towards the acquisition of wealth, but now"—Polycarp flicked the ash off his cigar reflectively, as though the ash represented wealth to be lightly cast aside—"I realise that the true ambition of man is not to secure wealth, but peace. Peace and a quiet domestic life. Ever studied human ecology?"

"Never heard of it, my boy, never heard of it!"

"I got a book on it from the County Library at the village institute. And all through the history, the economic history of man, you'll find that the underlying motive, although it manifests itself through battles and bloodshed, is for peace and a field to till and cows to milk. I realised that in time. I reckon, Joseph Kay, either you're a man who's big enough to do without this kind of peace and domesticity or you've just missed the turning. That's the tragedy of many lives—

missing the right turning. But not of mine—I turned in time, and here I am for life."

"Nonsense, Polycarp, nonsense. Why, if you would let me help you, I could put you in the way to make a name for yourself. I'm not the kind of man generally to start helping any lame dog—once you begin that you find that you're swamped by people wanting help—but when I see a man with ideas, then I'm ready to do something for him, and with your ability you could get anywhere you wanted to. Don't you realise, my boy, that you've got a flair—from what you've told me and what I've seen—for publicity, and today the man who can get into the headlines is in the way to make big money, as long as he doesn't get into banner type by murdering someone—"

"Even then he can write his life story for the sensational papers," put in Polycarp cynically. It amused him and tickled his vanity to have this important little man telling him what he could be if he wanted to; but Polycarp was not to be led aside easily from his new love of domesticity. He honestly imagined that he would find it easy to live the rest of his life in the valley with his dogs. He saw himself as a modern St. Francis, a new eremite sitting alone by the sun-filled fields, contemplating the joys of passivity as an Indian fakir contemplates his navel, and deploring the world over the ridge of the valley. Ambition and striving were for younger men; he had completely renounced his early vow to find fame and fortune; the people of Bristol, his aunt, his own private vows fell into nothingness alongside his new determination to rusticate and to let his roots grow deep into the steady soil of the valley. He had become a complete apostate within two years, and, what is more remarkable, his craving for peace had lasted longer than any of his previous longings.

"Nonsense my boy, nonsense! Why don't you stick to the point? If you like to sell up here and come to London, you can be my secretary and general sort of publicity man for a while until you begin to get the hang of things, and then something will come along and give you the chance to start for yourself. What do you say?"

"My answer, Joseph Kay, with a few alterations, will be found in the tenth verse of the fourth chapter of St. Matthew. I wanted peace and a simple life and I've got it, and I'm sticking to it for the rest of my life. Listen, Joseph Kay, I've had my share of hard knocks and shuffling around. Once I worked as a local government clerk, and hated it because of the restrictions and petty oppressions and jealousies. Then I left that, seeking for a purer, more decent kind of life, but everything I went into sooner or later went phut. Even the most romantic and exciting jobs had something about them, either they became monotonous or the people associated with me turned out to be scabs. Anyway, I went from one disappointment to another, always hoping that I should find something to satisfy me. I wanted to do big things, to do good in the world if it was only bringing a smile to someone's face by entertaining them, but you wouldn't believe how hard it is to make people smile and go on making 'em smile without getting bored and disappointed with yourself. And at last I discovered the eternal truth, that real happiness lies in a man's own garden. What did Voltaire say?—I believe it was Voltaire—first cultivate your own garden. And that's what I'm doing—"

"If looking after other folks' dogs is the same thing."

"Of course, it is. And I'm fortunate to have discovered that truth so soon. Some men never do! Joseph Kay—compared with you I may be young, very young, but in spirit I'm an old man." The full weight of Polycarp's spiritual senility lined his face, and in his own mind he saw himself, not as a healthy human striding along, enjoying the sun and breeze over his hair, but as a tottering old man, quavering and rickety. When Polycarp played a part he believed in looking the part. Mr. Winterton took no notice of this spiritual infirmity. He lit another cigar and champed the end restlessly.

"Nonsense, Polycarp, nonsense I You're just kidding yourself. I haven't known you very long, but I can read you. You get to be able to read men after a while. Now be sensible. In another twenty years, perhaps, you can begin to think of settling down with your dogs and domesticity, though you probably won't be so foolish then, but now you're young and there's a job waiting for you. Don't you see how selfish you're being by withholding your talent from the world? To live here is selfish. You could come to London with me and in a few years be doing something worth while. Plenty of men are capable of looking after other folks' dogs, but there's a greater work in life for you. Why you might be anything. Be sensible, my boy, be sensible. I've not only taken a fancy to you—perhaps because you were very kind when I was in a damned fix—but I recognise talent when I see it, even if it's only a talent for making yourself known. What do you think would have happened to me as a promoter if I could not recognise talent?"

But Polycarp was not to be persuaded. With all his acumen Mr. Winterton did not realise his initial mistake. The one way to make Polycarp idealise his present existence more than ever was by disparaging it. Polycarp's was a nature which strengthened and developed its loyalty through opposition. If anyone called him a fool, they only convinced him of his supreme sanity.

"No good, Joseph Kay. It's very kind of you, and you mustn't think I don't appreciate your interest. Of course, there's a lot in what you say about being selfish. I suppose men of the calibre and ability of Socrates, Titian, Cellini, and H. G. Wells haven't any right to hide their lights under bushels, but there's always the exception and I'm going to be selfish for once. I like the sound of my dogs, I like the smell of the firs and the dung-heap by the henhouses, and I like the long mornings, and I like being selfish—"

"Nonsense, my boy, nonsense! You just like talking and playing all the parts in a great renunciation drama. First you throw this ecology at me, then the Bible, and now a mixture of Greece, Italy, and modern Utopias, but that doesn't blind me. I'm used to mixing with people who can talk as though they'd swallowed the British Museum and the Kremlin, but the ones that matter most are the quiet chaps in the corner who never interrupt their eating and smoking by talking hot air. You'll get over this phase."

"Never. It isn't a phase!"

"Nonsense, Polycarp, nonsense!"

Often, after that day, Mr. Winterton came down and spent long hours at the kennels with the two. At first he would bring up the subject of Polycarp's future, but after a while he dropped the matter and contented himself with ordinary topics and showed an interest in the dogs and went for walks along the river with Polycarp. Sometimes he brought rods and they spent aimless hours flying for trout, and during these days he told Polycarp something of his life in London and his ventures. As their friendship grew, Polycarp was amazed at the multiplicity of deals and schemes in which the man was involved, and he developed the habit of looking in the paper for Mr. Winterton's name.

And he found, as is so often the way once one becomes interested in a certain topic or person, that it was almost impossible for him to pick up a paper without coming across some mention of Mr. Winterton or Mr. Winterton's schemes. There were times when Polycarp found himself on the verge of envying the prowess and ability of this little man who, with nothing more than his board-school education and a native sharpness, had worked his way from a Truro back street to a house in London where the provision bills were accounted for largely by the food eaten by his many servants. Winterton was the Stock Exchange, the theatre, boxing matches, football grounds, provincial entertainments, and now the talking films … they all owed something to the bald-headed, pop-eyed, good-natured fellow who enjoyed Polycarp's beer and saw nothing unusual in Higgins's sharing their conversation and meals. Polycarp's admiration vacillated, according to his moods, from envy to respect. Winterton seemed the prototype of all that he had once longed to be, less his delight in the sound of his own name. The name Winterton was only mentioned when it was absolutely necessary; at all other times he was the genie and master magus behind the substance of things seen and heard. Polycarp conceived a profound respect for Mr. Winterton, a respect qualified in his own mind with the statement that if he, Polycarp, wished to do so he could probably achieve as much, if not more, only he preferred the peace of his kennels and the quiet country life.

Sometimes Mr. Winterton sent the pair tickets for theatre shows, and they would borrow the ancient two-seater of the landlord of the Ugly Duckling in the village, and go up to London and sit for three hours in a box enjoying the novelty and gaiety of a musical comedy that had its genesis in Mr. Winterton's money, and the next morning Polycarp would find himself just a little out of harmony with kennel life. He would be thinking of the crowd and the lights, the upward drift of cigarette smoke in the foyer, and the constant tinkle of voices and laughter, and his mind would slip back to the days when he and Frank had held a crowd gaping, and to the times when the son of Solomon had startled crowds with his drum and robes … The feeling would wear off, and he would be as stout as ever in his protestations to Mr. Winterton of the delights of domesticity. But the tickets still came, and they never refused them, because, so

Polycarp argued to himself, Higgins took a low pleasure in dancing legs and vulgar songs.

"I wonder what me old mother in Abingdon would say if she could see me watchin' this parade of the Devil," he would say, with a satisfied chuckle.

Perhaps Mr. Winterton had realised his primary error in approaching Polycarp so directly; anyhow, he continued to send the tickets, and, although Polycarp was unaware of it, the little man knew, or guessed, of the effect upon him. He had taken a quick, inexplicable almost, liking to Polycarp and, what was more cogent in view of his private boast that what he wanted he got, he had determined that he would start Polycarp on the road to something big and important. Time was a minor element, he could wait, but in the end he would bring his desires to fruition—and Mr. Winterton was not to be disappointed.

One day in September two tickets arrived for a boxing match at Wembley Stadium. Polycarp sat beside the wriggling Higgins and watched two heavyweights punch one another fraternally until one had the misfortune to cut the other's eye open, and then they fought like wild men until the ring was an animated butcher's shop and the air reeked with the smell of leather and perspiration. When the fight was over, Mr. Winterton took the two out to supper with him, and, although the evening slipped by him in a pleasant blur of food, wine, and laughter, the next morning Polycarp remembered every detail with a clarity which hurt. He walked up the dying valley, where the leaves were tinged with the coming of autumn, and for once found that he was not drawing the same joy from the scene. He looked at it and saw, instead of the burnished trees and rippling stream, the barrenness and black trunks and sky-etched branches that would be with him in another three months. It would be winter, and the valley would be shrouded in the grey mourning of summer's passing. He arrived back at the kennels in time to answer the telephone-bell which was ringing.

It was Mr. Winterton speaking. He soon made it clear why he had telephoned.

"Have you got any money, Polycarp?"

"Money!" Polycarp did not understand.

"Yes, you know, the stuff the banks hand out. How much loose money have you got?"

"In hard cash, at the moment," said Polycarp, wondering what the joke was, "I think Higgins and I could manage about three and ninepence. You see, we paid the grocer this morning and we're very low."

"What about the bank? Haven't you got anything there? You know, capital."

"But what's the idea?"

"Never mind—have you got any?"

"I daresay I could rake up about three hundred, but that's all I've got to run the place on and meet my various expenses."

"Forget the expenses, Polycarp, and send me a cheque for as much as you can spare. Don't begin to give me a lecture on the gold standard or metallic systems. Send it, and I promise that you'll never regret it. And, when Winterton promises, that means something. Will you?"

"All right, Joseph Kay, but—" Polycarp pulled at his moustache.

"But nothing, you old hermit! Give my respects to Mr. Higgins and his mother, and don't forget to send that cheque right away."

Polycarp sent the cheque. He had enough confidence in Winterton to know that he was unlikely to lose his money. Then he settled back into the peace of his domestic existence and forgot London and prize-fights in the quicker, more insistent troubles of dog-fights and nursing ailing hens.

A month passed, and the only sign from Mr. Winterton was a pair of tickets for a new show. The two went, and, although they did not see Mr. Winterton, Polycarp refused to drive home through the stormy night and the two, after wandering about streets and sampling three restaurants and a dance hall, finished up at a cheap hotel near the British Museum. They drove back in the bright morning, and when they reached the kennels they found Mr. Winterton feeding the dogs, which were ravenous from their long fast.

"Fine business men, you are!" he called. "What's the good of running kennels and starving the dogs? That's not the way to go along. Where've you been? I've been here since eight."

"We spent the night in London, Mr. Winterton. And a fine bath I had this morning, though I had to run down the corridor in me shirt to it for fear them girls would see me."

"What's all this about baths and girls?"

"It's all right. Higgins hasn't been satisfying his libido. We stopped the night in London after the show. Too tired to drive home."

"Ah, tired, eh?" said Mr. Winterton, and he eyed Polycarp curiously. "Well I've got some news that'll cheer you up. Here, Higgins, there's a poodle in there won't look at dog biscuits—you'd better see to him. Come inside, Polycarp, I want to talk to you."

"What's all the mystery?" asked Polycarp, when they were inside the house.

"This. You know the three hundred you sent me?"

"Yes. What have you done—lost it or made a donation to the Dumb Friends' League?"

"No, here it is." He handed a cheque to Polycarp, and watched his face as he took it.

"Thanks," said Polycarp, and he started to fold it without looking at it. "Glad to have been able to help you—"

"Nonsense, Polycarp, nonsense! Look at it." Polycarp opened the cheque out, and saw that it was made out for fifteen hundred pounds.

"What the—?"

"Quite right—what the! There you are, my boy, there you are! That's how Joseph K. Winterton does things. Changes three hundred into fifteen hundred within a month—though usually it takes a bit longer than that, but this was an exceptional deal."

"Are you trying to tell me that my three hundred has become fifteen within a month through some financial business in London?"

"I am. And an honest financial transaction, too. Just a question of foresight and knowing your markets. Things happen like that in London."

"If you say so, I suppose they do. I'm very grateful to you, Joseph Kay. This'll come in handy. We were getting pretty low with dog biscuits, but we can afford a new sack now. By Jove!" Polycarp began to realise just what had happened. "You know, you're pretty smart to be able to do that—"

"Nonsense, Polycarp, nonsense! You could do the same. Makes your domesticity look small, doesn't it, eh?"

"It certainly does, but I'll bet that money means distress and want somewhere. It's been wrung from someone, you know. You can't get away from that. Economic sadism—"

"Ah, there you go. Listen, Polycarp. Why don't you come along with me and give it a trial? If you don't like it, you could always come back here. You can leave Higgins in charge for a time. I'll pay you a good salary, and while you're with me I'll guarantee that you get enough knowledge and opportunity to treble that amount in your hand within a year, and as soon as you see something worth while you can fire off on your own. Why I take all this trouble to persuade you, I don't know. It shows that I think you're worth it. What do you say? Are you going to stick to domesticity all your life?"

They stood in the window-place looking at one another; Polycarp in a dark grey suit which had rubbed a dirty line against his white collar, his light hair in its usual state of semi-tidiness, and his face frowning as he tapped his teeth with the edge of the cheque, and Mr. Winterton, an anxious, almost pleading figure, his bald head lying like the north pole cap just below Polycarp's eyes, and his two bottom waistcoat buttons undone to give him greater ease.

Polycarp was faced again with the old question, but now his determination had lost some of its dogmatism. He looked at Mr. Winterton tenderly; the fellow obviously wanted to do something for him, wanted to help him, otherwise he wouldn't be holding in his hand a cheque for fifteen hundred. Fifteen hundred—he had never owned so much money in his life. It was a fortune. With fifteen hundred a man could begin to do things. If he remained in his state of rusticity the money would not help him much, he would only use it in improvements which would detract from the charm of the kennels, but outside, in the world which knew Mr. Winterton, fifteen hundred could open up many doors. Then he thought of his ideal of continual peace and it had somehow lost part of its potency. The crest of his enthusiasm for domesticity had coincided with summer, and the benign influence of hot, lazy days had vitalised his enthusiasm until it had seemed that he could never lose his passion for peace. Now, however, the valley was preparing for winter. It would be cold and ... After all, Mr. Winterton had been very decent to him, and the least he could do was to give the suggestion a trial. He knew, he told himself firmly, that in the end it would be proven that domesticity was the only thing for him. He knew that within six months he would be longing for the peace of the kennels, yet if it would satisfy

Mr. Winterton's desire if he went with him, then he was not the kind of person to spoil anyone's happiness. He would go with him for a while to please him, and, when the truth of his contention that peace and a country life were the better was clear, he would return to the kennels and to Higgins, and neither he nor Mr. Winterton would feel disappointed. It was very likely that all that Mr. Winterton said about him was correct—in fact Polycarp himself was sure it was correct—and he might do big things, but he told himself reassuringly that, underneath it all, he would always be ready to sacrifice that life for the one he had been living so peacefully for the last eighteen months and more.

"What do you say?" Mr. Winterton asked.

Polycarp nodded, and put his hand with a dramatic gesture on the other's shoulder : "To please you, Joseph Kay, I'll give it a trial just to prove to you that I'm right. In six months I shall still feel the same as I do now about this place. It's worked its way into my soul and has become part of me, so that I can never love anything else or any other life but this."

"Nonsense, my boy, nonsense! How many men have said that about a wife, and, when she died, married again? But never mind that. You'll come with me. Ah, very sensible. I'm glad you have made up your mind. You'll never regret it, I can promise you. Why I almost wish I were in your shoes—going to start again ... You and your hermit ideas! Higgins! Where's Higgins? We'll get some beer and celebrate your new life." Mr. Winterton bustled round excitedly.

"This is no time for merriment and celebration, but rather for sorrowing and dejection," said Polycarp gloomily; and, "Higgins," he added, turning to the kennelman, "don't forget to take our empty beer bottles back at the same time and get the money on them. We mustn't let our jubilation get the better of our commercial instincts."

That evening they piled the fire high with logs, and sat round the fire drinking and smoking and discussing their plans. Higgins was, after some difficulty and a deal of beer, persuaded that he was quite capable of managing the Polycarp Kennels, and when his protests had transmuted themselves into avowals of the wonders he would work with dogs, Mr. Winterton outlined to Polycarp what his new duties would be.

"I'll pay you a thousand a year to begin with, and raise it as you prove your worth—"

"Gracious, listen to him! A thousand a year! It's not possible!"

"Higgins, don't show your plebeian upbringing by doubting such things." Polycarp reprimanded him. "I'll admit it's an indecent sum for any man to earn while some poor devils have to be content with thirty bob a week and the risk of death from falling coal, but—take what the gods send, I say. It won't be for long."

"That's true, Polycarp, it won't be for long. You'll be going off and making your thousands a year soon."

"You mistake me, Joseph Kay. I shall be going off—but to return thankfully to this quiet spot, this jewel, this ..."

"Heaven save us! Why did they never teach you to talk naturally?"

"Don't be silly, Joseph Kay, there's no such thing as naturalness in this life—"

"If you'd watched the dogs in the kennels closely, you wouldn't say that, sir," put in Higgins.

"Don't," said Polycarp, with severity, "be biological, Hi ggins!"

That was the last night Polycarp spent at the kennels, for the next day Mr. Winterton took him off to London to a new life.

XVII
Polycarp meets an actress
and is taken for a ride

For six months Polycarp lived at Kensington with Mr. Winterton and worked for him. Polycarp never called it work. It was more of a game to him—an exciting, fast-moving game. He became Mr. Winterton's general liaison officer with the Press and the public. He made himself known in Fleet Street, and, when the time came, saw that the papers were supplied with publicity stories to back any new venture of Mr. Winterton's.

He bought drinks for the reporters and men who mattered. He told them funny stories, and, while they laughed, managed to get what he wanted from them. He helped to sponsor the appearance of new plays, new stars, new boxing wonders, and new stadiums. He revelled in his ability to create public interest through the Press, and, when he could not find a genuinely interesting story to herald Miss Lydia Fingle's opening night in the *Rococo Rose*, he told a lie that was original and good for a column and nearly wrecked Miss Fingle's reputation—though the story did its work well.

At first he had not quite understood what Mr. Winterton wanted of him, but when he realised that he had a free hand to invent and carry out what schemes he liked—with certain provisos—Polycarp was as happy as a puppy with a carpet-slipper.

It was from him came the story that a new dog-racing track, financed by Mr. Winterton, had been erected over the exact site of a Roman arena used by the legions of Claudius, and that at night those with any psychic powers could see the ghostly chariots racing round the track cheek by jowl with the leaping greyhounds. Posters had invited the whole of London to come to the track and combine an evening's pleasure with a test of their spiritualistic receptibility. Crowds had accepted the invitation and paid their shillings; spook photographs were taken, women fainted, and one man, persisting that he had been injured by a protoplasmic chariot, claimed damages. So great was the interest created that the place was packed and the greyhound-racing was treated as a subsidiary amusement. A few sporting psychics wanted to lay bets with bookmakers on the racing chariots; but gradually the story was allowed to die out in the interests of earthly business and the breeding of greyhounds.

It was Polycarp who discovered, after a hint from Mr. Winterton, the Skinny Wonder of Willesden, and helped by his publicity methods to make him the heavyweight champion of England, a title which he held for three weeks and then disappeared to Australia with a Lyons' tea-shop waitress. Polycarp wrote the Wonder's life for the papers before the big fight which gave him the championship. In an interview he discovered that the Skinny Wonder's life had been about as interesting as the Tottenham Court Road on a foggy day, so he invented a new life for the man. The Skinny Wonder never really recovered from the trials and adventures with which Polycarp adorned his past, and Mr. Winterton always swore that it was the past which Polycarp foisted upon him that had sent him seeking matrimonial joys and seclusion in Australia.

Polycarp acted as an advance guard for people who wanted to see Mr. Winterton. He learned to tell at a glance whether a man was a crank or had genuine practical, commercial ideas. The cranks were generally well-dressed. He learned the arts of war and peace; he could be angry and indignant at imagined insult, and would threaten until rewarded by a capitulation, and he could woo an actress to Mr. Winterton's ideas like a diplomat. He knew how to make people go when they were not wanted, and he learned how to dress correctly and comport himself in this new world without appearing awkward or distressed. He learned even quicker than Mr. Winterton had thought possible, and after the second month in London he forgot his dreams of domesticity and found himself at times just a little annoyed that, while he could create so much publicity, the name of Polycarp never once appeared in print. It seemed to him that he was spending his life putting other people's names in the headlines, and, at times, this irked Polycarp. He consoled himself by thinking of his increasing capital, for he invested his money as Mr. Winterton advised, and Mr. Winterton seldom advised anything which was not profitable.

"What do you say about domesticity and kennels, now?" Mr. Winterton asked him one morning at breakfast, smiling over his paper.

"Ah—it's a comforting thing to realise that it's all there, waiting for me whenever I wish to go back. Still, I'll be honest with you. I think my enthusiasm for this job will last just a little longer. The only things I don't like are the rather tall stories I have to pull at times. Truth, Joseph Kay, would be a homeless child in London—"

"It would have plenty of company then."

"To have companionship is no comfort when you're an outcast. Do you know, I was reading a book yesterday which stated that half the population of the world's capitals was drawn from the criminal, destitute, and semi-destitute classes, and that—"

"What time does this lecture end?—I'll come back then!"

Polycarp shook his head sadly. "Ah, Joseph Kay, you're a clever man, but you don't read enough. Know what Francis Bacon said about reading? Never mind, you wouldn't believe it."

Occasionally Polycarp visited Higgins at the kennels, and his only joy then was to stare at the green and gold-lettered board and dream. As his duties and friends in London increased, he found himself with less and less time to spare for the kennels.

How long Polycarp might have remained under Mr. Winterton's wing, waiting for something to turn up, would be sheer conjecture had it not been for the peculiar commutations and perplexities that surrounded the lives of Peggy North and Lord Depping. Both of them had their difficulties, their triumphs, and their secrets, and both of them came swinging along their human orbits and crossed Polycarp's path at propitious moments.

There is something grand, and occasionally terrifying, about the chance which sends people to one another and arranges meetings which produce results sometimes magnificent and sometimes insignificant. It is as though the whole mass of humanity lay like currants in a bowl, and was moved occasionally by the stirring from a stick wielded by some unseen cook who only stops stirring to admire the changing patterns. It was one of these social stirrings which brought Peggy North to Polycarp.

Peggy North—although she was a very famous actress—was actually her real name, though there were few people in Portsmouth who could readily believe that the woman so famous from her part in the play *Dead Men Rise Again* was really Peggy North of Portsmouth, whose father had sold penny glasses of sarsaparilla outside the railway station until her mother had earned enough from taking in lodgers to buy a small grocery business. Peggy's mother and father were dead, but the grocery business still flourished.

Peggy North was as superb a human being as she was an actress. She lived as genuinely as she acted, and was the kind of woman who aroused men's admiration and respect. A woman of few regrets, her greatest sorrow had been that after her success in *Dead Men Rise Again* she had refused the love of a young man who would have made her happy, because she believed that marriage would interfere with her art. She had discovered her mistake, and recovered from her morbid act of self-immolation to find that the young man had disappeared from England. She decided not to allow herself to be so stupid again, and continued her life, hoping that one day he would return. He never did, and she tried to forget him in her generosity and sympathy for others. That was her one fault; her generosity could at times be so great that it would lead her into acts of doubtful probity on behalf of others. Whenever Peggy found the world into which success had carried her going to her head, she would take an excursion trip to Portsmouth, and spend an hour walking up and down its streets, looking into the familiar grocer's shop, and then, when her sanity had returned, she would go eagerly back to London.

It was on a Sunday in mid-winter that Polycarp met Peggy North. He and Mr. Winterton were waiting, in Mr. Winterton's London office, for the actress to arrive with her agent to sign documents and contracts referring to the new play which Mr. Winterton was backing, and in which Peggy North was to play the leading lady.

"Marshall said they'd be here at ten—that means eleven, if I know Peggy," said Mr. Winterton bitterly. "These people never seem to be able to call at an office at a decent time on a normal day, but must make it Sunday morning of all times! Still, I forgive her—she's probably got some good reason. There's a woman for you, my boy, there's a woman! Full of good reasons, and as generous as they make 'em—and a fine actress."

"A pleasant combination, eh?" said Polycarp.

"Absolutely, my boy, absolutely. Hullo, here they are."

Mr. Winterton looked up as the door swung open and Mr. Marshall came into the room. The man nodded to Polycarp and smiled at Mr. Winterton hesitantly.

"Hallo, Marshall. Keeping fit? Where's Peggy?"

"Where's Peggy?" Mr. Marshall threw his hands in the air in mock gesture and sat down. He was a long-faced man, with large ears that added a horse-like touch to his features. "Where's Peggy?" he groaned. "That woman—didn't I tell her that it wasn't right to keep you waiting? Didn't I say that you would be annoyed? But, no—she must go and do it because, so she says, she always does it! Joseph Kay, she's a nice little woman, but when she gets something into her head—there's no stopping her. She bundled me into a taxi and there you are!"

He punctured the end of a cigar with a matchstick, and looked around for a light. Polycarp held out a lighter as Mr. Winterton said anxiously: "What's all this about? Isn't she going through with it? I thought that was all agreed to?"

"No, not that—she's going to play the part, but—" Mr. Marshall shook his shoulders and grimaced.

"What—is she ill, gone away, or something?" asked Polycarp, trying to be helpful.

"She said you wouldn't mind waiting for her—but she won't come now. She never does when she goes to that place. It's her weakness."

"For heaven's sake, make yourself clear, Marshall!" Mr. Winterton got up. "Where is she?"

"She's in Petticoat Lane. She stopped the car by Broad Street Station and made me get out. She goes there every Sunday morning when she's free, and she couldn't pass it this morning. She said she'd be along in half an hour, but she won't be. She won't come. She'll stop there for hours, buying things ..."

Polycarp thought for a second or two that the man was going to weep at the depravity of Peggy's action. Mr. Winterton laughed.

"Good gracious, I thought it was something tragic. I don't mind waiting half an hour for her. She's done me many a good turn before now, and if she wants to visit Petticoat Lane …"

"She won't come. Not even if I went for her. I did once, and she kept me there. I nearly died …" Mr. Marshall was thoroughly depressed until he was given a glass of sherry, and then he smiled a little and puffed at his cigar, but at the end of half an hour Peggy North had not arrived.

"It doesn't look as though she's coming, Joseph Kay—and those things must be signed if you're going away tomorrow." Polycarp, though he could not help being amused at Marshall's helplessness, was slightly annoyed to think that the woman should keep them all waiting. It was hardly fair on Mr. Winterton or Mr. Marshall, he thought.

"Why don't you go back for her?" he asked Mr. Marshall, when she still did not come.

The man shook his head. "Not going to be caught twice. No good. Sorry, Joseph Kay, about this … but you see—"

"I'll fetch her!" cried Polycarp. "These women!" He breathed heavily, and put on his hat and coat.

"Nonsense, my boy, nonsense, you'll never find her in that place. Have you ever been there?"

"No, I haven't; but it's better than sitting here, waiting for her!" said Polycarp.

"She's wearing a black fur coat and a red woolly sort of hat," called out Marshall, as Polycarp left the room. "She's got her car—green one, somewhere. But you won't get her. You …"

Polycarp was out of hearing and trotting down the stairs. Outside the office he called a taxi and directed the driver to take him to Petticoat Lane.

Polycarp sat back in his taxi and told himself that he would stand no nonsense from Miss North. Business was business. A black fur coat and a red hat, and from what he had seen of her numerous photographs he knew he would easily recognise her.

The centre of London on a Sunday morning in winter is almost as grey and lifeless as the cold cliffs of the moon. The only life is the slow movement of patrolling policemen, who interrupt their beat to stand in shop doorways and rub their hands before trying the locked doors; the clatter of boys, mostly caretakers' children, on their way from Sunday school : the occasional rumble of an empty bus or swift taxi; and the shuffling parade of old men who push wheel-mounted soap boxes full of papers along the gutters and startle the dozing pigeons on the cornices with their forced cries. The buildings are shuttered and dead. Shops show no more than blue blinds that act as backgrounds for porcelain advertisements that span the windows with curving letters, announcing the names of chocolate firms and the makers of everything from blacking to tombstones. The colour seems to be sapped from the streets, leaving them long, dismal, echoing, and dull, as though they were mourning the departure of the hurrying thousands who throng the pavements during the weekdays. There is no flash of warm browns and bright packets from the tobacconists, no mounting hues of scarlet, blue, and gold from the florists, no white glitter from the eating-houses, no hawkers littering the pavements with jumping toys or lining the walls with mad pastel drawings of fish and politicians ... everything is grey, and the shops stare out to the few brave pedestrians with dead eyes. The only brightness comes from the red fire alarms and the electric lights shining over the top of the half-gauzed windows of the one or two public-houses which are opened to cheer the troglodytic denizens who live in the basements of office blocks, and from the gay hoardings that rise against every blank wall space ... and even these are tinged by the sobriety and loneliness which seem to stalk the city like wanderers in a city stricken by plague.

The taxi raced through the hollow streets, by accountants' offices and the huge buildings that enshrine mighty insurance companies, and then the silent city fell behind them and they came into a region of light and movement, movement that grew from idle groups of men outside tube stations to the swirl of a thin crowd passing along the pavements; a Sunday-morning crowd, men and women in the primness of church attire, and men and women in the collarless untidy slackness of Sunday leisure.

"Here y'are, sir!" The taxi-man opened the door and pointed to a turning off the long road. "Petticoat Lane, and look after your purse, sir, though t'ain't nothing like it used to be in my young days. Thank you, sir."

Polycarp left the taxi and entered the crowd which was swarming into the turning. He had never been to Petticoat Lane before—that noisy, colourful thoroughfare which is London's nearest approach to the oriental bazaar, and the solace of East Londoners who find in the curving lane all the pleasure and brightness which is denied to them by Nature.

Polycarp had no time to waste. His job was to find Miss North and to take her back to Mr. Winterton. He stroked his moustache seriously, and, with his eyes glancing from side to side in search of a red hat, he started to make his way up the thoroughfare. After he had gone twenty yards he realised that his task was not going to be so easy. He had not expected such a crush. The place was crammed with a tight mass of people, some moving one way and some another, and some standing still, hindering the wriggling flow of life. The sides of the roadway were lined with stalls and hawkers' carts, guarded by men and women whose faces all owed something to miscegenation, but whose voices were those of the East-End native. Men in grey-green shabby overcoats, with thick stubble growths and red scarves colouring their wrinkled necks, stamped their feet by the side of hot-chestnut carts, and occasionally plunged their hands into the mounds of nuts to serve customers who bought twopenny-worths to hold in their pockets, to warm their hands, before eating them.

Against the background of red brick wall and grey buildings, carts full of washed walnuts, polished apples, and winking oranges, were caravans laden with bright jewels. Men with flashing dark eyes stood on boxes and held up lengths of red silk and white satin, shouting and beguiling. Women with full bosoms and the soft, warm skin of the Israelite laughed quietly and bit their nails as they talked to one another, or suddenly interrupted their conversation by shrill cries and plucked at the sleeves of likely customers. In all his market days Polycarp had not seen so much itinerant variety and splendour at one time. There were carts selling fruit; carts that sold ice-cream with true optimism, and were decorated like Indian temples and gleaming with brass like a ship's bridge-house; carts painted red and black, and mounted with shining bottles like young carboys, and emitting from their boilers clouds of steam through which men tempted the cold mob with hot sarsaparilla, hot lemonade, cold ginger-beer, and boiling tea. At intervals came trucks loaded down with tins of floor polish that were stacked into pyramids more arresting in their black and yellow than any Egyptian creation. Everywhere stood stalls draped with long silk stockings and blazoned, in a frankness that was too funny to be indecent, with nightwear and knickers of every colour in the spectrum and of sizes to suit the extreme ranges of human cosmogony.

Polycarp pushed his way through the crowd, his eyes searching for Miss North but being continually attracted by some fresh wonder. Men, catching his glance, waved alarm clocks—" 'Ere y'are, guv'ner, something to wike you when the missus oversleeps!" A little man with a tarbrush moustache shot out from under the cover of a stall, hung with masks and scalps as a South Sea islander decks his house, and caught Polycarp's arm: "What about a nice face to amuse the kiddies, sir. Look!" He shot round, flashed up a hand, and a short, pop-eyed, rubicund-nosed devil was grimacing at Polycarp. Polycarp shook his head in dismay and negation, but the man was undaunted. He took off the mask, and again metamorphosed himself, this time to a paunchy Napoleon, complete with hat ... A swirling in the crowd helped Polycarp to escape before he saddened the man by confessing that he never went to children's parties. Men offered him gladioli bulbs and potted hyacinths, and retired hurt behind long mare's tails of raffia when he refused. If he had bought everything which was offered to him as he passed along the lane, he would have emerged at the far end with enough nougat to serve a healthy child for a year, five pairs of gents' tastefully decorated braces (elastic and washable), seven pairs of hose, four with blue clocks and three of good stout grey wool, a garden spade that could be used as a wireless earth, an indoor aerial that looked like a dado when placed around the room, three velvet evening dresses for his young lady (and should his fancy vacillate, the dresses were of different sizes), a box of soldiers (unbreakable), a bucket, a suit which had cost eight guineas and been worn once and was now offered to him for ten shillings, enough bananas to make the Zoo monkey-house delirious for an hour, a pair of green budgerigars, and a mouse-trap.

214

To escape from the siege of salesmen, he slipped on to the pavement at the back of the stalls and walked slowly, scanning the crowd in the roadway through the gaps in the stalls as he searched for Miss North. Once or twice he saw a red hat but no fur coat, and he often saw fur coats but no red hat. Most of the crowd seemed at home in the lane. For the majority it was their Sunday-morning outing and they knew each hawker and stall-holder. Polycarp felt a pleasurable sensation of well-being spread over him as he watched and listened. Young men, in smart, cheap suits and ties that glistened on their starched shirtfronts like veins of colour in marble, stalked through the press with high-heeled girls hanging to their arms, who were dressed in the pretentious finery of the Houndsditch fashion follower.

All the world was there: fat men with greasy necks and rumbling laughter, who carried thick parcels of fish and sausage under their arms and were followed by their tubby sons sucking nougat and chewing liquorice all-sorts; policemen standing on the corners disregarding the chaff of Cockney pedlars; Asiatics in long robes and turbans, who wandered through the fitter of people holding silk scarves and shawls over their arms and looking into the crowd with eyes that seemed to see not the occidental coldness and shrill humour, but to travel far away to the warmth and dignity of cities where the vulture casts his shadow on the flat house-tops and men walk without the aid of women on their arms; mechanics; house-wives looking for cheap meat and remnants; pickpockets looking for innocent provincials and persistent detectives; harlots taking the air and ready to forget pleasure for business; wealthy looking, astrakhan-collared Jews, who stood beside gown stalls and looked at their pudgy ring-decked fingers and let their eyes caress every fine figure in silk stockings that passed them ... Here was all the world. All its pageantry, all its love of pomp and noise, all its passions and inhumanities, all its jealousies and weakness, all its courage and despair, and the wonder of it gradually went to Polycarp's head so that he began to forget that he was looking for someone and just wandered up and down, enjoying himself and occasionally shriving his conscience by glancing about for a red hat and a black fur coat.

He saw men selling cures, as he had once done, and he smiled at their patter, and he knew that here in this lane peopled by sharping hawkers and cheerful Londoners, most of whom lived on less than three pounds a week, was the real land which he loved. Here rested all the qualities which made England famous. Here people drew their happiness from small things, from a joke or a patch of colour that lit the dullness ... and Polycarp loved them all. Out of sheer good spirits he paid half a crown for a toy racing-car and gave it to a dirty-faced, keen-eyed boy who had asked him for fag-cards.

He stood in front of a china-dealer's stall and watched the man juggle with dinner plates and coffee-sets, as he tempted the people to buy. He held up wash-bowls with pink rose designs that should have made Staffordshire blush, cups with the capacity of small jugs to appease father's thirst in the mornings, peltiform cheese dishes ravaged by dragon designs that would take the savour from the stoutest gorgonzola or Camembert, and when none of these seemed to fetch any customers he held aloft a set of three green and yellow jugs.

"Here you are then—perhaps it's jugs you want. Why don't you say? A set of three jugs, good sound Hanley ware, guaranteed not to crack, warp, or whistle. Look at the handles, look at the pattern—lovely." He kissed the largest jug reverently, and then, spinning it in the air, caught it and cried: "Come on, now—who says seven and six? No one—and very wise! Five shillings—it's a bargain! Three jugs for five shillings—try and get 'em in the shops at the price. Impossible. Ah! Here—tell you what I'll do! Not five shillings, not four and nine, not four shillings—but three and sixpence! Set of three jugs, three and sixpence!"

His assistants grabbed each a set of jugs and canvassed the edges of the crowd, repeating the cries of the patriarch. "Three and sixpence, a set of three jugs. Jugs, lady? Jugs, sir? Come on—three and sixpence!"

Polycarp knew the man's feelings as the crowd remained completely apathetic towards the jugs. The dealer wiped his forehead sadly as the crowd let his assistants go by.

"All right, boys, put 'em down, put 'em down. Nobody wants a jug. What a lot! What a lot! They don't use jugs; they're like our neighbours, they fetch their beer in a ruddy bucket!"

The remark was so sudden and unexpected that the crowd hailed it with delight and swayed with laughter, and, as they swayed, Polycarp went with them chuckling. He stepped back and felt his foot get mixed up with something soft. He flung out his arms as he regained his balance.

"I say, I'm … I'm awfully sorry." Polycarp turned quickly and apologised to the woman upon whose foot he had trodden.

"Thank you, young man, thank you." She looked down, and Polycarp saw that the ground at her feet was scattered with parcels. He bent down and retrieved them for her, and stood with them in his arms.

"Well, if that gentleman makes any more jokes like that I'm going to come prepared with shin-guards." She laughed at the nervous look on Polycarp's face and the sound of her laughter reassured him. He had stamped heavily upon her foot, and was afraid she might be annoyed.

"Cheer up, you didn't quite kill me. I think, if you don't mind carrying those parcels for a moment, I'll get out of this crush, and tidy myself after the blow."

She did not wait for Polycarp to agree, but wriggled through the crowd and found the comparative calm and freedom of the pavement behind a stall. She stood on the steps of a warehouse and straightened her hat and tidied her hair, and Polycarp suddenly laughed loudly.

"What a fool I am," he cried. "I've been looking for you, and I didn't realise I'd found you until this minute. You're Miss North, aren't you?"

The woman interrupted her tidying and eyed him humorously. She was some years older than he and much shorter. Her skin was dark, and her eyes fenced with long lashes under eyebrows which she used more expressively sometimes than words. Under the fur coat she wore a red dress with barbaric beads around her throat, and her hair was drawn tightly back from her forehead in two black sweeps to a small bun at the curve of her neck. Her mouth as she looked at Polycarp might have been a brilliant planet thrown off by the fiery nebula of her hat.

"I am. And is this the way you usually find people? Anyway, what do you want me for? I don't know you." She started forward as Polycarp was about to reply and grabbed a parcel from his arms. "Silly, keep it that way, will you? You don't carry potted hyacinths with the roots upwards!"

"I'm sorry, Miss North, I didn't know. I really must apologise for my rude way of making myself known." Polycarp had quite forgotten that he had set out to haul this woman back with him by force if necessary. "You see, I'm Polycarp Jarvis—from Mr. Winterton, you know. Mr. Marshall said you were here ... and they were waiting for you ... so, I ... you know, Mr. Marshall said you were in Petticoat Lane ... so ..."

"I see what you mean—with the help of Mr. Marshall and Mr. Winterton you gathered that I was in Petticoat Lane. And now you see you were right. Here I am!" She laughed again at Polycarp's confusion, and then took his arm. "You came to fetch me, eh?"

"Well, yes, in a way, Miss North. You see Mr. Winterton wants to get away."

"How awful of me, keeping the dear waiting. But this place is my weakness. Come on, I'll tear myself away if you'll help. Do you mind carrying those parcels? I always buy a lot of things."

She started down the roadway with Polycarp at her side, trying to control the wayward inclinations of the parcels in his arms. Before they reached the side-turning where her car was parked, Polycarp was laden with still more parcels, and secretly admiring this splendid woman who crushed the forwardness of men with a glance, and extracted courtesy and respect from stall-holders who usually only took off their hats when they went to bed.

When Polycarp followed Miss North into Mr. Winterton's office, laden with parcels, Mr. Marshall grinned and winked at him. Miss North saw the look and smiled.

"Now, Marshall, don't be brutal. If ever I go shopping again in Petticoat Lane, I'm going to take him with me—he's much more use than you were, and he has a method all of his own." She threw a grateful look at Polycarp as he rid himself of the parcels which she had refused to leave in her car.

When the agreement was signed, she came and talked to Polycarp while the two other men were busy discussing business. There was a charm and grace about her which captivated Polycarp. He had never met a woman like her before, and she was amused as she noticed his young enthusiasm and regard for her. It was not long before he was telling her how Mr. Winterton had brought him to London. He told her of his great discovery of domesticity and described the Polycarp Kennels and the Chess valley in summer-time. She listened while Polycarp, warming under her confidence and friendliness, proved to her, by illustrations from his own career, that the greatest thing in a man's life was to achieve peace, not fame and wealth, and she was too kind-hearted to tell him that she did not believe him.

"You must show me these kennels and the valley."

"I say, would you like to? Would you really? I'm sure you'd love it."

"Of course, I should. What about tomorrow?—I'm free then. Or will that be interfering with your big business plans?"

"No, no, really. I should be delighted ..." Polycarp could hardly believe his luck. Peggy North, the actress, actually asking him to take her to see the kennels.

Peggy laughed and shook her head at him. "Tomorrow then; I'll call for you and drive you down. Don't argue; I insist on driving you. Now, if you will be kind enough to carry my parcels down for me? Thank you. I got the most lovely haddock. How people can bear to buy things in shops when there are such beautiful stalls, I don't understand ..." She went ahead, talking happily, and Polycarp followed, clutching her parcels.

When he came back Mr. Winterton laughed and chuckled. "Wonderful woman—but a bit odd at times. Still, a great heart, a great heart. I wonder if she'll ever marry?"

The next day Miss North drove Polycarp down to the kennels in her car. Although he was no coward, Polycarp had always entertained a healthy regard for his own personal safety, and he decided that the temperamental qualities that made famous actresses were very far from the qualities needed to make successful drivers. She drove as she acted. Her hands left the wheel to make gestures, the car swerved to emphasise her conversation, she turned corners regally, and emboldened or subdued her pauses by fierce bouts of acceleration and gear-changing. That she never hit anything was entirely to the credit of the pedestrians and other drivers who used the road.

"I hope you're not nervous?" she said, after they had narrowly missed being annihilated by a petrol-lorry. "Some people refuse to drive with me. They say I'm too erratic."

"Well," said Polycarp, clutching at his hat as the car jerked forward, "I have often been in safer hands on the road, but never in fairer."

"I like you for that, Polycarp—you must call me Peggy—most people would have lied at first. You have a nice way of saying that you're a coward. I believe Joseph Kay hasn't put his money on the wrong horse after all. There's something about you ..."

They spent the afternoon looking around the kennels. Higgins introduced them to the new dogs, and then Polycarp took Peggy up the valley. The leaves had fallen long ago, and the tufts of grass were stiff with frost. As she walked by his side, hidden beneath a huge fur coat and her black hair showing like a raven's wing where it escaped from under a small green hat, Polycarp tried to explain to her just what it was about the place which held him to it, but when he tried to put his feelings into words for once he found them not flowing from him as easily as they should have done. His affirmations lacked colour and sincerity. He found himself wondering, even as he talked, whether after all he hadn't been mistaken.

"I like your sign, Polycarp," Peggy said, as they stood by her car before going.

"Yes—nicely proportioned lettering. Proportion in art is everything, you know ..." Polycarp stared at the sign, and the sight of his name cheered him up, until he remembered how seldom he was afforded the pleasure of seeing it elsewhere than the kennels.

"You know, Peggy," he confided as they drove back; "it's a very sad life. I spend half my time helping to make other people famous and well known, but I have to remain in the background. When I left Bristol I had very different ideas. I was going to do things. I was going to get somewhere, and I did. In my way, I suppose, I can't grumble at what I did. I made the name of Polycarp well known ... Gosh! If I wanted to, I still could, I suppose ..." He stopped talking and stared ahead of him, and Peggy turned sideways to watch him. She saw the Polycarp who dreamed of doing things and had somehow got his vision confused with his ideas of peace and a country life. She saw—what Polycarp was still, yet less determinedly, trying to refute—he was gradually recognising that, so far from being time for him to retire and live in peace, he had not begun to live; that the full measure of his capabilities had never even been attested.

And seeing this, because she was naturally one of those women who derive pleasure in helping and prompting the hesitant, she found herself liking this old-young man more than ever, and wondering how she could help him.

"Won't you tell me something about what you've done, Polycarp?" Her dark eyes captured his, and Polycarp knew what it was to have a woman suggesting that she should enter his confidence. He expanded with importance and pleasure. And then he began to tell her. He told her about his madness at Bristol and delighted in her sympathy with his position; he revelled in her laughter as he described the morning on the Downs, and answered her occasional questions as he outlined the rise and fall of the New Age Flying Company, and, when he described his first appearance as the son of Solomon at Oxford, they escaped death from an electric-light standard by two inches. As he retold his story, he found himself stirring to the ambition and enthusiasm which had prompted him in those days, he felt keen and eager again, and the thought of the peaceful kennels left him.

"Oh, Polycarp," she cried, when he finished. "How exciting! And you mean to say you were going to finish it all in that horrible, draughty, dirty place back there. Oh, I can't let you. Why—there's nothing to stop you from being as big as Winterton himself."

"That's true. If I once get going I'll show 'em. But it's getting a start. Do you believe I could, as well as Winterton, then?" Polycarp was stimulated by her interest.

"Of course, I do. And, if it's possible, I'll help you all I can." Her hands were dancing on the rim of the wheel, and Polycarp, as he looked at her, thought he had never seen anyone quite so beautiful. Beautiful women were generally uninteresting, but here he had discovered what all men seek, a woman who was beautiful and intelligent and who understood him. She was a goddess beyond his reach, yet full of human sympathies. With someone like that to believe in him, he could do things. He thought of Gracie, and his lips curled with scorn—Gracie and Peggy—why they were poles apart!

XVIII
Lords and coins of the realm

Peggy and Polycarp became firm friends. At first Polycarp had not thought it possible that such a woman would be interested in him for very long. She was a celebrity and he was merely Mr. Winterton's agent, and if she wanted a friend she had the pick of London waiting for her. He was elated to think that she enjoyed being in his company, and he drew a vicarious pleasure from being seen with her, apart from his quite genuine happiness at her interest in him.

She let him take her to tea at the Carlton, and he drew a great satisfaction from the feeling that he, alone, of all the males in London was at that moment her sole companion and the focus of her immediate thoughts. Polycarp's almost naive enthusiasm and delight amused and gratified the legitimate vanity in Peggy. She went for morning walks with him across Hampstead Heath, laughing with him and scuffling up the dead leaves under the beeches, and as she had just finished a long run he was able to take her to dinner and theatres, and he had to admit to himself that he enjoyed the cosmopolitan life and the opportunities which his friendship with Peggy gave him for becoming the cynosure of playgoers' and diners' eyes as he and she entered a theatre or restaurant.

He was not in love; he was very firm about that; and when—because Peggy one day said something about men with moustaches—he shaved his upper lip, this denudation was no concession to the pandiculated, dart-throwing Cupid, but a tribute to a goddess whom he was content to worship and respect.

A month after his first meeting with Peggy, Mr. Winterton took Polycarp into Oxfordshire to a point-to-point meeting, and it was here that he met Lord Depping. Polycarp, through Mr. Winterton, already had a slight acquaintance with the man, and had met him in the course of his business several times. They drove from London in Mr. Winterton's car, and as they passed through Oxford Polycarp smiled to himself and thought of the Red Dragon Company and of Mrs. Anstruthers. Somehow the place seemed much smaller and quieter than it had done on his first day there. The buildings were less imposing and aloof, the policeman at Carfax no longer a sphinx, and even the elms in St. Giles's seemed smaller and friendlier.

From Oxford they passed through a country hedged with dwarf oaks and hazel scrubs, and bordered with fields that showed the glitter of streams and willows. Patches of flat land flying dirty white cotton-grass flags bordered the road for a while, and then they were on rising ground where hedges gave way to low stone walls and streams lost their turbidness.

Polycarp had never been to a point-to-point meeting before, and as Mr. Winterton wished to hang about the paddock tent, and talk to his many friends there, Polycarp slipped away to enjoy himself alone.

He listened to the shouting bookmakers, watched them licking their chalky fingers and scribbling hieroglyphics on their blackboards and taking money with the slickness of bank clerks, while behind them their clerks (horsy little scribes sucking cigarettes or pipes) entered up the bets and carried on conversations in undertones. Polycarp put ten shillings on a horse named Ben Gunn and watched it straggle happily in the rear of the field round a three-mile circuit, apparently preferring to have plenty of room as it took the lumps and splashes. After that Polycarp betted no more but stood on the fringe of little crowds surrounding hucksters and tipsters. He had never appreciated the fine art of the tipster or the pantomimic dress which their calling insisted upon. He saw tipsters dressed in Eastern robes more gorgeous than he had worn as the son of Solomon, saw beady-eyed, red-faced men in yellow polo-jumpers yelling themselves hoarse with excitement, as they recounted the information that they knew what was going to win the next race from the mouth of the master of the hunt himself, and tall, languid men in scholastic gowns and mortar-boards who held packets of pink envelopes containing the names of certain winners. In odd corners of the field furtive men unfolded crown-and-anchor tables and dared the yokels to beat them, and others played the thimble-rigger's game or defied the crowd to find the lady and kept all the time an eye cocked for the policeman.

Along the finishing straight were stretched rows of cars, from the roofs of which men and women cheered and shouted as the runners breasted the slight rise before the winning-post. Polycarp watched the moving quarters of the straining hunters, saw their heaving, perspiring flanks, and his eyes sparkled with pleasure at the beauty of the swift forms and thundering drum of hooves on the turf, and he shouted as excitedly as the rest of the crowd as the field raced homewards with the jockeys crouched on their saddles, their bright colours splattered with mud and water and the peaks of their gay caps pressed back by the wind.

After a time Mr. Winterton sought him out and they watched together.

"Depping's in the next race," he said, holding up his card. "He's riding a black gelding and I think he's got rather more money on his own horse than he should have."

They watched the horses get away from the starting-line and swerve across the field for the first hedge. Over they went like trout leaping a lasher, and through his glasses Polycarp picked out the black gelding and the big form of Lord Depping wearing his purple and black colours. The field, after the first three jumps, thinned out and left three horses in the lead: the black gelding, a brown mare, and a chestnut gelding. Half way round the course Depping was lying third. Mr. Winterton chuckled: "He's got a good horse but the others are better. It's nonsense, my boy, nonsense to put money on your own horse when you know it isn't the best. But Depping's like that— plenty of cash to throw about and doesn't care what he does with it."

Polycarp was scarcely listening, he was watching Lord Depping. The man, seeing that he was going to have a hard fight, was using the switch cruelly, and Polycarp winced as he watched it rise and fall on the horse's quarters. The two horses ahead of Depping were running free and needed no switch except for a slight touch when they came to the rise before the winning-post.

As Mr. Winterton went back to the paddock, Polycarp caught a glimpse of Depping riding in. The black gelding was sweating and quivering and its muzzle was running with foam, while its rolling eyes showed their whites like a frightened child.

"Here—take him!" said Depping angrily to his man. "The swine let me down!"

Polycarp, who hated cruelty, wished he could use the switch on Depping, but he controlled his anger and followed Mr. Winterton, who wanted to talk to the man.

Mr. Winterton talked to him as he changed. He was a big man, about thirty-five years old and with a body as perfectly developed as an athletic public-school and university life could produce. As Polycarp stood and watched, he was reminded of a polite ape. The man's chest was powdered with black hairs and his heavy face had a petulant expression. He had come into his title and wealth very young and had gained a reputation as a man with a flair for failures. In a way he was a superior Harry Manning, always making new starts and putting his money into new ventures. His continual failures, while they had hardly affected his general wealth, had embittered him and changed his nature. Where success would have encouraged his generosity and kindliness, failure had fostered his savagery and harshness, though he was not without his sympathies. He loved three things: himself, his latest business venture, and model trains; and of these he obtained most satisfaction from model trains and was a constant customer at the Bassett-Lowke shop in Holborn.

"You had bad luck today," said Mr. Winterton in the course of the conversation. "But your horse was nowhere in it."

"Don't rub it in, Joseph Kay! I know I had bad luck—I always do have bad luck with everything. Horseracing! Do you know how much a year I spend on horses? Never mind. I could have killed that beast a few moments ago, but I've calmed down a bit now."

"You were unlucky certainly—"

"Unlucky! I'm cursed. Nothing goes right with me except my little railway. Do you know, Joseph Kay, that in another six months the *People's Paper* will be an absolute washout! It's the truth. My financial half-yearly report spoilt my breakfast this morning. When I bought that affair for more than I like to think of three years ago it was a fine thing, making handsome profits—and now it'll soon be dead, and there's not a man in England would give me ten thousand for it."

"Depping!" Mr. Winterton was astonished. "You don't mean that?"

"I do—it's going fast—and the sooner the better, I say. Damn the affair! I was keen about it at first, but even that's going round on me. I don't know what it is that makes me pick losers. I shall have to wind it up and give everybody the sack!"

"What?" Polycarp came into the conversation. "Sack all those people on the paper? That's pretty tough, isn't it?"

"Of course it's tough, Jarvis, but can I help it? I'm only losing money on it. I can't be philanthropic about things. They'll find something else; bound to."

"That's a pity." Mr. Winterton shook his head. The *People's Paper* was a fine old weekly of reputable standing, with a definite appeal to the middle classes of England and as well known as *Tit-Bits* and *Answers*.

"But think of the men and women involved," said Polycarp. "Couldn't you do something about the paper?" He was revolted by the unconcern with which Lord Depping contemplated the discharging of hundreds of workpeople. Now, definitely, he did not like the man; he disliked his cruelty and his ruthlessness. It was men like this, he thought, who made the workers savage and bitter and sowed the seeds of revolution.

"Don't be all intense about it. They will be out of jobs—that's plain; but they'll get something after a while or else go on the dole. I can't be responsible for 'em. They'll have to pull in their belts. After all, I shall be as cut up about the paper as they will. If you feel so much about it, perhaps one of you will buy it. Ten thousand I'll take."

"Don't be ridiculous!" snorted Mr. Winterton, and he left the dressing-room laughing at the absurdity of the request.

"What about you, Jarvis?" Lord Depping smiled grimly. "Like to become a newspaper proprietor for ten thousand to save a few lousy workers from unemployment?"

Polycarp controlled his anger at the man's taunting manner and rubbed his upper lip. If he had possessed ten thousand he would have bought the paper, just to spite Lord Depping and to try and do something for the people involved. He was repelled by the idea that so many people's destinies should be in the hands of such a man. He thought of the days when he had been a clerk, and he could guess what the feelings of the men and women would be when they were discharged. He put his hands into his pockets and turned away. Ten thousand—and he had about six, and thought that was a fortune.

"Not so philanthropic when it comes to paying out hard cash, eh?" Lord Depping laughed and reached for his coat. The laugh decided Polycarp. He turned back.

"Lord Depping, you're an Englishman and consider yourself a sportsman, don't you? I tell you what I'll do—I'll toss you fifteen thousand or five for your paper. What do you say?"

There was a silence while Lord Depping considered this offer, a pause enriched by the neighing of horses and the calling of people on the track. He nodded his head quickly. "All right. We'll toss. It's as good an offer as I shall get, I suppose."

Polycarp smiled, and took a coin from his pocket. "Tails, fifteen thousand; heads, five thousand!" he called, and at the same time spun the coin in the air.

Lord Depping watched it fall and then handed the coin back to Polycarp. "Congratulations, Jarvis—you're a newspaper owner at five thousand. If you call at my office in the morning I'll fix up details. I wish you more success than I had."

"Thank you, and if you don't mind, please say nothing to Joseph Kay or anyone else just yet."

"Right you are; it's your funeral." Polycarp watched him leave the dressing-tent and then, as he made to follow him in search for Mr. Winterton, he slipped back into his pocket a penny which Frank Burns had presented to him in a Birmingham public-house. He had no qualms at all over the probity of his action. Any weapon was honourable, he thought, to such an end.

The next day he saw Lord Depping and they went into details, and after that he had a private interview with the editor of the paper, Mr. Squires. Polycarp did not waste any time on useless preliminaries.

He told the man what was happening, and then asked for his candid opinion as to the gradual failure of the *People's Paper*. Mr. Squires, who was a rotund little man with a straggling moustache and an equally badly conceived villa at Streatham, passed his hand over his tonsured head and told Polycarp exactly what he thought.

The paper had gone downhill since Lord Depping's accession because it had professed no definite policy, and because Lord Depping now refused to spend money on it, and it was impossible for him to do anything without funds, and there were a few other subsidiary reasons.

"How can we get it back to what it was?" asked Polycarp eagerly.

Mr. Squires smiled at his enthusiasm and said: "Money—put money into it, adopt a definite policy and perhaps a new name. Advertise it well and get good writers. Given a good advertising campaign and people like Peter Walden, Professor Goldenstein, and E. B. Broker contributing to it and I could put it back and make profits. But if you tried to get those people now"—he shook his hands—"they'd either laugh at you or put up such a price that it would be impossible. It hurts me when I think how the old paper's gone down."

"Don't worry." Polycarp patted his shoulder. "We'll do something to save it—even if it ruins me."

He left the office and decided that he would go and see Mr. Winterton. He was rather apprehensive about his reactions.

Polycarp did not have to wonder long. Mr. Winterton was very definite about his purchase of the newspaper.

"Polycarp, my dear boy, this is utter nonsense!" he said when he recovered from his initial surprise. "Why did you do it? I brought you to London because I knew you could make good. You knew, as well as I, that you would have to wait your chance. I said you'd fall on your feet after a time, but I honestly did not expect this. It's nonsense, my boy, nonsense!"

"I thought it was a bargain. Five thousand for a weekly paper—"

"For a decent paper, yes! Surely you know the state of the *People's Paper*? And what about the capital to pay the staff and printing? Oh, Polycarp! You've let your heart get the better of your head. If you're going to keep it going you want to be able to afford to lose a thousand a week, and you haven't a cent after you've paid your five thousand, I know that."

"I know, Joseph Kay. I thought you'd be good enough to back me for a while until I could pay you out of the profits. Or you could buy a share in the paper—"

"Profits? There won't ever be any profits! Depping ruined that paper. Once it was a fine weekly, but now—why, they almost refuse to wrap fish and chips up in its sheets! No, Polycarp, I like you, and I still believe you can make a name—but not with a newspaper, and I won't help you. Remember, I'm a business man, and I don't put my money into obviously rotten concerns. It would be suicide, and not even for our friendship will I commit financial suicide."

Polycarp was not altogether surprised at Mr. Winterton's attitude, though he had expected him to be a little more sympathetic.

"You want me to chuck it up, eh? To let the paper fizzle out, and throw printers, pressmen, artists, clerks, and God knows who out of work?"

"Very crudely put—but that is it. Business men can't afford to have such fine feelings."

"Well, I won't do it, Joseph Kay. I've been in worse holes than this. Before, I've only had myself to think of. Now there are men, women, and children, and it's a question not of one man—myself—but of whole families. I'm not a saint; at times I wonder whether I'm even normally moral, for I do dirty tricks and take unfair advantages of people more fortunate than myself. I know this, though: that I'm going to sink or swim with the people attached to that paper. Do you realise that I've bought them from a silly fool of an English lord for five thousand, as though they were so many pounds of butter? If the inhumanity of that doesn't shrivel you, it should. I don't like that kind of thing and I'm going to do my best for them. I'm not begging for help. I only ask you for one promise. You say I shan't get advertisers for the paper; I shan't get the writers and big names to make the people buy the paper. That may be so—I certainly can't afford their present terms, it seems. But I will get 'em, and when I come to you and can say that Peter Walden is doing a serial story, that E. B. Broker is going to do illustrations, that Professor Goldenstein is going to be the political correspondent, and a lot of other famous people are going to contribute for half their usual terms—people whose names will make any paper—will you back me then?"

"Sure I will—that would be sound business. But, Polycarp, you have about as much hope of getting them to lower their scale for you as you have of getting the Fallen Angel to do you an exclusive article on his Descent to Hell."

"We shall see. You don't know Polycarp Jarvis. I'll get those names, and then the advertisers will pay high prices and the newspaper dependants will still have a job."

"Good boy, Polycarp, good boy! I admire your enthusiasm but deprecate its direction. Pure nonsense, my boy, pure nonsense! Why, Peter Walden would want at least a thousand for a serial and you've got about tenpence! And he won't write for any but established papers with fabulous circulations."

"I'll do it somehow." But just how he was going to do it Polycarp was not sure.

He saw Lord Depping and arranged that the *People's Paper* should go on publishing without the change of ownership being made public for a couple of weeks, and then Polycarp told his troubles to Peggy.

For the first time in his life he found himself glad to have someone to whom he could go and discuss the difficulties of his life. Now he had Peggy. Never once did Polycarp think of escaping from the turmoil and worry of his new venture to the kennels. They were gone from his life as completely as the New Age Flying Company and Solomon's Glory; these things were no more than a background for future exploits and indiscretions.

Over their tea he told Peggy everything, and of Mr. Winterton's promise.

"You see, Peggy, I've got to get those men somehow."

"Of course, dear boy. What a pity that most of them, although they are undoubtedly good at their jobs, are such scabs in private life. You might otherwise be able to talk to them and persuade them to help you for the sake of saving the paper and the workers, and not want so much money."

"Money-grabbers, are they?"

"They are, Polycarp. I know Walden and Goldenstein—success turned them like that, I think; and Broker, from all accounts, is a nasty piece of work. Now what can we do? We must think hard."

With a charming unconcern she immediately appropriated Polycarp's worries as though they were her own. She was impressed by his hot-headed rashness, and, knowing that his actions had been motivated from reasons which she could appreciate, she was anxious to help him as much as possible.

She touched the back of his hand and smiled encouragingly. Polycarp frowned as he concentrated. Peggy sat very still, her green velvet dress emboldening with its severe lines the straight beauty of her hair and the oval frame of her face. She wondered where this impetuous young man, whose serious face made such a ridiculous contrast with his floppy fair hair and sprawling, puppyish body, would finish in life.

"Peggy," said Polycarp slowly after a while, "some thing is coming to me. I see daylight; we can get those men, if you'll help me."

XIX
The influence of the cinematograph on morals

Before Justice it is as great a transgression to steal goods from a thief as it is to rob the toffee-apple from the sticky hand of an infant. This is so because justice is concerned with performing conjuring tricks with scales, and walks blind-folded where even policemen go in pairs. Both acts may be equally crimes before the law, yet in the minds of honest men there can never be any doubt as to the poetic justice of a thief having his safe rifled and the crude, rapacious meanness of stealing from an unsuspecting child. Popular opinion finds satisfaction in seeing a thief robbed and is prepared to condone the act. It was this easy virtue of popular opinion which Polycarp had offered up as an excuse for some of his less lawful and sometimes discreditable deeds; and it was upon this *lex populi* that he relied for help to make a success of his weekly. The law will never forgive a sinner because he sins with a certain charm and perhaps with an altruistic motive. The mother must not steal bread for her starving children, and Polycarp should not have broken faith with his higher principles in order to make the weekly flourish; but mothers do steal and the public gives them sympathy to temper the rigour of the law, and Polycarp transgressed civilised codes of conduct to keep a couple of hundred families from facing the terror and wearying waste of unemployment and degeneration, and although the public never knew of his apostasy it is more than likely that had they done he would have received their approbation.

A week after Polycarp purchased the paper Peggy gave a party in her rooms to celebrate his venture and to christen the paper, which he had decided to name *Polycarp's Weekly*, and, because an invitation from her was as good as a command, the gathering was enriched with more notabilities and notorieties than the gossip columns of a daily paper. The party was in spirit very much the same as the Friday evening carousal which Polycarp and Frank had enjoyed in the Golden Barbel, only here the singing was worthy of any music-hall and often in accents which the Golden Barbel would have disowned. Of drinking there was the same spontaneity, only the drinks ranged from homely ale to fiery kiimmel and cocktails with names far stranger than those of any racehorse. And, where at March there had been a frank amorousness and bussing upon the high-backed settles, here it sought out darkened corners and quiet nooks. Polycarp did not, however, repeat his performance of the Golden Barbel. He drank little and watched the gathering, under the guise of merriment, with anxious eyes, for this was a trying time for him; he was a Napoleon facing what might be his Moscow or Austerlitz, and particularly he watched those men whom he had sworn to acquire for his paper. There was Peter Walden, fat and treble-chinned, with pudgy hands that ended in hairy fingers like wooded promontories, who had a camel's capacity for drink but avoided that beast's necessity for prolonged abstinence; Ernest Benjamin Broker, who as an art student never raised a pencil without thinking of Tintoretto and now never raised his pencil without thinking of the Bank of England; and Professor Goldenstein, who knew so much about economics and political moves that he had made a nice fortune and a name from his prescience, which had not, however, saved him from the unpolitic act of marrying a jealous woman.

At three o'clock, when everyone had, with the exception of Polycarp and Peggy, drunk far more than was good for them, the party broke up. As Polycarp left, he said to Peggy:

"Thank you, Peggy. I shall never be able to repay you!"

"Don't be dramatic, Polycarp. I enjoyed it. It was just like playing the same part over and over with a different lead each time."

Two days later Peter Walden received a note from Polycarp asking him to call at the flat which Polycarp had taken close to Mr. Winterton's Kensington house.

As he drove through Hyde Park on his way to the flat, Peter Walden found himself wondering why he had not disregarded this request to call upon someone whom he personally regarded as a whipper-snapper, and who had got himself mixed up with a shaky newspaper scheme, and alternately trying to guess why Polycarp could want to see him. The note had been headed—"Most Important."

When he arrived he did not haggle with preliminaries. Peter Walden had a reputation which enabled him to disperse all formalities and practise a direct brusqueness even with influential men.

"Now then, Mr. Polycarp Jarvis, what do you mean by asking me to call and hinting about something important? I'm a busy man, and can't give you more than five minutes." He sat down as Polycarp waved to a chair, and flung his hat on to the table.

"And so am I, Mr. Walden. I won't keep you long. I've just bought a newspaper, as you know—a newspaper which, to put it mildly, is in a bad way; and I'm determined to see it on its feet again, and one of the surest ways to regain popularity is by offering the public something they'll pay for—and that's where you come in, Mr. Walden. You write stories that the public like reading, and I want you to write a story, a serial for the paper—"

"What!"

"That's right—a serial for my paper."

Peter Walden rose to his feet. "Ridiculous! I wouldn't write for that lousy rag if you paid me a million. I don't believe you know what you're asking. I'm sorry for you, Mr. Jarvis, but I won't do that."

"I'm not asking you to write for the *People's Paper*, Mr. Walden. I want a story for *Polyearp's Weekly*, which is going to be a very different thing from the *People's Paper*. The *People's Paper* ceases and a newer and better paper comes in its place, and I'm offering you the opportunity to be among the select band of famous men who will contribute to it. That is a tribute to you, I think."

"Who else is writing for you?"

"I am not at liberty at the moment to mention names, but I refer to men and women who are as fastidious as you, Mr. Walden." This information soothed the man, and he sat down.

"I hadn't appreciated that it was to be a new paper altogether. That puts a different complexion on the affair."

"I can promise you that it will be a paper you will be proud to be associated with—*Polycarp's Weekly*!" Polycarp mouthed the words lovingly.

"I'm not denying that. What would you pay me for a sixty-thousand-word serial?"

"What would you want?" Polycarp tapped his teeth with his thumb-nail and waited.

"A thousand, and to retain all rights of course; but you can fix all that up through my agent. Of course, it would have been better if you'd made all this clear from the beginning, Mr. Jarvis. I didn't know · you were going to make a splash …"

"Oh, yes, it's going to be a big thing. A thousand pounds—that's a lot of money. Still, one has to pay for good stuff these days. Are you interested in the development of the film industry, Mr. Walden?" Polycarp watched him closely.

"I loathe the talking pictures, if that's what you mean, though I must say they pay me good prices for my stuff at times. It's not an art-form … Oh, no!"

"I wonder if you'd care to see some of my stuff? I'm interested in film technique. I've got a little projection-room fitted up here. Would you like to see it?"

"Certainly. I have a little time to spare. I had no idea you had such a hobby."

"Good, come along and enjoy yourself for a while. By the way"— Polycarp paused as they crossed the room—"am I right when I say that it's a sort of slogan of yours that you always write good, clean adventure stuff. No sex or risque situations?"

"That's right. I couldn't afford to offend my public by writing doubtful stuff. Very awkward at times, you know." He laughed and followed Polycarp into a small room, which had been darkened.

He watched Polycarp fiddle about with a projector, and then, as the screen at the end of the room brightened, Polycarp, said:

"Take a pew and watch. These are only some scrappy shots I got the other day."

"Is this an old hobby of yours, Mr. Jarvis?" Peter Walden asked, as he sat down and left Polycarp to handle the projector.

"No, fairly recent; though I've always been interested. I'll run through, first of all, without the sound-track, and then, if you aren't bored, we'll have it as a real full-blown talkie."

The famous writer settled down into his armchair and forgot in his pleasure at a new commission and this little show, that he had an appointment with his mistress for twelve. He knew that it was policy to humour men who could give large commissions.

The machine clicked and whirred, and then the screen jumped to life. Peter Walden found himself looking at the interior of a comfortable little room, furnished with easy chairs. A divan faced him, and he noticed all the little appointments of a woman's room. Something about the scene aroused an impression of familiarity in him, but before he could isolate his memory the door on the screen opened and a man and woman, both in evening dress, entered. The next five minutes were the most harrowing and amazing of his career. He watched himself and Peggy enter the room, and the mute movement of the screen showed that they were laughing and he, obviously, unsteady with drink. He stared at the screen, unable to take his eyes away, all his senses disturbed by the shock, and during that five minutes he saw with cold, sober eyes how stupid a man seems when he is intoxicated and how foolishly he will act. Although he saw nothing flash across the screen which would have horrified a normal film audience, he saw enough to make him appreciate that, if the great British public realised that this was the Peter Walden of the slogan "Fiction for the Family," his sales would fall off, or if only a few of his acquaintances were privileged to see the film he would be involved in domestic tangles which would make his life untenable for years.

The light flickered and died, and, as though through an ugly dream, he heard Polycarp's voice say petulantly:

"Pity—the machine seems to have broken down. Never mind, you can see the rest some other time. The sound-track makes the whole thing very funny. Love scenes generally are, don't you think?"

Peter Walden got up from his chair and confronted Polycarp. Like most fat men he could command a noble anger.

"What's the idea? Is this blackmail?" He almost shouted the words, and his paunchy face wobbled with emotion.

"Of course, the real thing will be when we get coloured films." Polycarp ignored his anger and talked calmly. "I fancy experiments are even now being carried out towards that end. I see you were very impressed. It's so interesting to meet someone who is in sympathy with modern cinematograph evolution. There's a future in it—a great future. The possibilities are as unbounded and marvellous as were those of steam in Watt's day, or electricity when Edison was a boy." Polycarp talked on as they left the room. "Some time I'll give you another show. Well, to come back to business, Mr. Walden, it's been very nice having you up here and fixing things up. I'm sure you're going to be proud to be associated with *Polycarp's Weekly*. It's going to be the big thing in journalism very shortly, and you'll be glad to say yours was the first story in it. Of course, later on, when we begin to make a decent profit, I shall pay you as much as the wealthiest daily can afford, but until then we must be prepared to work for the good of humanity and accept a little less. I'll see your agent tomorrow, and fix up with him about the story, as you suggest. Five hundred pounds is a lot of money, but I think it will be worth it for a story from you."

"This is blackmail. I'll … I'll …"

"You're excited, Mr. Walden. Curious how films affect people. I often have a good cry myself. Still … it's all false emotion—that's how I bring myself back to earth. False emotion. You understand that? Well, goodbye, and thank you for calling. Some day, as I say, you'll be proud to be a contributor to *Polycarp's Weekly*. Thank you again for calling, and I won't forget to see your agent."

Polycarp held out his hand, and the overwhelmed Mr. Walden found himself grasping it and having his own pumped up and down vigorously.

"This is blackmail …" The man backed weakly, like a reluctant elephant, towards the door. "I won't do it … I … I … I … Oh, hell!"

"Now, now, my dear sir, don't take on so. Youth never objects to its folly; and old age and wisdom should learn to be indiscreet unobtrusively. Goodbye."

Mr. Walden found himself outside, and as he went down to his car he knew that Polycarp had got the better of him and that he would have to do the story on his terms. He snarled to himself and glowered at his waiting chauffeur.

"Where to, sir?" asked the man, as Mr. Walden stepped into the car.

"To hell! And drive quickly!" bawled Mr. Walden, to relieve his feelings.

"Yes, sir." The chauffeur closed the door and saluted.

In his rooms Polycarp was lying on the divan, fanning himself and sipping a glass of water. If Mr. Walden had appreciated just how nervous and anxious Polycarp had been, and how easy it would have been to have bluffed Polycarp by refusing to be intimidated by the film, he might have been even more annoyed with himself. Polycarp was finding his first adventure in refined criminology rather enervating but, so far, satisfying.

Later that day Ernest Benjamin Broker fell a victim to the same trick, and, because of his Bacchic indiscretion, accepted half price for his services, and the next morning Professor Goldenstein was so worried by the possibility of his wife's coming to know of his lapse that he offered to do what Polycarp wanted for a third of his first demand, but his first demand had been so exorbitant, far more so than any of the others, that Polycarp halved his second offer and the Professor could do no other than accept.

In all, the victims of Polycarp and Peggy were six, and five of them gave full proof of their craven spirit and human weakness by capitulating to Polycarp with as good or bad grace as they could command, but the sixth was a hawk caught in the net with the sparrows.

A versatile offshoot of a very humble family, who knew everyone in London worth being seen with and far more with whom it was as well not to be seen, and who could write a gossip column that might take form as a didactic epic or an ecstatic parade of epigrams, Alexander Macktolland Royston frankly called Polycarp's bluff.

"A very nice film, Polycarp. Very nice. Peggy played the part very well, though with hardly sufficient abandon, don't you think? I wondered what the persistent clicking was, that evening, too. Dear Peggy—the things that generous soul will do to help people. That was sailing very close to the wind, don't you think? Still—all for a good cause. You know you'll never be able to show it anywhere. It wouldn't do you any credit, though it would be nice publicity for me. What a pity that I'm not in need of publicity."

He shook his head at Polycarp and straightened his bow-tie.

"You win, Royston."

"Call me Alexander—everyone does."

"All right, Alexander. I can afford to pay you your price, I suppose, considering what I've saved on the others. You got into the wrong net."

"Yes; it's a habit of mine—that and getting into debt. I suppose the other stories are not for publication?"

"No—not until I write my memoirs. Thank you for calling, and I apologise for making such a mistake over you."

"Not at all; not at all, my dear chap. I shall be glad to be associated with you. I can see that the weekly is going to be a big thing. You've got the blood of an unscrupulous adventurer in your veins."

"Unscrupulous?"

"Well, bit harsh perhaps, say conveniently unconscientious. Goodbye."

With the six contracts in his pocket Polycarp called on Mr. Winterton, to hold him to his promise, and it was not until he had shown him the contracts that Mr. Winterton would believe him. He finished looking through them, and cocked his head at Polycarp.

"I've got to admit that you've surprised me. I didn't think you could do it. Well done, my boy, well done!"

"I've surprised myself a bit. And I don't think I could have done it alone."

"I believe I can guess who helped you, and I'd like to know how it was done, but I suppose that wouldn't be a fair question?"

"No—that's a secret which is to be buried at once, thank goodness. And now, Joseph Kay, you'll come in with me, will you, and buy some shares in the business?"

"I gave you my promise, didn't I?"

Polycarp nodded. "Yes. I couldn't have gone through with it otherwise. I feel a bit shabby about things, but it wasn't any more than some of 'em deserved, I suppose."

"Come on down to the office and we'll talk things over."

It was two weeks before Polycarp could really get to work on launching his weekly. Despite his humanitarian approach to his undertaking, he was by no means oblivious of the necessity and personal desirability of making his paper return him equitable profits. He had not, however, realised quite how much detail and procedure would be involved; but, the moment he had dispensed with all the formalities and got an idea of how the *People's Paper* had been run, he was not long in starting. He kept on all the old staff, making new arrangements and bringing in fresh men where necessary. He had a talk, first to the staff and then to the workmen, and fired them all with something of his enthusiasm, and then, content with the knowledge that he had the whole vast organisation for him, he set to work to wake the public to a realisation of *Polycarp's Weekly*.

London and the larger provincial towns were plastered with yellow and black notices announcing the first number of *Polycarp's Weekly*. Bills crying: Truth not Trash! *Polycarp's Weekly*—Facts not Fiction! *Polycarp's Weekly*—Good Reading! Great Writers! Grand Value! *Polycarp's Weekly*—A weekly that combines Scholarship with Entertainment and tempers Justice with Sympathy!—The Open Forum of the People!

The yellow and black bills spread themselves all over England, and Polycarp had the satisfaction of not being able to stir a step from his rooms without the name—Polycarp—soliciting his eye at every turn. He lived in a chromatic dream, and when the first number appeared it was almost as good as the advertisements had promised. The *People's Paper* had failed partly because the staff lacked enthusiasm, not ability, but under Polycarp they gave their best, and his special contributors did not stint their work because they had been virtually blackmailed into doing it. Peter Walden's story was a fine, virile masterpiece because he had written it in a towering rage which improved his style; Broker's drawings had a new vitality of resentment, and Professor Goldenstein's article was a marvel of scholarship and foresight and, in a way, an offering to the gods for his deliverance from the possible wrath of a jealous woman. Royston's page mixed epigrams, wit, and wisdom such as is only found in men who have to crave no favours of the world. If Royston had been born a Frenchman he would have rivalled Molière, as it was he was born an Englishman and became a gossip writer.

And so *Polycarp's Weekly* was launched. Perhaps not with such flamboyant or irreverent methods as had characterised Polycarp's earlier ventures, for he was older now and developing an eye for the finer things and he disparaged too obtrusive a vulgarity in his appeals. The posteriors of the public statues in London were safe from him, for he could not afford to outrage public opinion or to cheapen his message to the masses; and slowly those men and women who had abandoned the *People's Paper* under Lord Depping began to buy *Polycarp's Weekly* and to like it, and Polycarp had the satisfaction of knowing that he had vindicated his rash resolution in the dressing-room, and turned what might have been failure and consequent hardships for many into success and continued happiness for the people concerned with the weekly.

Of the actual journalistic work, Polycarp did little more than write an occasional editorial and to indicate any special policy. He believed in leaving the job to men who had been trained and were competent to do it. He was always ready with new ideas and schemes, and as the weekly flourished and began to show a profit he found himself becoming wealthy and with enough money to employ in other directions. He watched *Polycarp's Weekly* rise from an almost defunct paper to the position of an important national weekly, with a distribution service that sent it into every corner of England and Scotland, and as it grew so Polycarp grew with it until he began to appreciate that he, a young man of twenty-eight, was becoming an important figure in the public life of the nation. His dream of fame and fortune was gradually becoming a reality.

XX
Confessions

At the end of nineteen hundred and thirty *Polycarp's Weekly* was as much a habit with a considerable section of the English people as their weekly bath, and Polycarp's fortune seemed assured. Since the paper had commenced to make profits he had slowly begun to acquire interests in other concerns, under the guidance and advice of Mr. Winterton, until he realised that he was now in a position to regard pounds as he had once looked at shillings.

Polycarp had effected one of those sudden phenomenal successes which swing men from comparative nonentity into the limelight of a public life and prosperity which measures itself by the control of thousands of lives. Polycarp did not let his success coarsen his principles or dull the desires which had characterised him as a clerk in Bristol. His extravagances were too childlike to be vulgar and were more than balanced by a generosity towards those who were less fortunate than himself.

He was the chairman of a few companies, and his investments were wisely distributed throughout the financial world, but until the end of nineteen hundred and thirty his only personal concern was his weekly paper; that was the one thing which bore the name of Polycarp.

As soon as he was in a position to do so, Polycarp asked Peggy to marry him. He had done this more from his sense of gratitude towards her than from the love which he imagined he felt. She had laughed at what she called his nonsense, and when he had grown serious in his protestations she had told him not to bother her with puzzling questions until her show had finished running, hoping that he would forget his assumed passion before then. Polycarp did forget his love while the show was running—he had so many other things to think about—but when her play came off he remembered their previous conversation, and made his proposal to her again.

Peggy was amused to find that he had not forgotten all about his love.

"How noble of you, Polycarp, to remember all this time."

"It was not difficult to remember, Peggy. When a man's in love, he doesn't forget easily."

"No, I suppose not. Oh, look! Is that a pigeon or a ring-dove? I can never tell the difference, can you?"

They were walking in Hyde Park, and Polycarp swung his stick with a little gesture of annoyance at her irrelevance. The subject was serious to him, he mused.

He was a very different figure from the carefree, flannel-trousered proprietor of the New Age Flying Company. His yellowish hair was hidden beneath a black Homburg, his long body constrained within an expensively cut dark suit that was hidden almost by the loosely buttoned, heavy topcoat which he was wearing against the coldness of the December day, and his hands were warm inside yellow gloves. His upper lip was still free from growth. Peggy, in her fur coat, seemed not to have changed from the early days when he had first met her in Petticoat Lane, and later walked with her down the side of the river on their visit to the kennels.

Away across the worn green of the turf and the smirched skeletons of the plane-trees, the skyline of London cut the pale clouds into angles and curves, and peopled the blue with craggy cliffs and soaring pinnacles of masonry that housed pigeons and chattering starlings. Through the trunks of the trees Polycarp could see children playing around perambulators, the movement of uniformed soldiers and the coloured swirl of traffic in the roadway. Overhead a black-headed gull, dowdy in its winter plumage, swung towards the distant Serpentine to meet the calling, hungry company of other gulls and wild-fowl that shared the water with floating cigarette cartons and abandoned toy boats.

"I do love you and I want you to marry me," said Polycarp almost guiltily. He lit a cigarette to cover his nervousness.

Peggy laughed quietly and took his arm. "You don't love me, Polycarp. You only think you do, but you don't."

"But I do—haven't I waited all this time to ask you to marry me?"

When she told him that he did not love her, it only strengthened his idea that he did love her. The more she denied his feelings, the surer he felt about them.

"Stupid—you don't. I know; and, in any case, I don't love you, Polycarp. I don't hate you, of course, dear boy, but love you—no! I like you a lot …"

"You don't know what you're saying, Peggy. You're hurting me by saying such things." For a man suffering pain, Polycarp was singularly self-composed. "I love you and I believe you love me. Anyway," he cried, with grand disregard, "what does it matter about loving or liking? It's a very fine distinction, you know."

Peggy shook her head and smiled compassionately at him.

"Don't make so much fuss about it, Polycarp. You can't talk me into doing a thing like this. Why, it's ridiculous! I don't love you. I did love once, but I spoiled it all by acting very foolishly "

"Peggy, I'm sorry. I didn't know."

"It's all right. I've almost recovered. Although I'd do anything to get him back. He was a young man I knew, and I sacrificed him unnecessarily for my career. Since then there has been no one else … there couldn't be."

"But if you love him, why not marry him?" Polycarp was interested in this sad part of Peggy's past.

"If I knew where he was, I would—if he would have me. He went away long ago."

"Then why not marry me? I love you."

Her eyebrows lifted expressively. "You dear old thing, haven't I said, I don't love you? And I don't think you really love me—it's just a sort of loyalty that makes you think so. You'll get over it in time."

"Never," avowed Polycarp determinedly. "I shall always love you, and I shall be waiting for you when you want me. Remember that, Peggy … waiting for you." And, because he was young and the sharp sunshine was gilding the railings with running fire and turning the shadows of the tree-lined walk into a bower of golden dapple spots, he believed he would always be waiting, always loving her. At that moment, Polycarp was plunged into the delightful gloom of the rejected, faithful lover. What irony, he thought, Peggy loving some unknown man, and content to spend her life hoping, and he loving her, and content to spend his life waiting for her. If he had not loved her so much, he mused, it would be amusing, but his love for her only made it tragic for him.

Polycarp had never occupied a tragic role in the comedy of life until now, and the heaviness of the part interested him while it stimulated a peculiar misery in him. He excused himself from Peggy and left the park, wrapping himself in the grey folds of deliberate misery. He tried to forget his tragedy in an expensive lunch, but the bill depressed him further and the food warred with his internal secretions. He went into a cinema in Leicester Square and had his morbid attitude heightened by a screen drama, which might have been his own if he had taken his life after leaving the park, and Peggy had been with child by her vanished lover. Not even the Mickey Mouse cartoon cheered him up. He left the stuffy atmosphere of scented disinfectant and cigarettes, and the flickering shadows where lovers held hands and tall men fought to encompass their legs in the narrow gangways, and went out to meet the clammy welcome of a winter afternoon. For the next hour or two he wandered about the crowded streets and his dejection settled closer upon him.

Streets and voices passed him like phantoms of a film. He saw the Cenotaph grey and steady in the fresh drizzle of the evening, and leaned for a moment over Westminster Bridge listening to the thundering of Big Ben. His eyes went down-river, across the black, loathsome glitter of water, and he heard the lick of the current against the pillars as the tide sucked back towards the sea, taking a long trail of debris and refuse with it. The lights along the Embankment made a dark filigree of the trees, and the tall shadows of hotels and public buildings hung above the river like the outjutting scars of a wide ravine. Lights played about the darkness in wandering fingers, and limned with softness for a moment the rigid spars of ships and the solid hulks of barge and steamer. Through the night trams clanged and whined, newsboys shouted, and downstream a liner hooted dismally.

Polycarp walked about, nursing his sorrow to himself. The bright facades of theatres, tempting with their photographic displays of pulchritude, made a blaze of light to shadow his tall figure. He stopped outside the ill-lit windows of little eating-houses and watched heavily coated men—carters, taximen, porters, loungers—drink cups of thick cocoa; and he stood opposite a theatre queue in Shaftesbury Avenue and watched a Welsh miner wriggle his wiry body through steel hoops that seemed to him no bigger round than the lid of a saucepan. He had no wonder in his eyes as he watched another exhibitor evolve paper creations of grace and beauty from rolls of old placards with the aid of his thumb-nail. He felt sorry for the men on the streets, the down-and-out musicians who shuffled round the heels of the crowd playing banjos and violins, the blind beggars with their pathetic notices hung about their necks and their limp hands clasping wet strings of bootlaces. He stood for a moment in Trafalgar Square and looked up to the gloom that hid Nelson from the gaze of the streets, and then hurried by the warm posters of Jamaica and Port Said in the shipping offices, posters alluring with dusky-skinned girls and fat-tummied nigger-boys holding slices of melons.

At first he had enjoyed his dejection, but now he found that it had mastered him and he was under its control. He walked through the streets, dodging umbrellas and buses, scowling at the hawkers who monopolised the pavements to parade their Christmas toys, and wishing that he could plunge the whole of London into a gloom as deep as his own. He wanted to announce to the world, from the top of the Duke of York Steps, that he was a disappointed man; he wanted everyone to know that he had plumbed the depths of despair and exhausted the possibilities of misery. He stalked, still scowling, along Regent Street, and felt each burst of light from opulent windows searing at his own darkness of spirit. There was no sincerity, no goodness left anywhere; everyone was acting ... everything was false except his love.

When his feet were tired with walking, he turned into a wine vault and had four glasses of sherry as quickly as he could drink them. When he got outside, he found the lights and traffic only adding to his masochistic despair. The sherry moved his mind to anti-social thoughts, and he found refuge in a public-house with a pint of beer and a packet of potato crisps. The beer, entering an almost beaten man, combined with the sherry and sent him out into the streets again in search of a place where there was less noise and more companionship. He drank in hotel bars frequented by aristocrats and actors. He drank in low haunts where crime grew and ripened. He felt that he had to forget ... but he soon forgot what it was he had to forget.

For some hours Polycarp dragged himself through a slough of despond and drinking, hoping to reach the hilarity of careless intoxication, but drink only increased his moroseness and heightened his disappointment in love. Where once he and Frank had found a new joviality in tippling, Polycarp only found himself growing angry with life, and especially the little portion assigned to himself. He was a microcosm in revolt against a malicious macrocosm.

His clothes were crumpled and his hat stained with mud, where he had dropped it, and his coat pockets were filled with boxes of matches, bootlaces, packets of lavender, and a rosette which he had bought with any coin which came to his hand from hawkers and beggars in his peregrinations.

When he tired of his search after gaiety and forgetfulness, a grim idea came into his mind and, full of bitterness, at nine o'clock he was riding down Fleet Street behind a cabman who had portrayed no surprise on Polycarp's insisting that he should pay and tip him before starting. The taxi drew up outside the offices of *Polycarp's Weekly*.

At the office he pulled himself together and, with unswerving resolution written all over his face, he went up the lift and into the editor's room. The editor was not on duty. His assistant, a freckle-faced indecisive man, hovered round Polycarp like a frightened skylark.

"We go to press in an hour," he said in reply to Polycarp's bawling query.

"An hour? Then I have time. Send me a stenographer and a proof of the weekly. Quickly, quickly ... Speed, my man, speed is what you want to cultivate, and a firmer, less dithering manner. Ever read Dickens? No? Well, you should; he wrote about people like you. Great social reformer in his way, Dickens, and I'm going to be the same. Show up the shams and falsities of life. Where's that stenographer?"

The assistant shot from the room and left Polycarp looking through a proof copy of the weekly. Not even his name in big type on the front page appeased his mordant rage and savageness.

When the assistant and stenographer appeared, he shouted at the man: "Cut out that squitty editorial by Squires—cut it out. I'm going to write another for the paper. We want force in our editorials. I'm always telling Squires that! Force, do away with all this toadying. Tell the truth. Isn't that one of my mottoes—Truth, not Trash?"

"Yes, sir, yes, sir—shall I ring for Mr. Squires at his house, sir?"

"No, you damned fool, I don't want Squires. I can write this myself. Here, girl, take this and get it typed, and you, man, see that it's set up smartly. I'm going to wait and see it through the press myself. Tell them to hold everything until I've got off my mind the wisdom which I have accumulated this evening at the London, Dirty Dick's, the Cheshire Cheese, the Cock, Shirreff's, and a score of other places with names as fantastic as that of any meat extract."

The girl, who was in the happy position of merely having to do as she was told, and not required to accept responsibility for other people's foolishness, was amused at Polycarp's manner and secretly delighted at the assistant's obvious concern. He, poor man, did not know whether to shout for help and bind Polycarp until a doctor could be called, or whether to do as Polycarp bade him. Whatever he did, he was jeopardising his job. Torn between these two alternatives, he at last decided upon the easier and made no effort to interrupt Polycarp as that gentleman, with his battered Homburg perched like a moulty crow on his head, sat with his feet on Squires's highly polished desk and dictated an editorial which made the assistant wince at every sentence.

When the editorial was finished, Polycarp dismissed the girl and then, to fill up the time while the editorial was set up, he cornered the assistant and, with all the superb calmness of the completely but unhappily intoxicated, he held the man to him with a long discourse upon the effect of Rabelais on modern conventions and the influence of Daudet on French as taught in public secondary schools. He thrust a cigar into the man's mouth to stop his under-lip from quivering, and talked on and on like a patent gramophone until the proofs came. He corrected the proofs, still talking, and he did not let the assistant go until the editorial was tearing through the thundering, rolling presses for distribution all over England. When he knew that there could be no interference with his act, Polycarp left the building and called a taxi. On the way home, he went to sleep, and remained asleep despite the efforts of the taxi-man and his valet. He was carried by them up to his room and put decently to bed, and slept the dreamless sleep of a man who has weaved a purpose from his drink and carried his purpose into action on the crest of his carousal.

The next morning he was awakened gently by his man, who placed a tray on the bed, containing his breakfast, and, as was his custom, a copy of the new issue of *Polycarp's Weekly*. Polycarp picked up his paper and dismissed the food without a regret. The memory of his evening had gone from him, in detail, completely, until he came to the editorial page and read what he had dictated the night before. Polycarp's feelings as he lay reading may be likened with some felicity to those of a man who, dying, hears the sound of his funeral-bell tolled by order of some over-hasty cleric. The editorial was splashed with wide margins over the centre page and it was impossible even for the casual reader to miss it.

TRUTH NOT TRASH! FACTS NOT FICTION!

For some years now this organ has enjoyed the confidence and popularity of a wide circle of readers. We may not be considered boastful if we assume that the success of this weekly is due to the principles which it strives always to carry into practice, principles which induce both confidence and popularity.

Our great service has always been to give the public truth and not to subvert truth for any man, to give the public fiction which was entertaining rather than educative and, while we have been under the obligation of making a profit, never to allow dividends to divide us in our determination to serve our public first and ourselves afterwards.

And now we have a CONFESSION to make. While we have shouted "Truth" we have been condoning a lie to ensure our profits. We have subsidised Truth with the profits of deception.

Look at the advertisements in this weekly, the very blood which keeps it alive, and see how false they are, how misleading and dangerous—and yet we print them week by week to ensure our profit!

On various pages will be found advertisements for foodstuffs which only irritate the stomach, and never satisfy as the manufacturers say; for cures for every ill which, should a man trust to their vaunted efficacy, he would die within a week; for drinks which it is an abomination to pour into the local authorities' drains, let alone into man's body ... all these advertisements are false, abusing with misleading adjectives what little good may rest in the wares they shout.

This we CONFESS, and also crave your indulgence and forgiveness. In future a strict surveillance of all advertisements in this paper will be made, and none accepted which is in the slightest way misrepresentative.

POLYCARP JARVIS.

As Polycarp finished reading, he groaned loudly and dropped the paper to the floor. He could not imagine how he could have behaved so stupidly.

This was the end of *Polycarp's Weekly*; this was the end of him and of his ambitions. He could see himself faced with a couple of hundred lawsuits from manufacturers ... and all, he groaned, because a woman had been true to her feelings and he had been fool enough to try and forget his fictitious disappointment in drink. This was the end of him and—the thought suddenly occurred to him—the end of the scores of people who were dependent upon the weekly for a livelihood.

"Damn it! What an ignorant, selfish, unthinking ass I am!" He slung himself from the bed and glared at his reflection in the mirror.

Polycarp, who was not usually given to imprecations, enlarged upon his outburst with as choice a collection of tavern oaths and clerkly comminations as he could command. Once he had perjured his soul almost to start the weekly, to prevent the human sacrifices which would be made if the paper ceased publishing, and now he had in one wild night sacrificed five times as many men and women without a single thought.

How could he explain his act? He rubbed his upper lip and then, lighting a cigarette, strode up and down the room trying to see his way clear. Peggy could not help him now, and Mr. Winterton was powerless to prevent the smash-up; he had to swim or sink by himself, and upon his ability to survive rested the fates of hundreds of families. For the first time in his life, Polycarp realised that no man can ever be a completely irresponsible individual; that no man can live his own life regardless of other people; that man has a duty to man which limits, while it strengthens, his individuality. In those ten minutes, as he paced his bedroom before his man ushered in the pale, distraught, and furious Mr. Squires, Polycarp lived through an emotional experience which aged his spiritual body ten years and exercised his brain as it had never been exercised before. But the indomitable enthusiasm and resource which had made him a man of mark in London at an age when most men are financially infants and commercially children, this will to be Polycarp, and not a unit unrecognisable from the millions of other units in England, came to his aid and proffered him a loophole through which he might attempt to struggle to safety.

He looked up as Squires slammed the door, and his face was the face of the smiling, care-free Polycarp who had once flourished a bundle of coloured tickets in the faces of the inhabitants of March, but underneath his composure he was as perturbed as Squires was furious.

"Mr. Jarvis—I hand in my resignation at once! I refuse to be associated with such irresponsible ... damn-foolery! I ... I"—Mr. Squires's mouth opened and shut with agitation as he flapped his face with his gloves and marched pompously towards Polycarp.

"Sheer unbridled lunacy! What on earth you did it for I don't know. You'll have the whole country about your ears in twelve hours, and I do not intend to be involved. I'm speaking to you as man to man now, not as employee to employer."

"My dear Squires, calm yourself and have a smoke." Polycarp pushed the box towards the man, and so great was the other's confusion and distress that he took a cigarette and began to shred it over the floor as though it were a bus ticket.

"I hope you will always speak to me as man to man, Squires. That's the only way I wish ever to be addressed. And now what is all the fuss about?"

"Oh, don't prevaricate and beat about the bush. You know as well as I do," said Squires, picking up the weekly from the floor. "That damn' insulting, unnecessary, untrue, irresponsible editorial! Do you realise what this is going to mean? It's going to cost you thousands of pounds in lawsuits and means the finish of your paper. Means the finish—do you understand that? Are you completely mad?"

"Mad? My dear Squires, I'm as sane as you, though I must confess that you astonish me somewhat by your abruptness and lack of understanding." Polycarp's tone was that of a gently chiding father.

"Understanding and abruptness! What do you expect me to do? Thank you for making it imperative for me to resign a good job? Thank you for making a fool of my paper?"

"No, Mr. Squires, not that, but to thank me for making you the editor of the most famous weekly in London; thank me for privileging you to participate in the greatest journalistic scoop of the century; thank me for putting the name of Squires on the map, and thank me for giving the country its smartest advertising campaign."

Mr. Squires eyed Polycarp weakly and shook his gleaming skull in perplexity. "I can't fathom you. I still think you're deranged."

"No, no, Squires, not mad, I tell you. Listen to me. That editorial wasn't the rash act of an irresponsible fool. That was cold, clever business, and it's going to make *Polycarp's Weekly* famous and enable me to raise our advertising rates double their present figure ... Now keep calm and listen to me while I outline why I did it."

An hour afterwards, Polycarp and Mr. Squires left the house for the office in a closed car, and Mr. Squires's face was ruby with the glow of a secret which he alone shared with Polycarp against the world. Polycarp was taking a chance, and how slight that chance was may be measured by the fact that he had not easily convinced Mr. Squires of its authenticity, but to convince Mr. Squires, who had been weaned on printer's ink and knew no atmosphere so well as that of Fleet Street, was a creditable beginning.

The rest of that morning and afternoon Polycarp and Mr. Squires were locked in the editor's room, and, though the office was besieged by reporters all eager for the inside story, they could not obtain information from anyone, and all the office telephones were disconnected. Not even Mr. Winterton or Peggy could get into communication with Polycarp. In their shirt-sleeves, he and Mr. Squires battled—Polycarp to save his paper and himself, and Mr. Squires to bring off the biggest journalistic risk of the century— and the strain upon both men was evidenced by the appallingly untidy state of the editorial room with its scattered papers, crushed cigarette stubs, and the stacked beer-bottles and food remains which had been necessary to sustain them as they worked out their individual salvations.

It was not until the presses were thundering with a special number of *Polycarp's Weekly* that they relaxed and discovered that they were out of cigarettes. For twelve hours they had laboured, and during that time no one had left the building and no one had entered. Outside stood a curious crowd of spectators, including reporters and infuriated representatives of half the big commercial concerns in London. That day Polycarp became national news and the next day saw him a national genius, a genius so potent that no one, not even Squires or the harassed assistant editor, guessed how near to calamity and ruin he had come.

The special number of *Polycarp's Weekly* was not sold; it was given away. Newsagents, acting on instructions from the weekly's office, handed free copies to their customers, and boys distributed them in the street, and it contained a full account and satisfactory explanation of the outrageous editorial.

The weekly denied that the editorial had been written by Polycarp, although it carried his imprimatur. The front sheet was devoted to a full explanation. In simple, concise, but telling sentences, the assistant editor told of a realistic impersonation of Polycarp; how a fake Polycarp had entered the offices and by sheer bluff and superb acting had hoodwinked the staff so thoroughly that the editorial had been printed. In another article, Polycarp established an alibi, supported by his valet, describing how he had spent a quiet evening at home, and in another article Mr. Squires conducted a reasoned enquiry into the possible motive behind the impersonation of Polycarp and the attempt to wreck the weekly. He had clinched his arguments by hinting that the paper had inside information, which it was not wise to disclose altogether, that the dastardly act had emanated from a Bolshevik source, and was probably the first of a long series of schemes to sabotage the foundations of organised society. This hint, more than anything else, won the people's imagination and provided a glib refuge at a time when Russia was the convenient scapegoat of the world.

In the editorial, written by Polycarp, the paper made a full and unconditional apology for the upheaval.

> *While we must deprecate and join our readers in expressing horror at the malicious stroke at our popularity and esteem, we are, in a fashion, grateful to the evil instigators of this social crime for granting us this opportunity to assert our policy of truth and probity.*
>
> *This special issue contains all the advertisements so maliciously slandered by the unknown impersonator and, of course, no charge will be made to the manufacturers concerned for their insertion. As to the wares advertised, it needs but a moment's reflection to perceive how unfounded were the charges laid against them. Any advertisement in this organ has by virtue of its inclusion our supreme confidence, and readers may rest easy that, as our editorial policy is "truth not trash," so is our advertisement policy.*
>
> *As an earnest of our good intention and deep regret at this unfortunate incident, this number will be circulated free of charge; thus do we re-affirm our confidence in our public and repulse the dastardly attempts of subversive forces to overthrow one of the greatest influences in journalism today for truth and plain speaking ...*

The next day Polycarp made a personal call on the heads of all the firms involved and expressed his profound apology for any inconvenience caused to them, and he also gave a detailed account of the steps which were being taken to detect the impersonator. Before he left, he had convinced them—if any of them needed convincing—of the wonderful advertisement which the affair had provided for their goods.

The risk which he had taken brought him to victory, and at the end of the week he knew that *Polycarp's Weekly* would need no further advertisement stunts to endear it to the public, and he himself became a national figure. Crowds collected round his car in the streets; the daily papers printed his views and account of the outrage; the broadcasting authorities graciously allowed him ten minutes between the nine-thirty news and a talk on "The Stars at Night" to tell the listeners his experiences; and he knew that everywhere men and women and children were mouthing the word Polycarp. Two mornings after the appearance of the special number of his paper, a daily referred to him as the "Splendid Polycarp."

"I should like," said Mr. Winterton to Polycarp as they were talking a few days after the outrage, "to get hold of that impersonator. I could make something from a fellow who was as good an actor as that."

"Don't worry, Joseph Kay. How do you know that he isn't someone who's already been made by you?"

Mr. Winterton looked at him through his spectacles, quizzically, but Polycarp would say no more. Mr. Winterton did not press him for details. Apart from Squires and a few others on the staff of the weekly, Mr. Winterton was the only person who ever suspected that there had been no impersonator; and no one—not even Squires—suspected that Polycarp's editorial had not been deliberately planned, except the girl stenographer, who lived at Greenwich and supported an habitually drunken sea-captain of a father, and she guessed that Polycarp's inebriety had not been simulated, but such was the loyalty amongst his staff that she never mentioned her doubts to anyone.

Lord Depping, Peggy, and scores of others offered Polycarp their condolences for the impersonation, and he accepted them. Only Mr. Winterton bit his lips and smiled, and when he was alone smacked his leg and laughed.

Everything Polycarp had promised to Mr. Squires happened. Within a month the advertisement rates in the weekly were doubled and the manufacturers were glad to pay his price, for *Polycarp's Weekly* was cheaper, less easily mislaid, and as essential a factor in most British homes as a screwdriver.

In the excitement of those few furious days, Polycarp almost entirely forgot his love for Peggy, and, when the bustle and anxiety were done, he found himself with so many fresh things to occupy his mind that he gradually forgot his passion altogether, and he was so busy that it was only very occasionally that he saw her.

XXI
Polycarp returns to school

Polycarp had become a public figure, and he now found himself continually on the alert for fresh speculations and ambitious schemes to satisfy the driving impulses within him.

Not only was his weekly making him a wealthy man, but he found it a useful medium through which to announce his new schemes and to prepare his speculations, and it was not through his weekly alone that he reached the public, for all the other papers were eager for information from him. He found that he had attained that delectable, and sometimes damnable, glory of being "news."

When great dailies composed symposiums of what Jack Hobbs, Bernard Shaw, Steve Donoghue, James Maxton, and Bertram Mills thought of the modern girl or the economic depression, there would also be included the opinion of Polycarp Jarvis, which aroused as much comment as any other. Of the modern girl, he said: "As my experience of girls is confined to those in my own employ, all of whom have successfully passed an intelligence test, I can say nothing about the modern girl." Of the economic depression of nineteen thirty-one he was very scathing: "The depression is compounded of nine-parts fear and one-part flatulence and kept alive by a few men, who, for political reasons, have decided to get the wind-up about nothing." Not only did he give this as his opinion, but he backed it by disregarding the slump, and, at a time when economy became the shibboleth of shopkeepers and masters of commerce, Polycarp spent money and consequently bought cheaply.

At the height of the depression he bought up a huge block of slum buildings in Stepney, and housed the ejected families in a modern block of flats, which he had erected on the site of four disused warehouses by the riverside above Limehouse. For a time the cleared slum area remained untouched while he tried to decide what he should do with it.

He did not allow his growing success to alienate himself from his old friends. He was something to all men and, despite his wealth and the luxurious trappings of his house and environment, he was still Polycarp. He visited Mrs. Anstruthers at Oxford, insisted upon paying up the mortgage on her house, and gave her a whirling day of gaiety in London; a day which started with cocktails at the Ritz and went on to lunch at Frascati's, two hours shopping in Oxford and Bond Streets, tea at a Lyons' Corner House because Mrs. Anstruthers wanted to hear the gipsy band, a picture show at the Carlton, and then a quick dinner at the Café Royal before going on to a theatre. At the end of the day Mrs. Anstruthers was in a state of swooning contentment and was glad of the night run in Polycarp's car to Oxford—to which she insisted upon returning so that she might be up next morning to prepare the lodgers' breakfasts—in which to recover her normal stability. Polycarp steered her into her sitting-room at three o'clock, and, after kissing her heartily to cheer her up, left her murmuring weakly, "My, when things happen they do happen …"

On the way back he stopped at an all-night coffee-stall in the Uxbridge Road to buy himself a drink and a sandwich, and it was here that he had his great idea.

He had parked his car at the roadside, and was leaning against the counter, chewing at a thick wedge of bread and ham. Inside the stall, the proprietor was busy wiping thick mugs and shaking his head to keep his cigarette smoke from his eyes. In the early-morning greyness the coffee-stall was a cheerful note, with its brass boiler and dwarfed piles of sandwiches and buns.

"Gonner be a frost before sunrise," said the stall-man, affably, to Polycarp. "I can always tell by the way the salt comes from the dredger. Funny thing, salt—gives you fair warning of damp and dry. Let's hope it's a sharp one—that'll be good for business."

"Ah—that's how you think of it—good for business!" Polycarp had hardly noticed the other customer at the stall until now. He was a shabby, thin man, with a red, sniffling nose and eyes that shone hungrily from the shade of an enormous peaked cap. Under his arm he had a violin-case.

"Well—ain't it?" said the stall-man perkily.

"For you, yes; but what about the poor devils what are on the streets? T'ain't good business for them. You're all right in your snug buggy-hole, with hot cawfee and plenty of smokes—but what about us? How'd you like to be sleeping on a bench on the Embankment with a nice frost nipping you, or moving up and down Edgware Road, waiting for the park to open so you could go in and have a kip?"

"Ah, well," said the stall-man philosophically, "what's meat for one is poison for another. You can't get over that, so why bother?"

"Are you ... on the streets?" Polycarp asked the question with some diffidence, for he did not wish to hurt the man's feelings.

"Should I be buying a tuppeny cup of cawfee at this hour if I wasn't? Sometimes you 'as to toss for it, whether you'll spend a night in blankets, warm and snug, and do without food, or whether you'll spend a night with your belly warm from food and drink and your feet aching and cold from the streets. It's a rum go, life, ain't it?"

"It unfortunately is," agreed Polycarp.

"Unfortunate—that's puttin' it mild, mate. Tragedy, I says. Look at me, on the streets, scraping at me old fiddle for a few pence, when if I'd had a bit of luck I might be where Kreisler and Kubelik are today. I got talent, I know I have—but it's too late now. When I was young I could have done things, if I'd had luck and some money to help me, but I'm a dead horse now, playing lousy dance tunes to people what ain't got time to bother with street players. And there's plenty of talent like meself on the streets—plenty of youngsters waiting for a chance that'll never come, and plenty of old 'uns waiting for ... well you know."

"Ay, that's true enough!" put in the stall-man, filling the man's mug again at Polycarp's bidding. "There's plenty of talent in the world waiting to be given a chance. Like you say, mate, you might have been a famous player and in other things, too. I've seen it meself. Tike football, fr'instance. I'm fond of football, and there's plenty of youngsters keen about it, what would be as good as any professional, if they got a chance, but will they?—no, not they. It's just luck all along; some's lucky and some's not. I knows—being on a cawfee-stall opens yer eyes."

"Football!" scoffed the musician. "What's a ruddy game like that gotter to do with music?"

The two started a discussion on the relative merits of football and music, and while they argued Polycarp left the stall, slipping a note into the musician's hand, and went to his car.

"He's a gent! A real gent," said the musician, as the two watched Polycarp's tail light disappear down the dismal perspective of street lights.

The stall-holder's remarks about football, and the musician's talk of waiting talent, had given Polycarp an idea. He lay in bed that morning and thought about it, and as the idea crystallised in his mind he slowly found himself growing enthusiastic. A few days later he had all his plans formed, and started with characteristic fervour to carry them into operation.

For the next few months Polycarp, in company with Samuel Carter, one-time professional footballer and a player of international repute, travelled England looking for the football talent which he knew waited for him.

Sam Carter was a diminutive man, somewhat bandy in the legs, with a voice that was out of place in a drawing-room but would have suited a ship's deck in a storm admirably, and of a bluff, rude, generous nature which somehow did not accord with his twin fears of rheumatism and accidents. These fears he had retained from his professional days, when his livelihood had depended upon his physical fitness. Now he ran a small gymnasium, and could afford to hire physically fit instructors to do his work. Sam was rather doubtful, at first, of Polycarp's idea, but after a time he was infected with Polycarp's enthusiasm and he became as keen as his employer.

Those months of travelling about the country provided Polycarp with the happiest and the saddest moments of his life. When Sam, either by himself or through his scouts, discovered a likely player, he and Polycarp would travel by car to visit the man or youth, and it was these journeys, into towns and country places hitherto unknown to him, which made Polycarp realise how little he knew of England and how impossible it was to hope that he, or any man, could ever know it thoroughly.

They went north to Cumberland and Durham, and Polycarp saw houses and towns of incredible ugliness and monotony. He passed through miles and miles of streets, where families lived like rabbits in hutches and fed less often than rabbits. In the workless shipbuilding towns of the north he watched men digging their pitiful little allotment patches, growing vegetables to eke out their dole allowance, and finding a corner for a clump of chrysanthemums or Michaelmas daisies. The flowers were all some of them had left to satisfy their natural love of beauty. Street after street whose windows opened into rooms of poverty and despair; rooms where women hunched over their sewing-machines, or darned until their eyes and backs ached, and worried over the household's meagre budget and wondered, when their minds had time to forget the troubles of crying children and loafing sons, what it was all coming to in the end; houses where small fires burned with a feeble warmth that only mocked the inhabitants and made the cold seem more intense—fires built of coals stolen from railway yards and gas-works heaps by children whose morality of living had little in common with the morality of the religion they learned in the drab schools and churches; back-lanes where boys played football in the roadway with balls of stuffed rag and paper, and laughed and drew chalk drawings on blank walls; corners where men stood and talked, not of their misery, but of the past and the odd incidents of the everyday life about them ... and in the midst of the squalor and hopelessness people still found place in their hearts for laughter and joking, and made their sport amidst the black slag heaps of deserted mines and the gaunt skeletons of empty factories. In one of these towns they discovered a youth, who, Sam declared, had the makings of a football genius, hardly more than a boy—a youth who had never known work, but who had kept himself fit with sport and plain food.

James Morris was the son of an unemployed riveter, and one of a family that lived and laughed on less than thirty shillings a week.

"Won't you come home to tea and meet my people, sir?" the lad had asked Polycarp, when the arrangements had been made for his journey to London, and the request had been so simple a gesture of gratitude that Polycarp had no heart to refuse. He and Sam went to tea. This was the first time he had been inside a working-class home where work was a holy grail which all men sought and few found.

The room was small and tidy, the walls decorated with a few family photographs and a picture made from an old calendar. In honour of his visit there was a good fire burning—he never knew that the family went cold for three days afterwards to make up for that extravagance—and a clean tablecloth. Mrs. Morris made no apology for the tea, and Polycarp had eaten the bread and margarine, and wondered at the courage of this quiet woman who faced life so surely in spite of all the trials which it put upon her. Mr. Morris was a tall man with a humorous glint in his eyes and frankly glad that his boy was being given a chance to do something for himself. After a while the company had thawed, and they had spent a pleasant evening talking and joking, yet always behind their laughter Polycarp had sensed the feeling of tension and fear. When he left he made a resolution that he would pay all his men enough to allow them to send something home, and he was filled with an admiring regret when Mr. Morris refused to accept his offer of help.

"Nay, Mr. Jarvis, 'tis the lad you're interested in—not us. You're welcome to our home, but we don't want charity—if ye can find me a job, now?" he smiled at the absurdity, as it seemed, of the request and watched Polycarp and Sam get into the car.

After that they went east to the quiet roads and country of Suffolk. They passed through a land where the ploughed earth was greening with young corn, and where rooks marshalled in noisy squadrons above the tall elms. It was a fat land where there was good food and fine ale, and where men were ready to talk with him in country hotels. As he travelled about, Polycarp captured the spirit of his early days when he had bucketed over the country peddling his cures. He watched the winter scene wake into the fresh beauty of spring. He saw sheep folded in corners of fields, and marked the pride on the gnarled faces of shepherds as they held to their bosoms the first lambs of the flock. He drove through rain that swept across the Welsh mountains to ravage the great central plain of England, and he lost his way in thick fog that cloaked and hid the twisting curves of the Wye, and foliated the scarps and crags of the river valley with moving shapes and swirling wraiths of cloud. Primroses pushed their way through the wet, dead leaves, and the pale daffodil spikes pierced the earth to greet the watery sun. Whenever Sam discovered a new player, Polycarp left London gladly and drove for miles along the roads that stretched over moors and fens and climbed the sides of peaks and soared through tall passes.

Sam had little difficulty in finding players, and all the men were generally eager to accept Polycarp's offer. But not all. There was a farm labourer on the far side of Sheffield who stoutly refused to leave his home to become a famous footballer. He doubted not his ability, but Polycarp's integrity, and also he was scared to leave the countryside which he knew so well and his village friends. Polycarp and Sam had been unable to persuade him to join them, and as they were motoring Londonwards through the Peak country, a late spring snowfall had trapped them in the hills.

At first the snow had not interfered with his driving. The headlights had shown the road before them and limned the dropping flakes with quicksilver. Both he and Sam were a little dejected over their disappointment, for the youth had been a good player and they had wanted him. The road reached through the darkness over the ridge of a hill, and as they breasted the top a gust of wind came down at them like a hand and rattled the car in its outburst. Polycarp kept the machine on the icy road and wished himself safely at Derby. The snow came thicker, and on the far side of the hill was piling into little drifts.

"Seems to be going to turn into a real snorter," said Sam, beside Polycarp. "They get sudden storms like this in the Peak country."

"As long as it doesn't stop me from getting to Derby tonight, I don't care how thick it gets," answered Polycarp. They drove on for another half an hour, and then suddenly the lights lost the road and Polycarp was blinded by a brilliant dazzle of white. He shut off the engine and braked, but the wheels slipped over the soft snow, and before he could do anything the car had plunged nose first into a thick drift that filled a dip of the road. The car ploughed into the mass and then stopped, and in the silence Polycarp could hear the soft clinging sound of falling snow all around him.

He swore, and, pushing the door open, got out and looked around him. Deep in the drift he could see the spreading illumination of the headlights, but elsewhere everything was a blackness streaked with the faltering lines of the thick fall.

"Can you back her out and try another road?" Sam asked. It was quite impossible to attempt to break through the drift.

Polycarp tried to reverse the car from the drift. The wheels skidded round without biting the snow and threw up a fan of sludge as they spun.

"No good," he said. "Looks as though we're stuck." And stuck they were for the night. They spent the long hours rolled in their rugs with the engine turning over quietly, while the petrol lasted, to keep the car warm. Neither of them slept. They smoked their cigarettes, and amused themselves by watching the snow pile up about the car, creeping higher and higher up the windows. The snow over the engine thawed, and the moisture soaked into the car and made the atmosphere muggy and damp. When morning came they were tired, shivering, and bad-tempered.

As soon as it was light Polycarp pushed back the sliding roof, with Sam's help, and climbed out. Except for a small portion of the roof, the car was invisible and the whole countryside lay under a covering of white. The sharp slopes of the hills showed black knife-edges where the wind had kept them free of snow, but the ledges and valleys were piled high with drifts. Scrub oaks clung to the white hillside and leaned forward under the weight of the white burden which pressed upon their branches, giving them an umbelliferous appearance.

The sun struck a cold glitter from the plain below, and somewhere behind him a sheep bleated. Polycarp had never seen such a sight. Before him lay the plain, its whiteness checkered with the red and black of bare wall and traced with the shadows of piled hedges and broken telegraph wires. The snow added a clarity to the air and a keenness to the touch of the sun. A long way off he could see a man struggling over a field, and through the air he caught the ring of a spade as someone cleared the snow from a doorway. Within a few hours the country had been changed into a soft, clean expanse of beauty which denied itself colour and relied upon the play of dark shadows where ditch and sheltered corner or windswept ridge had escaped the fall.

"It looks good, doesn't it?" Polycarp was impressed by the grandness of the scene in spite of his annoyance at the hold up.

"It gives me the belly-ache," said Sam, with pardonable vulgarity. "They ought to keep stunts like this for Christmas cards. I suppose we've got to struggle through this to find a town?"

"I'm afraid so, Sam. The car's no good to us."

"Come on then, let's get it over. I bet I fall into a drift and break my leg, or catch rheumatism with the damp …"

With Sam to keep him company with his grumbles, Polycarp headed for the plain. They pushed and scrambled their way through the heavy drifts of the hills for an hour until they reached the plain, where the fall had been more even, and they could walk more easily. By mid-day the snow was thawing fast and disappearing from the land, except for the drifts in the hills. They made Derby at last, and, after giving instructions to a garage about the car, Polycarp and Sam caught the London train, Sam still grumbling but dry, and Polycarp finding that, now he could view it as part of the past, he had enjoyed the little adventure.

But three days later Sam was left to continue his searchings alone, for Polycarp was confined to his room with an attack of influenza. When he was on his feet again his doctors advised a few days' holiday and relaxation to hasten his recovery. He decided to visit his aunt.

He had always maintained a fairly regular correspondence with her, and occasionally had managed to visit her. But after his great advertising stunt with his weekly he had not been able to see her, as he had been so busy. From the first she had steadily refused to acknowledge that he was a famous man and would not let him help her at all. He wanted to buy her a new house and settle some money on her. She only smiled as he repeated his offers when he came to see her after his illness.

"Don't be stupid, boy, you've been reading romances lately. You don't want to waste your money on me." She dismissed his offer and went on with her sewing.

"Aunt, please, listen. Why won't you let me? What do you think I left Bristol for, if it wasn't because I knew that one day I should make a name and be able to do something for you?"

"Don't be foolish, boy. You left Bristol because it couldn't hold you—that's all. I don't suppose you'll put the truth in your autobiography, though ..." She looked up at him and smiled slowly.

"How on earth did you know that I was writing my autobiography?"

"Your father wrote three before his unhappy death. I've got them upstairs. The first is the longest—and funniest!"

"You're laughing at me. Well, if you like to stop as you are, I can't force you to move, but I don't feel that it's right that my only living relative should live in a potty little side street while I strut it in a London mansion. Won't you come and live with me?"

"No, boy. I want to end my days in peace."

"Humour, humour ..." wailed Polycarp, in mock despair. "But I can stand it—"

"Why, boy, that doesn't sound like you at all."

"It isn't. It's a man called Harry Manning, or the son of Solomon, but never mind that. Isn't there anything I can do for you. It seems wicked for me to have all this money and yet not be able to do anything for you."

She was silent for a minute. In all the years he had been away she had not changed. She sat by the window, sewing, as she had been sewing when he had come home and told her of his resignation from the office ... a quiet, grey-haired old lady in a high-necked black silk dress, her cameo brooch touching the wrinkled skin of her chin as she bent to her work, and her face glowing with a soft inward calm—a woman refusing to acknowledge him as Polycarp the Splendid, and seeing him always as "Boy." Polycarp felt, during the pause while he waited for her to speak, that he had treated her very harshly while he had lived with her. He wished now that he had been more considerate. Now, it seemed, not all his wealth could enable him to do anything to please her.

"There is one thing you might do—though not for me."

"What's that?"

"Mr. Simmonds, the headmaster of your old preparatory school, asked me if I thought I could persuade you to give the prizes away at the next speech-day. He wanted you to make a little speech to the boys about your trials and so on. The man can't be so sensible as I thought he was. I wouldn't let you give advice to any boy I cherished."

"He does, does he? The old goat-bearded buffoon. When I was a boy, he thought I was good for nothing but spanking: now, when I'm well known, he's ready to toady to me. The sycophant; still, I'll persuade myself to do it—although I'm supposed to be an invalid—on one condition."

"Poor boy—you have enjoyed your illness, haven't you? However, what is it?"

"That you put on your best dress and come and sit on the platform beside me and share some of the glory."

"Oh, I couldn't do that."

"Then no prize-giving for me. Please, aunt ..."

She dropped her sewing, and then, seeing the look on his face, she nodded.

"All right, boy, I'll come. You'll want someone to look after you."

When Polycarp, in company with his aunt, entered the school which he had attended before going on to the Bristol Grammar School, he was appalled by the thought that he had once been deliriously happy inside the mid-Victorian walls and terra-cotta trimmings, and amazed to think that he had once regarded Mr. Simmonds to be a very Joshua among schoolmasters. Now the place stunk of books, boys, and chalk, and the headmaster was no more than a pince-nezed, fluffy-bearded old man who thought Garbo was a mouth-wash, and who was ready to wipe Polycarp's boots for the favour of a speech from him.

Polycarp applauded politely while the school gave various recitations, songs, and acts from plays. When the concert was done, he handed out the form prizes under the direction of Mr. Simmonds, though the master's eagle eye could not prevent Polycarp from blissfully presenting Jones minimus with Jones secundus's prize for English, and handing Jones secundus Jones minimus's prize for biblical knowledge. As the English prize was a volume of *Treasure Island* and the biblical prize a *Moffatt New Testament* there was a scuffle at the back of the hall when Jones minimus, hardly crediting such good fortune, refused to restore Treasure Island to its real owner. The subversive scuffling of the two contestants punctuated the whole of the ceremony and provided adequate pauses for Polycarp during his speech to the boys.

"It is a privilege for me," he began, and immediately forgot everyone in the hall but himself, "to come back here today and visit the scenes of my boyhood labours and triumphs. Under this venerable roof I was once happy and care-free—"

A scraping of chairs as Jones minimus nearly lost possession seemed to grate—"Liar!"

"You boys, who are perhaps a little resentful of the restrictions and severe routine of school and long for the freedom of mature life, must not forget the restrictions and impediments which the responsibilities of manhood bring."

Jones secundus grunted as he tugged at the end of the book, and in Polycarp's pause his grunt seemed to echo—"Garn!"

"Here, in this building, you have only one responsibility—to yourself. You are here to fit yourself in preparation for the great battle of life. And make no mistake, boys, it is a battle. I, who perhaps have been more fortunate in the struggle than some, can tell you that it is one long battle; and were I given my time in these venerable halls over again I should not do as I did before, when I frittered my time spent here so that my good friend Mr. Simmonds—though I did not then regard him as such—had more than once to correct me in no uncertain fashion."

During the titter of laughter which arose from the audience Jones minimus definitely lost possession of the book and changed from defender to aggressor.

"No, boys, I should prepare myself more thoroughly than I did do, so that I should be able to face the world well equipped to meet its buffets and blows. It is a trite, but none the less true, remark that one's schooldays are the happiest, and it is more true that they are the most important days of one's life, for by your endeavours at school so shall you be rewarded in life outside of school. Merit always gets its reward, though the reward may seem long in coming. I want you to remember that, boys; and, when you feel rebellious of the time required for the preparations of your lessons, say to yourselves, 'An hour spent working now means two hours saved when I am a man—two hours which I shall need some day,' and then go back resolutely to your work instead of heedlessly to your games. There are two difficulties which you as boys are faced with. The difficulty of exercising control of your desires, and the difficulty of controlling your exercise. Master these difficulties and the world is yours, and remember, if you have to choose between your books and your bat— choose the books. Books make for learning, and learning makes statesmen, and, while statesmen are always good sports, good sports are not always statesmen …" Polycarp was very satisfied with that bit, and even Mr. Simmonds nodded his head in approval, as he handed a note to a prefect to go round to the back of the hall and suppress the scuffling prizemen. Polycarp's aunt smiled behind her black gloves.

"Face life squarely, boys—that is my advice. Never do anything you can possibly be ashamed of; never play a mean trick; never act rashly without thought; always let your brain be the master of your desires—and you will succeed in your endeavours. I speak not from hearsay, but from actual knowledge. I have tested and tried those precepts in my own fife, and I think I am justified, though I do not boast it, in saying that the name of Polycarp Jarvis is respected wherever it is heard today. And such respect and honour are within reach of every boy here if he follows my advice."

Polycarp sat down, and, in the burst of applause which followed this somewhat inconsequential but sweetly platitudinous speech, the crash of toppling chairs as the Joneses resentfully left the hall accompanied by the ungentle prefect, was swallowed up.

Polycarp and his aunt took tea in the headmaster's study afterwards, and they were introduced to the staff and their wives. Polycarp suddenly found himself shaking hands with Gracie Hayward, a slightly stouter, more soberly clad Gracie than he had known.

"I fancy you have met Mrs. Coombes, the wife of the science master, before, haven't you, Polycarp?" said his aunt.

"Why, of course he has," said Mrs. Coombes, and her body half started its twisting and then stopped, as though she had remembered something. "Why, of course, Polycarp and I are old friends, aren't we?" This time Mrs. Coombes giggled loudly, and her body corkscrewed so that she slopped the tea from her cup. Polycarp saw the science master, a man with a body as thin and anaemic as one of his own pipettes, frown, and he wondered how long the poor man had been trying to break Gracie of her epicyclic laughter.

"Certainly," replied Polycarp, in a dignified voice, finding himself filled with a strange solemnity as a result of the lingering platitudes of his speech which still filled his mind. He tried to evade the contrast which flashed into his brain between Gracie and Peggy. "Certainly, Mrs. ... ah ... Coombes was a very good friend of mine in my ... ah ... my struggling days. We must have spent many happy hours together, though to be sure it was all so long ago that I scarcely remember any particular incident. Very happy days ... I'm charmed to meet you again, my dear lady. May I pass you a pastry?"

"Oh, Polycarp, how you do go on ..."—then, catching her husband's eye, "Thank you, Mr. Jarvis; thank you, I will have a cake. I think your speech was adorable."

Polycarp winced at the adjective, and he was glad when his aunt said she was tired and he could get away from the cake-eating, tea-slopping, laughter-repressing Gracie.

"How long has she been married?" he asked his aunt, as they drove away.

"Four years—silly girl. Two children—boy and girl, I think. When are you going to get married, boy?"

"Never! The ascetic life for me."

"Poor boy, you sound as though you'd started to read poetry."

"Humour, again, and from my aunt—the one person in the world I am entitled to expect respect from. Oh, human relations are as cold-blooded and cruel as those of reptiles! Is there no pity or compassion left in the world for me?"

"What do you want me to do—weep crocodile tears, boy?"

The car stopped with a jerk which killed Polycarp's retort.

XXII
A little man from Wandsworth

It was in the following winter that Polycarp satisfied the curiosity of the papers as to his movements about England. All the summer, men had been working behind huge hoardings on the empty patch of ground which was his in Stepney. Although he wished to keep his intentions secret, it was soon known that he was building a fine sports ground and stadium. While the stadium was under construction, Polycarp's footballers had gone into strict training, with Sam Carter, in a secluded part of Scotland.

When he adjudged that the time was ripe, Polycarp announced, through his weekly, that his team—composed of unemployed men drawn from the depressed mining, industrial, and agricultural areas—would challenge any First Division football team in England, and, if they lost, he would hand over to the Mayor of Stepney the sum of one thousand pounds to be used for any charitable work which should be decided upon by the council.

The challenge of the Polycarp Players, as they were called, provided a sporting topic and sensation which roused the interest of the country. Polycarp's audacity and faith in his players amused the public, and, while it amused them, endeared him to them, for they were ready to love a man who was willing to take a risk. There was something so simple and yet sweeping in his gesture that the country, which could remain cold when a Premier launched a new political idea, seethed with interest at this new factor in the football world. Within a week the challenge was accepted by the Thameside United, a First Division team representing the cream of professional football players. Newspaper men pressed Polycarp for details of his players, but he refused to make any statement, for he well understood the box-office value of mystery, and he kept his men well hidden in the country until the day of the match. Polycarp himself had little doubt of the result. He knew now how true it was that there were more geniuses outside of London, and begging in its streets, waiting for a chance to make themselves known, than were ever likely to achieve recognition.

He and Sam had found what they wanted—young men who had thought and dreamed of nothing but football since they were old enough to kick a ball, and grown men who had kept themselves fit during long periods of unemployment by playing on waste patches of ground and vacant lots, and in his team was a fine selection of players, strong with the strength which comes from hardship, and keen with the keenness which has battled against despair of improving conditions ... men and youths who had somehow escaped the demoralising influences of unemployment and poverty.

There is a mentality which finds it easy to sneer at men whose minds hold little else but thoughts of football. Yet, in a country where more provision is made for mental exercise than for bodily health, where public gymnasiums are much rarer than public libraries, it is a tribute to the nobility of the human spirit that men, who have every justification for sinking to the feral level of degenerates, still are capable of corporal enthusiasm and ambition, even though that ambition be represented by football and not Freud, and their enthusiasm be for a sport and not a spirituality.

Ten minutes before the match Polycarp descended from his grand-stand box to the dressing-room, and asked Sam to call the players. They came, eleven yellow-and-black-garbed athletes with huge black P's for pocket badges, and Polycarp's heart quickened its beat as he looked at them and remembered whence they had come; from Welsh coal valleys, from Bristol slums, from Durham drabness, from the misery of the Midlands, and some from London's own chaos ... He looked them over and noted their clear eyes and healthy flushed skins, and at that moment he went as near to sentiment as it is advisable for any man of business ever to go. He began to talk to them, and guessed a little of the feeling of Henry V before Harfleur.

"I'm not going to make you fellows nervous with a lot of words," he said. "You know what this afternoon means. You may think I'm nervous because of my thousand—forget it! That will be paid whether you win or lose. The real struggle this afternoon is for yourselves. I can only help you to this point and no further. You're going out to play against a team which is one of the best England can point to in the football world; you're going to play against men who eat, sleep, talk, dream, and worship football, and who are used to playing before huge crowds—and you're going to beat them! Yes, beat them! And I'll tell you why. Whether they lose is only a question of honour—they will still be paid footballers. Whether you win is a matter of life or death. And the man who fights for his life fights harder and fiercer than the man who fights for his honour. If you lose, you'll probably be the laughing-stock of England—that's the risk you take—and you'll go back to where you came from, to the poverty and misery which I won't stress because you know and hate it more than I ever can."

He paused. "But if you win—the world's yours to use as a football. It means a settled job, for this team will go on having lucrative engagements and may possibly end as a recognised league team, and you'll know security and comfort. I won't say any more; but remember you're going on to that field and when you come back it must be victorious—or …"

"Nay, Mr. Jarvis, don't you worry. You've given us a chance, and we'll show whether we're worthy of it. Won't we, lads?" The captain of the team, Walter Plaister, a dark-browed Hercules of a northerner, turned to his men. "Ay! We'll show 'em how to play football."

"That's the spirit!" boomed Sam, rubbing his hands.

"Remember," cautioned Polycarp. "Play clean football, but play hard. You carry my name now, and I don't want any dirt thrown on it. Good luck, and I'll be shouting for you from the stand—and swinging a rattle if necessary!" He patted the captain on the shoulder and then left the men. A few minutes later and the teams trooped on to the field. A roar like the combined mutter of a hundred avalanches met them as the yellow and black stripes of Polycarp's men and the blue shirts and white knickers of the Thameside United splattered the field with moving colours. Here was a modern tourney to be fought before thousands. It was an early spring day, with enough frost in the air to keep the players stamping their feet and smacking their arms until the kick-off.

Around the rectangle of fresh green turf was a thick barrier of faces and caps. Thousands of men and women circled the field, so that it might have been a green lake defended by high black and white pebble ridges and afloat with coloured wild-fowl.

The two teams were hailed with partisan cheers by the crowd. Policemen walked up and down the touchline, ignoring the remarks made to them from the fringe of the crowd. Amongst the spectators, programme-sellers whined and hawkers carted round their trays of popcorn, peppermint, and chewing-gum. Small boys wriggled through the legs of tall men to find their way to the grass verge, coloured rosettes tossed and flapped in the breeze, and high over the grand-stand a long yellow and black pennon floated in idle sensuous curves against the blue and white virginity of the spring sky. Thousands of hearts beat expectantly; thousands of mouths opened and shut as people chewed and talked and spat; thousands of chilly torsos warmed inside coats as the press of bodies increased, and thousands of feet grew colder with the keen draught that whipped along the ground. There was an atmosphere of delightful tension over the stadium, a sense of surprise which titillated the minds of the spectators and kept them in good humour. Not a square foot of space remained empty, the crowd covered the roofs of refreshment canteens, the top of the stands; and, even round the base of the pole carrying Polycarp's pennon, men were grouped like flies, and along the tall palings that marked the boundary of the ground street-boys had climbed to vantage posts to see the great match, the match which had been the topic of bar and ballroom, of house and hotel, of street and office for weeks.

"Polycarp's Latest," the papers had proclaimed. "Polycarp Does it Again." "A Challenge to British Sport."

The teams took up their positions, the linesmen clutched their flags, the referee bent down, whistle in mouth, and the whole ground was enveloped in a waiting silence through which came the faint noises of London—the hooting of a steamer, and the distant clang and growl of traffic. The thin pipe of a whistle echoed in the stands, and the statues of players leaped into coloured, kicking life as the ball moved from the centre of the field.

The first half of the game filled Polycarp with misery, and not even the slip which his manager pushed into his hand, showing the amount of the takings, cheered him up. His men were obviously nervous before the crowd, and lacked all the cohesion which had characterised their secret practice-matches. They were now no more than an odd collection of individuals, each with the possibilities of a great footballer, but warring against one another because of their indecision and nervousness.

Although the crowd cheered them in the way that a crowd does cheer the underdog, against the machine-like precision and clean skill of the Thameside United, Polycarp's Players showed up like schoolboys, and when they came off the field at half-time they were two goals down, and would have been in a far worse position had they not been kicking with a wind which had played tricks with some of the movements of the other side.

"Not much hope for them, Polycarp, I'm afraid," said Mr. Winterton, as he watched them disappear into the dressing-room.

"Don't you believe it. They're my men, and I've told them to win, and they're going to. You'll see. They've got to win, for their own sakes." Polycarp refused to be downcast in front of him.

"Of course, my boy, of course. But, even though I don't know much about this game, I don't think they will. Though I'm praying for them for your sake ..."

"You'll see," said Polycarp, though in his heart he was inclined to agree with him. The performance of the players had not fulfilled his hopes of them or the promise they had shown.

"Your luck's held too long, Polycarp," Mr. Winterton went on. "Now you've got your money on a loser. Still, your popularity can stand it, I suppose."

"Joseph Kay—such a defeatist attitude in you dismays me! I never back losers—"

"You have this time—and not a good loser, either."

It certainly looked as though Mr. Winterton were to be correct. At the resumption of play the Thameside United, with the wind in their favour, penned Polycarp's men in their own half, and had it not been for the heroic work of the goalkeeper they must have scored time and again. The crowd grew tired of urging the Polycarp Players to "Give 'em socks!" and, "Roll 'em in the mud!" Their encouragement died, and grew again in the form of boobs and caustic remarks; and a football crowd, when it begins to criticise, takes no regard for personal feelings. The crowd jeered the yellow and black men. They objected to the conformation of Walter Plaister's face, and they went through the history of each member of the team with an inexact but colourful plethora of intimate detail. The men played on gamely, and it was clear that they played with the conviction of beaten men ... Polycarp's words in the dressing-room had slipped from their minds, and their one objective was to last the time out, and then disappear from the crowd's disturbing candidness which was making each moment of the game a hell. And then something happened which proves that men resent most that which may legitimately appear to be the truth. For a long time Polycarp's men had been listening to a fantastic litany and description of their forbears' defects, of their own anthropoidal features and puerile prowess. They had been likened to camels, to codfish, to children, to sleep-walkers. They had heard themselves announced by roaring voices as the sons of maggots, as invertebrate nit-wits, as sanguinary fakes, and other epithets dear to the heart of a football crowd that feels it is not getting its money's worth. And they had not unduly resented the remarks because they were so very far from the truth—which was, that they were no more than good footballers who were suffering from a tenacious sense of inferiority. And then, from a corner of the field, a piping voice shouted mockingly:

"Come on the charity boys!"

The slogan caught, and in a few seconds the whole field seemed to be chanting: "Come on the charity boys!" It was then that something happened to the team. Walter Plaister heard the roar, and he knew how near to the truth and yet how unjust the words were. It was not only Polycarp's charity which had given them their chance, but their own skill and genius—and they were muffing their opportunity.

Walter Plaister spat from his muddy mouth, and his dirty face creased into angry lines as he swore to himself. In that moment he ceased to be a man, he became an avenging demon, scorning any man's charity. He looked round and nodded sympathetically to his men, who were all smarting from the false truth of the jibe. A miracle happened—a rushing, tearing, muddy, panting, sweating, pushing, kicking, thrusting, miracle. The team jumped into a sweeping solidity, held together by a determination to throw the he back into the faces of the chanting crowd.

Each man felt himself bound to wipe out the insult, and their only way lay towards the Thameside United goal. There was barely half an hour to go, and the Thameside United team never knew what happened in that half an hour. Plaister suddenly took upon himself the divinity of an archangel and the immunity of the Devil. He was here and there, the ball was attracted to him as though he were a magnet, and, when his foot repulsed it, it travelled, with a sureness that was uncanny, wherever he wanted it to go. For two rushing minutes the ball never touched a Thameside United man, and the yellow and black jerseys swarmed towards the goalmouth until a fast, low shot from one of the wing men sent it spinning through the keeper's hands into the net. Five minutes later another goal followed, and the crowd stamped its feet and sent white combers of frosted breath fading into the afternoon gloom as they bellowed their approval. They changed their tune; they shouted madly to the "charity boys," and now there was no sting in their words. Their first jibes, however, had done their work. Polycarp's men became a team, an invincible combination that swept from one end of the field to the other and performed prodigies of skill with the ball. They found a rich confidence in their anger that nothing could destroy, and the professional footballers went down before them as foot soldiers fall before cavalry in battle. At the head of his men rushed Plaister, eyes sparkling with fury and joy, and his mouth working in foul curses to relieve his wild spirits. He was a modern Taillefer leading his men into battle, and on his lips, instead of *Song of Roland*, were the dear, dirty oaths of Manchester and the Midlands.

The Thameside United left the field a defeated team four goals to two. Polycarp's men ran, laughing and smacking one another, into their dressing-room, and in the murk of the afternoon the crowd strained towards the grandstand where Polycarp was, and sang *For He's a Jolly Good Fellow*, and would not let him go without making a short speech. He had captivated their admiration and brought off a risk which excited all their love of daring and bravery. He and his men were heroes.

"You're the luckiest dog that ever walked," said Mr. Winterton, as they walked away.

"No luck in that, Mr. Winterton," put in Sam. "Good hard football and clever selection of men. Anyone could do it."

"Maybe it was a bit of both," said Polycarp. "Anyway, this is the first time I've ever felt as though I'd done something worth while. I'm glad for these fellows … Joseph Kay, if you'd seen what I have …"

They drove away from the ground, and in the press about their car was a little man, going home to a supper of tripe and onions at Wandsworth, who never guessed how large a part he had played in Polycarp's life by shouting, "Come on the charity boys!"

The Polycarp Players became for a while almost a fable, and for the rest of that season they played team after team and beat most of them; they were inspired men, and their inspiration brought them happiness and Polycarp large sums of gate money, so that he was able to lower the rents of his new flats for slum dwellers and subsidise his losses through his stadium receipts.

XXIII
How an Atlantic Flight began in Charing Cross Road

The world was a very grey place, so thought Polycarp as he sauntered alone through the thin drizzle along Charing Cross Road. Whenever he was oppressed by fits of dejection, which came at times to temper his superb optimism, it was his habit to walk down the road and immerse himself in the bustle of life which seemed peculiar to this road alone in the whole of London. He moved slowly along the edge of the pavement, swinging his stick and watching the roadway through the blur of rain-drops which he allowed to collect upon his eyelashes. Tall red buses swayed along the road, distorted by the water into fantastic red elephants with piggy yellow eyes; long private cars swirled in and out, their tyres dribbling with water, and adding to the mutter of the roadway with their gentle susurrus; errand-boys in the livery of cleaners' and outfitters' establishments performed mad convolutions around the other traffic, and let the sooty rain and grime of the city caress their faces as country boys lift their broad cheeks to the rough touch of upland storms. Charing Cross Road had a soothing effect on Polycarp.

The bright windows of the shops were filled with gaudy song-hits that lyricised anything from rain-soaked sugar to a year in jail, and outside in the rain stood men who bore on their faces the marks of vicissitudes which come to those who will not acknowledge that life has overtaken them. There were shops filled with brightly coloured shirts and ties, with figured hose and decorated braces, shops warm with thick fur coats and gleaming leather jerkins, and eyeing these, as though they drew some comfort from the garments which they were denied despite their need, stood men whose trousers were jagged at the heels, whose shirts were too old to face washing, whose ties had given up their design and colour to the dirt and drabness of doss-houses and park benches, and whose filthy, thin coats only advertised the poverty which they were intended to disguise. There was neither envy nor anger on the faces of these men; they just stood and looked, and edged away from the comfortable theatrical agents and plump citizens who rushed up and down the streaming pavements, as if they feared that they might be prevented from looking at the unattainable if they hindered these more fortunate men. Around the bookshops little clusters clung like swarming bees to the cheap shelves, and tried to forget their poverty and coldness in the pages of Anatole France and Edgar Wallace, and with them were lean-framed students whose eyes ran over the book titles with the appraising and discriminating glance of a producer selecting a beauty chorus. It was a road of men fat men who stood like bulwarks against the pavement scramble as they feasted their eyes on the frontispieces of nudist magazines and let their eyes wander pornographically over the photographs of foreign journals; thin men, with dirty collars, who held brown copies of Voltaire in their hands and chuckled as Pangloss sweated at the galley oars, and then replaced the books in the shelves and went off to spend their money on an A.B.C. meal; tall men who stooped to the medical shelves and read with apparent ease the German titles; short men who reached up to the fiction shelves in search of first editions; men— with faces that spoke of breeding, and clothes that bred lice and told of reach-me-down tailors—who held in their hands fat, comfortable volumes as though the warmth from the masters should uncramp their fingers for a while before they put them back and went away into the clanging turmoil and wet misery of the day.

Polycarp had come to know nearly all the types: the students; the halting provincial; the down-and-out teacher; the pensioned bibliophile, starving himself to feed his library; the sensualist, lingering over the plump posed women of the health magazines; the foreigner, greeting Goethe with little cries and Mann with reverence; the American, picking up everything bound in battered leather; the clerk, skipping the cloacal Rabelais and the grand Johnson for the earlier Wells novels, and the omnivorous readers of sensational paper-backs. For Polycarp it was a street of interest, for others it was a street of adventure and tragedy. Here, from black portfolios, were produced the songs which acted as narcotics to a million love-sick girls and disappointed swains; here came the hot-music mongers and laughter-makers of three continents; here congregated those sons of Israel who had forgotten the warrior splendour of the son of Nun and the dark deed of Ehud the left-handed, and here, when their fortune had turned full circle, came the favourites of a fickle public to haunt the offices which had once welcomed them, to commune with other unfortunates and to while away their long hours with tales of past triumphs and present hopes. It was a whole world in miniature, containing every class distinction, every joy and despair, every tragedy and triumph, each sorrow and sin—and the glaring cars and buses that swam along the wet road with their loads of men and women were no more than outer planets, swinging for a moment in their orbits by this world and then gone, never dreaming of the cosmic forces which swarmed in that narrow stretch of road between St. Giles' Circus and Trafalgar Square.

As Polycarp walked along the wet road, thinking of his own oppression and the mixture of misery and splendour around him, he regretted that he had ever left his kennels and come to London. His triumphs, though they were accorded more acclamation, never quite recaptured for him the joys which had accompanied his early successes when he and Frank had founded the New Age Flying Company; the success of Polycarp, the newspaper proprietor, was not so satisfying as the triumph of Polycarp, the son of Solomon. The atmosphere of money, the glitter of high life and London laughter, seemed to devitalise his efforts, and at times as he walked he wished he were still jockeying around the countryside in his little van. He had been happy in those days, he told himself, without any adamant desires to thwart his peace of mind; in those days there had been few responsibilities to cumber his intellect and destroy his sleep; no committees, no telephones, no meetings, no agents, no lawyers, no necessitous petitioners ... he had been free and the world had been his. Now when he was miserable, his degenerate impulses sent him walking for relief through an artificial valley of houses and shops; in those other days he had taken his troubles into the fields and laughed away his sorrows and disappointments in the keen air of the moors. For motors he had had the slow movement of cattle, knee-deep in tall grasses starred with dusty kingcups; for songs he had heard the sharp call of tits, searching in the walnut-trees, and the long whistle of blackbirds volleying from dew-spangled briars; and for company he always had the sound of the wind in the leaves, and the pleasant grumble of the river over its rocky bed. He thought of Sussex and the long lazy Downs, with the blue heat haze covering the sea in the south; he thought of the immeasurable distances of the fens, and the steady beat of a hawk against the mauve and yellow sky; of Wales and the comfort of craggy hills and lakes like disturbed quicksilver; and of the Pennines, where time had lost its meaning. Some day he was going back to all that ... unless ... He was now Polycarp—Polycarp the bold; Polycarp the grand; Polycarp the splendid: Polycarp who did not ask but intimidated. He was—He was going on to outline to himself all the things he imagined he was, flourishing with his stick to preserve the rhythm of his thoughts, when a voice said in his ear:

"Hullo, Socrates, how'd you like to buy yourself a jumping dog to amuse the kiddies at Christmas?"

Polycarp came out of his reverie and halted. A man was addressing him from the gutter—a short man with a thick bushy beard and carrying a tray of jumping toy dogs.

"My good hawker," said Polycarp pompously, and a little annoyed at the interruption. "I have no kids, as you phrase it, neither have I need to amuse anyone with jumping dogs. Laughter should be spontaneous, rising from the soul, not extraneous and motivated by the artificial actions of toys. Here is five shillings—buy yourself a meal and a shave."

He turned to go, when the man dropped his tray and seized his arm with a familiar movement.

"Well, I'm damned! Eight years, and you haven't got out of the habit of talking to people as though they were students at a lecture. No wonder they made you front-page news. Don't you recognise your old comrade in misfortune? Don't you recognise beneath this dirty beard the once-loved face of the functioning half of the New Age Flying Company and the sordid, potential, but unexpressed, architect?"

"Good Lord! Frank Burns!" cried Polycarp, as he recognised his friend.

"Frank Burns—the English Immelmann himself—now selling Japanese manufactured dogs to support the anatomy which once risked death to make England a land fit for heroes. Men play grim jokes on one another, don't they? There you are—lousy with wealth, and here am I—just lousy!"

"Frank—you must forgive me for not recognising you. It's that beard. What on earth's happened to you? And why didn't you look me up? I did make enquiries for you at one time, but I couldn't find you." Polycarp was genuinely concerned at Frank's condition.

"I didn't fancy pushing myself on you … You know, a fellow may be damned low, but I guess all that bunk about pride still means something—"

"Here—taxi! We can't talk in the street. Chuck your tray away and come with me."

A taxi sidled up to the curb at Polycarp's signal and he pushed Frank into it. Polycarp gave the driver his address, and added, as he pushed the jumping dogs into the man's hands, "Here's something to hand out to the children in your street when you go home. Drive quickly, will you?"

"Right y'are, sir. Very good of you, sir." The taxi driver accepted the present with an unconcern which was probably a commonplace thing when the gods lived on earth. They shot away into the traffic towards Polycarp's house.

"Don't talk. We'll leave all that until I've made a new man of you," said Polycarp. "You fool; you utter, senseless idiot. Why on earth did you let a damned silly thing like pride stop you from coming to me? Here I am with so much money that I don't know what to do with it—and you on the streets! Don't talk, I said. Just relax. You're a damned fool, Frank."

Half an hour later Polycarp was looking at a very different Frank Burns—at a Frank Burns who was warmly clad, fresh-shaved, and bathed, and starting in to a good meal.

"You haven't changed a bit," said Polycarp, watching him eat with much the same satisfaction a mother gets when her ailing child begins to show signs of returning appetite. "It was that beard confused me."

"And you haven't changed so very much. You're famous, but you're still the same amiable, talkative gas-bag that bombed Brinton. Remember that day?" Frank chuckled, and stuck his fork into a potato.

"You bet I do. Gosh! Things have happened since then—nothing quite as exciting as that, though."

"They have. You went up and I went down."

"What happened to you?" asked Polycarp gently, with the hesitancy of a man who knows that he may possibly be treading on dangerous ground. Frank was not reticent over his downfall.

"Oh, the usual things. Going from bad to worse, and always hoping things would look up. I never seemed to be able to hold on to money. I won't recite the gory details, but you can see where I'd got to—selling toys on the curb. You know, you begin to open your eyes a bit when you stand on the curb instead of walking along the pavement. And that reminds me—you've given my stock away. That'll cost you a few shillings."

"Don't be foolish, Frank. I'm not letting you go back to a job like that. I'll see you get another job somewhere."

"I've about as much chance of getting and keeping another job as I have of flying the Atlantic."

"Flying the Atlantic …" Polycarp started at the words, then he looked keenly at Frank and his face tightened with an idea. He had a genuine regard for Frank, and his present condition pained him. Something was wrong with a system which kept Frank in the gutter and himself in luxury. He wanted to help the man, but he knew enough of Frank's temperament to understand that no ordinary job would hold him in check for very long. The man lived only for excitement, and his chance words gave Polycarp an opening for his generosity.

"Say, Frank—how would you like to have a shot at flying the Atlantic?"

Frank seemed far more interested in his steak than the Atlantic, and his principal concern was the warm sea of gravy on his plate, not the cold rollers of the ocean.

"How would I like to sleep with the Queen of Sheba? Wealth is turning your brain, Polycarp. I've as much hope of doing one as the other. Though," he added, with a sly grin, "if I had to choose between Sheba and the Atlantic,

I'd choose the Atlantic. It was Kipling, wasn't it, who said, 'I've had my pick of the women'?"

"Don't be coarse, Frank. Listen—I'm Polycarp, and I can make you or break you. I can get things done. It's an awful responsibility at times. You've given me an idea, and you're going to carry out that idea and make a name for yourself. You're going to fly the Atlantic for me!"

"Do you mind if I finish my steak first?" said Frank, with a calmness which is supposed to have characterised the English since Drake's day.

"Not a bit. You hang on here, I want to talk to my editor." Polycarp left Frank, and went into his study to telephone to Squires. He talked to Squires for half an hour, and then returned to Frank, who was making himself at home with one of Polycarp's cigars.

"You seem pleased with yourself, Polycarp. Still you ought to be—living in a place like this! Ever slept on the line in a threepenny doss-house? I never realised until now how much eating off a clean tablecloth improved one's appetite."

"Frank Burns, late Royal Air Force—you're made," said Polycarp, in a pontifical voice. He stood over the ex-aviator, running his hands through his yellow hair. Responsibilities and wealth had given a dignity to Polycarp's face, but it was a dignity which struggled always with a resurgent impetuousness and youthfulness. "Tomorrow you will be news—Squires will see to that. Our meeting in Charing Cross Road is going to become historic."

"What are you driving at?"

"This—you are going to fly, not just across the Atlantic, but across and back. Don't shout. You can do it in the plane I'll provide you with. I'll ring the aeroplane manufacturing people today and get things started. You'll fly across, rest, say, three hours for food and sleep, and then come right back. Gosh! What a story; and what a sensation! What a triumph of man over the elements!"

"Do you mean you're ready to finance such a flight?" Frank sat upright and threw his cigar away.

"I do. Why not? I know you can do it? This is your chance, and I'm damned glad to give it to you. It's a chance for you to put your finger to your nose at all the years you've wasted. Of course, your exclusive story belongs to my paper, and all the details of the flight are in my hands! It's your great chance."

"Polycarp, you're mad! I'm out of condition. I'm a broken-down aviator—a drunk, a nervous wreck, unhealthy, and unstable Oh, don't try to stop me, I know what I am. I'm a useless good-for-nothing who's never been able to forget the war days. I'm not a man, I'm a memory. You're gambling your money!"

"Rats! I'll give you a week of life; rich food, plays, late nights, and what you like—after that you are under my orders, and you'll live like a Cistercian, or a Benedictine, you can choose which, and within a month you'll be the antithesis of all you say you are now. You're not afraid, are you?"

"Don't be a fool, Polycarp. Of course I'm afraid. That won't stop me from doing it, though."

"I knew it. Then you'll do it?"

"If you like to put your money on me. Wheeeeo!" Frank whistled: "And thus morning I was wondering where the next meal was coming from. Polycarp, you're a Briton!"

"I'm a keen man of business—which is the same thing, I suppose—and also I have a weakness for you because part of my success is due to you."

The next morning the papers proclaimed—Polycarp's Latest! Polycarp Finances Atlantic Flight! Polycarp Takes the Air! Polycarp's Discovery—The London Lindbergh!

"You see!" said Polycarp, as he and Frank read the morning papers. "Anything is possible once you know how it's done and if you've got that little something."

"I understand—if you own a paper, eh? The thought of all this publicity is going to make me nervous."

"Forget it. Nerves are good publicity, only the reporters spell it temperament."

Polycarp fitted Frank out, gave him a hundred pounds, made him stay at his house, and told him to enjoy himself for a week before he went into monastic training for the flight. Frank, with a thoroughness which a puritan would have admired, and which made Polycarp smile, as it reminded him of the old days, celebrated his new self by coming home drunk every night for a week, and bringing with him trays of toys from the men in Regent Street. His bedroom was decorated with pecking hens, climbing monkeys, tumbling clowns, and a fairly representative collection of the genera of mechanical toys in which modern children delight.

While Frank was enjoying himself, Polycarp was busily inventing news stories for him and conferring with the aeroplane designers about the machine which Frank was to fly. Within a week Polycarp had things started, and it was arranged that the flight should begin in the early spring of the next year—nineteen hundred and thirty-two.

From Christmas until the time of his flight Frank was held by Polycarp at his house in the Chess valley, and there, under the skilful hands of doctor and physical-training expert, his body was brought back to as perfect a state of health as any body can achieve which has subsisted for several years on whiskey and irregular meals. Although Frank rebelled at times against his confinement, Polycarp was adamant, and detailed Higgins to keep an eye on the aviator. Once or twice Frank gave them all the slip and made what he called "whoopee" at the Ugly Duckling. As the day set for the flight drew nearer even Frank became impressed with the importance of his coming venture, and when the call of civilisation and the chatter of bars pulled at his heartstrings, he stifled his ache by whistling loudly and forcing Higgins to put on the gloves. On an average Frank sublimated his desires through pugilism three times a week, and Higgins slowly began to develop cauliflower ears and to pray for the flight to be over.

The aeroplane was finished three weeks before the flight, and Frank spent most of those last weeks testing and making himself accustomed to the aeroplane. It was a twin-engined monoplane of absolutely new design, and constructed solely for the purpose of the flight to America and back. It was painted in black and yellow stripes and christened the *There and Back*. Frank had half, expected that Polycarp would call it after himself, but he had insisted that his name should not be given to the machine because he knew that this would detract from the prominence which he wanted Frank to enjoy. This venture, although he could not help but derive some glory from it, was prompted entirely by his desire to do something for Frank. Yet, inevitably, when Polycarp indulged his generosity on the behalf of others he instinctively endowed his actions with his own theatrical effects.

"It's a grand machine, isn't it?" Polycarp said, to Mr. Winterton, as they stood in front of the gleaming monster. He let his eyes travel along its smooth lines and curves.

"It frightens me a little," said Mr. Winterton. "It looks ust like a big wasp preparing to sting."

"That's your imagination. It's nothing of the kind—it's a great dragonfly which is going to swallow up the fear of the Atlantic and turn three thousand miles into a third-class return to Brighton. Do you know"—Polycarp turned to him—"I'd gladly give up all my money and position in exchange for the ability to conceive and design such a creation as that? All the things I've done are nothing compared with that machine—that stands for science, for workmanship, for labour, and marks a period in the evolution of the human race. Can't you see the history behind it? Once man went in fear of the forests, and then he conquered them with paths. Man dared the deserts with his camels; he tempted the fury of the seas with his cockle-shell boat; from his rough carts came the motor, from his rude paths came the main roads, and from his coracle developed the ocean liner. All through history man has been fighting the time element in his life. Speed, speed, and more speed. His motors move now at two hundred miles an hour; his liners chase across the seas; his paths have explored the whole world; and now the air is struggling against his domination. Next week Frank will fly to New York and back and make history, and after him will come men, adventurers to dare and designers to conceive, who will fly to the moon and back, and make a trip to Mars as commonplace as an excursion to Margate is today. All that lies before us—and what have I done towards it? Nothing. All the credit belongs to the designers of that machine, and to Frank who will fly it. It's a sad thing when a man finds that he's lived the best part of his life to no purpose."

"Don't be dramatic, my boy, don't be dramatic!" Mr. Winterton took his arm and laughed.

"You forget that none of these things are possible without money. You provide the money, the life-blood, as it were, which makes these things possible. With your money you can command these things, but a designer without money is like a monkey without a tail."

"Money—you tell me that anything can be done with money! It can never buy a man the spiritual things, the essential things in life …"

The record flight started well. Frank left Hendon in the early morning of a fine day, and, despite the batteries of cameras, wireless microphones, and reporters, he preserved a calm worthy of a Roman hero. His last act as he stepped into the aeroplane was to wink at a pretty special correspondent from a London daily. Twenty hours later he stepped out of the plane on to the Floyd Bennett flying-ground and repeated the wink for the benefit of a pretty reporter from the *New York Times*. He had two hours' rest and some food, while the *There and Back* was refuelled and attended to by mechanics, and then, while all the cables in the world were humming and burdened with the news of his triumphant first stage, he took off into the air for the last lap of his record flight, and the lewd grin on his tired face as one of the flying-field officials finished telling him a story as he helped him into the machine was the last thing the world saw of Frank Burns. He disappeared into the sky and out towards the sea. For a while details of his progress were radioed from ships over which he passed, and then he merged into the long distances of the Atlantic, into the infinitude of storm and fog, of lone gulls and complacent plankton, and was heard of no more.

Frank Burns and the yellow and black *There and Back* vanished, as so many daring people have started upon long trails and vanished. Polycarp sat in the *Polycarp's Weekly* office, reading the cables and messages as they came through. When the messages ceased, he sat for hours, waiting. The hours passed until the time of Frank's arrival was overdue. Liners deviated from their course to search the waters, aeroplanes took off from the Irish and English coasts to watch the sea … but no sign of floating wreckage, no scrap of painted fuselage or torn wing indicated where Fate had overtaken Frank Burns. He made history in a record flight across the Atlantic, and, as Polycarp announced in the weekly, put a nation into mourning by his disappearance on the return journey.

Polycarp was acutely depressed by the tragedy. He called up Alexander Royston, and got him to write an appreciation of Burns for a special edition of the weekly. Royston wrote an article which would, if Frank had had the slightest claim to only one tiny miracle, have resulted in his canonisation. He put him amongst the famous discoverers and voyagers of the world. He made Marco Polo a day-excursionist against Burns's brilliance; Drake was no more than a clerk taking a motor-boat trip round the bay, Mungo Park a suburban hiker, and Columbus a man whose only claim to distinction was the introduction of smallpox to the Americas. He belittled the ancient heroes, and then put Burns among them so that he shone like a new star in the firmament of travel and adventure, and Polycarp printed his paper with a black edging and announced an exclusive life-story of the hero in future editions.

He wrote the life-story himself, and then went down to his Chess house to try and forget the tragedy for which he felt he was so actively responsible.

XXIV
Tonight—The Children of Destiny

Polycarp was distressed by the death of his friend. He felt that he was solely responsible for Frank's end. If he had not lifted him from the gutter to send him off on a mad venture for fame, Frank would still be living, perhaps unhappily, but anyway still living, and an unhappy life was better than death. And as he had reached that stage in the extreme twenties when tragedy, because of its infrequency, is the more felt, Polycarp refused to allow himself to forget Frank.

He reproached himself that he had not sought him out earlier while he lived, and made him share his fortunes. He saw the tragic end of his friend, when he was trying to help him to fame, as a punishment for his tardiness. He should have found Frank sooner. He became obsessed with the idea that he should have done more for Frank while he had lived, and when this obsession had taken toll of his sleep by restless nights, and curtailed his appetite for a week, it finally manifested itself in a powerful determination still to do something for Frank, though anything he could do now would only be in the nature of posthumous glory. But even posthumous appreciation is better than silence and the forgetfulness of the grave, thought Polycarp.

While looking through an instalment of the life-story which he had written, Polycarp conceived his great idea. In life Frank had found death as an aviator, though he had wished to be an architect; in death he should be remembered architecturally.

Before the papers had time to drop the mystery of Frank's disappearance, they were enabled to plaster the hoardings with:

POLYCARP TO BUILD BURNS MEMORIAL
THEATRE!
NEW THEATRE TO COMMEMORATE
ARCHITECT-AVIATOR
POLYCARP'S LATEST!

Polycarp outlined his plan to Mr. Winterton, and his opinion was clear-cut and definite.

"Nonsense, my boy, nonsense! It'll never pay you. I think you're making too much fuss about Burns—he was a nice chap, but, from all you tell me, you only knew him for a few months. Surely you don't really feel so cut-up about him?"

"I feel as though I were personally responsible for his death," said Polycarp. "And, anyway, I promised Peggy North once that I'd build a theatre which would show up the rotten affairs that London owns."

"It won't be difficult to build a better theatre than most of the present ones, I'll admit. You'll have a job to make it pay, though."

"Polycarp always makes things pay. I'll find some way of attracting the crowd. But that's beside the point. The Burns Memorial Theatre is going to be the biggest in London, and the best. Any play that goes on there is, by virtue of that fact, going to be a success. I owe such a building to Frank. He used to tell me sometimes about his dream buildings. If it hadn't been for the war he would have been a famous architect. He had ideas, and I'm going to concrete one of them to keep his memory green."

"And incidentally try and make a profit for yourself, eh?" Mr. Winterton laughed.

"That is unfortunate but inevitable, and I'm doing my best to forget it."

And Polycarp did almost forget the profit element as he threw himself into the task of building his new theatre. He called a panel of architects, and, after he had decided in consultation with them on the main features, offered a prize for the best design. He threw the competition open to all architects and architects' assistants in

England, and, refusing to be intimidated by the lure of a famous name, he chose against certain opposition the design of an unknown architect's assistant from Dover.

Within two months of Frank's disappearance, the foundations of the theatre were being laid. There were to be only three prices—five shillings, half a crown, and a shilling—for Polycarp was not insensible of the competition offered by the cinemas, and he knew that he would have to attract a good crowd to make the theatre pay. The building was constructed of reinforced concrete, and was of a bold, utilitarian design. Gradually it began to take shape. Rising in a great white tower from the morass of streets, its tall façade was stepped like the crags of a cliff and decorated above the main doorway with symbolic figures and a medallion of Burns's head. High in the tower a clock starred the darkness, and on the roof was a restaurant which offered one of the finest views and best meals in London. Inside the building everything was furnished with Spartan comfort that abhorred sharp angles and inaccessible corners; the seats had ample leg-room, and a special draught apparatus made smoking possible and prevented the smoke from reaching the stage. The stage itself was an intricate mechanisation which Polycarp, although he pretended he did, never understood. He knew that it moved, but never did he fathom quite how it did move. It was the dream theatre of all good theatre-goers. The doors from the bars and foyer closed a few seconds before the beginning of a scene, and any unfortunate who had not returned to his seat, as requested on the programme, in good time after the bell rang, was locked out until the next scene. To make this possible Polycarp had to have constructed special emergency exits from the auditorium to satisfy the London County Council's regulations; he maintained the expense was worth while to avoid the nuisance caused by vandals who returned noisily to their seats when the play was on. There were no boxes, and from each seat it was possible to obtain an uninterrupted view of the stage, and to hear, provided the actors spoke normally, every word.

The papers were full of the new wonder; some said it would never pay, others said it would be a riot, and the people, who held the inert power to make it either, just passed up and down in front of the growing marvel and held their opinions to themselves or forgot them in the rush of their workaday lives. Polycarp was a force, and they knew that whatever he did they could expect something interesting, and of the value-for-money order, from him. Polycarp was aware of his reputation, and he did not intend to do anything to impair it.

Since her refusal to marry him, and his subsequent madness with his weekly, Polycarp had drifted away from Peggy North and almost forgotten her existence. There had been so many things to occupy his mind that he had dropped his grand passion and immersed himself in his schemes. When they met, he never mentioned his formal avowal of love, though he still enjoyed her friendship.

Not long after his announcement that he intended to build a theatre, Peggy had called upon him full of enthusiasm to hear his plans and congratulate him upon his intentions, and when the building was almost finished he took her over it, demonstrating and explaining, as best as he could, its unique features.

"It's marvellous, Polycarp darling. It's everything a theatre should be—except those seat prices. Are you sure about them?"

"Of course—that's what the public wants. Make the theatre as cheap and comfortable as the films and you'll draw 'em in. Yes, it's a dream theatre—your theatre, in a way, because I've built it according to your wishes. And you have promised to open in the first play here, haven't you?"

"Yes, I want to terribly, Polycarp. But what about the play? Have you thought about that yet?"

"Well, it's got to be something good. I've had one or two suggestions floating round in my head. We shall probably get someone with a reputation—"

"That doesn't sound like you, dear boy. Relying upon reputations. Why don't you pick up some struggling nobody and make him famous?"

"I can't take that risk with the first play. When we open this place it's absolutely imperative that the play goes with a bang—slick and successful from the first line of the first act. You know what theatre people are No, the first play must be a success before we begin to rehearse it."

"Yes, there is some truth in that. But, Polycarp, it would be a much better opening if you could use an unknown man. Think of the boost that would give you! The theatre not only commemorates Burns; it also makes an unknown architect and an unknown playwright famous. Why, you'd be a philanthropic institution."

"I've no desire to be an institution. I can't take the risk. I've put a lot of money in this thing because I feel I owe it to Frank—but I've put such a huge amount that sometimes I wonder whether I do owe him so much. Still, that's disloyal."

"Nonsense, you must be business-like. Have you ever heard of Felix Ollard?"

"No—what is it?"

"He's a youngish playwright who's never had any success—in fact, I don't think he's ever had anything produced. I think he's a genius, myself."

"I don't want a genius for my theatre, I want a craftsman—a good playwright."

"I think this man is that. I met him the other day. You must see him some time. He may be able to help you."

"Help me—an unknown genius! Why, even a new play by Shakespeare wouldn't altogether make me feel comfortable on the first night. You know what they're like, and so do I, from my Winterton days. The times I've sat shivering and waiting for that weak clapping or lusty applause!"

Although Polycarp dismissed Felix Ollard from his mind then, he met him a few days later when he called at Peggy's flat.

Felix Ollard was a large, clumsy man. His long silky, fair hair swept back from his high forehead, and his eyes swam and vacillated behind thick-lensed glasses like two tadpoles. He was obviously one of those happy mortals who instinctively excite the maternal instinct in a certain type of woman, and who, while they will suffer no compromises in their ethical theories, will cheerfully wear the same pair of trousers for a year and use string for shoelaces. Polycarp discovered later that, despite an impenetrable egotism, he exercised a certain pathetic charm which made some people enjoy his company.

"This is Felix Ollard," said Peggy, and Polycarp wondered if she were apologising for the man. "He's brought a play for you to read."

"One of my latest works, Mr. Jarvis," boomed the man, with a voice which was surprisingly strong and mellow. "I think you will like it. The moral force in it is simply terrific ... terrific ..." He caught the word to himself, and repeated it for a while as though he were sucking an acid-drop.

"Thank you, but I'm afraid I shan't get much time for reading until all this theatre business is fixed up. Besides, I never read plays for recreation ... only novels."

"Don't take any notice of him, Felix," laughed Peggy. "He's being dictatorial. Polycarp"—Peggy turned to him with a quick bird-like movement and caught at his hands—"Polycarp, don't be stupid. I want you to read this play and see if you like it enough to put on at the Burns Theatre. I think you will. I think it's a masterpiece."

"Peggy—" Polycarp stopped. He did not wish to enter into any argument before a stranger. "All right, Mr. Ollard, I'll have a look at it. What is it, a farce?"

Felix Ollard laughed hollowly for a few seconds, as though he liked the sensation of his vocal vibrations tickling the lining of his stomach.

"As it is an epic, it necessarily contains an element of farce, Mr. Jarvis ... an element of farce ..."

Polycarp joined wonderingly in the laughter. "Quite; an element of farce ..."

"It also embodies an entirely new technique, Mr. Jarvis."

"It's marvellous, Polycarp. I'm sure you'll like it!" Peggy stood between the two, her eyes shining, and her long fingers playing in quick, impatient movements on Polycarp's sleeve. "I can just see myself in the part ..."

"All right, I'll have a look at it. But—" Polycarp took a cigarette, and let his "but" die with the wisdom of a man who has decided to reserve his judgment until he has had time to consider the play in the sane comfort of his own bedroom.

"Thank you, Mr. Jarvis ... thank you ... I'm sure you'll appreciate the earnestness of the play. A play with a purpose one might call it ... a purpose. Not like so many of these modern plays. I have not long been in London, Mr. Jarvis, but the few plays I have seen have revolted me by their obvious sterility ... their obvious sterility."

"You wouldn't say that if you knew what the box-office takings of some of them were. Ask Peggy which of her shows lasted longest—the farces or the tragedies."

"Oh, it's true, I suppose, that the audience like to laugh rather than to cry, but sometimes they should be made to cry."

"Not in my theatre, they won't. Have you ever had any stuff put on, Mr. Ollard?"

"Only a very slight sociological drama—*The Demented Demagogue*—which was quite a success ... quite a success."

"Where?"

"At a students' theatre in Munich, Mr. Jarvis. Quite a success. It ran for two nights, and then the municipal authorities closed the hall, but the effect was explosive in its penetration ... explosive ..."

"The only time I ever dabbled with bombs I lost a job and a friend," mused Polycarp.

"Poor Polycarp—here, take this cup of tea and drown your sorrows." Peggy smoothed his elbow and led him to the settee, and left him there while she went back to Felix Ollard.

Polycarp, much against his will, but because he knew Peggy wished it, read the play in bed that night. The room resounded to his derisive laughter and groans as he read, and when he at last sought sleep it was to find only a nightmare. He awoke the next morning with a bad headache, and a pessimistic outlook on life which he attributed entirely to the play.

"You don't seem yourself this morning, sir," said his man, as he moved about the room.

"No, Bickford, I don't. I'm worried about the theatre and various things, and, on top of that, misguided friends made me read a play last night."

"Read a play, sir?" There was almost disapproval in the man's voice as he folded a tie with the care of a shepherd folding sheep.

"*Children of Destiny*, Bickford! And I'm ready to bet that the Demented Demagogue had something to do with it! Children of Ruddy Destiny, and look at me this morning!"

"You certainly seem a little overwrought, sir, if I may say so."

"You may, Bickford, and I am overwrought. So were those Children of Destiny, and so would an audience be if they saw it—and I, conscious of my responsibility to the public, am going to shield them from this horror."

That was all he told Bickford about the play. When Peggy called upon him, he had much more to say.

"Did I like it?" Polycarp stood by the window after handing her a cigarette. "Did I like it, you ask? I think it's unique, I think it's stupendous. How could the man think of such stuff and imagine that it would make a play?"

"I don't understand, darling. Did you really like it or not?" Peggy tapped her cigarette expectantly.

"Peggy"—Polycarp turned and faced her—"I think it the most awful slush and rot I've ever read. That fellow's a wash-out. Where on earth did you rake him up from?"

"Polycarp—I don't understand you. Rot and slush—why, it's perfect stuff. I thought you would be wild about it."

"So I am—raving wild that I should have wasted my time. Do you seriously want me to consider putting that thing on?"

"I certainly do. I think it has definite possibilities. It shows genius."

"I wish you'd forget genius for a minute. Listen, Peggy darling, I'm going to be brutally frank. That play is terrible. There's not a man in London of any sense would dream of reading beyond the first act, let alone put it on a stage. Yet, because you asked me, I read it right through—that itself was an achievement. No—forget the thing, and I'll find something much better for you, a sort of mixture between Lonsdale and Hackett. Let Ollard go back to the murky region from which he emerged to torment me!"

"Polycarp, don't say such things about my friends! I think you're being perfectly horrid. Darling, do you think you have honestly thought about it enough? I'm sure the play would go well. It's unusual and would attract people, and with me in it. Won't you put it on to please me?"

Polycarp rubbed his head desperately. Peggy was going mad, that was the only explanation he could find for her obstinacy.

"Peggy, can't you see that I can't afford to take the risk? Peggy, you don't want to be in a flop, do you? And you know I'm all for encouraging deserving people, but Ollard hasn't got anything. I can't understand quite why you're so keen about this play—"

"I'm keen, dear boy, because I want to help the man, and because I think the play can be made a success—no matter what you may say to the contrary."

"Peggy," Polycarp was confused by her attitude. "You know I'd do anything for you. I'm eternally grateful to you for many things, and I've tried to show it—"

"Polycarp, I think you're losing your nerve. Success is making you a coward. You're afraid to take risks these days. A few years ago you would have said you could put the play on and make a success of it—"

Polycarp smiled dryly. "Never, Peggy. I've always had some foundation for my boasts."

"Well, Polycarp, my dear"—Peggy assumed a nonchalant air—"if you won't put it on—that's that; but I must tell you that I refuse to act for you in any play but that one. I believe in it as I once believed in you. We proved what we could do in those days—and I helped you as much as I could. Now, I feel the same about Ollard. I know the poor man's had a bad time and I want to help him, to give him a chance, and I want to act in that play at the Burns Memorial Theatre. Once, when you loved me, you swore you would do anything for me …"

"I did, and I still love you … Oh, Peggy!" It hurt Polycarp to see her almost imploring him, and yet at the same time he was secretly pleased to think that the famous Peggy North should be asking favours of him. She was still lovely and desirable to him, and, as he faced her, he found himself wondering why she had slipped from his mind since that day in the park. Once she had jeopardised her good name for him, and now he was refusing to do something for her.

"You still love me?"

"You know I do. I always have done. I'd marry you tomorrow, if you'd let me." Polycarp spoke with a determination and persuasion that convinced even himself. He loved her, this elusive woman. As he made his avowal he was amazed that his passion could have rested so quietly in his bosom for so long.

"Why don't you prove your love for me by putting on the play, by backing my judgment?" Peggy came up to him and caught at his coat lapels. "Such courage might make a difference, you know."

"What do you mean, Peggy? That you would?"

"Now, dear boy, don't get excited. I'm making no promises, but there's a saying that faint heart never won a fair lady."

She stood in front of him, smiling, her dark eyes shining, and she was to him a syren, a Circe, a nereid holding before him a golden bubble in which he saw the future, saw happiness and contentment ... Peggy North, who had once sent him away, had now come back to him to hold out the promise of ... Polycarp felt a sudden resolution grow within him. He was a knight to whom a gage had been thrown down. For this woman he could dare anything; her brilliance, her power and good nature overcame him—he was a slave, and at her bidding ... and she would honour him as few men in England could ever hope to be honoured. The possibility filled Polycarp with splendour and hope.

"All right—I'll put it on. I'll make it my Ilium. But Peggy, it's going to be hard, even with you to inspire me. We shall have to have a conference and alter the thing a bit."

"Dear boy, I knew you wouldn't fail me. Ever since you nearly crippled me in Petticoat Lane, I've known you were a man of courage. Darling—" She slipped up to him quickly and kissed him on the cheek, and then was gone from the room, leaving Polycarp alternating between despair and delirium, a delirium that derived all its sweetness from her beauty and the possibilities of love, and a despair that rested in the *Children of Destiny*. Between his groans, as he thought of the play, his heart hymned a wild epithalamium.

XXV
Three bottles of whiskey

It was over nine years since Polycarp had left Bristol to seek his fortune in the great world. In those young days he had been a very awkward figure, awkward with an inward clumsiness which he still possessed though he was now able to disguise it more adroitly.

There had been a time when he had been overcome with self-consciousness on entering a restaurant; now he felt as much at home in public places as he did in his own sitting-room. He no longer hesitated before correctly garbed supercilious shopmen, but spoke to them with the commanding air of a feudal lord to his serfs. He, who had once hesitated to take an olive from the free dish on the bar counter of a Bristol public-house, had accustomed himself to the public pleasures of hotel life. He knew what the foreign names on a menu meant, though he still argued that they should be printed in English. He knew when a man was trying to get something for nothing from him and he had modified his old belief that all men were at heart honest. He could enter into the syntaxless jargon which in some circles was entitled conversation, and make himself as incomprehensibly clear as any unpublished poet or juvenile lead, though he still preserved his love of the heavy phrases and involved sequences derived from the books he read. In his Bristol days, food and drink had been mere incidentals; the mind, the brain, was everything; but now he knew how important were good foods and fine drink. He was careful not to let this importance develop into an obsession, and he kept up his exercises, so that his body was as fit now as it had been when he had lived the strenuous life of the proprietor of the New Age Flying Company, only his hands and nails were softer and cleaner. He was a man of the town, well dressed, austere with a statuesque composure which comes from authority and wealth, and owning no overlord beyond his own desires ... and yet underneath his fine clothes and new manners, beneath his silk shirt and expensive hat, he was more Polycarp the irresponsible and generous than Polycarp the splendid; he was still the young fellow who accepted life in a spirit of serious fun and knew that he could achieve anything in the world if he really wanted it. His facile optimism would have disgusted Voltaire and pleased the paranoiac Rousseau.

Despite his inherent optimism, however, Polycarp was worried. He had some reason for anxiety. He had on his hands a new theatre and a new play. The rest of his enterprises were in the hands of competent men chosen by himself and whom he knew he could trust. Until his schemes were assured and established successes, he always handled them himself, and of all his ventures, from his paper to his football players, the Burns Memorial Theatre was the most stupendous. He calculated that by the end of the year the theatre would be finished and ready to open, and that left him three months to make the *Children of Destiny* acceptable to the great British public, a public whose attitude towards children was reflected in the falling birth-rate, and whose most aggravating characteristic, so far as the theatre was concerned, was that they never knew what play they might like, and when they saw it they were not quite sure until they could go home and read the critics' reviews in the morning papers.

At the end of those three months, Polycarp swore that never again would he commit himself to such a period of strain. In retrospect he might enjoy the struggle. While it lasted he had no time for retrospection. He became a living information bureau and reference library. He attracted to himself designers, costumiers, authors, painters, scenic artists, carpet manufacturers, electricians, managers, secretaries, composers, conductors, out-of-work musicians, theatrical agents, wealthy friends who wanted to get their nieces into his play and forgot they would have to be able to act, pressmen, publicity agents, L.C.C. officials, carpenters, caterers, hard-luck stories, bawdy stories, and a whole procession of requests for favours of one kind and another; and he dealt with them as he could, shouting instructions as he got into his car, filling telegrams with cryptics, yelling from the spotlight gallery, talking over luncheon-tables, exhorting through his bath-sponge, demanding over the telephone and muffling his words by attempting to masticate at the same time, threatening in taxi-cabs, pleading in parks and swearing as he walked up the Strand; and his greatest worry was the play itself. Sometimes he knew he was mad to attempt to put it on. As it stood, there was not a genuine laugh in the whole script. It was just about as interesting as the back of a gas-works on a rainy afternoon, and yet because he loved Peggy, or thought he did, he was attempting the impossible.

He saw Felix Ollard, and had a long talk with him and made him re-write the play. The man's second attempt was worse than the first, so Polycarp said nothing and adopted the first version. He showed it in confidence to Mr. Winterton, and the fat little man brought it back, looked fixedly at Polycarp, and then turned sharply towards the fireplace, saying:

"Nonsense, my boy, nonsense!"

So impossible did it seem to make a success from the play and— except for Peggy's laudatory encouragement and Felix Ollard's booming self-praise—so cold was the attitude of the few people who read it that Polycarp woke one morning and found that the challenge thrown down to him of making the impossible possible was not going to be passed by. He determined that he, Polycarp, would make a success of it. Nothing, not even the impossible, should be impossible for him. From his brief pessimism he constructed a policy of optimism and cheerfulness which lasted for a few days, but in those few days he had set to work on the play.

He collected a cast, and announced to the disappointed Ollard that he might have written the play, but he certainly was not going to produce it. He, Polycarp, would produce it, and not even Peggy could persuade him from his purpose.

Polycarp was averse from paying a high figure to a famous producer when he knew that the play was not good enough to merit such attention; and he doubted very much whether, had he wished to engage a good producer, he could have secured one willing to undertake so evident a risk. He started rehearsals and, when the watching Ollard began to make objections, Polycarp had him locked out of the theatre and kept out, and Peggy agreed that it was the best policy. It would have taken a brave man or a stupid woman to have interfered with Polycarp as he thundered down from the stage into the echoing well of the nearly finished auditorium.

"Ollard! You can go to hell and stay there! You might have written this play—I don't dispute that; no other man in the world could have done it—but I'm producing it, and while I shan't alter a word of your precious script, I'm in charge here, and what I say goes. Now get out and rusticate in the country for a month until I want you again! Now then, everybody, attention, and let's try that piece again without the melanic influence of the author to distract us. And remember, Miss Pegrin, I want you if anything to over-emphasise your distress. Don't restrain yourself. Let yourself go! Now then—let's have that pistol-shot again."

He sat back and watched the scene, and he saw that, with a bit of luck, he could carry out a design which was slowly formulating in his mind.

The rehearsal went on, and occasionally he would leap to his feet and storm, for although this was his first experience of producing, he knew from the American films that all producers stormed. Occasionally he did have a genuine cause for anger. The small cast were all, it seemed—except Peggy—infected by the dolefulness of the play, and Polycarp sympathised with them, though he did not show it. Only Peggy played her part as if she were inspired, and her inspiration, while it filled Polycarp with admiration and doubts as to her sanity, only served to depress the company more than ever.

One evening he sat alone in his room with the script and made a decision. There were two weeks to go before the play went on, and in those two weeks Polycarp took every single member of the cast—except Peggy—out to his Chess valley house, one at a time, without letting anyone but Higgins know, and there he talked to them as he walked alongside the frozen river and bound them to a vow of secrecy.

He said nothing to Peggy of these interviews, and she was not suspicious when he suggested that it was no longer necessary for her to be present at every rehearsal. To allay any doubts, he pointed out that if she stopped away occasionally from rehearsals, it would give her understudy an opportunity to perfect the part. Peggy, who knew her part well enough to feel justified in not attending each rehearsal, and who did not share the usual desire of leading ladies to thwart the possibilities of their understudies, readily agreed with Polycarp's suggestion.

After that, Polycarp directed the rehearsals in a more settled state of mind, and he arranged that there should be plenty of rehearsals without Peggy's presence.

As the opening day approached he began to drop hints to the Press about the play.

The Burns Memorial Theatre was to be opened on a Thursday. In the afternoon there was to be a ceremony when Lord Proudservant, one of the leading figures in civil aviation in the country, would open the doors with a golden key and after that there were to be speeches from the stage about Burns, Polycarp, and the theatre. In the evening, the play would open. Polycarp, while he looked forward to the day, saw it only as twenty-four hours of suspense and wonder, of anxiety and starting fears.

Three days before the ceremony, the newspapers were noisy with the same announcement which starred and splashed nearly every hoarding in London.

FRANK BURNS MEMORIAL THEATRE
OPENING NIGHT—THURSDAY, DECEMBER 8TH
PEGGY NORTH
CHILDREN OF DESTINY
A Play of Dramatic Elementals,
as Modern as Pirandello
and as sincere as the first Miracle Play
by FELIX OLLARD

Special Announcement:
Mr. Polycarp Jarvis, as a special mark of his appreciation of Frank Burns's heroic venture, announces that on the first night, all seats in the theatre, except the first four rows, will be free.

Polycarp knew that the public were guided in all their actions by an underlying desire to get something for nothing at any price;

suburban dwellers would use a half-gallon of petrol to motor into the country and pillage hedges for free holly when they could buy it for twopence a bunch in the shop round the corner; housewives would take a penny ride in a bus to buy meat a penny a pound cheaper than they could get it at their local butchers' shops, and Polycarp was going one better—he was going to give them something for nothing at his expense, and hope to make up his losses by turning the venture into a success.

"You're mad, and you'll finish up a bankrupt," said Mr. Winterton.

"I may, and I may not. Remember, Hannibal crossed the Alps with his elephants—and that couldn't have been much harder than making the *Children of Destiny* a play London will fight to see. What Hannibal can do, so can I."

"Fine talk, my boy, fine talk! We'll see. I suppose half the society folk in London will be scrambling for those four front rows?"

"Half the society folk in London have scrambled for 'em already and I've had to be very careful in handing them out—at a price!"

"Well, it'll be the first time I've lined up for the gallery."

Polycarp laughed. "Don't worry, Joseph Kay, I'm keeping a block of seats for my acquaintances, and you're my greatest friend. What should I have been without you to help me with my money affairs all these years?"

"I shouldn't like to answer that question, my boy."

The great day arrived and the opening ceremony went without a hitch. Polycarp, top-hatted and morning-coated, hovered by the side of Lord Proudservant as he twisted the golden key in the doorway, and then conducted him, followed by distinguished officials and celebrities from every profession, into the building and showed him its glories. Now that the day was here, Polycarp was not so nervous as he imagined he would be. He walked by Lord Proudservant's side and answered the tall, aristocratic peer's questions calmly. He even made a joke, and the pressmen took advantage of their mirth to photograph them. Press photographers are astute folk; they know there is nothing the great public likes so much as to see great men displaying human traits. A great man laughing impresses them more than a great man tapping the top of a foundation-stone with a ridiculous little silver trowel.

The theatre was decorated with red, white, and blue ribands and hung with futuristic aeroplane propellers and wings. It was like a great green-mossed cave, full of flowers and swaying tub-palms, and silent with the cloaking softness of thick carpets. While Polycarp was demonstrating the mechanical marvels back-stage, the public were admitted to the theatre and took their seats in readiness for the speeches from the stage.

When the curtain went up, it revealed the stage, containing a long table set with chairs, on which, ranging from Lord Proudservant in the centre, sat Polycarp, Peggy, Mr. Winterton and other dignitaries. Alexander Royston, who was in the spotlight gallery and was going to write a special description for *Polycarp's Weekly*, grinned as he saw Polycarp's serious face, and restrained a desire to shout down "Boloney!"—an expression of which he was fond, and entertained himself by compiling in his head an estimate of the sum total of the incomes of all the people at the table. Felix Ollard, looking uncomfortable in a morning-coat, sat at the far end of the table and itched for all the ceremony to be done and for the night to come, so that London might recognise his genius. He was proud of his genius; he had nourished it in poverty and obscurity for the prescribed number of years and he felt that it was time the etiolated growth saw the sunshine of fame. Polycarp did not intend to hurry things for anyone. Lord Proudservant made his speech in the concise, meaningless phrases of a skilled politician and diplomat. Famous aviators added their little, ungrammatical tribute to Burns's genius, though few of them had ever seen him for more than two minutes, and those who had had disliked him. Peggy dropped a few demure phrases in his honour on behalf of the profession which she graced, and a patriotic member of the Stock Exchange regretted that there were not more like him in business as well as in aviation, and Polycarp wondered if he had heard of Frank's two-headed penny. Then Polycarp added his testimony to all the others.

He stood up and faced the great crowd which stretched away into the coloured distances of the theatre, and every nerve in his body responded to the satisfying thrill that came from knowing that every person out there was looking at him; seeing him as Polycarp, the distant wonderful Polycarp who had burst upon London like a shell and risen from comparative poverty to the dizzy, undreamable heights of wealth and fame within a few years; seeing him as a swelling South Sea Bubble which, refusing to burst, threatened to spread until it held the world within its soapy tension and formed a new universe for them. He loved them all. He served them; he gave them what they wanted and they applauded him. It was not his fault if they liked meretricious shows and flashy exhibitions. His duty was to serve them—and at the same time, of course, himself.

His speech was short.

"What I have done by building this theatre," he said simply, "I have done for Burns, because he was my friend. Nothing in the whole world can ever replace his loss in my heart. In life he wished to be an architect, and dreamed of such a building as this, but life was cruel and denied him his wish and added instead his name to the long and noble roll of aviator heroes. He died in an attempt to further the greatness of this country, and it is for men like myself, who can only guess at the danger he faced, yet know the courage with which he met it, and know my own cowardice beside his bravery, to honour his name ... He went out into the unknown, as we all must go at some time, and he left me full of memories and sorrow. Let this building, then, be his memorial and my sorrow."

Polycarp sat down and the crowd was so touched by the sincerity of his tones that it remained hushed and quivering with growing sentiment which the orchestra, as arranged by Polycarp, cleverly emboldened and smoothed into admiration by playing a selection of tunes commencing with *Abide with Me* and finishing with *Land of Hope and Glory*.

When the ceremony was done, the speechmakers departed and the crowd, after satisfying its curiosity by looking around the building under the care of guides provided for this purpose, made its way into the streets. Polycarp was left alone in his room, glad that the first part of his trial was over. He sipped a whiskey to give him strength for the evening. Outside the room he could hear people talking and walking about, but he was alone, and thankful for his solitude. Tonight he would be so busy that he would have no time for reflection, and after tonight, if all went well, there was Peggy ... He lay back in his chair and blew a smoke-ring at the electric light. The ring floated upwards, circling the dust-motes that danced in the beams, and, widening against its tenuous periphery, slowly dissolved into the air. Polycarp shut his eyes peacefully and blew another ring. His whole body was tingling with nervous apprehension, and he told himself that he would be glad, infinitely glad, when the day was over and he could live normally. He thought of his speech in the theatre, and in retrospect he knew that, despite any bombast and ostentation which had crept into his remarks, he did feel deeply about Frank. He was dead, gone ... He half guessed that the tragedy had probably been the result of Frank's own weakness, but he stifled those thoughts and no one knew that the officials of the American flying-field had sent him a confidential note that Frank had shipped three bottles of whiskey before taking off. Where were those bottles now, Polycarp wondered? Somewhere in the Atlantic? And, wherever they were, he was almost certain that they would be empty.

He shut his eyes and tried to recall the distant days of the New Age Flying Company. He dozed off and slept until the theatre manager awakened him, and then, although he had not forgotten Frank, his mind was full of the thought of his play. That night the *Children of Destiny* would either add to or detract from the monument which he had built to Frank's memory.

XXVI
Polycarp progresses

The moment Polycarp entered the theatre he forgot Frank Burns. He was in a new world—a world of hurrying individuals, some half-dressed and some, so he thought, half-witted; a world of stage-hands, call-boys, lights, props, stage-managers, and all the abracadabra of back-stage which presents an appalling muddle to the untrained eye, and yet when the curtain goes up resolves itself into a perfect organisation.

Peggy was in her room, making up. She nodded at him in the glass as he came in.

"Nervous, Peggy?"

"Just a little—I always am—even on the hundredth performance."

"I hope this goes to a hundred performances."

"Silly, dear boy, of course it will. It's going to be a success. Seen the house?"

"Yes. Every seat taken, but what could you expect when every seat almost is free? If only it looks like that a week from today, or even tomorrow night …"

"It will—the public will recognise Ollard's genius and your success." Peggy was confident.

"Or my genius and Ollard's success, eh? This is a great night for you, and for me"—he looked at her, and wanted to move across and take her by the shoulders—"and for Ollard."

"Particularly for you and Ollard. Oh, Polycarp, darling! I know the play'll go all right. Now, go away and let me change."

Polycarp left her and travelled round to the rest of the cast, spending a few moments with each one, and then he went to the front of the house and took his seat alongside Mr. Winterton and Felix Ollard.

"I hope you don't mind, Ollard," said Polycarp, as he sat down, "but at the last moment I had to make a few minor additions to the prologue—I didn't alter any of your other stuff, don't worry."

He waved Felix Ollard into subservience and turned to Mr. Winterton. "This is the great moment, Joseph Kay. Are you praying for me?"

"You're beyond prayer, my boy—beyond it. And the age of miracles is over."

"Pessimist."

Polycarp sat back in his seat and tried to appear calm. He would be glad when everything was over. He almost wished he had never seen London. As he sat there, he thought of the morning on top of the Sussex Downs when he had severed his connections with the Red Dragon Company, and his face creased into a smile. He was mad then, and he was mad now, he supposed. Then he thought of the play, and wondered whether it would be a failure in spite of all his labour with it.

Felix Ollard's *Children of Destiny* in the original script was actually as bad as Polycarp knew it was. Felix had explained to him that not only did the play out-Shavian Shaw, but it also went back to the fundamentals of drama. It started with a spoken preface which, so Felix Ollard purported, explained the point of the play, though Polycarp saw it only as a jumble of words, and it was to this preface that he had made a few last-moment additions. Felix Ollard was very proud of his preface. Shaw, he pointed out to Polycarp, always wrote his prefaces for the book publication of his plays, but he, Felix Ollard, gave the public the preface and the play at the same time. Polycarp could never understand why the play was called the *Children of Destiny* as there were no children in it and only one mention of destiny. It certainly went back to the fundamentals of drama. There was a villain, a heavy father, a weeping mother, a jealous sister-played by Peggy—an outraged milkmaid, a younger brother, an elder brother, a rich man, a poor man, a good man, and three or four bad men … and all these characters did what they traditionally should do. The villain betrayed the milkmaid. The elder brother paid the younger brother's debts, on certain conditions. The weeping mother wept at the heavy father's heavy-handed treatment of the poor man, who was very poor. The good man was robbed at intervals by the bad men, and the bad men drank and were very bad. And all the characters lived and spoke as though they had no more emotion than cardboard dummies in a boy's peep-show. Not even its naive charm of dialogue—and Polycarp had to admit that if Ollard had any genius it lay in a certain skill with words—could disguise the paucity of the play's theme and well-worn situations.

Polycarp had said more than once that the whole thing reminded him of a funeral—lovely flowers adorning a dull coffin. And all this was done under the guise of genius and had to be acted with a seriousness which, so Ollard and Peggy declared, was demanded by the loftiness of the preface and the play's theme.

That Polycarp should have been foolish enough to put on such a play was good cause for Mr. Winterton's pessimism. He had had years of experience in the theatre and he knew what the public did not want, if no one knew quite what they did want, and he knew that Polycarp was booked for a failure, and Polycarp knew that he was booked for a failure, if the play were presented as Ollard intended it. Polycarp also knew that there were five hundred different ways of saying "I love you" and of kneeling before a woman, and it was this knowledge that gave him a little confidence as he sat in the front of the auditorium and waited for the orchestra to finish and the curtain to go up. His confidence alone was not enough; the people that could endorse it stretched behind him in a solid layer of heads and shoulders. A good critical laughter-loving, sentimental crowd who held the power in their hands to break Polycarp's fortune with their nod or frown. There they were gallery-girls, autograph hunters, tradesmen who had shut up their shops early to get in the queues for free seats, clerks and their girls, roues and their painted consorts, students and their spotted faces and horn-rimmed glasses, electricians with knobbly hands and minds facile with Ohm's Law and alternating currents ... a great concourse, not very different from the crowds which had cluttered the Roman arenas to watch the Christians make game for wild beasts, or thronged the streets of Rome to witness Caligula's triumph and spit at the bonded Germans; a concourse that could be as suddenly kind as it could be cruel, and was quicker to love than to hate. And it was upon these people, not many of whom received as much in a year as Polycarp earned in a month, that his success depended. He stopped thinking about it and watched the curtain rise into the dimness of the roof as the music ceased, and he wondered if his secret interviews with the players would be as fruitful as he hoped.

The babble of the audience stopped, the automatic theatre doors closed and the play was on. From the wings a dark figure, heavily cloaked, strode steadily on to the stage, and, letting slip the cloak from his shoulders, shone like a silver beacon against the dark backcloth. He started to speak the preface.

After the first six sentences, Felix Ollard began to suspect that Polycarp had hatched a plot to frustrate his genius, and the audience were chuckling gently to themselves. Polycarp had indeed made a few additions, and the effect of these turned the serious sections of the preface into hyperbole and fun. The herald declaimed with extravagant flourish and gesture. He cracked topical jokes in asides, and turned a prologue into a monologue that puzzled the audience as it made them laugh.

"The single purpose of the drama is to present to man a picture of his esoteric life—and to give chorus girls a chance to show their legs ... Ladies and Gentlemen, you are now to see *Children of Destiny*—but don't let that worry you, there are special exits in the auditorium ..."

Felix Ollard sat in his seat and pinched the arms of the plush chair as he saw Polycarp's "minor alterations" come trotting in one by one.

"I have not touched the script at all," Polycarp leaned over and assured him, as the curtain went up on the first scene. What Polycarp said was strictly correct. He had not altered a word, but he had rehearsed the whole cast—except Peggy, who knew nothing about the scheme—to play their parts with the utmost extravagance and to burlesque as much as they could, telling them that it was the only way to make a success of *Children of Destiny*. And it was. As a straight play it would not have held the audience for ten minutes. Played as a wild burlesque, as a travesty of Felix Ollard's original intention, it reached the level of good-class comedy.

The audience, still a little puzzled by the prologue, were quick to appreciate the play's ridiculousness. Polycarp soon had the satisfaction of hearing the first plebeian hearty guffaw which signals possible commendation and success. Every player, except Peggy, whose severity and dignity only pointed and clarified their wildness, made a mockery of the lines. The heavy-handed father cut his erring son off with a shilling, using Ollard's own words, and then waited in silence while the son gave him change for half a crown. The villain villainised with hisses and rolling eyeballs.

Felix Ollard writhed in his seat as he heard the audience roar where they should have wept, and desecrate the auditorium with laughter when they should have been silent. Death-bed scenes became pantomime, and the weeping mother was no more than a fat old trollop with a knack of making the wrong entrances and exits. At the end of the second act Polycarp knew that it could not be an absolute failure.

The audience approved the burlesque and looked for it, and Polycarp looked across at Mr. Winterton and nodded.

During the interval the audience composed their minds to the acceptance of the unexpected, and from the first line of the third act the play lived because they knew what to expect.

At Polycarp's side sat Ollard, and to his surprise as he heard round after round of applause he found himself feeling curiously half-angry and half-amused. He was not such a fool as to think that the burlesque was unintentional, and he knew that no one but Polycarp could have ordered it. The play went on, and when the final curtain came down and the cries of "Author!" filled the smoky vault of the theatre, Felix Ollard forgot his ire almost completely in the superb joy of climbing on to the stage and bowing to the crowd with Peggy by his side. After he had made his little speech of thanks, the crowd shouted for Polycarp, and would not leave until he had appeared and waved his hand to them. As he stood alone on the stage, he could see Peggy and Ollard and others waiting in one wing for him, and the prospect of facing them all and entering into arguments filled him with despair. He had made—so it seemed—a success from Ollard's inanities, and now he was entitled to escape from everything and to be himself for a while. He slipped off the stage through the other wing and disappeared into a taxi, which he directed to drive him the thirty miles to his Chess valley home.

He stopped and telephoned a few instructions to the theatre manager, and told him he would be back in the morning. Then he leaned back in the car and forgot everything but Higgins and the little valley.

When he arrived he woke Higgins, and they spent the rest of the night playing solo whist and drinking coffee, and telling one another distorted tales of their past lives.

As they talked, the affairs of the last few days and months began to take their proper perspective in Polycarp's mind. He chuckled to himself at the thought of the consternation and possible publicity which would arise from his dash away into the country after he had made a success of an almost impossible play. It was good news. The exultation in his heart repaid him for all the worry and care with which he had lived so long. He stretched his long legs, and, flicking his cigarette-ash over the floor, put his feet on the mantelshelf.

Higgins looked across at him with a smile on his rough, red face. "You'll soon have to break yourself of habits like that!" he said.

Polycarp did not understand for the moment. "What do you mean?" he asked.

"When you're married, the missus won't allow it."

Polycarp had almost forgotten that. When he was married ... Things might be different then. He thought of Peggy. He had made Ollard's play a success for her; he had done that in the face of difficulties which most men would have regarded as insurmountable. He knew she would not cavil at his methods, though it had not been possible for him to let her into the secret of the burlesque. And if she did object ... To his surprise he found himself hardly caring what she might think. He tried to efface this heresy from his mind, but the idea remained with him. What did it matter what she thought? He was Polycarp. A loyalty to Peggy, and to his love for her, helped him to dismiss his rebellious thoughts for a while, but they continually crept back into his mind so that he rose and, leaving Higgins to find some breakfast, walked out to the river.

The morning was grey over the tops of the firs, and a row of poplars tossed themselves like mares' tails in the first breeze of the day. He sauntered along the bank, his feet crackling over the dried quitch stems, his eyes marking the dark swirl of the river, muddy with flood water. Everything was the same here, not a tree, not a leaf, it seemed, had changed. Here it was as it had been, and always would be, a slow steady progression from birth to death, from seed to flower, a cosmic circle that marked its circumference with the dropping of an acorn and the squeal of a leveret in death. Here life and death were moulded into an infinity of peace, and death was only the gateway to another adventure.

And he had left all this to go to London, to become famous for no other reason than that he had wanted to be famous. He thought of Higgins, jolly and rough, of the dogs, and the country—soon he would be married and these things would be further away from him than his London life had already made them. He would have to think of Peggy now, not himself. He walked, with the crows rising in black knots from the trees to punctuate his mood with their caws, and the thought which had come to him in the house returned to him with enforced life, and he could not dispel it. In one quick flash of blinding vision Polycarp knew, as definitely as he knew that he loved excitement, shouting, and colour, that he had never loved Peggy. He had only been in love with the idea of love.

Late in the afternoon of that day, Polycarp stopped in Great Portland Street, as he walked towards Peggy's flat, to buy a paper. The prospect of the coming interview was worrying him a little. He scanned the paper for news of the play, and was satisfied at the publicity which his dash from the theatre had provided. Then his eye caught another paragraph, and he shook the pages eagerly. For a few seconds he was entirely oblivious of the great London life around him. He forgot the streaming traffic, jostling crowds, shouting newsboys and dingy pigeons, forgot everything except the few inches of black print before him. Peggy had been married that morning, at a registrar's office, to Ollard. He read the news item in a daze ... romance of the stage ... actress marries old love ... success brings happiness ...

Then he understood. He swore loudly, threw the paper from him and called a cab. He knew now why Peggy had insisted upon having Ollard's play produced. He was mad, mad, mad, at the trick which had been played him. He sat back in his seat and let his mind range over the whole gamut of tortures which might be inflicted on the human body, while the cabman performed the aimless function of "driving round." Then suddenly from the midst of his black disappointment Polycarp began to laugh, and his anger, which was more emotional than logical, passed away like a cloud-shadow from a sunlit field. His laughter started from a fierce rasp of breath into a paroxysm of chuckling and thigh-slapping. He remembered his walk by the river that morning, and, still laughing, he gave an order to the astonished cabby.

Some hours later Polycarp sat with Higgins again, and, when they had eaten and drunk, he raised his feet with elaborate ceremony and placed them on the mantelshelf as he flung ash into the air from his cigarette.

Higgins eyed him hopelessly. "Miss Peggy'll have a fine time breakin' you of your dirty habits. You'll have to act differently when you're married and settled down—"

Polycarp laughed light-heartedly. "But I'm not going to be married and settle down. There's still a lot more excitement waiting for me around the corner!" He moved his feet to comfort against the clock, and stared at the dusty-shouldered bottle of Solomon's Glory which held the place of honour at the end of the shelf.

Preview

In a mid-life moment, Paul Morison travels from America to England to discover his mother's roots. A chance encounter and uncanny resemblance leads him to agree to assume the identity of a famous singer for a while. But it's not just the unnerving attentions of the adoring public that he must deal with.

Seeking to regain his freedom, Paul flees the length of Britain from Southampton to the Scottish Isles. On the run, he discovers he has let himself in for much more than he bargained.

This gentle comic caper and love story was hugely popular on first publication in the 1930s and retains a timeless appeal today.

Fly Away Paul, by Victor Canning

Also Available

Mr Edgar Finchley, unmarried clerk, aged 45, is told to take a holiday for the first time in his life. He decides to go to the seaside. But Fate has other plans in store...

From his abduction by a cheerful crook, to his smuggling escapade off the south coast, the timid but plucky Mr Finchley is plunged into a series of the most astonishing and extraordinary adventures.

His rural adventure takes him gradually westward through the English countryside and back, via a smuggling yacht, to London.

Mr Finchley, Book 1

OUT NOW

About the early works of Victor Canning

Victor Canning had a runaway success with his first book, *Mr Finchley Discovers his England*, published in 1934, and lost no time in writing more. Up to the start of the Second World War he wrote seven such life-affirming novels.

Following the war, Canning went on to write over fifty more novels along with an abundance of short stories, plays and TV and radio scripts, gaining sophistication and later a darker note – but perhaps losing the exuberance that is the hallmark of his early work.

Early novels by Victor Canning –

Mr Finchley Discovers His England

Mr Finchley Goes to Paris

Mr Finchley Takes the Road

Polycarp's Progress

Fly Away Paul

Matthew Silverman

Fountain Inn

About the Author

Victor Canning was a prolific writer throughout his career, which began young: he had sold several short stories by the age of nineteen and his first novel, *Mr Finchley Discovers His England* (1934) was published when he was twenty-three. It proved to be a runaway bestseller. Canning also wrote for children: his trilogy The Runaways was adapted for US children's television. Canning's later thrillers were darker and more complex than his earlier work and received further critical acclaim.

Note from the Publisher

To receive background material and updates on further titles by Victor Canning, sign up at farragobooks.com/canning-signup